YANKEE MISTRESS
ASHLEY SNOW

ZEBRA BOOKS
KENSINGTON PUBLISHING CORP.

ZEBRA BOOKS

are published by

Kensington Publishing Corp.
850 Third Avenue
New York, NY 10022

First printing: May, 1989

Printed in the United States of America

10 9 8 7 6 5 4 3 2

One

"Mark my words, there's goin' to be a real fight out thar a'fore this night is out!"

As he spoke the old man half-rose from his chair and made a wild gesture with his arm that all but knocked Selene's tray out of her hands. She made a quick genuflect to right it, then moved cautiously around Caleb's chair to set it on the table.

"I think not tonight," the old man's companion across the table intoned solemnly as he reached for one of the tankards on the tray. "All that marching and that little spat wore everybody out. But it'll be soon. Maybe tomorrow."

"Tonight, I tell you! We'll all be dead a'fore the sun sets."

Though heartily sick of talk about war, Selene was glad of the chance to stand for a moment and catch her breath. She smoothed her apron and set her hands on her hips, waiting.

"Will you gentlemen be wanting anything else," she asked as the more sober of the two looked up at her.

"No thank you, Selene. Caleb here has had more than enough for one afternoon and I think I have, too. Why don't you go and see about the rest of them fellers."

"Best you go and make peace with your Maker a'for you have to stare Him in the face," Caleb intoned, shaking a calloused finger at her nose.

"I'm not afraid to face my Maker, Caleb Hartshorn," Selene said, laughing at him. "But you'd better give a thought to it. He might want to know about all that ale you've put away these sixty years."

5

"Humph, saucy tongue you got, girl. I kept yer uncle in business all these years, ain't I?"

Selene moved away before Caleb could launch into another long tirade, easing her way between the cramped tables and chairs. She had never seen her uncle's taproom so crowded before. Every table was filled, and still men stood lounging around the perimeters of the room, waiting for someone to get up and leave. Most of them wore civilian clothes—black frock coats or farmers' smocks—but there were a number of slate gray uniforms scattered among them, too. Through a group of these soldiers clustered at the bar, she caught her uncle gesturing to her and fought her way across the room, weaving among the sweaty bodies to his side. The noise was heightened by an undercurrent of anxious excitement left over from the gunfire earlier in the day. The heat was almost unbearable. July in Virginia was bad enough without all these people crammed into one room.

"Those railroad workers are wanting a meal," her uncle said, nodding to one corner as he ran a dirty rag across the counter. "Call down to Rosie in the kitchen and ask if that stew is ready yet."

"Uncle John, Caleb Hartshorn is claiming there will be a serious battle near here before sunset. Do you think he's right?"

"You know Caleb, Selene. He's always hanging crepe before the corpse is cold. Pay him no mind."

"But everyone's talking about a major battle. And you know we're sitting here so close to both armies. Those guns this morning . . ."

"I know. But they didn't bother us, did they? Don't go looking for trouble before it finds you. We're too busy this afternoon anyway. Blast that Matilda. Of all days for her to go running off after her soldier boy!"

Selene wiped at her damp forehead with the end of her apron. She would like nothing better than to take a broom to Matilda herself for running off and leaving her with the bulk of the work on one of the busiest days they had ever had. After all, serving was Matilda's job. Selene had occasionally helped out when times got busy, but never before had the whole burden fallen on her shoulders. She was hot and tired and the noise and commotion of the overcrowded room was making her head throb. The thought of going down to the kitchen where the heat would rival the furnaces of hell was more than she could bear.

"I'll speak to Rosie, Uncle John," she said. "But first I'm going to go outside and get a breath of air. It's unbearable in here. Give me that pitcher. I'll bring back some water from the well."

"That's Cato's job, carrying water. I need you here."

"Let Cato wait on these men for awhile," she said stubbornly, grabbing up the pitcher. "I'm going outside."

Her uncle turned his best authoritarian expression on her, ready to order her to stay, but a shout for two beers from the end of the counter diverted his attention. "Go ahead then, but don't linger. Doing slave's work! It's that highfalutin nonsense your Pa filled your head with again."

Selene turned her back on his grumbling and pushed her way to the door, the wooden pitcher under her arm. She stepped out into the stableyard where the heat hit her like a blast from a furnace. The tall, two-story stone house stood on a grassy knoll open to the sun except for one corner where a huge, old oak tree stood shadowing a low stone well. Selene hurried across the yard to its canopied shade. It was cool there and quiet. She leaned against the well and turned her face up to the shadowed leaves while wiping her apron across her damp neck. Drops of perspiration trickled down between her breasts and she eased down the lace-edged bodice of her dress, exposing their creamy softness to the air.

She was not surprised to find that tears were smarting behind her eyes, brought on by that familiar slur her uncle had made against her father. She ought to be used to it by now, yet it still hurt. And it did seem that Uncle John never missed a chance to make some unflattering reference to that good man, Theophiles Sprague. It had not taken her long to learn—after she came to live with Uncle John—that he had never understood why his sister had married her father in the first place. Selene suspected that he still blamed her father for the early death of her mother, instead of the yellow fever epidemic

7

that actually killed her. It was just that the two men were so different. Pa had been a teacher and a philosopher, and Uncle John had made it clear that he did not consider such pastimes to be in the same league with honest work. Yes, her father had taught her that slavery was an evil that ought to be purged from the face of the earth, but Uncle John had been well aware of that when he brought her here to Manassas to live. It wasn't what he believed, or the way he lived, but why must he always throw it in her face and make her father sound like an evil man? It was slavery itself that was evil.

She looked off to the east where a thin line of ragged trees blocked her view of the bridge and the road beyond. Somewhere over there General McDowell's fine Federal army sat waiting, with their smart new blue uniforms and gleaming weapons. Maybe there would be a battle today or tomorrow, or maybe there would not. But someday they would see to it that this evil scourge was wiped from Virginia's soil. Cato and Rosie and all the others would be free then, and her father's dream would be realized—the dream he had not lived to see, but had made certain his daughter would keep alive.

Laughing and shouting from the open tavern windows brought her back to reality. Enough dreaming. There was too much work to be done to linger here in the cool shade. Reluctantly she turned the winch and lowered the bucket into the well. Leaning over the edge she felt a cold draft of air from the dark depths below and she savoured it, so enthralled that she failed to notice several horses cantering into the yard. The first she realized she was not alone was when a hand grabbed at her through the folds of her skirt, clutching at her. With a gasp, Selene dropped the rope and swung around to face a young man leaning down from his horse and smirking at her lewdly.

"Now here's a pretty piece," he said, amused at her indignation. Behind him two other men sat watching, one of them sitting a huge white stallion. They all wore Confederate gray uniforms that looked very new with brass buttons sparkling in the bright sun.

"You . . . you cad!" Selene sputtered, spitting words in an effort to express her outrage.

"Come now. No sympathy for a soldier about to give his all for his country? Come, pretty girl, give us a kiss."

"Hanson!" the officer on the white horse snapped. Something in his voice brought the man sharply upright in his saddle. "We've no time for dalliance. Leave her alone."

Reluctantly the soldier turned his horse and trotted off to join the other two. Selene glared at them all. Wouldn't you expect as much from arrogant Southern slave owners! Soldiers giving their all for their country indeed. It wasn't her country and they could die in a ditch for all she cared. And if that officer on the white horse expected her to be grateful for his help, he would be disappointed. All the same, she made certain they had disappeared into the stables before quickly filling her pitcher and ducking around the back way to the kitchen where she took her time inquiring about Rosie's stew. By the time she got back to the busy taproom her uncle was looking around anxiously for her. The crowd had altered while she was gone, with half of the old group having moved off and a new set taking their place.

"There's three tables over by the windows waiting for their beer," Uncle John cried, shoving several tankards at her at once. "And that fellow alone near the door wants a toddy once you've got these taken care of. Oh, and there's three officers upstairs in a private room wanting some supper. Is that infernal stew ready yet?"

"Yes, it is," Selene said, glancing at the door as she set the tankards on her tray. Her eyes were caught by a figure sitting there who somehow managed to be by himself in this boisterous crowd. All the other chairs had been pulled away from his table, leaving him enveloped in a solitary haze that somehow discouraged friendly overtures. His countryman's felt hat was pulled low over his thin face, and yet there was something vaguely familiar about the stance of his shoulders that held her gaze. Then she caught her uncle's words and realized the men wanting their supper upstairs must be the louts who had accosted her in the yard.

"Let Cato serve them," she muttered. "I won't go up there."

"You'll serve them," her uncle snapped, leaning over the bar and into her face. "A private room means extra brass. And

9

they're officers."

"I don't care if they're Julius Caesar and Mark Anthony. I'm not going!" She grabbed up the tray before her uncle could splutter an answer, and began working her way around the room, determined to send Cato upstairs in her place no matter what her uncle said. The leering eyes of that lewd young soldier were too insinuating, too unpleasant. She moved around the room, finally reaching the single gentleman near the door who was the last to be served. As she set the glass on the table, he glanced up at her from under the brim of his round black hat without raising his head. Selene's absent glance was riveted and she peered closer.

"Why, I know you—"

Deftly he raised a finger as though to his lips and glanced cautiously around the room. "Hello, Selene," he said, so quietly she barely made out the words over the noise around her. Motioning his head to a chair which had just been vacated at the next table he indicated to her to join him. She eased down, never taking her eyes from his face. "I'd rather you did not speak my name," he said, leaning toward her over the table.

"It's been years," Selene said quietly. "And there's a beard now where there was none before. But I remember you."

"I still recall the many pleasant hours I spent in your father's front parlor. He was an admirable man. One of the most admirable I've ever known."

Selene was washed in a flood of memories, brief and sparkling like faint jewels in the dimness of the room. She could see so clearly her father's face, rapt and enthralled as he leaned with his elbows on his knees speaking to the men grouped around him, some of them sitting on the worn Turkey carpet, all of them listening in rapt attention. The room itself was so clear, the oval portrait on the wall of her mother in an old-fashioned gown with huge, billowing sleeves: the oil lamp on the round oak stand surrounded by books and daguerreotypes: books everywhere, scattered around on tables and the piano top, littering shelves, opened carelessly and piled on top of one another. The grate giving off iridescent heat, a shabby coal scuttle to the side.

10

It was so familiar, so dear, and so lost, that for a moment Selene was overcome with nostalgia. She leaned forward to set her elbows on the table and rest her head in her hands.

"It's been a long time," the man said gently.

Abruptly she placed the familiar voice. Simon Lazar. A poor government clerk in a second-rate job who came faithfully every Sunday afternoon seeking the insights and knowledge her father loved to share. He was only one of many young men who sought out Theophiles Sprague, but something about him had lodged itself in her memory. Perhaps it was because he was so often silent while the others reveled in argument and hot debate. But she remembered him well.

"It is very strange to see you here," she said, smiling up at him. "Have you turned into a Southern sympathizer?"

"Far from it," he whispered. "I thought perhaps you had though, since your father's unfortunate death. I was told you had come here to live with relatives."

"My Uncle John gave me a home when none of my other relatives cared, and I try to repay him when I can by helping out. But none of my ideals have changed. My father taught me too well."

"I'm relieved to hear it," Simon said. "I should have been disappointed if they had. And I suspect that good old man would have been disappointed as well."

"What does bring you here? Are you still in government service?"

Simon shrugged. "In a way."

"Not the army," Selene asked, lowering her voice and leaning closer. "Somehow I can't imagine you—a thoughtful philosopher—being swept up in this craze for war and glory that I hear from all the other men in this room."

"No, no. I have no use for guns and violence. But there are other ways to serve your country besides throwing cannon-balls at one another. Ways that require intelligence and cleverness."

Selene stared at him a long moment.

"Oh, so that's it. Now I understand the beard and the clothes and why you didn't want me to say your name."

Simon gave her a hard look. "I trust I can depend on you to

11

keep that confidence."

It was a question as much as a request. "Of course," she whispered back. "I have no love for Southerners even if I am surrounded by them. *Especially* since I am surrounded by them. I'll guard your secret."

Under the beard she could see Lazar's thin lips lift in a half smile. He had never been a pleasant-looking man—his sharp features and naturally contemptuous expression tended to put people off rather than invite friendship. Yet she had a grudging respect for the way he could quietly sum up personalities and ideas. And it was good to find someone in this place whose beliefs were similar to hers.

"I had rather hoped you might do even more," he said quietly. He had a way of speaking with his lips barely moving that intrigued her. She leaned closer and caught the faint whiff of stale snuff that she recalled from her father's parlor.

"What can I do? I won't hurt my uncle, and all I ever see here are farmers and regulars. I know as little as everyone else."

"I'm not asking you to become a spy. Just to keep your eyes and ears open, and to pass along any scraps of information you're able to pick up when I stop by from time to time. That's not too much to ask, is it? Besides, I have a feeling you will soon be seeing a few high-ranking Confederate officers in this taproom, as well as privates.

Across the room Selene heard her uncle bellowing for her. Quickly she gathered up the stray dishes on the table, rising from her chair. "I must go."

"Wait," Simon added, reaching out to lightly touch her hand. "You must realize that something very significant is about to happen near here which will effectively set off this war. Both sides now have a sizable army poised only a few miles apart and ready to fight at the drop of a hat. This is an especially significant time, Selene. Bear that in mind. And it is only the beginning. Anything you can learn now or later— *anything*—would be a valuable service."

Selene called to her uncle, then turned one last time to lean close to Simon. "But General McDowell's army is three times the size of Beauregard's. He cannot fail to defeat the

Southerners. Perhaps this war will be over before it's begun."

"That's what we all want and expect. However, there is another large Confederate army currently pinned down in the Shenandoah Valley by our General Patterson. If they should get away—either to reinforce Beauregard or move south to protect Richmond—it could alter the odds against us dramatically. We don't know for certain where they are or if they've moved. They've got some good leadership. One of them, Brigadier General Jackson, is especially clever and crafty. It would be an advantage for us to know that he's unable to leave the valley."

"I don't know how you can expect me . . ."

"I personally believe that the Southern army will move to protect Richmond. But at all costs, they must not be allowed to reach Manassas Junction before this battle. General Jackson was one of the most respected men in his class at West Point, and if anyone can spring a trap, it's him."

He was speaking so low that Selene had to strain to hear his words over the noise of the room. She looked uneasily around and satisfied herself that no one was paying them any mind.

"Would it make such a difference if he did leave the valley?"

"He commands several crack regiments. And there are three other battalions besides his own in the valley. If they were to join Beauregard, it would make our job that much harder. As long as he's pinned down, we can strike the enemy with every chance of success. I'm on my way now to reassure General McDowell of that fact, and to urge him to move swiftly."

Selene stirred uncomfortably at the word "enemy." It was still difficult for her to think of people like her Uncle John or foolish old Caleb Hartshorn as the enemy. Yet she had only to remember the evils of slavery and how tragic the dissolution of the Union would be to ease her conscience.

"I must go," she whispered. "My uncle will begin to wonder why I'm taking so long. Will I see you again?"

"Yes. I should be stopping by again within a week. It would be better if you pretended not to know me. Try to learn anything at all."

Selene stood and rested the tray against her hip. "I won't forget." She made her way through the crowded room back to

13

the bar where her Uncle John waited impatiently, feeling as though she had suddenly become part of something much larger than the enclosed, self-centered world that concerned her only a few moments before. Though Simon Lazar was not exactly a friend, or even someone she much admired, it was inspiring to think that he would be risking his neck to travel through this stronghold of Southern sympathy in order to learn those pertinent facts that would end the war that much sooner. It gave her a thrill of excitement to think that she, too, could contribute to such a cause—one which her father would have wholeheartedly supported had he lived. For the first time since his death a year ago she began to see how she might truly carry on his work.

"For God's sake, girl," her uncle exploded, jarring her out of her thoughts. "Of all times to pick to stand about flirting with the customers! I'm going a little daft here. Damn that sorry Matilda!"

Selene's full lips lifted in a half smile at the thought of flirting with Simon Lazar. But let her uncle think that. It would relieve her of the need to explain her long conversation.

"Why not ask Rosie to help, Uncle John. Or her daughter, Sadie. It's too much for me, too."

"Sadie's only a child. But perhaps you'd better call her anyway. She can do some of the simple things, and I need you to take that tray upstairs."

Selene groaned. "Oh, Uncle John, do I have to? Those fellows were very rude to me in the yard. One of them even laid his hands on me. I don't want to go up there."

"Now Selene, don't go antagonizing our brave Virginia boys. Leave the door open and if one of them bothers you, scream like the devil and I'll come running. But take their tray up and be quick about it."

She toyed with the thought of refusing yet again, then gave it up. If she was able to get in and out of the room quickly enough, they couldn't bother her too much. She had strong lungs and, if need be, could yell loudly enough to bring half the house to her aid. It wasn't so much that she feared them —cheeky as they were—as much as she was filled with a distaste of having to even serve them. Resigned, she moved to

14

the kitchen to send Sadie to the taproom and collect the tray Rosie had set out. It was covered with bowls of stew and slabs of fresh bread and it was heavy as she made her way up the back stairs. At least up here it was a little more quiet since the racket below was cut off by a door to the stairwell which someone had closed. The hall was empty since there was only the one private sitting room on the upper floor of the stone tavern, along with several bedrooms occupied by the family and kept locked during the day. As Selene started down the hall, she noticed that the door to the private room was slightly ajar, and as she approached it she could make out low voices from within. She was about to push it open and enter when she caught a name that stopped her in her tracks.

"As long as they think Jackson is pinned down in the valley, we have nothing to worry about."

Selene stood frozen, straining to hear the quiet words inside the room.

"But we're not certain where Jackson is. Or the rest of Johnson's army. Don't you think . . ."

She lost the next few words and strained closer to the door.

"Well, we know he's not the man to be thwarted by a timid old woman like Patterson. And I don't think he'll go to Richmond, either. He's bound to try to reach Manassas Junction, once he knows McDowell intends to attack us. You could never keep him away from a good fight."

"Yes. But does he know McDowell intends to attack?"

"He knows. Everybody north and south knows. It's my guess he's on his way here now, and we've only to find him and let him know how urgent it is that he . . ."

The voice moved away and grew indistinct. Selene recognized the one asking the questions as the cheeky young man who grabbed her at the well, but the other voice was unfamiliar. She was listening so intently that it was a second before she realized all conversation had stopped. The quiet creak of a floorboard alerted her to the fact that someone was crossing the room, coming towards her. Pulling up her shoulders, she pushed the door boldly open and entered the room, nearly colliding with the officer on the white mount in the yard. He was standing close enough to her that she caught

15

the familiar scent of leather and horse, and he was staring at her, his dark eyes frowning with suspicion. She knew at once he suspected her of eavesdropping and she gave him her most glowing smile, hoping she could reassure him that she was perfectly innocent.

"Good evening, gentlemen. Would you like your supper now? There's a delicious stew and some of Rosie's good fresh bread and Uncle John's best beer. I'm sure you'll enjoy it after your long ride . . ."

She was talking too much and too fast. With flustered motions she set the tray on the table and started removing the dishes, all the while noticing out of the corner of her eye that the suspicious officer—the tallest and most mature of the three— had followed her back into the room and was still eyeing her.

The young man who had grabbed her in the yard has no such reservation. He reached out and ran a finger down her arm under the elbow-length sleeves of her dress.

"That looks scrumptious, my girl, but I can think of something I'd rather have than food."

Selene yanked her arm away and for an instant the glare she turned on him revealed her true disgust. Then she caught the tall officer studying her face and forced her lips into what she hoped appeared to be a pleasant smile.

"Supper is all you'll get tonight, I'm afraid, sir. We're too busy for anything beyond that."

The young man stood closer to leer over her, peering down at the deep cleavage above her lace-trimmed bodice. "Perhaps later . . ."

"You did say 'Uncle' John, I believe," the tall officer broke in, allowing his critical gaze to shift for an instant to his junior officer.

"Yes, I did. My uncle owns this tavern." Selene answered, her voice slipping back into its usual genteel tones. "I'm only helping him out today because our regular girl has run off."

Keeping his dark eyes on her face, the officer went on. "You had better remember that, Lieutenant Hanson. We don't want any trouble from the proprietor tonight of all nights, now *do* we?"

Lt. Hanson at least had the grace to look embarrassed. "Well, I didn't realize. Please accept . . . apologies . . ."

"Of course you didn't," Selene said smiling at him. The third officer had already begun helping himself to the stew, uninterested in either a flirtation or the possibility that there was a Northern spy among them.

"Well," she mumbled, easing toward the door. "I suppose I had better get back downstairs."

The tall officer—a captain if she read the three bars on his collar correctly—watched her until she reached the door, then turned back to the meal on the table. Nothing more was said, and finally in desperation Selene stepped out into the hall, not quite closing the door behind her. She was about to put her ear to the crack, when she heard the Captain's heavy boots cross the room and the door slammed.

She knew he suspected her of eavesdropping and her good sense told her to go back downstairs and stay out of trouble. And yet she could not give up so easily. Already she had learned that Simon's information about General Jackson was wrong. These men had indicated with some certainty that he was on his way to Manassas, but when would he arrive? If only she knew that, she could hurry and catch up with Simon before he reached Centreville and McDowell's headquarters, and prevent him from passing on the wrong information—a mistake which might well cost them the first battle of the war.

She had to hear more. But how? At the end of the hall the small door leading to the attic stood closed and shuttered. The old floorboards up there were not tightly sealed Selene remembered. If she put her ear close to the floor, she might still be able to make out what was being said in the room below.

Running lightly she hurried up the attic stairs. The dark, musty room was crowded with old furniture scattered about haphazardly, and the heat was searing. Yet Selene paid it no mind. She eased over to the area above the sitting room and quietly knelt to get as close to the floor as possible. It was impossible to prevent a few groaning creaks from the dry timbers, but she hoped they would be ignored by the men below intent on their supper.

Small chinks of light filtered through the tiny cracks in the

17

ceiling. Placing her ear against the rough planks, she strained to hear the voices below. To her dismay they stopped completely, and Selene pictured in her mind quizzical faces turned up to the low ceiling in the room below, as though they could see her through the boards. She knelt, barely breathing against the long, heavy silence until, at last, the quiet voices began again, and she inwardly breathed a soft sigh of relief. It was difficult to make out their words, though now and again she caught the loud clink of silverware against china clearly enough. Then one of them seemed to move directly under her and his voice rose clearly upward.

"My guess is he's somewhere between Winchester and Ashby's Gap. I scouted that area with him once on a field trip when I was a student at the Lexington Academy. I think I can find him somewhere about . . . here."

The rattle of a parchment map being rolled out drowned the muffled replys of the other two men. Then she heard the first one speak again quite clearly.

"That little skirmish this morning was nothing compared to the slaughter we'll have, if we don't get those reinforcements. It's been no secret that the Federal army was marching out of Washington to meet us. You can bet that information reached Winchester almost as soon as we knew it here. Wild horses couldn't keep the First Brigade from joining the fight."

"But suppose they can't get here in time. That attack could come any moment."

"I don't think so. McDowell is a cautious bastard. He won't move until he's forced to. And don't underestimate General Jackson's ability to march quickly when it's absolutely necessary. Our part in all this is simply to make certain that he *knows*—it's absolutely necessary and I intend to do that."

Selene eased her cramped legs as carefully as she could without making too much noise. One of the old boards underneath her gave a crashing groan and she immediately froze her body while her mind went on working furiously. The Shenandoah Valley. She knew little of Virginia beyond the area close to Washington City, but she recalled her Uncle John talking about the area of prosperous farms enclosed by mountain ranges in the middle of the state. Johnson's large

18

Southern army could be anywhere in there. If only she could catch a name, a town or village or landmark. Anything.

She realized the voices had grown quiet again. Then the main speaker's voice came through clearly, almost as though he had heard her unspoken request.

"We know he was near Winchester. If he's making his way to Manassas, then he's probably going to go along this route, eastward."

"Why not this way, through the Manassas Gap?"

"I don't think so. I believe he'll take Ashby's Gap and try to join up with the railroad junction. I can probably find him somewhere around Millwood."

"But suppose General Johnson divided his army, sending part south to protect Richmond. We ought to cover that route just in case."

"That'll be your job, Casey. And yours, Hanson, will be to scout the Massanuttan range just in case he goes that way. Finish your meal, both of you, then we'll have a short rest before heading out. Hanson, you report to Beauregard and tell him what we're doing before you start west."

"I'd rather go with you."

Selene did not hear the reply. Already she was easing toward the attic door trying desperately to keep the old floorboards from revealing her presence. She had a route and that was all she needed. Now it was time to follow Simon and warn him that the Confederate forces were about to be reinforced with Johnson's army of the Shenendoah. Her uncle was never going to forgive her for running off right at this busy time, yet with such a crisis at hand, surely her country's interest came first. She would do what had to be done and apologize later. After all, what would Papa say? He would tell her to put the bigger issues ahead of the lesser ones and to follow her ideals. Wherever they led.

Breathlessly she ran downstairs, peered into the hall long enough to see that it was clear, and hurried through the house to the stables, avoiding the taproom. Lolly, the aged mare who was the only horse her uncle allowed her to ride, turned her softly eyes on Selene as she hurried around her throwing on the saddle, silently protesting this sudden interruption of her sedentary afternoon. Selene pulled on the bridle and fastened the cinch without much caring if it was well done. All she could think of, as she pulled the reluctant mare through the stable doors, was how long it had already been since Simon started down that road to Centreville. It was in her favor that he was not in a hurry, and if she rode swiftly she might still catch up with him. Anyway, she had to try.

She never saw the tall Confederate officer at the upstairs window watching her as she swung up into the saddle and slapped the reins on Lolly's neck. Without a word to his fellow officers still eating at the table, he rushed from the room and down the stairs. By the time he reached the stables Selene's mare was already trotting sedately down the road toward the stone bridge, unwilling to hurry in the heat of the afternoon. Even as he vaulted into the saddle, he mentally calculated how he could cut her off by ignoring the road and crossing the fields to reach the bridge before the girl. His magnificent white stallion was not fresh, but he had never failed yet to come up with the speed his master asked of him, and he did not fail now. He bounded over the field as though borne on the wind, reaching the bridge just ahead of Selene's loping mare. With a lunge that brought the white horse rearing on its hind legs, the man bounded in front of the girl on the mare, just as they were about to clatter onto the bridge. He tried to reach for Selene's bridle to steady her mount, but the terrified mare, screaming in fright, reared up just high enough for her startled rider to slide out of the saddle and land in a heap on the road.

Free of her mistress, Lolly backed away, spun in a circle, and lit out across the field for the familiar comfort of her stable. Behind her, the man reined in his own horse, slid out of the saddle in an effortless motion, and knelt beside the girl lying on the road.

"Damn," he muttered peering down at her. "I didn't intend to kill her!"

Selene opened her eyes to a world whirling dizzily around her. The throbbing in her head and the labored breathing of her chest brought back her spill. She groaned and reached up to still her aching head. Her eyes slowly began to clear, revealing the man bending over her, his dark eyes enigmatic.

"Lolly . . ." she moaned.

"She threw you," he replied in a calm voice. "How do you feel? Is anything broken?"

Deftly he ran his fingers down her arms, his fingertips lightly pressing her wrists.

"I don't think so," Selene murmured, pulling her arms away from his hands. "Where is my horse? I've got to go on . . ."

She tried to sit up, but was so woozy that at first it was impossible. He laid a steadying hand under her arms and helped her first to kneel and then to get to her feet. She leaned against him until her head cleared and she found her footing.

"I don't need your help, thank you. If you could just be so kind as to retrieve my horse."

The man released her and stood back, crossing his arms over his chest.

"I can't. She headed straight for the stables at that tavern back there as soon as you slid off her back. She's probably nearly to her stall by now, still dragging the bridle."

Slowly Selene became aware of an ache in her shoulder where she had landed on the hard earth. She rubbed it gingerly and eyed the officer with a growing suspicion. "I remember now. She was frightened by your horse. You deliberately ran out in front of us."

He nodded, almost imperceptibly. "I regret that I had to. Unfortunately I had no time to devise a less traumatic method of stopping you."

"But why? I don't even know you."

"Perhaps it's time you did. Captain Wade Kinsolving of the 26th Virginia. Your servant, ma'am."

It was said with the civility worthy of a drawing room. Selene glared at him, her eyes narrowing. She had a very strong suspicion of why he had stopped her. It was clear enough that he had been the officer on the huge white stallion who had spoken so forcefully earlier at the well. She even recognized his voice now from her intense listening in the attic. She rubbed at her arm and shoulder, trying to get the feeling back into them. "How did you know?"

He seemed relieved at her frankness. "I saw you gallop out of the yard from the upstairs window. And though you tried to

21

be quiet above our room, I could make out your footsteps. What I don't understand is why. Why should a good daughter of the South go hurrying to the Union army to tell them what she had overheard in a Southern taproom?"

"Daughter of the South!" Selene sniffed. "I'm not from Virginia and I detest your beliefs. I also detest your mock civility—pretending to be so polite when you have just frightened my horse into throwing me. I could have been killed."

"I regret that, ma'am, more than I can say. But sometimes circumstances call for extreme measures."

"Don't call me ma'am," Selene said angrily, her frustration growing. While they stood here exchanging barbs, Simon would be gone.

The tall man pulled off his hat and brushed back his hair with his hand. It was a dingy gold, almost brown, and fell in natural waves to his collar. "There you have me at a disadvantage. I have introduced myself, but who are you? Other than the niece of the proprietor of that tavern back there, I don't even know your name."

"My name isn't important. I will appreciate it if you will simply go on your way and let me get back to my uncle's inn. Since you've so effectively prevented me from completing the errand I was on, that should satisfy you."

Wade Kinsolving frowned and carefully placed his hat back on his head. He appeared to be thinking this over as he looked her up and down. The massaging she had given her shoulder had caused her blouse to slip halfway down her upper arm. The lace-trimmed edge pulled tightly across her arm and over the fullness of one swelling breast, revealing its ample contours. The deep shadowed cleavage between her rounded breasts riveted his attention and he felt a sudden hot swelling in his loins. He forced his gaze back to her face. It was a lovely face, he had to admit, now that he had a chance to scrutinize it so closely. Oval in shape, her eyes were slightly slanted, quite large, and heavily rimmed with dark, thick lashes. She had an unusual combination of dark brows and eyelashes with golden hair that caught the sunlight filtering through the trees like flaxen thread. Her lips were full and inviting, shapely as a cherub's and tinged with pink. Her neck was graceful and long and so slight he could put his hands around it, yet below her ample breasts and slim waist her hips looked full and broad—made for loving.

He tore his eyes away and mentally shook himself. It didn't matter a whit that she was beautiful and luscious. The important thing here was that she knew things she ought not to know and posed a danger to his country. But what in hell was he going to do about it?

Selene recognized something of the struggle going on in the man who faced her. She knew that look he gave her—appraising and admiring all at once—and she knew it had nothing to do with generals and armies. Yet she also sensed that it was not strong enough to deter this man from what he considered to be his duty. Something warned her he was not going to let her go. In fact, there was a coiled alertness about him that suggested that if she even tried to make a sudden break, he would be after her in a second. And she would be no match for him. He was at least six feet tall, broad-shouldered, narrow-waisted, and the muscles of his long legs were readily apparent under the tight-fitting gray trousers of his uniform. When he glanced away she studied his face from under her long lashes. It was not unattractive—lean, intense, a full mouth, narrow patrician nose and eyes that revealed every nuance of the intelligence behind them. He had unusually thick lashes for a man, but there was nothing weak about that square firm chin and determined stance. She should have paid this man more attention back there when she was so busy concentrating on Hanson, that silly flirtatious roué. This man was the dangerous one, and because she had ignored that fact she was now caught in a bad situation with no way to get to Simon and warn him of what she had learned.

"Look," she finally said, deciding it was best to be completely honest. "I did overhear a few remarks back there and it seemed at the time that they might be useful to General McDowell. But since you've stopped me, and it's too late now to pass the information along, why not just let me go back to the tavern? My uncle needs my help today, and heaven knows, I can't cause you any harm there. It's too

23

near the Southern lines."

"How can I be sure of that?"

"I give you my word. My promise."

Captain Kinsolving did not even attempt to suppress a laugh. "Oh, of course. That will make everything all right then."

"You don't need to be sarcastic. My word is honorable. I'm not a serving wench in a tavern, you know. I was only helping out today because our usual girl ran off. I was brought up a lady, and my father was a distinguished professor."

Wade waved a hand, cutting her off. "It's not important to me who you are, or how distinguished a lineage you spring from. All I care about is the safety of our army which is about to be involved in a crucial battle. What's to prevent you from taking another horse and galloping off to the Union lines the moment I ride away? I can't risk that."

"But if I give you my word—"

"Hush, madam. And since I don't know your name, it will have to be 'madam' or 'ma'am' for the time being."

"Selene," she muttered, glaring at him, her anxiety growing. "Selene Sprague." He was never going to let her go!

"Hush then, Selene, and let me think."

Absently he walked toward his horse grazing contentedly nearby and pulled up the dangling leather bridle, running the strings through his hands. He was tempted to send her back to her uncle. It would relieve him of an unexpected burden. If only he had the leisure to sit and keep an eye on her for the next two days he would willingly do so. That way she would be out of harm's way while also providing him with a pleasant diversion. The trouble was, he had no time right now for dalliance. He had an urgent mission to accomplish, and even now time was wasting while he struggled to figure out what to do with this troublesome girl.

Selene studied Wade as he concentrated on his next move, half-fascinated by his lithe attractive figure, while the other part of her mind raced about trying to discover some possible means of escaping from him. The set of his shoulders, the strength of his hands as he fondled the bridle, the intensity of his lean face as he bent toward his horse, all of them set her blood tingling in a way she had never experienced before.

Mentally she shook herself. This was no time to be drawn toward this young man's obvious sensual appeal. She had an important mission to accomplish, and he was standing in her way. Unless she found some means of escaping from him the entire fate of an army and a country might hang in the balance.

The big white stallion raised his head and shook his mane impatiently. With a gentle manner Wade began to stroke the sleek neck, soothing the horse. And Selene chose that moment to run.

Two

Selene had inched far enough away from him to have a good start toward the woods. Yanking up her skirts, she dove for the shelter of the trees, certain that if she once made the thickest part she would know the area well enough to outwit him. Her heart gave a leap as she realized she was almost there. She heard a startled cry behind her and pushed herself to run even faster, her breath tearing at her throat. The canopy of limbs closed over her as she darted around the slender saplings, heading for the dark thicket that loomed ahead. Almost there!

A weight like a stone wall slammed against her, knocking her to the earth. Her breath went out with a loud *humph* as her shoulder crashed against the hard ground. Strong arms, like an iron vise, clutched at her legs even as she struggled against them. She was thrown over on her back as if she were no more than a sack of potatoes, the man straddled her, his heavy weight pressing her into the damp earth, pinning her arms above her head.

"Let . . . me go," Selene gasped. "You're . . . you're hurting me!"

His face was an angry mask, dark and severe. "That was very foolish."

"Please, you're hurting my chest . . ."

He eased his weight up on his knees but kept her arms tightly pinned over her head. "I don't want to hurt you, miss, but you asked for it. You should have known you couldn't outrun me."

Selene went limp, her eyes soft and pleading. "Please let me go back to my uncle. I won't run away again, I promise. Please."

His hands closed firmly around her wrists. Throwing one knee over her body, he pulled her up until her face was inches from his. There was something in his look, something of pleasure at his strength and her helplessness, that frightened Selene. For the first time she realized how dangerous this man might be.

"You've made it quite obvious that I cannot afford to let you go, my girl. You probably won't believe this, but you are as much a trial to me, as I am to you."

"You're right. I don't believe it."

"All the same . . ." his words trailed off as he studied her face intently for the first time. Keeping one hand firmly on her wrist he allowed the fingers of his other hand to lightly trace the outline of her cheek and then wander to her full, parted lips. Without a word he bent and kissed her, at first lightly and then more sensuously, forcing her mouth with his tongue. Then abruptly he pulled back.

"All the same, you are most decidedly a nuisance. You'll have to come with me. Nothing else is safe."

Standing quickly, he pulled her to her feet. "What do you mean, come with you," she spluttered. This was one possibility that had not crossed her mind. She had thought he might murder her, or carry her back to the tavern and watch her, but kidnap her . . . it was unthinkable. "I can't go with you. I don't have a horse, remember. I don't even have any other clothes. Be reasonable."

Holding tightly to her wrists, Wade pulled her back to the bridge where the white stallion waited obediently. "There's nothing reasonable about it. I have to move and move quickly. Bringing you along is a pain in the neck and something I would much rather avoid. But I can't risk letting you go." Grabbing a rope from his saddlebags, he began lashing her hands together, holding her tightly in spite of the way she strained against him.

"But you can't! My uncle will come after me. He'll kill you. It's barbaric. You're no gentleman if you do this!"

He stopped to look fiercely into her eyes. "Madam, the only other choice I have is to put a bullet through your pretty head

27

and you can be grateful that I'm too much of a gentleman to do that. Though the thought has crossed my mind. Now, get up."

"I won't!" Selene cried, even as he lifted her and threw her up on his mount in front of the saddle. Bounding up behind her he grasped the reins, gripped his arm tightly around her waist, and with a cry to his horse, cantered off into the woods. Selene soon gave up struggling and prepared to scream her head off the first time they encountered anyone on the road. As though Wade anticipated her plan, he kept to the woods, skirting the main roads and moving even deeper into the underbrush when it appeared that someone might be approaching.

They rode so long that soon Selene was too weary to scream, even if she had seen someone to help her. She had to admire the way the stallion picked his way with lithe feet and obedient manners, never hesitating to go where his master asked. Unused to sitting on a horse for so long, she soon found that the muscles of her thighs were screaming in protest and her back slumping more with each new hour. Though she tried not to lean against her hated abductor, soon her aching back had no strength to keep her away, and she slumped against him, almost grateful for the support.

As the afternoon light began to give way to dusk, she realized that she was both hungry and thirsty. Once only during their long ride had he offered her a swig from his canteen, and this she had disdainfully rejected. Now her throat felt as though it was filled with cotton, and she would have gladly taken the drink, had he had the courtesy to offer it again.

She had no idea where they were except that they were heading west. Any small towns and farmhouses in their path were carefully avoided. Unerringly her abductor seemed to know what fences to skirt and what settlements to circle, and even as they moved farther into untamed, uncultivated areas he seemed to have a confidence about his direction. Selene was hopelessly lost. Had he untied her hands and put her down to find her way back, she would not have known in which direction to walk.

When it was finally becoming so dark she could not make out the trees thirty paces ahead, he pulled his tired horse to a stop and slid out of the saddle.

By this time Selene had almost fallen asleep. Waking quickly she looked around her. They were in a small clearing, where the solitude and surrounding brush were so thick that it had to be deep in the woods.

"We'll stop here for the night," Wade said, pulling her off the horse. Her weak knees gave out from under her and she would have fallen had he not grabbed her.

"You're not accustomed to riding for so long, are you?" he said almost gently.

"I'll manage," she snapped, pulling away and slumping to the ground. "But it would help to have my hands free."

"In a moment." He turned to take care of his horse, leaving her sprawled on the ground. There was a tiny stream close enough for her to ease her way over to it and lap up some of its pristine water in her hands. Never had anything tasted so good! When Wade had finally got his stallion bedded for the night, he returned to begin setting up some kind of shelter for the two of them. With a practiced manner he made camp, something he had done many times before, but which for Selene was a new experience. Although the thought of finding a way to run was never far from her mind, she nevertheless managed some grudging measure of admiration for the brisk, efficient way Wade went about building a makeshift hearth and crude shelter. Everything he needed was in his saddlebag. He deftly stretched a large strip of canvas between four poles to form a roof. Underneath he rolled out a narrow blanket with one swift movement. Gathering twigs and leaves and a few solid logs, he soon had a fire sputtering and crackling against the gathering dusk. A soft misty rain, more damp air than actual rain drops, had dampened Selene's thin dress and long hair and she gladly edged closer to the fire's warmth.

Producing an iron skillet from his saddlebag, Wade cut a slice of bacon and soon had it spitting in the pan.

"I thought soldiers only ate salt pork." Selene noted glumly.

He sat on his haunches, shaking the handle of the skillet, and smiled mischievously up at her. "The regulars do. Officers know how to take better care of themselves. Otherwise, they shouldn't be officers." He frowned at the sight of her rubbing her arms against the chill. "Here, come closer to

29

the fire," he said brusquely. "You women never wear the proper clothes."

"I didn't plan on taking a trip," Selene added, her voice dripping venom. In spite of his mild attempt at conviviality, she was not going to forget that she had been dragged here against her will. Or that she was still a prisoner.

Wade studied her for a moment, her wide skirt and petticoats protected her below the waist well enough, but the low scoop of her bodice left her neck and shoulders bare to the increasing rain. His eyes lingered on the clinging, damp fabric of her dress which emphasized the swelling fullness of her breasts tantalizingly. Then he forced himself to look down at her hands, still tightly bound in her lap, trying to ignore the sudden hot surge in his loins.

"I suppose I could loosen those a bit," he murmured, reaching across to tug at the ropes that bound her wrists. "You must understand that I cannot take them off completely."

"But why not? I don't have the slightest idea where we are. I couldn't get back to the Federal army even if I wanted to."

"And don't you?"

Selene shrugged, hoping to appear resigned to her situation. "I'm so tired and uncomfortable right now, that I don't want to even think about escaping."

Wade stirred the bacon over the fire. He was convinced more by the pathetic picture she presented than by her words. She was only a bit of a thing, not strong at all, and undone by the miseries of a long ride and the wet, open campsite. Yet, he wanted her where he could keep an eye on her and make sure she would not escape. And he had to admit that he enjoyed watching her. The fire glow made a golden nimbus of her hair and emphasized the graceful shadows on her narrow cheeks and the fullness of her lips, so enticing that he was overcome with the desire to draw the sweetness from them with his own.

Mentally he shook himself. She was having a disturbing effect on him and he must guard against it. There was no time or energy for anything but finding the General as soon as possible. And yet . . .

While Wade struggled to ignore her, Selene stretched the ropes between her hands as far as they would allow and casually studied the shadowy woods around her. Soon it would be completely dark and she would have no chance at all of escaping. Even now it was only by straining her eyes that she could make out the thin open curve of what appeared to be a road through the branches of the surrounding trees.

She had to get away from this man! She was disturbingly conscious of the intensity of those side glances he threw her way, and she could sense the waves of excitement underneath them. Once, looking up at him from under her long lashes, she felt a tremor grip her own body. His shoulders, bent over the fire, strained against the fabric of his shirt when he had removed his coat. In spite of the anger she felt toward him her eyes lingered on the high forehead, the firm curve of his cheek and the strength of his chin, the narrow hips and the long thighs, the high boots, and most of all, his hands, with their long, graceful fingers that moved so deftly.

Ignoring all the covert glances between them, Wade kept up a running banter that helped to take his mind off this disturbing girl and the fact that she was his prisoner.

"Not only do we not have to eat salt pork but we're spared hardtack as well," he said almost jovially as he removed a thick slab of crusty bread from the saddlebag. He already had a small pan of water boiling and he threw in a handful of peas and some grains of salt, stirring them with his knife. The pungent aroma of the bacon made Selene's mouth water and she remembered she had eaten little all day. When Wade got some coffee boiling, its nutty fragrance complementing the bacon, she wondered whether she would be able to leave the campsite at all before supper, even if she got the opportunity to run away. By the time everything was ready, she was as anxious as Wade to dive in.

The food was delicious. The added ingredients of open air and a hard day's ride were all the sauce it needed. By now she had nearly a foot of rope between her hands which made eating easy, yet seemed to satisfy Wade that she was still bound. She devoured every morsel and then sipped the hot coffee, feeling as though her body was slowly reviving. By the time the food was all gone and the remains cleared away, there was only the last lingering gray of dusk before darkness fell completely, and

31

Selene was beginning to resign herself to having to spend the rest of the night as a prisoner.

"We'll only sleep until the first light of dawn," Wade said, almost as if reading her mind. "The sooner we are up and back on the trail, the better."

"And do I have to fear for my life when we finally come across this general you're looking for?" Selene asked sarcastically.

Wade laughed. "What do you think we are—barbarians? I have no wish to harm you, madam. Once I've accomplished my mission, you will be free to go."

"In the middle of the Confederate army. Oh, thank you, sir. How gallant."

A flush of anger colored Wade's face. "There is no finer gentleman in the world than Thomas Jackson. Nor are the rest of his officers lacking in genteel refinements. You will be completely safe."

Selene gave him as scathing a look as she could manage. "And I suppose that is true for you as well. You have a strange idea of what constitutes a gentleman."

Fiercely Wade reached out and clamped a hand over her wrist. "And you do not strike me as much of a lady."

Her flesh felt hot under his hand while the defiance in her flashing eyes sent a thrill through his blood. He made himself drop her arm and turn away.

"We might as well turn in," he muttered, and rose to step into the deep shadows surrounding the faint firelight. He had his back to her just beyond the edge of the trees, when Selene realized that he was relieving himself before going to sleep. She looked around wondering if they were supposed to share the small space under the canvas cover, or if he would be gracious enough to leave it to her.

And then she heard it. The soft clip-clop of a horse on the narrow road back through the trees. It was so faint that she almost missed it completely. The rider sneezed and then coughed, the sound carrying through the woods.

It was her only chance. In an instant she was on her feet. Wade was across the open campsite, in the trees at the edge with his back to her. She grabbed up her skirts to strike out through the thickets.

"Help!" she screamed as she ran crashing through the thick undergrowth. Her skirts tangled immediately, torn by the thorny branches of a blackberry bush, catching her and holding her there.

Had she really screamed? Or had the hand that closed over her open mouth prevented even that? She felt the crushing weight of his body as they fell into the tangled undergrowth, his arms around her, pinning her to the ground. Struggling against that terrible force, Selene writhed and thrashed under his weight, and struggled to call out against the imprisoning hand that pressed against her mouth.

"Damn you!" Wade muttered between his teeth. "Be quiet or I really will be forced to kill you!"

The muffled sound of their struggle hid the distant steps of horse and rider, but Selene knew they were passing her by and taking with them any possibility of escape. She was drowning in a white-hot searing anger at this powerful, despicable man who thrashed on the ground with her, pinning her down and preventing her from getting away with his heavy body. She fought like a tiger while Wade, gasping and struggling, tried to muffle the sounds of their struggle as he managed to get both arms around her, clutching her into stillness and pressing her into the ground with his weight. He listened with one ear on the road until he felt certain the rider had moved far enough away to no longer be a threat. Then he rose, pulling Selene to her feet, still keeping her in his steel grip and half-dragging her back to the fire. She twisted and struggled in frustration and fury. She dug her heels into the soft earth, tried to clutch at branches, and, finally, as they got back to the camp, managed to sink her teeth into the hand he still held over her mouth.

"Damn you!" Wade cried without releasing his hand. Rudely he thrust her down on the blanket under the canvass, then fell beside her, gripping her as she twisted, still trying to elude his iron grip. Her sleeves had slipped down over her shoulders, half-baring one breast. Her rumpled skirts were yanked up around her thighs. With a sudden horror she realized she could feel his swollen manhood firm and tight against her, and remembered how her escape attempt had

33

caught him half-undressed.

Wade was intoxicated by the twisting, voluptuous body beneath him. His anger at her—coupled with the longing she had already evoked and the fact that they were both half out of their clothes—sent him reeling beyond an ability to stop. He wanted her body, he wanted release from the hot torment in his loins. And he wanted to hurt her, to have power over her, to show her that she was completely and wholly his prisoner.

In one searing instant the struggle between them was transformed. He tore away the fabric of her bodice, cupping his hand around the hot fullness of her breast. Selene slashed at him with her hands and he caught them both in one free hand and threw them over her head, pinning her arms down while his mouth closed on the taut nipple. Her back arched and the breast rose in his lips and he sucked wildly, smearing the sweet projection with his lips, licking it in ever-widening circles, then working his way back again to the erect, tight nipple where he sucked with abandon.

Selene began to feel her fury fading under the excitement of Wade's insistent gyrations, his thighs sliding against her legs. She felt his hands tearing at her skirts, laying bare her thighs. His fingers thrust into her, twisting and pushing, firm against the increasing wetness that welcomed them. His body was heavy on top of hers, and yet the sensation of his searching fingers and lips drove away everything but the longing for completeness, for being filled with him. She could feel his exposed manhood, hard and throbbing, pressing against her thighs wet and sticky. With a moan Wade forced it into her, pushing and thrusting ever deeper as Selene fought not to cry out. Dimly she determined she would not give him that satisfaction. He was beyond caring. Wildly he probed at her, his body throbbing against hers, his iron-hard spike violating her with its force.

No, Wade thought. He wanted her with him. It was not enough to reach this thrilling summit alone. His fingers sought out the soft seat of her passion, massaging back and forth, carrying her along on a torrent of pure sensation.

Selene gasped as the fires began to build within her. Her struggles ceased, became instead a melding of their bodies

34

riding the crest of a thunderous, roaring tempest. Dimly she heard herself cry out as they both went sweeping over its edge into the shattering void beyond, where the world went spiraling into a million shining fragments of ecstasy.

Wade's body slumped against her. Her body felt as empty and weak as it had been before she heard the horseman on the road. His breath came in heavy gasps as he fought to calm his raging body. Selene, gasping heavily, turned her face away from him and tightly closed her eyes.

During their struggle her hands had slipped over his head, where they still gripped his shoulders tightly, the length of rope between them holding him prisoner. They lay spent together for several long minutes until calm returned at last. Wade lifted his head, looking at her pale face shadowed by the dying fire.

She was so beautiful. Her hair lay floating around her like a cloud, as golden red in the firelight as the embers from the flames. Her long lashes fluttered against her cheek, a dark crescent on creamy rose. Her lips were still parted, the last lingering residue of her wild, passionate abandonment. Her long neck, as graceful and aristocratic as a statue, rose from her white shoulders and spread gracefully to the full roundness of her breasts, the dark nipples still taut.

Her passion had more than matched his own. For Wade this was a new experience. Up until now the only women he had ever made love to were either loose women who pretended to a false passion or the occasional gentlewoman whose purity and gentility suffocated her like a vise. This was a woman to treasure, he thought. His fingers slid lightly up the arch of her graceful throat. He had treated her brutally, his lust overpowering his every intention of remaining a gentleman. She had intoxicated him into taking her like the lowest serving girl, when she deserved better. He would make it up to her, given the chance. He would show her he could be gentle, he would win her acceptance and her joyful participation.

Selene slowly turned her head to look up at Wade. Her eyes were open now, only inches from his. She did not try to read what she saw in his gaze. She ignored the softness and repentance in the face so near her own. He had shifted his

35

weight so as not to be completely on top of her and her hands were free enough to raise, slipping the rope over his head. She forced down the warmth radiating from the soft tickle of his hand lightly stroking her neck and deliberately, forcefully, she lifted her hand and dug her nails along his cheek, forcing them into his flesh. A thin red stain sprang to life the length of Wade's cheek. With a cry of pain he grabbed at it, his eyes narrowing.

"You vixen!"

"Did you expect me to thank you!"

"You might have given me a chance to . . . Never mind. Get up."

He moved to sit up on one knee, grabbing Selene's hands again in his own. Forcing her to face him, once more he gripped her chin and brought her face close to his. She glared at him murderously, and would have spit at him but he kissed her hard and brutally. When he let her go, she spat on the ground instead.

"That's what I think of you," she said bitterly.

He laughed. "It doesn't matter what you think of me. We are forced to be together until I can turn you over to General Jackson, and whether you like it or not is beside the point. We have very little time to sleep since we must get off again at the first light, so you needn't expect a repeat of this performance."

"I suppose I should be grateful."

Wade forced down the hand he so longed to slap her with. "You can take the shelter," he said, standing and grabbing at one of the blankets. He wrapped it around him. "I'll sleep by the fire."

Selene did not argue. As confused and angry as she felt, the chance of being away from him was too welcome. And she might still be able to escape.

As though he read her mind, Wade picked up his saddlebag and removed another length of rope nearly six feet long. Deftly he tied one end around her ankle, using a complicated knot that she knew she could never work loose. The other end he tied around his own boot. Then wrapping himself in the blanket and pulling his hat down over his face, he stretched out close to the fire.

There was still a thin mist in the air and for one half a second Selene felt a little sorry that he had to be out in it. Instead she toyed with the delicious thought that perhaps he might get pneumonia from exposure. She lay down under the canvas square and wrapped a blanket around her as closely as she could, considering the bounds on her hands and feet, and tried to sleep. She was weary, sore all over, so tired that breathing was an effort, and her mind was in a turmoil. Her body ached where she had been violated and her spirit raged at the fact. Yet she needed to rest and sleep, in order to face the new day and try to devise some way to get back to Simon Lazar with the news about Jackson's army. It was so critical. She was the only person who knew it and she was helpless to tell the people who ought to know. Frustration was added to her other aches. Tossing and turning, she finally slipped into a fitful rest, never deep enough to help her forget the lumpy, uneven ground beneath her.

Just before dawn she slept at last, a short, deep unconsciousness from which she woke with a start at the first sound of waking birds above her head. For a moment she could not remember where she was. The fire had all but died, and the figure lumped beside it was so dark and still that at first she thought it was another log. Then the soft sound of Wade's breathing broke the stillness and she remembered.

Selene sat up very quietly and easily, in spite of the pains that shot through her body when she moved. She ran her hands through her hair, disheveled and tangled beyond hope. It had grown quite chilly and she pulled the blanket up around her shoulders, wishing she had some coffee or even a little water.

Wade stirred in his sleep. Above her head the stirring birds warbled their welcome to the dawning day. Selene leaned her arms on her knees and rested her head against them. What was she going to do? How was she ever going to get away from this despicable man and back to her own people. He was never going to be careless enough or relax his vigilance enough to let her get away. And would there be a repeat of last night? She forced down a traitorous thrill at the thought. He was hateful and a monster. She would kill him before she would allow him to force her again.

And then she saw the saddlebag.

It lay on the ground halfway between her canvas shelter and the man sleeping by the dead fire. She remembered now that Wade had thrown it there last night after removing that second rope. The outer flap had fallen open, exposing the edge of folded paper beneath.

Cautiously Selene slid her hand toward the leather pouch, watching Wade for any sign of movement. His back was to her and his soft regular breathing never altered. Her fingertips touched the bag, caught the edge of the papers, and carefully slid them out.

The gray light of morning had begun to deepen, but the clearing was still dark in shadow. As quietly as possible, hardly daring to breathe, Selene spread the papers in her lap and bent close to them, straining to make out the letters. The bundle was quite thick when folded, but proved to be only several pages. The one on the top looked like official orders relating to the search for Brigadier General Jackson and his battalion. It was signed by General Lee, the Commander of Virginia's Forces, and empowered the Captain Kinsolving to take whatever measures necessary to find and alert Brigadier Thomas Jackson about the storm brewing at Manassas. Selene didn't bother to try to read it, but put it underneath, and examined the second page.

This appeared to be an official paper commissioning Wade Kinsolving as an officer with the rank of captain in the Army of Northern Virginia, the Confederate States of America. Selene threw it aside in disgust and held the third page near her eyes, squinting in the poor light.

A letter of some sort, but an official letter. The signature at the bottom was once again that of Commander Lee, and the orders included in it riveted her attention. As nearly as she could make out, Wade Kinsolving was empowered by this letter to attend at once to Norfolk where the frigate *Yamacraw* would carry him to Barbados with all speed. There he was to meet with Sir Reginald Simms, Lord Candelby, her majesty's representative from Great Britain, with the intention of establishing preliminary guidelines to effect a treaty between the aforesaid government of Great Britain and the Confederate States.

Selene caught her breath. She knew enough of the ways of politics and government from her years growing up in Washington to realize the far-reaching implications of such a treaty. If the South could gain recognition of a country like England—a country whose insatiable appetite for cotton made the southern states almost an economic necessity—it would give them a double-sided advantage: the prestige of recognition by a major power and the continuation of a badly needed economic market. Surely that would be a blow to the Union. It would extend the war. Perhaps even lose it for them. What was she to do? Did Mr. Lincoln's government realize what was afoot here? Did they have any idea of how close such a treaty was to actually being signed? Was she the only person who knew the true mission that had been entrusted to this Confederate captain, and if so, what on earth could she do to stop him?

Wade stirred in his sleep, half-turning onto his back. Selene froze, waiting for his regular breathing to resume, then quickly folded the papers, and returned them to the pouch. Very quietly she slipped the pouch back in the saddlebag, all the while keeping her eyes on the sleeping man. Then she eased away from the fire and back under the canvas. Just as she resumed her old place, Wade reached up to wipe his eyes. He was waking.

He came awake with a start, sitting up and looking around cautiously, checking the ropes that linked his boot with Selene's foot. She had pulled her blanket around her and was feigning sleep, and it seemed to convince him. Roughly he shook her shoulders.

"Get up," he said brusquely as he deftly untied the rope on her ankle. "It's getting light and we've got to be going."

Selene stirred lethargically, hoping he would believe she was still half-asleep. "I'd like some coffee first," she said in as pitiful a voice as she could muster.

Wade was already busy dismantling their camp. "No time for that now. Maybe after we've gone a bit. If we catch up with the First Battalion, we'll share some of theirs."

"It's not fair," Selene muttered. He pulled her up on her feet, then turned to bring up his horse and throw on the saddle blanket and saddle.

"Fair or not, it's the way it is. This is not a pleasure trip."

"You hardly need to tell me that!"

She smoothed down her skirt and pulled her sleeves high up on her shoulders. She was feeling so unwashed and grimy that she would have gladly given a year of her life for soap and water and a good stiff hairbrush. But Wade barely allowed her time for the simplest of necessities before heaving her up on the saddle. She noticed that when he reached for his saddlebag he paused momentarily over the open flap, but the suspicious moment was quickly gone and he did not seem to suspect anything. His one concession to her comfort before leaping up behind her was to offer her a piece of hardtack to chew on. It turned out to be so grainy and pasty without anything to wash it down with that she quickly returned it.

They had ridden nearly an hour when a first faint rumble warned Wade they were nearing their destination. Selene had thought to pick up some distant sounds of drums beating or even pipes playing. An army on the march to her meant flags, neat rows of uniformed men marching in step, the rumble of caissons and wagons, all pomp and panoply.

She was not prepared then, when Wade brought his horse to an abrupt stop and sat motionless, listening intently. All she could make out were the cries of birds and the soft rustle of water in the distance.

"Listen," Wade whispered. "I think we've found them."

Mystified, Selene would not give him the satisfaction of asking what led him to that conclusion, though she was convinced he was wrong. When he spurred his horse forward, she all but slid from the saddle. Wade's arms tightened around her, while the white stallion went cantering out from the protection of the woods and onto a narrow road.

The dust ahead soon told her that Wade's intuition had been correct. Soon they met the advance cavalry, their horses lathered in the morning air. Behind them, strung out for what looked like miles, men filled the road. They carried haversacks on their backs and their long muskets rested on their shoulders. Their uniforms were every assortment of colors and civilian dress. What struck Selene the most as Wade guided his horse easily along the side, was the quiet. No laughing, no singing to pass the hours, indeed, barely a sound save the tramping of their boots on the road. There was a purposefulness in the dogged way they went forward, the pace brisk and unrelenting. Wade guided his horse against the traffic for what seemed an eternity to Selene, tired and hungry as she was. Occasionally he called out to a familiar face in the eternal rows of men, or returned a hello from them. He never bothered to explain to her who they were, but Selene guessed from some of the remarks exchanged that they knew him from his home, wherever that was. They all seemed in remarkably good humor considering the circumstances. She could not say the same for herself.

A sharp bugle cry swept along the lines, and almost as one, the men fell out, half of them emptying the road, or making for the grassy banks along the side, while the others fell where they stopped. They sprawled, content to rest, and Selene was disappointed to see that no one made a fire, though she hoped this was to be a breakfast break. With the road more empty Wade made better progress and he soon pulled up beside a group that by its hats, swords, and handsome horses swishing their tails nearby, were obviously the higher echelons of the corps.

"I'm looking for the General," Wade said, riding up to an officer who had pulled off his hat and was mopping at his brow with a checkered handkerchief.

"He went down the road to check on stragglers," the man said without interest. "He should be back in a minute." His eyes fastened on Selene sitting in the saddle, too weary to try to hide her still-manacled wrists. "Where did you get that, Captain? Spoils of war?"

"None of your business," Wade threw back over his shoulder, as he spurred his horse back onto the road. He caught sight of Selene's lingering glance at a group on the side of the road who were passing a canteen between them. "Well, perhaps we could wait here," he muttered, and turned off the road to the group of men seated on the bank. Slipping out of the

41

saddle he reached to help Selene off and supported her when her knees buckled beneath her. "I don't need your help," she said through clenched teeth, trying to pull her arms away. Wade lowered her to the ground. "Sit here. I'll bring you some rations."

Selene did not exactly like the way the men on the knoll were eying her. She sank to the ground, leaning gratefully against a tree, but turning so that her back was to them. Wade was only gone a minute, and when he returned he thrust a plate at her with cheese and biscuits and even a little honey upon it. Selene took it because she was too tired and too hungry to refuse. She was even more grateful for the canteen he offered her which turned out to be filled with a bitter-tasting water. Still she drank it greedily.

Wade crouched near her, helping himself from the same plate. When Selene next looked up it was to see that one of the men from the group beyond had risen to walk toward them.

"Somehow I never expected to see you here, Wade," the man said, thrusting out a hand to the Captain who had risen also. "You were in Richmond just two days ago. What did you do? Fly?"

"I might ask you the same question," Wade said, smiling in a way Selene had not seen before. "I thought you were with Beauregard."

"Staff sent me to Winchester as soon as we learned of McDowell's Washington dances. You should have seen the way Old Jack foxed that Yankee Patterson. Fancy that old woman keeping us pinned down in the valley when there's a battle going on twenty-five miles outside of Washington itself. We slipped him as neatly as a greased porker. It was beautiful. Who's this?"

Selene glanced up at the older man who was standing with his hands on his hips examining her from above. He was older than Wade, and had a patrician, lean face with a long nose and deeply set eyes, so blue they all but disappeared in his tan brown face.

"This is my prisoner," Wade said in a matter-of-fact voice. "And a dangerous one, too."

"Wade Kinsolving, trust you to take a beauty for a prisoner." He swept off his plumed hat. "Your servant, ma'am.

42

Clive Atwell, Major, Virginia Artillery."

"You needn't bother to be so gentlemanly with this one, Clive. She'll scratch out your eyes the first chance she gets."

For the first time Clive seemed to notice the long flaming red line along Wade's cheek. He laughed. "She's already made sport of you, I see."

Selene opened her mouth to protest that she was the one who had been made sport of, but Wade gave her no chance.

"She's part of the reason I need to see the General," he went on. "I've information about McDowell's plans . . ."

"That's no secret, man. Why everybody north and south knows what Lincoln and McDowell plan. Thanks to our spies in Washington, it might as well have gone out over the wires."

Wade hesitated. "Still . . . I should see him as soon as possible. Doesn't he ever rest when the men do?"

"Not that I can see. For all he drives us, he drives himself even harder. Look here, Wade. This girl's got ropes on her hands. Aren't you carrying this a little far? That's no way to treat a decent woman."

Selene noticed that Wade's color rose slightly. At least he had the grace to look uncomfortable. "This is war, Clive. Some graces have to be put aside for the common good. She'll have her freedom soon enough, but not until I'm satisfied that she can do no harm to us."

Selene decided to get involved, since Clive Atwell gave every indication of being someone who might help her. Hurriedly, she rose to her feet. "I thank you, sir, for reminding this . . . this ruffian of what constitutes civilized behaviour. I am not a threat to anyone. And I *am* a decent woman. He has forcibly kept me prisoner and treated me in the most shocking manner and . . ."

Wade put his hands on her shoulders and thrust her back down on the ground. "Sit down and be still. You'll be taken care of in the proper manner at the proper time."

"You see how he treats me . . . !"

"I do say, Wade, that's a bit ungentlemanly. What would your father say?"

"Father is dead. It's General Jackson now who'll decide whether this 'decent woman' constitutes a threat or not. And once he knows the whole story I think he'll agree that everything I've done is correct."

Selene wanted to ask, "Everything?" but the thought of the way he had taken advantage of her the night before was still too mortifying to share publicly. She gave Wade a murderous glare and clenched her lips together. Somehow she'd get even with this barbarian, and get her information to the proper persons, too. She must bide her time until the right opportunity came.

Clive was watching her closely, looking first at her and then at Wade, thoughtfully weighing what he saw. For a moment she thought he was going to side with her, but then he shrugged and turned away. At the same time a ruckus arose, a clatter on the road, and clouds of dry dust scurrying around the horsemen advancing toward them. There was a sharp yell from the seated men and several of them jumped to their feet, grabbing up the hats and gear they had thrown down a few moments before.

Clive looked back at Selene, his eyes narrowing. "I don't rightly know what is going on here, but it doesn't matter. Here comes the General now. I suppose he'll straighten it out."

Three

Wade turned with relief to face the stern ramrod figure who rode up on a small sorrel horse. There was a thin film of lather on its sleek sides and the man in the saddle sat as straight and tall as Wade remembered. He had known Thomas Jackson since taking classes under him at the Virginia Military Institute in Lexington. There was still something in that stern face, with the piercing eyes and the long salt-and-pepper sideburns, that captivated his attention. Even as a youth he had been mesmerized by those eyes and the fiercely honest character of the man. He walked toward Jackson as the General swung out of the saddle, saluting smartly. "Good morning, sir."

Jackson slapped his horse's flank then extended his gloved hand to Wade. "Didn't expect to see you here," he said, laying a hand on the young man's shoulder and directing him back to where his subalterns had risen. "Thought you'd be in Richmond. Have you something to report?"

One of the officers handed the General a tin cup which he raised to his lips, studying Wade from under stern brows.

"Yes, sir. I do," Wade answered.

"Didn't expect any of those armchair generals down there to search me out," Jackson said, smiling. "You ought to be nosing around Winchester right now."

"I know you a little better than that, sir," Wade answered, opening his saddle bags. "Though it wasn't easy. You move so fast and so adroitly I might as well go looking for a mouse in a rabbit warren."

Jackson seemed pleased at the compliment. "That's the nature of war, son. Even now, we've had all the rest we can be allowed. So show me what you've got in that diplomatic pouch and let's be on our way. I wouldn't want to keep McDowell waiting."

Wade threw back the leather cover of the saddlebag and pulled out the smaller pouch, frowning over it. He glanced back at Selene still sitting under the tree.

"Who's that woman?" Jackson asked, his eyes peering over the edge of his cup.

Wade explained as he drew out the papers and spread them on the ground at Jackson's feet. The General knelt, still watching the girl slumped by the tree, as Wade spoke quietly.

"She's my prisoner and she's dangerous. I had to bring her with me or risk allowing her to get back to the Union lines and tell them you were on your way here."

Jackson nodded. "I don't want my little surprise ruined. It is my fondest hope to give General McDowell the shock of his life. What's the word from Manassas? Do we know when to expect the attack?"

"Our spies informed us it was set for yesterday, but I guess after their march they were too worn out for anything more than that little skirmish. It could be anytime."

Jackson frowned. "We'll get there, but not quite as early as I had hoped. However, any reinforcements—no matter how late they arrive—must be welcome to Beauregard. Without them we'll be badly outnumbered."

"May I congratulate you, General, on slipping away from Patterson's army so successfully. We've done our best to convince the other side you can't possibly get to Manassas in time, and I think they are going to be very surprised at the numbers facing them."

Jackson frowned. "We're not there yet, Captain. These look in order." He glanced up at Wade and smiled. "Quite a little task they've set you, Captain Kinsolving. But it's one I'm sure you can manage. If I remember the adroitness you showed at the Institute."

"It, too, depends on the utmost secrecy," Wade said,

glancing back at Selene. The General folded the papers and handed them back to Wade, obviously anxious to be off again. His eyes followed the younger man's to the girl slumped under the tree.

"She may be a prisoner, Captain, but she is also a woman. I trust you have treated her with respect."

"Oh, of course, sir."

"Let her go now. She can put up at the Harrow farm, which is only a couple of miles distant, and then find her way back to her own people. By that time we should be in the thick of the fighting."

Wade shook his head. "With your permission, sir, I should like to keep her where I can watch her. Just until I feel sure she can do us no harm."

A young corporal led the General's horse back to him. He swung easily up in the saddle, rested both hands on the pommel, and observed Selene with surprise. "Why, Captain, you've got her hands fettered. Is that really necessary?"

"I felt that it was, sir," Wade said testily. "Otherwise I should never have done it."

Selene, leaning against the tree, rubbed her eyes from sheer weariness. When she glanced up, her eyes met the General's high above her. The older man paused, seeing something there that held his gaze.

"It is not necessary now. Free her hands. And let her ride in one of the wagons. We can't have a woman riding pillion on a forced march."

Wade folded the letters and stuffed them back in the pouch. He felt that in a small way he was being unfairly reprimanded by his General. There was probably no way a gentleman like Thomas Jackson could understand the problems a girl like this could cause. Or the stern measures that had to be taken to prevent her from bringing ruin on them all. Jackson liked to think that all women were ladies.

"Sir, I respectfully request that we at least assign a guard to watch her."

The General was already pulling his mount around. "Let her ride with Murdock. And if you like, take one of the privates to walk alongside. You are coming with us, I trust."

47

Wade thought ruefully of the ship waiting at Norfolk. He had a day or two of grace but that was about all. And yet, did it matter if he was late in arriving? They'd wait for him—they couldn't go without him. They'd just have to hope for good weather to make up the lost time.

He called after Jackson, who rode off surrounded by his staff, their horses stirring up the dust of the road.

"General, I wouldn't miss it for anything in the world."

Selene was almost happy, she was so grateful to have her hands free and to be sitting in a wagon, instead of crushed into a saddle up against a man who treated her like a common doxy. Looking ahead at the long serpentine stream of men and horses, she noticed for the first time how few other wagons there were. An army ought to travel with many more accoutrements—cannon, caissons, pontoons, wagons both covered and open, extra horses, cattle. Here there were only miles of men marching endlessly, or stopping briefly to throw themselves down on the grassy fields along the road, several supply wagons like the one on which she swayed, and a few caissons with ammunition and cannon tied securely.

Such was the nature of a forced march, she supposed. The lighter they traveled, the sooner they would reach their destination. Something in her chest tightened at the thought. They were on their way to reinforce the Southern positions at Manassas, and there was nothing she could do to warn her own people about it. It was frustrating and demeaning. She had only been given this one opportunity to help her country and she had failed miserably. Unless . . .

The young corporal walking alongside the wagon stumbled, struggled to catch his footing, then smiled up at her sheepishly. She had already noted the guarded admiration in his surreptitious glances, and she was prepared to take advantage of his interest.

"You must be very tired," she said with as much sympathy as she could muster.

It was not difficult to get him into a conversation. He was very young, idealistic, and terrified at the thought of the coming fight. He loped along, growing more and more garrulous while Selene mentally examined what means she

48

might use to turn his sympathy to her advantage. When he casually remarked that he was the eldest of ten children, she forgot her concern in her amazement.

"I wonder your mother allowed you to leave," she said, thinking of the farm he was so obviously removed from.

"They couldn't of stopped me, ma'am. Once I heard that my native state of Virginia needed men to fight off the Yankee invaders, old Beelzebub himself couldn't have held me back." He looked up quickly at her frozen face and the color rose on his freckled cheeks. "Pardon, ma'am. It's hard to recall you're the enemy, you being so dainty and pretty and all."

Selene forced a smile. "Perhaps 'invaders' is not quite the right word for us Yankees. Still, your father must have needed you. Was it difficult for him to allow you to go?"

"Oh, yes'um. Me and my two younger brothers as well. My Pa would've gone, too, but that my Ma wouldn't hear of it. She can be awful fiesty when she gets up a head of steam, my Ma."

"And your home?"

"In Fairfax, ma'am. Or near there. Close enough to Washington City to hear the drums beatin' reveille."

"I lived in Washington myself . . ."

She was interrupted by Wade Kinsolving who rode up, pulling his mount to a dusty stop beside the young private.

"Don't talk to this woman!" he barked. "Take the other side of the wagon. I'll ride here."

The chagrined private fell back hastily and darted around to the other side of the driver, a weather-beaten, grizzled old fellow who chuckled in amusement.

"We were only being civil," Selene snapped as Wade's mount fell into a sedate walk alongside the wagon. He glared at her briefly then stared straight ahead. Selene shifted her weight on the hard plank seat as her spirits fell. It was going to be a lot harder now to find a way out with this captain eternally dogging her heels. But she'd think of something. She had only to keep her vigilance up and wait for the right moment.

By mid-afternoon they reached the junction twenty miles east of Piedmont where the Confederate troops from the valley were lined up waiting to embark on flatcars for the rest of the trip to Manassas. The wagon on which Selene was riding pulled up to form part of a large group of vehicles bivouacked in an open field opposite the tracks. She got down and stretched her stiff muscles by walking around the wagon while Wade stood nearby watching her. When a mounted rider on a lathered horse came hurrying into the compound, word spread quickly through the waiting troops. Farther down the road, the tracks had been torn up by Union raiders, and there would be no more trains until they were repaired.

Her heart gave a leap when she heard this news. Surely in the confusion of a long wait she could find some opportunity to slip away. When Wade moved off to consult with some of the other officers, she even dared to hope that he was concentrating so much on the problem of reaching the battlefield that he had forgotten about her for once. That sanguine hope died half an hour later when he came striding up to the wagon and ordered the driver to ready his horses. It had been decided that most of the supply and some of the medical wagons would push on to Manassas without waiting for the railroad. Wade tied his mount to the rear frame of the wagon and climbed up beside Selene and the driver. They pulled off, a long, serpentine row of open and covered vehicles, horses and mules wobbling and swaying along the road to Manasses Junction, guarded by a small military escort. Selene was surprised to see that there were women in the group, camp followers and wives who had been straggling along behind the men on the hurried march from the Shenandoah. They rode now, along with her, slowly inching their way toward war and destiny.

The wagon train pushed ahead as long as the animals could continue to plod. Finally, well into dark, a halt was called and campfires sprang up over the landscape. At a nearby farmhouse small A-frame tents appeared like mounds of snow, covering the yard as the soldiers made camp. Selene was tired but so hungry that she gratefully fell to helping the other women get a supper going. It was a hot night and the weary travelers stretched out in their clothes on blankets underneath the wagons while the horses grazed nearby. She had three other women sleeping around her, with Wade just beyond the shelter of the wagon bed. But it had ceased to matter to her by then, for she was too tired to attempt an escape. When she was

50

dragged awake the following morning she wanted nothing so much as to sleep for another four hours. Yet once breakfast was made, and she had downed a strong cup of coffee, she felt better.

She had rinsed some of the cooking utensils and was piling them into the back of the wagon when Wade came up leading his horse.

"I hope you slept well," he said, admiring the way the growing sunlight glinted on her golden hair in spite of himself. "This is likely to be an important day for all of us."

"I suppose a victory would send you off to Norfolk with quite a feather in your cap."

He frowned at her. "How did you know I was going to Norfolk?"

Selene bit her lip. That was a slip of the tongue she ought not to have made. If only she hadn't been so groggy . . .

"I suspected you had sneaked a look at my orders," Wade went on angrily, tying the reins to the back of the wagon. "You foolish girl! *Now* how am I ever going to let you go?"

"I haven't said anything to anyone."

"Only because you haven't had an opportunity to see the enemy. Whatever am I going to do with you now? And with a battle to fight! Come on, get in the wagon. I'll have to think of something."

He grabbed her arm and pushed her rudely toward the front of the wagon. Selene climbed up beside the driver on the seat, mentally cursing herself. By now the Federal army must be aware that General Jackson had joined Beauregard and *that* information was useless. But the treaty! It was so important. And now this monstrous captain was never going to allow her out of his sight. All she could do was watch and hope. There might yet be a chance.

They heard the thunder of the guns long before they neared Manassas. It began as a slow rumble, impossible to distinguish from an approaching storm except that the sky was cloudless. The word was quickly passed through the ranks that the fight was on, and weary steps quickened in spite of the ground already covered. Selene herself felt a cold thrill at the thought that these two armies were at long last actually facing each other in combat. She strained forward on her seat, but at Wade's frown, sat back. The roar grew louder, thundering in a bombardment that began to make her ears hurt. She gripped the edge of the seat at the thought that this noise was the symbol of men dying and maimed. When the big guns paused they were replaced by the sharp rapid fire of muskets. Then soldiers appeared from the distance, riding at a furious gallop to direct them. Then Selene could see that the first of the line reached the summit of a low hill, then fanned out to disappear over its crest. Other lines behind them seemed to be running to take their place. She thought she could make out a roar of cheering from the men on the left at the sight of the relief column.

The face of the man riding beside her was a study in contrasts. She could tell that he was eager to gallop forward, yet he was caught and held back by his determination to keep her in sight. His horse—made nervous by the big guns—danced in restrained circles while Wade jumped into the saddle and fought to hold him back. When one of the couriers came tearing by, he called out: "What's happening up front?"

"We've fallen back to Matthew's Hill, but we're giving them as good as we got. Get up there quick, Captain. We need every man."

He was off before Wade could answer. The captain was within a hairsbreadth of letting his mount loose. Selene saw and caught her breath. With his attention turned elsewhere . . .

Wade glanced back to see the intensity on her face. He forced himself up to the wagon.

"Come on. You're coming with me."

Reaching out, he grabbed her wrist and pulled her toward him.

"That's crazy," Selene protested, holding on to the seat with her free hand.

"Don't argue!" With a tug he had her off the seat and half on to his saddle. Clinging to him as the big white horse tore away, Selene bounced and twisted, but his grip was like iron. He rode to the first group of entrenched soldiers he could see, a squad of artillery men dug in about four hundred yards behind one of the cannons. He pulled up long enough to ask them where the nearest field hospital was.

"There's a dressing station just over the rise, I believe," one of the men called. Their faces were black with powder and the whites of their eyes stood out starkly.

Wade looked to his right and spotted a low shed, well behind the fighting. Ignoring the shaking of the ground and the thunder around him, he pushed his mount across the open patch of earth, pitted and torn from random shells. It was a low building with one open side that had once been a sheep feeding station.

Though the battle had not been in progress for more than two hours, there was already a doctor at work, bent over a table. Around him men lay on the ground, some in grotesque positions, a few upright and holding a bandaged arm or leg. The earth was trampled and bloody around the table. Wade stopped long enough to set Selene on her feet.

"You can be useful here until I get back," he said, keeping a firm hold on her wrist.

The surgeon looked up, his eyes widening in amazement.

"You can't leave a woman in this hospital," he said in shocked tones. "This is no fit place . . ."

"You can use another pair of hands, can't you?"

"Yes, of course, but . . ."

"You two men there," Wade said, summoning two of the young soldiers who looked more fit. "Take this pistol. I order you to watch this woman, and if she tries to escape, shoot her."

The two men looked at him stupidly. "Did you hear what I said?" he barked. They nodded and one of them reached for the pistol.

"She is a spy and if she gets back to the Federals, it will mean the loss of more of our men. Do you understand that? I mean every word. Shoot her if you must, but don't let her out of your sight." He circled his restive mount and glared down at Selene. "As for you, madam, I suggest you make yourself useful until I return. It's better than a jail."

"I hope you don't return!"

With a derisive shout he took off, riding almost joyfully toward the crest of the hill where the fighting was thickest.

Selene watched him go, then turned to the dumbfounded surgeon. For the first time she noticed that the man's shirt sleeves were rolled up around his elbows and his forearms were thick with blood. Her gaze lowered to the figure spread on the table and she clutched at her throat. Bile rose in her mouth but she fought it back.

"Do you know anything about surgery," the doctor asked in a very matter-of-fact voice, as he went back to his grim work.

"No."

"Then you'd better begin learning. Look over there in the corner. There's a bag there with some vials in it. Bring me the tan one, the one with the green label. And hurry, woman, hurry. This man's bleeding to death while you stand there gawking."

Selene started to ease her way around the table and inside the shed. She had to step over two men almost as bloody and severely wounded as the man the doctor was striving to help. Darting finally into the shed, she located the bag and searched quickly through it until she found the right bottle. As she rose to her feet she managed to get control of herself at last. She didn't want to be here, but these men had needs that went far beyond her concerns. She would do what she could, and hope that her chance might come. As for being shot by one of those wounded privates—that did not seem likely. They both looked to be in shock, even though the lesser wounded of the two did keep the pistol pointed at her by resting it on his good arm.

By the time she reached the surgeon's side two more stretchers had been deposited at his feet, accompanied by three or four walking wounded. As she darted about, responding to the surgeon's quick orders, fighting down her revulsion at the horrors around her, Selene soon realized that escape was going to be unlikely, not because of the watchful vigilance of the privates, but because there would be no time.

By the end of the first hour, she knew she had assessed the situation accurately. She even forgot about trying to escape, so engrossed was she in the work forced upon her. It was like nothing she had ever seen before. Her arms were scarlet to the elbow from trying to wipe away the blood that flowed from the surgeon's table and the men on the ground. A steady stream of stretchers lumbered over the crest of the hill, often accompanied by the limping wounded, leaning on another not-so-badly injured comrade, or a makeshift crutch fashioned from a shattered tree branch or gun stock.

Gradually she became numb to the horrible wounds of the men hastily ferried from the battlefields. Though the shattered limbs and mutilated bodies were bad enough, she heard the men talking of even worse sights.

"A head rolled right past me," one young soldier kept repeating over and over, his white face still in shock. "Like a melon it was, the jaw still working!"

"That's nothin'," another added. "There was arms and legs hanging from the tree over my head after that last volley from the right. I was thankin' the Lord it didn't hit me, when I felt this here hole in my shinbone. At least it's still attached," he said, glancing warily at the surgeon. He had good reason to worry, Selene thought. The severed limbs of the worst of the amputees had been thrown to the side in a ghastly pile. The surgeon worked ceaselessly, spending little time over the hopeless who were swiftly moved to a spot beyond the severed limbs. There was no time for the dead, the demands of the living were too great. Selene could not help but admire the way the surgeon worked, even though he soon became callous to the pain he was forced to inflict on the patients before him. She fancied she saw some admiration in his eyes for her as well, for the way she did what he asked, no matter how awful or demanding. He was a Southerner and an enemy, but he was a doctor first and she admired that.

The screams and moans of the wounded never stopped, though at times they were almost drowned by the roar of the big cannon over the ridge. That terrible thunder came in waves, sometimes fading to a sharp crack of musketry, at others so ear-splitting that she expected to see swarms of fighting men sweeping over their makeshift hospital. The action seemed to waver close to them, then later, as the afternoon wore on, over to their left and farther away. At one point it almost stopped altogether and for a blessed half hour there was a subdued quiet. Selene and the surgeon both exchanged glances, their eyes saying what they dared not speak, that perhaps it was all

55

over at last. Then it started again, louder and more fierce than before. This time there was no break in the racket, and Selene could only dread the casualties that would soon appear to swell an already unmanageable overcrowded field hospital.

Her fears were soon confirmed. The stream grew to a torrent. When one young soldier was carried up with half his face blown away and horribly mutilated, Selene had had enough. Throwing down her pail of bloody water, she gathered up her skirts to run in any direction, as far away from this battle as she could go. She had only gone a few steps when the surgeon barked at her:

"The chloroform is being used up too quickly. Get the whiskey from my bag under the haversack. It'll make it last longer."

She hesitated. But as she looked into his stern eyes, she could almost hear her father speaking, words he had often said to her. "Bravery is doing what you have to do, no matter how hard it is, or how much you don't want to do it."

Turning back to the lean-to she knelt to search for the whiskey, idly wondering how he had managed to conceal it this long, and stayed there until she had herself under control again. Though the surgeon made no comment, she could sense his relief when she handed him the small bottle of spirits.

"Mix it with water and give some to that fellow," he mumbled, nodding to the young man with the terrible face wound. Forcing herself to follow orders, Selene knelt to dribble some of the liquid onto the half of the lips that still formed a mouth. She saw then that he had died, and she laid a cloth over the shattered face. For the first time that day she fought back tears. But there was no time to cry. No time to think that differences in noble ideals had brought on this terrible destruction. No time to wonder if any ideals were really worth all this.

She had just got back to the surgeon when Wade galloped up. He was on a different horse, a brown gelding, and Selene hoped his beautiful white charger had not been killed. According to the wounded men there had been almost as many casualties among the animals as the human beings.

"How does it go?" the surgeon asked, taking time to walk

away from his table for the first time in hours.

"We held them this morning on Matthew's Hill. Kirby Smith has just arrived with the last of Johnston's troops, and it looks as though we'll beat them yet. The Federals are just beginning to leave the field. It should be a great victory." He circled his mount. "We'll chase them right back into the streets of Washington."

Selene, saying nothing, glared at Wade's triumphant face looming over her. Both his uniform and his face were black with gunpowder, and his teeth stood out white against his grimy skin. She hated the glowing victory in his eyes. While the surgeon gave thanks, Selene gritted her teeth. It was impossible that the Union forces should retreat in a battle where they so outnumbered their enemies. What a setback that would be to the cause of justice. There would be no quick, easy resolution of this war now. Oh, if only she had been able to reach McDowell with the information that those reinforcements were on the way!

She looked toward the battlefield, hidden by the crest of the hill. Her uncle's stone house had to be involved if there had been heavy fighting around Matthew's Hill. And old Mrs. Henry's house. If both armies had fought over that hill, the old lady's little home was right in the middle. She hoped the woman had got away somehow, bedridden though she was.

Then she heard Wade speaking her name.

"You haven't had any trouble with Miss Sprague?" he asked the doctor.

"On the contrary. I don't know what I would have done without her. She's been invaluable, doing jobs without complaint that no lady should ever be forced to do."

Wade threw her a questioning look, but Selene did not bother to examine it. All of a sudden she felt such hatred in her heart toward this bully who had prevented her from carrying the message that might have saved the day for the Union, who had tied her hands and forced himself into her body, with no regard for her feelings or desires. She loathed him. Despised him. And silently she vowed that someday she would get even. Someday he would be forced to pay for the injuries he had done her and the righteous cause she believed in.

57

"You're going to have to move from here," Wade went on, shifting his attention back to the surgeon and the work at hand. "Most of the action now is on the road to Centreville, and this station is too far to move the wounded. Can you swing around to the Chinn house? You'll find other surgeons there and better facilities. And we can get some of the worst of the wounded inside."

"What about these men?" the surgeon asked, gesturing at the ring of dead and wounded thick on the ground.

"Leave them in charge of some of the men who are not so bad off. We'll send some regulars along to bury the dead when things quiet down."

The surgeon nodded, relieved to leave the carnage in this place.

"And keep a watch on Miss Sprague," Wade added. "I cannot stress how important it is that we keep her within our lines."

The surgeon threw Selene an oddly bemused glance and turned to collecting his surgical tools. A few of the men were already on their feet and determined to follow the doctor, but he ordered them to stay to watch over those men who could not be moved. Wade had galloped away when Selene, who moved around helping to gather up the necessary materials to take with them, noticed that among those ordered to stay was the young soldier who had been watching her all day. He had limped to his feet and, leaning on a crutch, was hopping off in the doctor's steps. The handle of the pistol was stuck carelessly in his belt.

"Do you think you could carry that satchel of linens" the surgeon asked her in a sympathetic voice. "I know you worked hard all day but they're sure to be needed where we're going. And can you gather my field chest, Miss Sprague?" the doctor muttered, as he went on thrusting scapels, forceps, and saws into his leather surgical kit. Reaching for a particularly long and vicious scapel, which he had only used fifteen minutes before to relieve a young private of his shattered forearm, he quickly wiped it back and forth on his trouser leg, and thrust it into the bag along with the other implements. "Don't forget what's left of the chloroform. It's worth its weight in gold in

58

this place. And we're likely to need it just as much down there. More, in fact. They've probably run low by now.''

Silently Selene gathered the vials and bottles which had been so urgently needed all day and placed them with the others. Most of the bottles remained in their compartments. There was no time in a field hospital for spirits of ginger, powdered rhubarb, or sugar of lead. Out here it was a matter of ether, morphine, chloroform, and maybe quinine. These other medicines would probably be needed later at the Chinn house.

She looked down at her dress. It was literally covered in blood, the whole front sticky and stiff where the stuff had dried. God! she thought. There was no way she could take more of this. She belonged with the boys in blue, passing on the information she carried in her head. They must know about that treaty between the Rebels and the British. Once that was delivered, if she was needed to nurse wounded men, let them be Federal soldiers.

Her hand rested on the implements carelessly lying on the ground, where they had either been set or thrown in the confusion. Among the bottles she saw a spring-mechanized scarificator lying beside its open wooden case. The surgeon had only asked for it once during that long day. It was not such a necessary instrument as to be quickly missed, but it was an important part of a field surgeon's kit all the same. Carefully with her foot she edged both box and implement underneath some of the tall weeds that spread like a fan near a corner of the shed, then closed and fastened the lid to the chest.

"I'll carry that, Miss," a young man said, hobbling up to her on a crutch. She did not recognize him, so many faces had passed before her that day, but she did remember the wound—a foot now swathed in bandages, that had taken a minié ball cleanly through.

"Do you think you will be able to?" Selene asked.

"Put her here, under my good arm," the young man smiled. "You've done yeoman service today, and you shouldn't have to carry that awkward thing so far. Besides, it gives me a good reason to leave this place."

Selene helped arrange the chest under the man's arm, then picked up the bundle of linens and rags. The doctor was already halfway over the crest of the hill toward the road, his steps dogged by all the men who could manage to walk. Selene hurried to catch up with them. She didn't want to be too far away to be sent back.

With her heart in her throat, she paused just over the crest of the hill to exclaim that she had forgotten the scarificator. For a terrible moment the surgeon paused to look back at the shed, and Selene felt certain he was going to tell her to forget it.

"There are probably more at the Chinn house," he said while Selene's heart sank. "But I'm fond of that one. Do you have the strength to go back for it, Miss Sprague?"

She paused before answering, hoping her reluctance was convincing.

"Of course, if you really feel you need it."

"I could go back, Miss," one of the wounded men offered. He could barely walk and was weak from loss of blood and a shoulder wound that had left his arm protruding at a crazy angle.

"No. It was my carelessness," Selene said quickly. "And you need rest badly. I'll catch up."

She had already started back toward the shed, trying not to hurry much, but not lingering either. If the surgeon remembered Wade's orders at all he preferred to ignore them and had already started at a lope down the road. And why not, Selene thought. With the kinds of injuries and trauma he had dealt with this terrible day, one lone spy barely mattered. He would probably be more sorry to lose her help than think she might have carried information to the enemy.

She hurried back over the hill just far enough to make certain the surgeon and his wounded were out of sight. Then, without a thought for the bloody shed and the men lying around it, she lifted her skirts and ran for the cover of the woods. Though she half-expected some outcry behind her, she heard nothing save the distant, incessant roar of gunfire, and that no longer mattered. The ground was littered and broken with small craters and torn ruts that tripped her up twice. Even when she finally reached the welcoming dark coolness and shade of the woods she dared not stop. The thickness of the ground cover where no shells had reached slowed her down, but she did not stop to let her thundering lungs rest until she was certain she had penetrated the dense thickets and pinewoods far enough to be completely out of sight. Then she sank down in the first open spot she came to, gasping in long ragged breaths.

She was free! She had done it! She had escaped from the clutches of that monstrous beast, Captain Kinsolving, forever. The thought was almost too delicious to bear and she allowed herself time to savor it while gradually her tired body relaxed.

She had never been more weary in her life. The sleepless night, the long ride, and then the endless hours working over the surgeon's table had drained her strength completely. Her last run had taken all that was left of energy from her body. She knew she ought to get back on her feet and move, but when she tried to stand, her legs refused to hold her. She only had a vague idea where they were—somewhere south and east of the battleground. Off to her left she could hear the confusion of the Federal retreat like a quiet murmuring punctuated by a scream of a horse, a distant shout, the crackling staccato of musketry, an occasional low boom of cannon. The afternoon was late now and the sun cast mottled shadows on the forest floor.

"I've got to rest," Selene muttered to herself. There was a large fern growing close to where her head rested on the soft ground. Its wide cascading arms would make a good cover. She rolled underneath it, curled up so as to be completely encased in shadows, and let herself sink into the loamy ground. With any luck Wade would not come back to the shed or the Chinn house for hours, and when he did he might assume she was making for the Union lines, not curled up under a bush in the forest. With any luck . . .

A thundering crash of cannon woke her abruptly. Selene sat up, ducking under the leaves of the fern, her body poised to run. Then she realized the thunder was not cannon but actually what it sounded like—thunder. A soft misty rain was falling, cool on her face. Twilight had come while she dozed, a gray mysterious darkness, skewered now and then by a white flash she could see above the tops of the trees.

Selene stumbled to her feet with every muscle protesting.

She must find the Union lines before it got completely dark, and there was still some glimmer of light to guide her. She started off, realizing for the first time that the occasional bursts of thunder had replaced the constant boom of cannon. In fact, there was no gunfire in the distance at all now— nothing but the soft, increasingly strong patter of the rain. The battle must have ended at last.

Off to her right there was a loud cry of an owl. Selene looked cautiously around. She was not used to forcing her way through woods at night and the thought of predatory, ferocious animals gave her a moment's pause. And yet, with all the gunfire she had seen this day, surely most wild creatures would have been frightened away. She must go on. She must at least tell someone in the Federal army that the Confederates were about to make a treaty with England.

She walked for nearly an hour, until the forest was so black that she began to fear she would fall into a ravine or stumble over a rocky ledge and break her neck. Then, just when it seemed there was nothing for it but to find a spot to wait out the dawn, she saw a light flickering through the overgrowth. Inching toward it, she heard the low murmur of men's voices. But whose side did they belong to? It would not help her at this late hour to walk into a camp of Confederate soldiers.

Very cautiously Selene crept close enough to see the figures spread on the ground near a small, flickering campfire. There were three of them and they had their backs to her, but the fire gave enough light to make out the dark blue cast of their uniforms.

Federals! Thank God. Straightening her dress and squaring her shoulders, Selene walked boldly out of the woods and up to the startled men.

Four

The Union rout was so unexpected that it took Wade several minutes to realize what was happening. Only a moment before a minié ball had torn through his hat, narrowly missing his scalp. It was the closest call he had had all day, but he was almost too preoccupied to realize it. The carnage, the noise, the choking, never-ending smoke, the horrors of seeing a long line of men advance up a slope to stagger and fall, until only a scattered few remained—his numbed senses had long ago refused to take in any more. He concentrated his whole attention on forcing his tired horse to carry him where he was needed, ignoring the screams around him and the dead and dying, the explosions and bullets streaking like rain. The miracle of his survival would only sink in later—he had no time to wonder at it now.

And then the Union line broke. At first it seemed an orderly withdrawal, but that soon turned into a full-scale rout. Though the jubilant rebels followed close on their enemy's heels, they were too tired, worn-out, and scarred by losses to follow up on this unexpected victory.

Wade pulled his lathered horse up under a tree so shattered by gunfire that only a skeleton of tangled branches remained. He slipped from the saddle and leaned on the flanks of his stallion who stood with head sagging, snorting wearily now and then.

Patting his mount's wet neck he spoke soothingly to the animal, for he had carried Wade long and bravely that afternoon after Wade's own white stallion had given out.

63

Now he wondered if either of them would have the strength to go back to the field hospital to collect Selene Sprague. Or was it the Chinn house? He vaguely recalled ordering her to move there, but that memory had almost been obliterated by that last successful charge. She ought to be safely installed there by now under the surgeon's watchful eyes. There was no hurry. He was not actually a part of the 47th Virginia whose officers were trying to galvanize their troops into chasing the Union army into Washington. Though he had served well with them this day, he could now go his own way. His real mission was far from this battleground, and he ought to be about it as soon as possible. The fact that his country had won a great victory this day would no doubt make his cause much easier to accomplish.

For the first time Wade noticed that the guns had grown more silent, the thin scattering of musketry and growl of cannon was irregular and intermittent now. Leading his horse by the reins, he turned away from the Centreville road and started back toward the Chinn house just over the next ridge. The slopes were crated and pockmarked, covered with a gruesome debris of dead bodies—both men and horses. He picked his way carefully, trying to avoid seeing the worst of the mangled bodies. Scattered groups of living moved among the dead, medical personnel looking for those who were still alive, soldiers seeking a friend or relative and, as always, scavengers, out to find a good pair of boots or any article of value. He ought to chase them away, but he was too tired. Ignoring them, he moved on, wading over ground that was still wet with blood in places.

The Chinn house infirmary was a mass of confusion. Its grounds were so littered with wounded that Wade was forced to tie his horse and pick his way through them to the door. One of the officers in the crowded hall—John Sounder, from Jackson's brigade—told him that a tangle of civilians on the stone bridge had blocked the road back to Washington, creating a panic among the Federals that had turned the retreat into a wholesale rout. "The Great Skedaddle" they were calling it.

"It was touch and go there a few times," Lieutenant Sounder went on. "This morning before we lost General Bee it looked as though we would be the ones to have to run. General Jackson saved us then. They're calling him 'Stonewall' Jackson for the way he stood firm and refused to give up his ground."

"I'm not surprised," Wade said. "When Thomas Jackson believes he's in the right, the devil himself couldn't dislodge him."

"We can all thank God for that."

Inside the house the confusion was even worse. It took Wade ten minutes to locate the surgeon from the shed who had set up an operating table in the formal dining room. When he was finally able to get the man's attention, the doctor looked as though he could not remember who Selene was. Then comprehension dawned.

"Why she went back for my spring-mechanized scarificator," he said numbly, as though seeing into a distant past. "Come to think of it, I don't think I've seen her since."

Wade grabbed the man by his shirt collar. "You let her go back alone? You let her out of your sight!"

The doctor's eyes flashed with sudden anger. He pulled Wade's hands away. "I've had more important things to do than keep track of your young women."

"But I asked you to watch her. It's important . . ."

"Captain, do you realize that I've done nothing for the last seven hours but try to patch up men whose bodies have been blown apart. I'm exhausted and discouraged by the enormity of pain and suffering which I cannot alleviate. I'm out of morphine and chloroform and nearly out of bandages. If you want this woman you'll have to keep track of her yourself. Now take your hands off me and let me get back to my work."

Wade stepped back, realizing the truth of the man's words. Without an apology he turned and stalked away. He was tired and discouraged, too, and he wanted nothing so much as to sink onto the ground and lie there for hours, blocking out the scenes he had witnessed with restful sleep. Instead he must go traipsing after that damned, misbegotten wench who was nothing but a nuisance and a distraction. Damn the girl anyway!

One look at his horse told him it was impossible to ask the poor beast to go any further. Instead he made certain the animal had some water and a few oats, then left him in the charge of two of the young privates from Jackson's brigade whom he recognized from the day before. Taking along some hardtack to gnaw on, he set out for the shed where he had last seen Selene. From there he would try to determine what way she might have gone, if that was even possible.

Selene stepped from the darkness of the trees into the dim circle of light flickering from the campfire. She stared at the row of gritty, streaked faces turned toward her, the whites of their eyes gleaming in the fire's glow. They stared back with open mouths at the ghostly figure suddenly before them, unrecognizable as a young woman with her tangled hair straggling beside her dirty face and her disheveled dress, blotched with brown streaks of dried blood. One of the men gave a startled cry and jumped to his feet, ready to run in the opposite direction. Another went for his rifle. It took all three a moment to realize the apparition was actually a girl standing here, wobbling on her feet.

"God almighty," one of the men whispered. "For a minute I thought it was a spirit."

Selene gasped, "Help me . . ." and took a step toward them before her knees gave out and she sagged downward. The trooper nearest her lunged forward to catch her in his arms, then lowered her easily to the ground.

"Jerry, quick," he said. "Hand me that canteen."

"Is she shot?"

"No, just exhausted, I think. Here, Miss. Drink a little of this blackjack. It'll get your color back."

He lifted the dirty canteen to Selene's lips and without thinking she sipped at the liquid, then coughed as it seared her throat. She could feel it burn all the way down.

"No . . . no more," she managed to gasp, limply shoving away the canteen. "Please, you've got to help me."

"Of course we will, ma'am. You lie back here a minute and get yourself together, and then tell us what happened. How did you come to be wanderin' these woods at night?"

"Was you in the fightin'?" the soldier who had been ready

66

to run asked, bending over her.

"Must have been," one of the others said. "Look at her dress. Darn near caked with blood it is."

"I was working with the surgeon," Selene said, grateful to be supported by the one trooper who did not seem afraid to touch her.

"God, that explains it then. Bloody work."

"Please, I need your help," Selene muttered as she managed to sit up.

"You still look like you're about to faint, Miss. Have another drop of this whiskey."

"No! No, thank you. Have you any coffee?"

"'Fraid not. It's this whiskey or nothin'. But it'll do you a world of good if you can just keep it down. We got a few biscuits and some salt-pork if you're hungry."

"Oh yes. I haven't had a bite since this morning. Thank you."

The two men bending over her both rushed for their haversacks, returning a few seconds later with the food. It looked stale and unappetizing but, Selene thought, hunger makes an excellent sauce and she bit into it with relish. They watched her, now and then looking at each other with speculative glances, still uncertain what to make of her.

After the first bite of biscuit, her stomach threatened to send it up again along with the whiskey. Selene threw down what was left and gripped the sleeve of the man who still supported her.

"You must get me to McDowell . . ." she mumbled.

"McDowell? Why he's probably back in the Miller hotel in Washington City by now, hidin' his head."

"Can you get me there?"

"Why, ma'am?"

"It's very important that I speak with him, or at least with someone on his staff. I have vital information. He must know."

The men looked at each other. One of them started to open his mouth but the seated one spoke up quickly. "Well, we weren't really headed that way . . ."

"Could you direct me then. Just get me started in the right direction and I'll find my way to the lines."

"Do you mean Centreville?"

"If that's where the retreat has halted."

"I don't think it's halted this side of Alexandria."

"Alexandria, then. I must see General McDowell."

"But, miss. You don't look as though you could walk twenty-five feet, much less twenty-five miles. Wouldn't it be better to rest here for awhile, then go on in the daylight?"

"It'll be too late," she said, looking around. She had not forgotten Wade Kinsolving. He was bound to be after her, and the more distance she could put between herself and him, the better. "Besides, I'm stronger than I look. I'll be all right. Perhaps if I get a little farther on I'll be able to find a horse."

One of the men leaned on his long rifle. "We'd like to help you, ma'am, but it seems like a far distance to be travelin' tonight. We had a pretty hard day of it, too."

"I know. But believe me, what I have to tell the General may help prevent any more tragedies like today's. Please, won't you show me the way to go?"

"We'll do better than that," the man who had supported her said, rising to his feet. He seemed to be the oldest of the three—the other two were little more than adolescents—and had the authority in the group. "We'll take you to headquarters."

"But, Wally . . ."

"Be quiet, Jerry. This lady needs our help and we can't be any more tired than she is after this day's work. We'll have to escort her. It's the patriotic thing to do."

Selene managed to thank them as she struggled to her feet. The effects of the whiskey on her empty stomach and tired body made her head swim and she had to grab for the nearest tree to keep her footing. But she was determined that if these men would show her the way, she would keep putting one foot in front of the other to her last measure of strength, as long as it would enable her to escape Wade Kinsolving and reach Union headquarters.

"Stamp out that fire, Tom, and let's get started."

"I don't like it," Jerry hissed at him as Wally took Selene's arm politely, half-supporting, half-guiding her. "Why can't we wait? The captain's bound to come up shortly."

"Because you heard what the lady said. It's important that

she reach headquarters. It might save another day like the one just past. We all want that, don't we?"

Grumbling, the two men fell silently in behind the soldier they called Wally who led Selene back into the woods. Though it was very dark, he seemed to know his way well enough. Before long she realized through the numbness of her brain that they were on some kind of a path which made walking easier. It became almost an automatic reaction, placing one weary foot before the other, leaning on the strong arm that stayed firm around her waist, pulling again when her knees began to weaken.

It seemed as though they walked for hours. Selene was half asleep on her feet, but she kept going, dimly hoping with each step that they might reach the rest of the lines and maybe even stumble on a carriage or a horse. And then the winding path through the deep woods, which ought to be strange and unfamiliar, all at once seemed to bring back fogged memories. Surely she knew this turn, that bank alongside the brook, that broken oak once destroyed by lightning. She began fighting to keep awake and alert, pieces of the direction they were traveling began to fall into place and she sensed that up ahead was a road, one she knew well, one leading across an open field to a two-story stone house . . .

She stopped in the road, pulling away from the soldier who had helped her along for the past hour.

"You musn't stop now, Miss," he said kindly. "We're almost there now."

"Where?" Selene rubbed at her eyes, trying to focus through the darkness, wearily conscious that she was headed in the wrong direction. There were voices ahead, through the trees. Someone was crashing through the underbrush, calling out, asking who came.

"Where are we?" she mumbled, pulling away, wanting to run. The two soldiers behind her stepped up to hem her in.

"Now don't go getting upset, ma'am," Wally said, positioning himself in front of her. She was not going to be able to get away from them. Terror closed into her throat.

"You said you would help me . . ." she said, her voice rising on waves of hysteria. "You promised . . ."

69

Through the trees, the footsteps grew louder. A voice called out. "Who's there? Identify yourselves." She knew that voice.

"Over here, sir," Wally yelled, and at the same time reached out to grab her arm, pinning her beside him. A figure came crashing through the thickets, standing not three feet away.

"Damn it! I said identify yourselves!"

Wally managed a poor salute even though he held fast to Selene's arm. "Private Walter Grady of the 33rd Virginia, sir, bringing in a prisoner."

Selene stared at the soldier beside her, then at the officer who returned his salute, his lips smiling thinly as he saw who the prisoner was.

"Good work, Private Grady," Wade answered. "I know this woman and I know where she was headed. You've saved me a great deal of trouble."

She could see his hateful arms reaching for her, closing her in. She tried to summon up the strength to run, but there was nothing left. The welcoming darkness closed around her as she slumped into his waiting arms.

She awoke to sunlight pouring through a window, patterning the floor beside her bed. She tried to turn over and groaned as every muscle in her body protested. The room was so familiar that it took her a moment to realize she was not supposed to be there. How had she got back here, ensconced in her own bed in her own room on the second floor of her uncle's tavern? Memories came rushing back—the battle with its blood and noise and gore. How had this building managed to survive all that? And what was she doing here when she should be halfway to Washington? She must have slept for hours, precious hours that were lost now forever.

At the soft sound of steps on the landing outside her bedroom door, Selene ducked under the covers, unwilling to face anyone until her questions were sorted out. She heard the door open and a familiar clucking sound. A voice said, "La, chile, is you still asleep?" Selene knew that voice and she knew its owner was no threat. Quickly she threw off the covers and sat up in bed.

"Rosie! Oh, Rosie, is it really you?"

"It's me, right 'nuff," the Negress said, smiling broadly as she crossed the room and sat the tray she was carrying on a table beside Selene's bed. She reached out a hand so black as to be almost shiny and smoothed back the straggling tendrils of hair from Selene's brow, still clucking with her tongue.

"I believes you looks a mite better than when dey drags you in here, but den dat wouldn't be sayin' much. I seen drowned cats dat had mo' life den you when dat cap'n brung you in ma kitchen."

Selene frowned at the word 'captain' but clasped Rosie's dark hand and held on as if for dear life. "I can't believe I'm really here in my own room. I don't even remember how I got here. And I'm starved. Rosie, is that really food?" She flung off the white napkin that covered the tray. "Blessed Lord, real ham . . . and your biscuits. And tea . . . oh, Rosie, I'm famished. Quick, put it here in my lap!"

"Woah, now. Don' wolf down yo' food or may'ap it'll come right back up again. My, you was hungry. How you come to be in the state you was in, chile? Dat dress—why I had to burn it. Weren't no savin' it."

Selene answered with her mouth full. "I was helping the surgeon during the fight yesterday." She swallowed and stopped to reflect. "It was yesterday, wasn't it? This is Monday?"

"La, no, Miss Selene. Dis here's Tuesday. You done slept Monday away. No wonder you is so hungry, you been without food so long," Rosie perched on the side of the bed and pushed the tray closer to Selene. "I hopes dat was the right kind of surgeon you was helpin'. It were a Federate doctor, weren't he?"

"Yes he was. And how you, of all people, can think that is the right side is more than I can undertand. Don't you know they want to keep you in slavery!"

Rosie clucked with her tongue as she smoothed the covers on the bed. "All I know is I'se a Virginy-ian, born and bred and I'se a Virginy-ian till I dies. Ain't gwine go 'gainst that. Now you finish dat breakfast and then I come combs your hair. Dat handsome cap'n, he's waitin' to see you."

Selene let her cup drop on the tray. "Well, I don't want to see him. Tell him to go away. It's all his fault I was half dead and nearly starved when they brought me here."

"Can't do dat, Miss Selene. Yo' Uncle John say dat captin he be an important man for Virginny and I gotta do lak he say. Come on now. Get yourself dressed afore he busts in while you ain't decent."

"No!" Selene's eyes searched the room for a way out. There was only one window and she knew from experience that it was too high off the ground. Maybe if she tied the sheets together . . .

A sudden brisk rap on the door made Selene freeze with her legs already over the sides of the bed.

Rosie jumped to her feet. "La, I knowed it'd be too late." She pushed Selene back in the bed and yanked the covers up around her throat. Without any further announcement the door flew open and Wade Kinsolving walked into the room, looking quickly around. Selene noticed even in her anger that he had replaced his dirty clothes with a clean, neatly pressed, trim gray uniform. He was clean-shaven and his long hair hung neatly in waves to his shoulders. But the look on his face was one of arrogance and impatience. She slid further down in the bed, pulling the covers up around her chin, and threw him a look that the devil himself would have blanched at.

Wade nodded to Rosie. "Get out."

"No!" Selene cried. "You stay right there, Rosie. This man is no gentleman and I fear for my honor if you leave me alone with him."

Rosie's eyes grew round and large. "Why, chile, yo can't be tellin' the truth!"

"Ask him!"

Very carefully Wade took Rosie's arm and started her toward the door. "This lady and I have something very private to discuss. You have my word as a gentleman that I shall not lay a finger on her person."

"Much good that's worth," Selene snapped from the bed.

"But Captin it ain't fittin' . . ."

"It's fitten. She'll come to no harm. Now go back to your stove. Mr. Carpenter already has two customers calling for their dinner."

Before she could protest further, Rosie was eased out of the

72

door into the hall with the door closed tightly behind her. Wade turned to face Selene across the room, folding his arms across his chest.

"Don't try to go out through the window. I've got a man on guard down there with nothing to do but make certain that you don't leave that way."

"And I suppose the door is locked, too."

"That's right. I have two days here before I can leave for Norfolk, and I don't intend to let you get away again. You can go about your business serving in the tavern—as soon as it's a tavern again—but if you try to run off once more, I'll have you shot."

"You don't frighten me! What kind of a man would shoot a lady for doing her duty to her country?"

"This is war and in the eyes of my country you are a spy. I could shoot you now and be done with it. In fact, that tempting thought has occurred to me. I could have you put away in a jail, but I'd rather have you where I know you aren't up to your usual tricks and slipping off again to the Federals."

Selene grew so furious she forgot her modesty. She sat up in the bed, her eyes blazing, her gown slipping down around her shoulders, emphasizing the fullness of the heaving breasts. "You bastard! You can't mean to drag me off to Norfolk with you."

"That's just what I mean to do, but only as far as that. Once I'm safely out to sea you will be turned over to some other authority. You've already run me a merry chase and I don't want to risk my mission being further endangered."

Selene caught his eyes lingering on her expanse of white breast and grabbed the sheet up again. As Wade made a step toward the bed she cried, "Don't you touch me," and scrambled out the other side, wrapping the sheet around her and getting as far away from him as was possible.

He stopped and gave a sharp laugh. "You make a tempting target."

"I'll scream. I'll scream so loudly they'll think it's the battle all over again."

At the mention of Manassas he seemed to pull back, and weightier matters took over. He shrugged and walked back to the door.

"By the way, Surgeon Mackenzie said you were a great help to him that day. I suppose I should thank you for that."

Though the compliment pleased her, she was not about to let him know it.

"Just tell me one thing," she said more softly. "Those men who brought me here—they were Union soldiers. How could they do that?"

"No, they were part of a Virginia Regiment, who had become conveniently separated from the rest of their group and planned to spend a restful night around the campfire before joining them again. I suppose their patriotism won out over their discretion."

Mentally Selene chided herself. If only she had been more careful to make certain she was with friends before blurting out her mission. But she had been so sure they were Union soldiers.

"Don't let your mistake bother you too much," Wade went on. "Earlier that day their blue uniforms had tricked a Northern battery into thinking they were reinforcements, just long enough to enable them to capture it. It was one of those incidents that gave the victory to us instead of to the Union army. Now, get dressed. Your uncle said he could use your help if you're up to it. And from the daggers I'm getting I'd say you've recovered from any ill effects of the battle."

"I only wish they were real ones!"

"One of my men is outside. He will escort you downstairs and stay by you until he is relieved. I'll be back this evening."

"I can't wait."

He threw her a look as bitter as the ones she had levied on him. Then without another word he left the room, slamming the door behind him. Selene heard the metallic snap of a lock striking home, and with a furious cry grabbed for her cup and sent it shattering against the door. A quick rush to the window confirmed the presence of a Confederate soldier standing below, leaning on his long rifle.

Selene took her time getting dressed and brushing her thick hair into a chenille net. When she stepped into the hall, a young soldier who had been lounging against the wall half asleep sprang suddenly alert and followed her down the stairs. She stood at the entrance to the taproom gazing around the room in amazement at the changes just two days had brought. All the tables had been stacked hastily against the wall when for a brief time the room had served as a hospital during the battle. The tavern was too close to the big guns to be used as such for very long, but little had been done to undo the damage. Most of the tables had been broken and lay around the sides of the room like firewood, casually thrust aside. Two had been restored to use and a few men sat around them, nursing tankards.

The floor had been scrubbed, she noticed, yet still bore the signs of the dark stains she recognized so well. Rubble and dust covered everything, while plaster on the walls showed signs of damage and was cracked and broken in places.

Selene walked over to the bar where her uncle was working and tied a long apron over her dress.

"Glad you're back, Selene," her Uncle John said without interrupting his work wiping off dark bottles that had been buried during the battle. "We can use you."

"Did Matilda ever show up?"

"Never. I guess she's gone for good, following her Johnny boy to the wars. Cato cleaned up some, but he's too old, and Sadie is too young to do much good. I can use another pair of hands."

"Why don't you get those soldiers to help. They were the ones to bring all this on us in the first place."

Uncle John's round face fell into a frown. "Now, Selene, I won't have you starting that kind of talk. I was relieved, I'll confess, to hear that you helped out Surgeon Mackenzie last Sunday. It crossed my mind that you might have run off to the enemy, with all your strange notions and all. I don't think I could have borne the shame if you had. You made me proud, my girl."

Selene studied the round, not unkindly face of her uncle, biting her tongue to keep from confessing she had been coerced into helping the rebels. She wondered briefly why Captain Kinsolving hadn't told Uncle John the truth, then decided it was best to say nothing. Let sleeping dogs lie.

75

"Where shall I start?"

"Help me clean what's left of these glasses and bottles, and then we can try to set up a few more tables. There's plenty to be put right."

Selene set to work, trying not to notice that the young soldier, who had followed her downstairs, was deliberately lounging nearby. She absolutely refused to ask him if he wanted anything. Let him do without. From across the room old Caleb's voice came floating toward her, as usual high-pitched and loud and fraught with the imagined importance of his experiences. The old man's thick brows moved up and down with the flights of his narrative. His thin pointed chin, jutting out as far as the end of his nose and covered with an iron-gray stubble, gyrated with his words. He paused now and then, long enough to take a swipe at his glass and wipe at his lips with his sleeve. Selene tried not to listen but it was impossible.

". . . I was at that church in Centreville and I tell you, I never seen nothing like it. Bodies piled around the sides as high as the ceiling of this room. They just dragged them out as they died and throwed 'em on the pile. Never knowed such horrors could exist as did that day . . ."

The man he was relating all this to, a stranger to Selene, occasionally added a quiet sentence, but was quickly drowned out as Caleb rambled on, overflowing with his own importance.

She worked quietly all day, saying little but constantly observing, her mind darting back and forth between possible methods of escape. Wade Kinsolving was as good as his word—she was never alone. Her guards even followed her to the necessary house and stood close by outside waiting for her. They were unobtrusive, they seldom spoke, and for the most part, they faded into the background. But they were there and she could devise no way to avoid them. By the end of the day she knew there was going to be no way of escaping Kinsolving's grasp until they left Manassas for Norfolk. Perhaps he might let his guard down on that trip just enough to allow her the right opportunity. Then the next morning her uncle dropped a casual comment that woke her hopes once again.

"There was a fellow askin' for you Monday morning," he said. "I forgot it until now. Said he knew your Pa and you back in Washington City before Theophiles died. I think his name was Simon something."

Selene felt a sudden start of excitement. "Simon Lazar?"

"Yes, I believe that was the name. I didn't want to wake you, you was so played out when they brought you in. He said he'll be back this way anyhow and would see you then."

Selene tried to choose her words carefully, trying to hide how much this news meant to her. "I wish you had called me, Uncle John. It's always . . . always gratifying to speak with an old friend of my father's. Did Mr. Lazar say when he would be coming back through?"

"I believe it was the end of the week. He made a point of that, come to think of it. He had to go to Richmond, but would be back by next Friday, and would be pleased to see you then."

Friday! Today was Wednesday and tomorrow she had to leave for Norfolk. Her high hopes began to go gray.

"I'm glad to know that at least a few of your Washington friends chose the Southern side," her uncle went on.

"I really would have liked to see Mr. Lazar, but I won't be here on Friday. Captain Kinsolving tells me I shall have to go to Norfolk with him for a few days. Uncle John, do you think if I left a note for Mr. Lazar you could see that he got it safely? He has a few of my father's books which I would like to have returned. I can make a list if you will see that he gets it."

"Why must you go to Norfolk? I need you here."

"Ask Captain Kinsolving," Selene answered smugly. "Let the captain explain that one! But my note—you will see that Mr. Lazar gets it?"

John shrugged. "Certainly."

Later, when she could get away, Selene went straight to her room and worked on her note for Simon Lazar. After deliberating about the best way to pass on what she knew about Wade's secret mission, she decided it would be much more expedient to write two notes, rather than say everything in one. She carefully wrote out one letter for General McDowell himself, sealed it, and then wrote a second to Simon, asking him to be certain that it was delivered into the General's hands. If Lazar was as eager to pass on information as he had led her to believe, he would see that her letter was safely delivered. And that was as much as she wanted. Once the government knew of Wade's traitorous treaty with Great Britain, she did not care where he dragged her.

She carefully sealed the letters and concealed them in her pocket until she could unobtrusively slip them to her uncle. For the first time she felt as though a great weight had been lifted from her shoulders. She could almost hear her father's beloved voice whispering in her ear: "Well done, my girl. Well done."

Though Selene continued to look for a way of escaping from Wade, there was never a moment when she had the opportunity. Her guards were diligent and all the exits were barred. It was frustrating, but not nearly so much if she had not been able to leave those notes with her uncle. As it was, she went about her work almost merrily, even to the point of giving a grudging civility to the Southern soldiers who filled the tavern.

As the day wore on, her pleasant feelings began to be replaced with a furious resentment. This hateful man, who so cavalierly expected to drag her off wherever he wished, would one day pay for his miserable behaviour. She did not know how yet, but she would find a way. She was determined.

And then he came back early—Wednesday evening before they were to leave the next day—and announced that she must be ready to go with him in half an hour. Selene was outraged, but her angry pleading was to no avail.

"My plans have changed. We have to be in Norfolk as quickly as possible."

"But travel at night? I'm not ready. My uncle needs me. I don't see why this is necessary anyway. I gave you my word . . ."

"You'll forgive me if I do not put too much stock in your word. I've managed to keep you from running off to Washington. I'm not going to have you undoing all my plans at the last moment. Half an hour!"

All Selene's determination to remain icily aloof evaporated under her fury. "You're not my husband! I don't have to go anywhere with you. You're an overbearing tyrant and you have no right to drag me around like some kind of slave."

78

Wade reached out and grabbed her wrist, twisting it cruelly. "Until I'm on the high seas you are my prisoner, and you'll do as I say, or you'll find yourself in a far worse place than any you ever imagined."

"I'll tell Uncle John . . ."

"I've already talked with your uncle. He believes I have good reason for wanting you with me and he trusts my judgment. You'll get no help from him or anyone else here. Now get your things together or we'll leave with only what you're wearing."

Selene rubbed her wrists as she watched him stalk out the door. There was nothing for it but to throw a few of her clothes in a heavy cloth bag and sullenly make her way downstairs. She was surprised to see that a carriage was waiting, rather than a single horse. That at least promised a little more comfort. She hoped to have it to herself but Wade climbed quickly in as it began to roll out of the yard, settling himself beside her. The damp leather was old and smelled of mildew but Selene shrank back into the corner as far as she could, trying not to allow her skirt even to touch his thighs. Wade knew what she was doing. He gave a short, mocking laugh and slid down in his own corner as the carriage bumped along the road. Pulling the brim of his hat down over his eyes, Selene thought he must be planning to take a nap. Relieved, she leaned against the hard leather cushion and closed her eyes, hoping she might doze off herself.

The road was too pitted and lumpy for sleep. With every lurch she was alert, eyeing Wade suspiciously. When they hit an especially pitted section of corduroy road, she was thrown against him, landing almost in his lap.

The quickness with which he caught her warned her he had not been asleep. His hands clutched at her waist, inadvertently slipping underneath her cloak. She felt his fingers tighten through the thin fabric of her dress. Selene tried to pull away but his arm slipped around her snakelike and he pulled her against him fiercely.

She shoved at his chest. "Let me go. You promised . . ."

Wade looked down at her in the darkness. He had had every intention of keeping his hands off her body when he climbed into the coach. But with every passing moment he had grown more conscious of her nearness, the intoxicating fragrance of her sharpened the memory of what they had once shared. Now, with her suddenly thrown into his arms, he found he could not let her go. The heat in his loins was too strong. The warmth of her waist beneath his hands, the feel of her hair against his cheek drove him beyond his good intentions.

"Let me go," Selene cried, struggling against him. The cab seemed to shrink, closing around them, pinning them in. Wade's hand slid up, closing over her breast, lightly rubbing against the hard, erect nipple. As furious as she was, Selene felt a lightning streak of fire through her body. He leaned against her, forcing her back against the seat, slipping one arm around her shoulders. His lips came down hard against hers, his tongue forcing her mouth, searching inside for the warm depths. Selene fought him, but of themselves her lips opened, allowing him in, wanting him there in spite of the outrage she wanted to feel. His hand slipped under the bodice of her dress, closing around the fullness of her breast and lifting it free. His lips slid sensuously down her chin, lightly dabbing her throat with a flower-soft, maddening sensuality. Selene groaned, pressing him against her with her hands but unable to force him away, arching her back as his soft lips traced circular patterns over the exquisite softness of her breast until they found and grasped the taut nipple, sucking lightly enough to drive her mad. She forgot she was supposed to be outraged under the insistent, hot waves of desire that he created in her yielding body. Sliding down farther on the seat he fell against her and she was conscious of the rock-hard shaft beneath his clothes pressing against her thighs. His hand was under her skirt, slipping up her leg, tracing light patterns in its search. She was conscious of her own moans as his fingers found its goal, plying the moist softness, thrusting into the waiting, longing emptiness.

"Please . . ." she moaned, not knowing if she was asking him to stop or to go on. With deliberate intent Wade worked at the soft sensitive flesh, rubbing lightly at first then harder, forcing waves of exquisite delight through her body. Searching and finding that most sensitive spot, aggressively and deliberately gyrating while he held her forcibly, helpless in his arms. Selene's hands slipped away from his chest, her back arched. Gasping, she lost all consciousness of everything except the exquisite pain and pleasure of the fast-building delight within. As her excitement peaked his own grew and she was conscious of his moaning in concert with hers. Her thighs rocked beneath his, sending his own senses soaring. He tore at his trousers, pulling out the hard, thrusting shaft that wanted nothing so much as to push its way into that open, moist waiting receptacle.

"God!" he cried as Selene went crashing over the edge, soaring among the stars, oblivious to where she was, who she was with. She cried out in ecstasy, a long, sighing wail.

The coach lurched wildly. A horse screamed, bucking in the harness and sending the cab rocking like a boat in a storm. Both Wade and Selene fell forward, landing in a heap on top of one another on the floor of the cab.

"What the devil . . ." Wade said, trying to lift himself up from the tangle of their bodies. The coach gradually ceased its rocking and in the ensuing quiet he could make out angry voices over the loud hawking of the night insects. He pulled himself up onto the seat then reached to help Selene.

"Are you all right?"

"No thanks to you," she snapped, ignoring his hand and trying to yank her dress back up over her shoulders. All the heat was gone, suddenly dissipated in their heavy fall. She could barely remember the intense pleasure he had coaxed from her, and in the void her anger at being taken advantage of came roaring back.

Wade straightened his own clothes. His longing was now a dim hunger between his legs but it was manageable. Snapping the window down he leaned out of it, trying to see in the darkness.

"What do you think you're doing, you idiot? Why have we stopped?"

The driver was already in the road, attempting to quiet his restive horse. He walked back to the window. "Sorry, Captain, but there was this person in the middle of the road. It was run over him or pull up. Gave my horse a terrible fright."

"What person?"

A cheery face came bounding up out of the darkness. "Why, sir, I believe your good driver is referring to me. What a godsend you are, too. Here I was thinking I'd be forced to spend the rest of the night languishing by the side of this lonely, interminable road when help appears like an angel sent from heaven itself."

Again Wade reached down to help Selene up from the floor of the cab, but she thrust his arm aside and climbed to the seat, smoothing down her skirts and squeezing as far in the opposite corner as she could get. He looked back at the stranger who already had his hand on the door handle.

"You fool. Don't you realize you might have injured our horse, not to mention spilling the coach on its side. Then we'd all be stranded."

The stranger, without missing a beat, swung open the door and crawled into the cab, his bulky coat and large portmanteau filling all the empty space.

"Now see here . . ." Wade started, but the stranger was already settling back on the leather cushions.

"Oh, sir, or rather, officer, for I see you are one of our stalwart Confederate saviours, you cannot know how relieved I am to be here. Oh, the terrors, the torments of sitting in the turgid dark of a lonely road."

"But you can't just barge in like this. We're in a hurry to reach Norfolk on urgent business."

"Norfolk! So that is your destination. Not what I intended, but one I shall nonetheless accept with eagerness. Yes indeed. Norfolk . . . a fine town."

"Who the hell are you?"

"You have the honor, sir, to address the honorable Mordacai Granberry, prominent performer of theatricals and refined entertainments. Also available for private readings. Temporarily between engagements, but on my way to your fair town of Norfolk to fulfill my next professional prospect."

Wade groaned and pulled his coat around him in his corner. Mordacai Granberry took up most of the middle of the opposite seat, his legs extending between Wade and Selene. He set his box on his knees and leaned back, smiling at them both benignly.

"An actor!" Wade muttered loud enough for that gentleman to hear. "I should have known. Only an actor would have the gall to force a coach on the run to a sudden stop."

"Fear not, good sir, you shall be fully reimbursed for your trouble," Mordacai intoned, resting his plump fingers on the handle of his box. "Though my pockets have often been bare as a baby's behind—your pardon, ma'am—Mordacai Granberry is not the man to ask favor with no thought of reward. Indeed, you have my word on it."

"I suppose that means after your next engagement."

"Why sir, not only have you generosity, but sagacity as well. Fortune insists that I must wait until then, but experience tells me it will not be long after my arrival that that happy moment will ensue."

"No doubt your bare pockets were the cause of your languishing alone by the side of the road in the middle of the night."

"Why, good sir, that did have something to do with it. A reckless driver with the soul of a reptile refused to give me further passage, may his bilious soul rot in— Oh, forgive me, ma'am." Granberry touched his hat and beamed at Selene, who slid deeper down in her seat without acknowledging his presence. She was fervently hoping that her disheveled dress and straggling hair did not reveal too much of what this verbose actor had interrupted.

"The lady wishes to sleep," Wade snapped.

"Oh, certainly, certainly. I would not think of disturbing her."

The driver appeared briefly at the window, asking if he should throw this person back in the road or move on. "Let him stay," Wade said grudgingly. He could happily club the man for interfering when he did, and yet now that he was here and the moment gone, he might as well stay.

Yet disturbing thoughts returned to trouble him as the coach resumed its familiar roll. He glanced over at Selene in her dark corner, her head turned away from him. Should he apologize when they finally reached Norfolk? He had not thought of taking advantage of her on this trip when they

83

started. In fact, it would have made everything more simple to leave her alone and keep his distance. Once he was on the ship and she was turned over to the proper authority, she was not going to matter to him ever again. That was the sensible way to handle the problem.

But damn it, she had such an intoxicating effect on him. He had only meant to taunt her a little at first, but then her soaring reaction had sent his own blood boiling. Even now the unresolved longing for her was beginning to eat at him again, filling him with a desperation he vainly fought to force down. He had never fallen prey to a woman in this way before. He had always been the one who walked away, unconcerned whether or not the lady followed. With a pang he realized that it was going to be difficult to give her up once they reached Norfolk.

The garrulous Mr. Granberry droned on in his cheery voice, endlessly commenting on every subject that flitted across the vast acreage that was his mind, from the wonderful victory the South had achieved on Sunday last, to the various theaters he had played throughout the state of Virginia. Wade soon tuned him out, shuffling down in his seat with his hat pulled down over his eyes, pretending to doze. But his mind refused to give up its fixation. How was he going to leave this woman behind him when they reached Norfolk? The question haunted him as the gray streaks of dawn began to pierce the darkness of the sky.

Simon Lazar rode into the yard of Carpenter's tavern late Thursday evening. He had been in the saddle nearly two days and was bone weary. The dust of the road seemed to have permanently lined his throat, making his voice raspy when he tried to talk. He had covered very nearly every Confederate bastion in Virginia and had not been able to pick up anything of importance anywhere. The next move of the Confederacy, after their unexpected victory at Bull Run, seemed as unknown to them as to their enemies.

He slid out of the saddle, pulled off his dirt-encrusted saddlebags and turned his horse over to the young Negro boy who came running up as he rode into the yard. His spurs made a soft clinking accompaniment to his steps as he walked to the door, barely aware of the noise within. Inside it was as smoky as the road had been dusty, and it took him a moment to see his way clear to a solitary table near the stairs. He sat down heavily, threw his saddlebags over the back of the other chair to discourage company and ordered an ale and a meat pie from the simple-faced girl who approached. He was disappointed it was not Selene Sprague, since he was expecting to see her. Glancing around the room he noticed idly that she was not there at all—somewhat surprising considering their last talk. He had hoped she might have something for him by now.

He was halfway into the pie when John Carpenter ambled over.

"Your name's Lazar, isn't it?" the owner asked, standing with his hands on his broad thighs.

"What if it is?"

"No offense. I've been waiting for you to get back. You left a message for my niece, Selene, the last time you was here. But if it's a bother to mention it, then sir, just forget the whole thing."

The innkeeper had turned and was a few steps away when Simon thought better of his abrupt answer. "Just a moment," he cried. John turned and eyed him suspiciously.

"Where is Selene?" he asked, not bothering to apologize. "I was hoping to see her."

"She's gone. And she won't be returning any time soon."

"Did you give her my message?"

"Aye. And she's left one for you, though you came close to not receiving it. I get enough customers here that I don't need to take any man's gruff."

So Selene had left him a message. That was worth a small apology. "Been in the saddle nearly three days. It takes the edge off a man's manners."

John dug into the pocket of his large apron and produced the two letters Selene had left him. Grudgingly he handed them to Simon. "She said these were important and I was to be sure you got them direct from my own hand. Now that's done, I'll get back to my work. Don't expect I'll be seein' Selene for awhile and that leaves me short-handed."

"I'm obliged to you," Simon muttered, his interest almost wholly absorbed by the two letters. He looked them over carefully, then slipped them into his saddlebags to be read in private. A second ale arrived as he closed the leather pouch and after hurriedly devouring it he made his way outside near the necessary house where he hoped no one would bother him. There was just enough light left to make out the writing on Selene's letter addressed to him. She begged him to deliver the second letter to General McDowell and no one else, assured him of her devotion to their cause, and warned him that something significant was in the works and she would be eternally obliged to him if he would trust her enough to follow her instructions. Simon skimmed the letter long enough to get the gist of it, then took the second one and abruptly tore it open.

As he carefully read the second letter a thin smile flitted across his lips. This was more like it. Just to make certain he read it a second time, folded it carefully, and placed it in the pocket of his coat. Then he hurried back inside the tavern. There were plans to be made.

Five

The gentle rolling of the coach soon began to lull Selene into a groggy half-consciousness in spite of her determination to stay awake and watchful. The presence of Mordacai Granberry, distasteful as it was, at least removed fears of any further indiscretion on Captain Kinsolving's part. Deep down she knew that some of the rage she felt toward him was also directed at herself for instinctively responding to him the way she had. How was she ever going to curb her treacherous body! It did little good to detest the man when the mere touch of his fingers wandering over her breasts sent her into a frenzy of longing. He was never going to let her alone unless somehow she convinced him she could not abide the touch of his hands.

Her thoughts drifted into a restless sleep from which she was suddenly awakened when the coach gave a sudden lurch and she was thrown heavily against the side, bumping her head on the frame. She sat up and realized that a dim thread of daylight was seeping around the leather window curtain. Outside there were noises—the cacophany of horses' hooves on pavement, the cries of drivers hollering others out of their way, the racket of iron-shod wheels on cobbled roads. Norfolk!

With a groan at the stiffness of her muscles, Selene sat forward and straightened her rumpled dress. Pulling down the window she peered out, searching for some sign that would tell her where they were. The salt smell of the sea was in the air and the congestion of carriages and wagons on the busy street confirmed her suspicion that they had arrived at their destination. She was grateful that she had been able to sleep a little since she would need all her wits about her once they got to Confederate headquarters. Glancing out of the corner of her eye at the slumped figure on the far end of the seat, she saw that Captain Kinsolving looked as though he had not slept at all. He was staring out at the traffic through a thin slit in the window, his hat pulled down to shade his eyes, and his arms folded across his chest just as he had been earlier. On the seat across Granberry slumped, his chin resting on his chest and his mouth half-opened in a raspy snore.

Selene expected the coach to pull up at any moment, but instead it continued its slow way through the congested streets for another twenty minutes before finally coming to a halt. Mordacai Granberry, who had snored loudly the whole way, woke with a start just as the driver appeared at the window.

"We're here, Captain," he said, opening the door for Wade.

Without waiting for help, Selene opened her own door and stepped down, her stiff body complaining at the unaccustomed activity. She leaned against the cab and looked around while Wade and the driver hurried around to her side and began pulling off their boxes.

Selene saw she had been correct about the smell of the sea. It lay before her, a blue expanse of river with the sweeping ocean dim in the distance. Closer to hand, ships' masts dotted the wharf, jutting into the misty air like a pine forest. Sea birds whirled and cawed, lighting on the rounded posts of the wharf or the planks to examine the clutter of garbage thrown there. Off to one side men were working on a ship, the clatter of their hammers filling the air. The morning air was cool to her cheeks and she breathed deeply of it, glad to be out of the close confines of the reeking coach.

The coach rocked and swayed as Mordacai Granberry hauled his bulk from the cab and stepped heavily onto the street. "A beautiful morning, is it not," he intoned, pulling at his neckcloth. "Ah, the pungent smell of fish and seaweed—not my favorite aromas, of course, but one must make do with what fate sends. Good morning, my dear," he said, doffing his tall battered silk hat to Selene.

She barely nodded, not wishing to have to deal with this man in any way, in spite of the fact that he had saved her from her worst instincts a few hours before.

"My goodness, but you are a lovely creature. The darkness of the night hid your beauty, but Mordacai Granberry was never one to turn an admiring eye from anything so lovely. Allow me, Madam, to escort you to yonder tavern for some breakfast. I feel sure you must be in need of it after such an uncomfortable and difficult ride."

"The lady is having breakfast with me," Wade said emphatically, reaching for Selene's arm. "As for you, if you have any blunt to give my driver for your passage, do it now. If, as I suspect, you do not, then be on your way. You've had enough of our hospitality."

Granberry was already reaching for his box but not his purse. "Good sir, I can only repeat my heartfelt thanks for your kind charity. And if you find yourself in this thriving metropolis with time on your hands, by all means come round to the local theater where I shall, I have no doubt, soon be presenting the public with performances that will remain in memory through a lifetime."

Wade pulled Selene's arm through his and urged her toward the tavern. "I'd prefer to see the color of your money," he said over his shoulder. Selene grudgingly followed him, trying to get her arm free as unobtrusively as possible. She had no wish to escape from one captor only to have to deal with a tiresome, pretentious actor.

"Let me go," she hissed under her breath. "We're here now in Norfolk. This is what you wanted. Now let me free."

Wade's face was a blank as he went forcefully on. "Not until I know you won't run to the nearest Union spy. Come on. You must be hungry and tired. A little freshing up and a decent breakfast might help to improve your disposition."

"My disposition would be greatly improved by being away from you."

"No doubt. But you'll have to make do with the breakfast for now."

A little food and a cup of chocolate did sound very tempting. Selene gave up and followed him into the tavern, dark panelled rooms that reeked of smoke and cooking odors. It was none too clean, but the food turned out to be surprisingly good and she soon fell to devouring it with enthusiasm. Afterward she was given a room to wash her face and comb her hair and she walked back downstairs feeling more able to deal with her unpleasant situation than at any time since Wade announced she had to go with him to Norfolk. Surely it would not be long now until she would be turned over to other Confederate authorities, and if she couldn't find a way to escape from them, her name wasn't Selene Sprague.

She found Wade sitting at a table with a burly fellow opposite who wore a long pigtail down his back. The man looked to be not quite intelligent, though the dim eyes he turned on Selene were appreciative enough. The muscles of his arms beneath his short-sleeved sailor's shirt bulged formidably.

"This is Seaman Hawke," Wade said in his infuriatingly cool voice. "He is going to sit with you here while I go aboard his ship to talk to the Captain about passage."

"But I thought . . . You said you would turn me over to the government."

"In good time. Before I can do that, I have to make certain that I'm safely on my way."

Selene sat huffily down at the table. "For heaven's sake. We're stuck here in this Southern port. Where could I go? I should think you'd allow me some freedom now."

"Too many Northern sympathizers around, my dear. And may I remind you that just outside the harbor, Federal ships are blockading this port."

"I suppose you think I am planning to swim out to them. And I'm not your dear!"

"I just like to cover all fronts. You be a good girl and wait here with Seaman Hawke until I return. It's not such a bad place to be."

"To you, maybe." She glared at his back as he left the tavern. Through the window she could watch him walk up the planks to the deck of a large ship whose thick cables fastened her to the wharf. Selene turned back, glaring at the sailor who was watching her with a patronizing smile on his thick lips.

"You maybe like some coffee," he said in a gutteral voice.

Despair flooded over her. What was the use. She must wait a little longer for her freedom. She nodded and Hawke waved a burly arm at a serving girl across the room who had just come up from the kitchen. "Two coffees," he yelled.

Selene stared at the planks of the table crusted with the grease of many meals, as a stoneware cup filled with steaming liquid was thrust in front of her.

"Here you are, miss."

At the sound of that voice her head shot up. The serving girl was bent over the table and one thick braid of hair hung over her shoulder, partly concealing her face. But Selene recognized her all the same.

"Matilda!"

The girl's startled eyes grew round. "Why, as ever I live, it's Miss Selene. What on earth brung you here?"

"Matilda! I can't believe it. I thought you were following your soldier boy. Imagine meeting you here in Norfolk, and just now when I need a friend most."

"But did you run off from Mister John, too? He must have been fit to be tied with both of us gone."

"You were very naughty to go off the way you did, but it's worked out for the best. You cannot know how glad I am to see you now."

The sailor across the table watched both women with growing confusion. In a sudden move he reached out to take Selene's hand just as she tried to rise. "Sorry, Miss, but I was told to keep you waitin' here till the Captain comes back. You'll have to sit down, please, ma'am."

"Take your hands off me," Selene snapped, yanking hers away. Grudgingly she resumed her chair. "Matilda, are you working here? Will you be in this place for the rest of the morning?"

"The rest of the day more like. It was the only place I could get to take me on after . . . after my Willie took off. He was a brass-faced liar, Miss Selene. Told me we was going to be married, but when we got here and he saw his regiment moving off, nothin' would do but he must go, too. He didn't care a fig about what become of me. I hope I never see him again."

Under ordinary circumstances Selene thought Matilda's

round plain face devoid of feelings or even of much intelligence. But the hurt in her eyes moved even Selene, absorbed as she was with her own circumstances. She was a simple girl, too trusting to be suspicious of her soldier's motives. Yet she had a stubborn streak underneath that kindly exterior. No one could have argued her out of leaving to follow her Willie, even if she had confided in anyone.

"Don't worry about it, Mattie. When I get free of my . . . business in this port, we'll go home together."

Matilda glanced back at the bar where her employer was busily polishing glasses. In another moment he would be calling her away. "I don't really want to go back, Miss Selene, but now there's really no place else to go. I'd be obliged if you'd take me with you."

"I'll come back here for you. Later today, I hope."

It somehow improved Selene's prospects just to see Matilda moving around the taproom serving the few customers who sat at the tables. When now and then she disappeared into the kitchen Selene waited anxiously for her to return. Just to know there was a familiar face from home nearby made her more hopeful. When, after a half an hour, Wade Kinsolving came striding through the door, her anxiety returned. He looked very tired and very angry, not too hopeful a sign. Wade threw a coin at the seaman and took a firm grip on Selene's arm, pulling her to her feet.

"Come with me," he said brusquely. She fought to pull away but his fingers dug into the soft flesh of her arm.

"Where are you taking me now? I demand to be turned over to someone else. Someone who'll treat me with respect."

"No one's going to hurt you . . . for the moment at least. I do wish you wouldn't always make such a tragedy out of everything I try to do. Now, please come quietly."

"I don't trust you." He half-pulled her toward the door. Selene looked wildly around but Matilda had disappeared into the kitchen and was nowhere in sight. "Wait," she cried. "I . . . I'd like to take something with me to nibble on. I'm still hungry."

"There's plenty of food where we're going."

At the door she glanced wildly back in time to see Matilda

emerging from the kitchen with a large tray in her arms. The girl's startled eyes filled with dismay as she realized Selene was leaving without her. Then she saw Wade and the dismay turned to admiration and resignation.

"Matilda," Selene called. "It's not what you think. I'll come back for you, I promise. Wait for me . . ."

Selene stumbled down the cobbled street as Wade pulled her toward the wharf. He looked back long enough to see Matilda standing in the doorway watching them, then strode purposefully on with Selene in tow. They went only a short distance before turning to the water and climbing a long, low plank bridge to the deck of a ship moored there. Selene's heart sank as she clambered on board. It was a clean, trim vessel but it was a *ship*, and that did not give her much hope of being turned over to the town authorities. A thin, tall man in a ship's officer's uniform stepped up to her and spoke politely.

"Welcome aboard, Miss Sprague. We are so pleased to have you. I assure you we will try our best to offer you a pleasant journey."

"Jour—!" Before she could finish her startled exclamation, Wade broke in.

"I know you will, Jonathan. Miss Sprague is very fatigued after last night's trip from Manassas. Perhaps you might take us to our cabin."

"Down the steps to the right, Wade. You'll excuse me if I don't accompany you, but there's much to do if we're to sail with the tide. I'll send one of the mates down to make certain you have everything you need."

Wade lost no time dragging Selene across the deck and shoving her down the stairs. Her shocked surprise was beginning to give way to outrage, but he hustled her down the hatchway so quickly that she had no time to protest. Not until he shoved her inside the cabin and closed the door was she able to turn on him in a cold fury.

"You . . . You cad! How dare you! You're holding me a prisoner and you promised . . . you PROMISED I'd be turned over to the proper authorities in Norfolk. Where are we going? I don't want to be on this ship. I don't want to be with you! I demand you release me!"

Her voice grew strident, angry with frustrated disappointment.

"Now please try to be reasonable, Selene. I can't let you go."

"Reasonable! Damn you for a lying jackal. How reasonable can I be when I'm being forcibly kidnapped. I demand you take me off this ship this instant!"

Wade leaned back against the door, folding his arms across his chest and eyeing her with cold resolution. "That I cannot and will not do."

"You're contemptible. What cock-and-bull story did you tell that officer this time? How can I possibly jeopardize your 'secret mission' when you are on the high seas and I'm stuck in a Confederate prison? Let me out of here, I demand it."

"Think of it as saving you from jail—which is certainly more confining and not nearly so pleasant as this ship. You ought to be grateful. As for what I told Jonathan, he thinks we are running away to be married and, being something of a romantic at heart, he's delighted to have a part in our escapade."

Selene gasped in amazement. "You can't mean that he believes such a wild story. Is he blind? Couldn't he see you had to practically drag me aboard this vessel? Run off to marry you . . . I'd rather face a firing squad!"

"I rather doubt, given the actual choice, you'd prefer the bullet. However, I might as well be frank. The truth is, I do not trust you and this mission is too important to take even the slightest chance that you might spoil it for me and my government. Therefore it seemed far the better part of wisdom to keep you under my eye. In order to accomplish this, I have asked Jonathan to perform the ceremony once we are underway."

"The ceremony!" Selene sank down on one of two chests that were bolted to the wall. "You don't actually intend to marry me . . . You don't really believe I'd go through with such a wild idea."

For the first time Wade unbent and walked toward her, still determined but with a slight softening of his rigid stance. "It may be a wild idea but you'll go through with it, my girl, no matter how detestable it may seem to you. I intend to make you

94

my wife, as least in Captain Carey's eyes, and to keep you under my watchful 'protection' until I know this treaty is executed. At that time you can do what you please—call the marriage invalid, sue for divorce, take a new identity—whatever you wish. But that's the way it's going to be and you might as well accept it."

"You bastard! I won't do it! I'll scream bloody murder at the top of my lungs. I'll force that Captain to see that you're coercing me into this."

"Go ahead. And I'll tell him the truth—that you are a dangerous spy and must be kept under lock and key for the duration of the trip. He may relent and just imprison you in this cabin, but I assure you, I will do my best to convince him that some place less congenial and more fortified would be a better place for you. And there are many such places on this ship. Very dark, very cold, and several of them with rats to keep you company. How long is the trip—one week, two? Not a pleasant prospect."

Damn! Selene fell silent, thinking this over. Above her head she could hear the irregular thump of feet on the decks and the voices of the sailors crying orders. They would be underway soon. Tears burned hot behind her eyes but she refused to give way to them. This whole scheme seemed impossible, and yet she could see no way out. Wade obviously had too much influence with the captain to persuade him to see her distress. She must find some way to pretend to go along with this wild scheme until she found a way to escape. Even if that meant killing this detestable man while he slept—a not too unpleasant thought at the moment.

"If I go along with this quietly, will you do one thing for me?" she asked, taking on an almost normal tone of voice.

"What is that?"

"I met a friend from home back in the tavern. Matilda Rollins. She's a simple girl and she's stranded alone in Norfolk. Let her come along as my maid. After all, it would seem more appropriate for me to be traveling with a lady's maid."

"So the two of you can hatch further schemes against the Confederacy?"

"I doubt if Matilda has the intelligence to hatch schemes

against anything. But it would be a comfort to me to have her companionship."

Wade recalled the girl's bland face and was inclined to agree with Selene's assessment of her capabilities. He was aware too that a single woman on a ship filled with men was in an awkward position. It might assuage his conscience a little to do something for his prisoner. For she was his prisoner and that was how he planned it. He really had meant to turn her over to the officer in charge at headquarters in Norfolk when they left Manassas. But here in Norfolk, when the time came to act on his good intentions, he found himself unable to do it. The truth was he wanted her with him. Ravishing her would be easy, but it went against the grain to make a habit of forcing himself on any woman. The guise of marriage was a convenient solution to both problems. It made him responsible for her and it gave him the right to what he wanted—her body.

"I suppose even this little request is too kind a thing for a man like you," Selene muttered bitterly, thinking he was going to refuse her.

"You can have your Matilda. I agree, a lady needs a maid. I'll have her sent for at once."

Selene spent an anxious half hour wondering if Matilda would actually be sent for, or, if she was, would really come. She might think it the height of folly to pack her belongings, leave her employment, and follow an unknown sailor aboard a ship, all because of a tenuous friendship. Yet more and more, she felt that if the girl did not come, she would have no hope at all of getting back home again. Not that she expected Matilda to be of much help. But the moral support of another woman and a familiar face from her uncle's tavern would give her strength to face the future, no matter what it brought.

She was relieved at length to see the door thrown open and Matilda Rollins thrust rudely inside. With a cry of joy she threw her arms around the girl's shoulders and hugged her.

"I was so afraid you wouldn't come," she cried, reaching for Matilda's pitiful bundle of clothing.

"I almost didn't. I couldn't imagine if that awful man was

telling the truth or not. If I hadn't seen him with you in the tavern earlier I'd of never listened to him."

Selene drew her to the bed and sat beside her. "Listen to me, Mattie. I don't know what they told you, but I'm being forced to sail on this ship against my will. I want to go back to Uncle John's but that horrible officer won't let me."

"You mean that handsome Captain? Why, Miss Selene, he seems like a gentleman right enough."

"Sometimes what people seem, and what they really are, are not the same thing. Stay with me, Mattie. I'm terribly in need of a friend. Please come with me, and when we get back home again, I'll make everything right with Uncle John for you."

The girl shrugged her shoulders and a pleased smile framed her plain face. "Well, as far as that goes, I didn't really have nowhere to go anyway. I'm glad to come along with you, Miss Selene. What do you want me to do?"

"I told Captain Kinsolving you would be my maid. You don't really have to be, as long as you keep up the pretense."

"Oh, but I'll be glad to serve you. It's a sight better than hauling trays in that tavern. Only, you don't seem to have much in the way of clothes," she said, looking around the bare room.

"No, I've never had the chance to really pack. But I can make do with what I've brought, as long as you stay nearby. Promise me you won't leave me alone with that awful man, ever."

"But Miss Selene . . ."

"Not for a minute, I insist. That will be the best service you can give me."

"Well, I'll certainly do that, then, Miss Selene. You can count on me. Now, why don't I at least lay out what's here so we make this place a little more liveable. Then I'll brush your hair for you. You always did have the prettiest hair."

It was sometime later that afternoon that Wade appeared once again in the cabin, long enough to order Selene to change her dress and fix herself up a bit.

"Why?" she demanded curtly. "Does the ship's master expect us for supper?"

"We're waiting in the harbor for the tide. I expect to have

97

the wedding take place once we're under way, which should only be a few more minutes. So make yourself presentable. I'd rather Jonathan thought this was a mutually agreeable ceremony."

He was barely gone before Matilda turned a startled gaze to Selene. "You're going to marry that man! But I thought . . ."

"You thought right. I hate him. He's forcing me to go through with this marriage. It's his reward for not locking me on the orlop deck and for letting you come with me. But he'll be sorry. I'm determined to see to that."

Selene refused to go up on deck even when, a short time later, they could make out the unmistakable signs of the ship getting under way. The activity on the deck above them grew heavier and the swaying of the cabin suggested the seas were not going to be too gentle. Selene refused to allow either Mattie or herself to go above for a last look at the shore. As for making herself look nice, she did exactly the opposite. She didn't bother to arrange her hair and she wore the poorest and shabbiest of her three dresses.

"It's not very presentable for a wedding," Matilda said with a note of disappointment. In her eyes a shipboard wedding with a handsome, virile man like Captain Kinsolving smacked of high romance, and she began to wonder if Selene might not be letting her prejudice blind her.

Slowly the cabin began to grow dark as the afternoon light dimmed. Selene was beginning to grow hungry since breakfast had been much earlier. They waited so long for someone to fetch her that she was beginning to think Wade had changed his mind. Then Hawke, the burly seaman who had kept her company that morning, appeared at the door and told them to follow him.

The Captain's cabin was just down the hall. It was larger and more spacious than the cramped quarters Selene had sat in all day, but not by much. There was a table to one side loaded with trays of covered food which gave off tantalizing odors. Two men rose from chairs on the other side of the cabin as the women entered, Wade looking very neat in his full dress uniform and Jonathan, the ship's captain, looking more cadaverous than ever in a blue naval tunic.

He greeted her politely but indifferently, as though this business was a distraction to the more serious work of sailing his ship.

Wade stepped up beside her. "We'll get this ceremony done first, then the Captain has been kind enough to have a supper laid for us."

"I'm not hungry," Selene snapped.

He grabbed her arm, pinching the flesh. "Nevertheless, we must have some festivity to mark the occasion. Proceed Jonathan, if you please."

The ship's captain turned a formal face to his friend. "Wade, you're sure about this?"

"Absolutely. Please do the honors."

"Miss . . . What was the name?" Jonathan lurched toward Selene, wobbling his upper body in a narrow circle long enough for her to catch a strong whiff of pungent whiskey on his breath.

"Miss Sprague," Wade said quickly. "Selene Sprague."

"And is this rather—unusual ceremony also your desire?" the ship's master went on. There was a barely perceptible trace of a blur in his speech and Selene's heart sank. She was going to get no help from this quarter, that was apparent. She felt a sharp twinge as Wade's strong fingers squeezed her elbow.

"Yes," she muttered, just loud enough for the captain to hear.

He wobbled again, then opened a tattered book, and began reading in a monotonous drone. Resigning herself to something that she had already decided was a meaningless charade, Selene paid little attention to the man's words. She only knew she was supposed to answer when Wade pinched her arm again. Her attention was focused by choice on the gentle swaying of the lamp swinging from the ceiling and the mesmerizing way the cabin walls moved up and down with the motion of the waves.

"And so I pronounce that you are man and wife . . ." she suddenly heard Jonathan Carey intone and came back to the present. The words had barely left his mouth when they were followed by a loud crashing boom and the walls of the cabin lurched crazily.

"You may kiss the bride," the captain murmured hurriedly.

"What was that?" Selene cried, grabbing for the table edge to steady herself.

Wade looked up toward the ceiling, on the deck above the thump of running feet was very apparent. "Later," he said and ran for the door. Matilda came rushing to Selene's side, gripping her arm. A second thundering boom set the ship shuddering. "Good Lord, Miss Selene," she cried. "Are we sinking?"

"What's the matter, Captain Carey," Selene cried as the captain turned a myopic gaze toward the door. "Excuse me," he said. "I think I'm needed above."

He hurried across the room very stiff-legged to keep his balance. Selene ran after him, throwing herself in front of the door before he could open it. "But what is it? What's happening?"

"Why, Miss—or it's Mrs. now, isn't it—I imagine it's something to do with the blockade. If you'll just excuse me . . ."

Shoving Selene aside he was quickly gone. "Did you hear that, Mattie," Selene said breathlessly. "The blockade! Union ships! It's our chance."

Matilda, who understood nothing of all this but found the shuddering and the increasing noise more and more frightening, followed Selene up the stairs to the deck, keeping close by her. They found a scene of wild confusion there as both Wade and Jonathan barked orders to the sailors who were flying around the deck to their posts and scrambling up the sheets to alter the sails. It was difficult to make out anything on the sea since night had fallen so heavily, but by straining to see in the dark, first on one side and then on the other, Selene was finally able to spot tiny shards of light on the horizon. As her eyes grew more accustomed to the dark, she was even able to make out the thrilling silhouette of a full-rigged ship bearing down on them. She couldn't see the flag it was flying, but she knew well enough it would be the good old Stars and Stripes.

She longed to lean over the rail to scream and wave at them, but that would be useless given the roar of cannon. The ship did not seem to be trying to hit them since the cannon spewed tall spouts in the water all around them. Yet with every shot the ship shuddered more under the increasing amount of sail.

"The wind is from starboard," Wade yelled above her on the captain's deck. "Bring her around and we can outrun the devils."

"But that's not our course," Carey yelled down at him.

"For God's sake, man. We can get back on course later. We've got to escape that runner now."

"I'll give the orders, thank you, Wade. I'm Captain here. Hard to port, Seaman Jess. Come about," he shouted as the sailors scurried up the masts.

If only Wade Kinsolving would mind his own business, Selene thought, while Wade cursed the Captain under his breath. For all their former friendship he sometimes wondered if Jonathan Carey was not too fond of drink to carry the responsibility of a ship. That he should have one, spoke volumes for the state of the Confederate navy.

The lights on the Union runner were growing brighter. Selene cast around her for something she might do to help the Yankee ship. Everyone was too busy to pay her much mind. The concentration of the sailors and the contest of wills between Wade and Carey had to work to her advantage. But what could she do?

There was a lantern hanging near her but even if she were able to wave it from the highest yardarm, it would mean little to the Union vessel. On the other hand . . .

The stronger wind had caught the altered sails now and she could feel the thrust of the ship as it pushed through the waves. Unless she did something to stop this vessel they were going to outrun their pursuer.

She darted under the shadows of the higher deck and began pulling pieces of debris into a pile. There were shards of wood, a few lengths of rope, no paper, unfortunately, but that was no surprise. Reaching under her skirt she tore off a length of her petticoat. Then she spied the bucket. It was made of leather and hard as stone, but it contained what looked like pitch. Hopefully it would help. She got the makings of a small bonfire

101

together in just a few moments. Grabbing the lantern, she threw it down on top, splashing the oil on the flame.

Her heart surged upward with the sudden bright flames.

"Miss Selene," a terrified Matilda yelled. "You'll sink us all!"

Frantically Mattie tried to stamp out the fire. "Stop it," Selene yelled, pulling the girl away. "Don't you see. This is our only chance."

"But if we all drown . . ."

Wade had been concentrating so hard on the swell of the sails above him that for a long moment he did not notice the acrid smell of smoke. When he did recognize it, he thought the ship must have been hit. Looking wildly around he realized that it had to be coming from somewhere below.

"Captain Carey," one of the sailors yelled from over his head. "Look there . . . on the deck . . ."

The Captain turned his eyes from the ship they were trying to outrun and blearily searched the quarterdeck. Wade recognized at once what the man was trying to indicate, rushed to the rail, and leaned over. The flames were spurting upward, already a foot high, and in their scarlet glare Selene's face took on an almost devilish gleam.

"God damn!" he muttered, and yelled to one of the seamen on the deck to put that fire out at once. Bounding over the rail he was able to grasp Selene around the waist and pull her away just as the sailor grabbed up a bucket of sand, kept handy for just such an event, and throw it over the flames.

"Let me go," Selene cried, struggling and twisting. With a swift movement of her shoulders, she was able to throw Wade off balance long enough to grab one of the sailor's hands and tear it from the handle of the bucket. The sand went flying.

"You vixen," Wade said as he lunged for her, his eyes smarting from the sand. Grabbing her around the waist, he twisted her against him, one arm around her throat. She was not going to get away this time, he determined as he forcefully dragged her back over the deck, far enough away from the fire to allow the men to put it out before it did any real damage. Some bond of reason snapped in Selene's mind and she fought him wildly, mindlessly, until Wade, in a burst of passion and futility, hauled back and hit her on her jaw, knocking her cold. There was a sense of satisfaction as she slumped in his arms.

Mattie stood beside him, wringing her hands and crying, the fat tears rolling down her cheeks. "You didn't have to do that, sir," she moaned. "You hit her too hard. You've probably killed her, sir, I just know it."

"That would be too good to be true," Wade muttered. Picking Selene up in his arms he started toward the stairs. "There was no other way to stop her. She nearly had us all drowned. Come below now and stay with her."

Mattie followed him, still sniffing as they went back to the cabin. Her tears flowed anew when Wade dumped Selene on the bed and stalked to the door.

"I'm going to lock the both of you in," he said, "and if by any means you get out of here and come up on deck, I'll have you both shot on the spot. Is that clear?"

"Oh, sir . . ." Mattie's wails reached a new height. "You're too cruel. What if the ship sinks? We'll never get out. We'll go to the bottom . . ."

"Then you'd better start praying it doesn't."

Slamming the door, Wade locked it and put the key in his pocket. Then just to be certain—for with a girl like Selene, he decided, you have to think of everything—he dragged a chest from the captain's cabin nearby and propped it up against the door.

"Let her get out of that!" he said, kicking the chest. Back on deck he was satisfied to see that the pursuing ship had slipped a little farther back while the scorched place on the deck, about the size of a table, was the last sign of the fire Selene had tried to start. He stepped up beside Carey, who was still peering into the night with his eyeglass even though Wade suspected he must not be able to see much.

"Do you think we'll evade her?" he asked the Captain. When Carey lowered his glass and looked at Wade, he seemed a trifle more sober than he had been earlier.

"If this wind keeps up, yes. I recognize her. She's the *Baltimore Star* out of Annapolis. I had a run with her once before and she's sluggish for a blockade boat. The *Yamacraw*, on the other hand, may not be too steady but she's trim and fast with a fresh wind like this. I think we'll get away right enough."

"And then what? Will we lay off Boston?" he said sarcastically.

Carey gave a grim chuckle. "Not quite. We're heading northeast now, but once we've got enough distance we can come about and swing back south. These blockade boats are easily discouraged. If they don't take their prize close to shore, they won't venture out too far."

"Well, that's encouraging, at least."

Carey closed his spyglass with a snap. "What was all that commotion on deck? Is your new wife some kind of Northern sympathizer?"

"In a way. You'll do me a big favor, Jonathan, by not asking too many questions. I promise you Selene won't try anything like that again."

"You do know this whole thing seems very strange."

"I know, but trust me. It will work out for the best for everyone."

Carey shrugged. "It's your business. As long as you say it will be to the advantage of the Confederacy, I'll go along. Look, that Yankee ship has dropped away even further."

The tiny lights that pinpointed the *Baltimore Star*'s position were now so dim as to be almost invisible against the ebony sea and sky. Wade leaned against the rail, crossing his arms over his chest and breathing deeply of the cool air. The breeze touched his face with refreshing fingers and for the first time since he stepped aboard the ship he began to relax some of the stiff tension of the past twenty-four hours.

This was one ship at least that the blockade would not net. Every thrust of the *Yamacraw* that carried it away from America was that much nearer to the completion of his mission. Once they turned and started south, he would feel even more assured that he would be able to accomplish the important task his country had entrusted to him.

Yet Barbados was days away, and Selene was a matter that must be dealt with. A new sense of anger swept over him as he thought of her face in the glare of the flames. "Vixen" he had called her and so she was. A wild, untamed vixen.

A satisfied smile touched the corners of his shapely lips. Taming her was going to be a pleasure now that he had the time. She was his prisoner and his wife. There was leisure and time to take on the task of breaking her. And he intended to enjoy every minute of it.

Six

The wind picked up so quickly that the *Yamacraw* was carried like a feather on its gusting breath. Wade stayed on deck long after the pinpoints of light from the Yankee cutter were visible on the dark horizon. Down below in the dark cabin Selene lay on the bed where she had been summarily half-thrown and dug her fists in the coverlet. What a stupid thing to have done, she berated herself. If there had been more time to think, she would never have been so naive as to expect to get away with starting a fire on a ship—the one place where fire was dreaded more than anything. Yet there had not been time to calculate alternatives. Everything had happened so quickly, and all she could see was the need to do something to attract the attention of the Yankee ship and distract that of the men trying to evade her. She ought to have known, though, that Wade Kinsolving was not going to let her get away so easily.

The motion of the ship dipping in the troughs of the waves told her clearly enough that they were outrunning their pursuer. Another opportunity lost! And God only knew when there would be another one as good. In the meantime she must somehow put up with this man who could now call himself her husband, taking advantage of her while she lay as much a prisoner as any felon in irons.

"Oh, Miss," Matilda moaned from across the cabin where she sat kneading her fingers in her skirt. "I was never so scared. I wish I hadn't come aboard this vessel. I wish I was home in Manassas!" The fat tears slipped down her cheeks and her face wrinkled with the effort to keep from bursting into loud sobs.

"Oh, for heaven sake, stop that wailing," Selene snapped. "I'm in for a lot more trouble than you." Her brusqueness only increased Mattie's tears and she added more gently. "Please be quiet, Matilda. We are in no danger of drowning. You'll get back home, I promise."

Selene moved to the door to try the handle which was (as she knew it would be) firmly locked. She looked around the small room but there was only one window and that one high up. Through it the pitch black of the night was like looking into a deep hole.

"But where are we going?" Matilda wailed. "I don't even know."

"I know. It's an island called Barbados. There are civilized people there. My Papa told me once about these islands in the Caribbean sea. They have heathen natives but they also have settlers from Europe. We'll just have to see which are the most numerous when we get there." And, she added mentally, once there I'll find some way to get back home or die in the attempt.

"But it won't be Virginia," Mattie cried, refusing to be comforted.

"No, it won't," Selene muttered. She sat down on one of the chests against a wall and rested her elbows on her knees, her chin in her hands. Barbados was a long way off. What was she going to do in the time it took to sail there to help her country and escape this oppressive man? The whole situation seemed more hopeless than ever.

"I've got to get out of this room," she said grimly. "I've got to get that door open."

"Oh, Miss Selene," Mattie wailed, "I don't understand any of this. I don't want to drown!"

"Hush, Mattie, or I'll drown you myself. There must be a way. I've got to think of something."

The ship, catching the wind, gave a creaking heave and lumbered almost on its side. Mattie howled and threw her skirt over her head while Selene scrambled to the door, twisting and yanking at the handle. It was locked tight and refused to budge no matter how she pulled at it. Glancing around the room she

107

spied a two-foot long iron bar used to shutter the windows. Grabbing it up she pried at the handle, but the old, hardened wood refused to yield. She pressed her ear to the pane trying to make out the voices above, but they were too muffled. In frustration she kicked at the door, managing only to bruise her toe through the slipper. Then as suddenly as it had started the sea grew quiet, and the ship, which had been wobbling in the water, settled into a gentle drift. She could hear the rhythmic luffing of the sails above the scrape of the chest in the hall outside as it was shoved from the door and a key rattled in the lock.

Selene caught her breath and stepped back, her eyes round with suspicion as the door was thrust open. She held the iron rod across her breast, tight in her fists, ready to use it on the first head that appeared.

The swaying light from the lantern threw elongated shadows on the doorway, now yellowish gold, now gray murkiness. As it grew still and settled, Selene made out Wade's tall form filling the entranceway, the shadows carving long streaks on his lean cheeks. His eyes were hard even in that poor light. He stood, slightly hunched forward, fierce with determination, one hand clutched around the neck of a green wine bottle. Selene involuntarily moved back against the wall of the cabin, pressing the rod against her chest.

Deliberately Wade stepped into the cabin and held the door open. "Get out," he snapped to Matilda, still cringing in the corner.

"Don't you move a step!" Selene ordered. The poor girl looked from one to the other.

"Oh, oh, oh . . ." she began whimpering.

Striding across the room, Wade grabbed her shoulder and pulled her toward the open door. "I said leave!"

"But, sir . . ."

Selene started to pull her back, then thought better of getting that close to Wade. "Matilda, stay where you are!"

"Get out or I'll have you fed to the sharks."

That seemed to settle the matter. The girl fled to the door, throwing Selene a guilty, frightened glance. So much for her standing by me through thick and thin, Selene thought.

"But where shall I go?"

"Anywhere you please," Wade said, slamming the door behind her. On the other side Selene could hear the girl still whimpering. "You might have found her a berth," she snapped angrily. "You told me she could stay with me."

"She'll find a place to sleep." He moved into the room and set the bottle down on one of the chests standing against the wall. In a dingy wooden cabinet above it he found a tin cup. Selene shrank against the far wall and watched as he filled the cup and drank it down.

"A little celebration," he said, wiping his arm across his mouth. He refilled the cup and held it out to her. "Your turn."

"I don't want it. I don't want anything from you!"

She could see his eyes flood with anger and a thrill of satisfaction went through her. When he gave a bitter chuckle and downed the second glass himself, she deliberately went on. "That's right," she said smugly. "Add drunkeness to the rest of your vices. I'm not surprised. Nothing about you surprises me anymore." While she talked she took stock of their respective positions. He stood between her and the door, but it was unlocked now. If she could distract him long enough, she might be able to get to it before he could stop her. She sidled around, still keeping the length of the room between them. His eyes followed her but he managed to refill the cup again and sip it as he watched her over the rim.

"Perhaps if your expectations were a little higher, you might find me more responsive," he replied. There was a slight blur to his words, as though his tongue could not quite manage to get around them in its usual way. He set down the cup. Though the wine numbed his anger and conscience, still he did not want to lose control. Selene would take advantage of that in the blink of an eye.

"You've given me no reason to expect anything more." Now they stood at right angles to the door. If she could just manage to get his attention away from it.

"You're my wife," he mumbled as though not quite believing it himself.

"Wife! You call that mockery of a wedding valid? It was nothing more than your excuse to hold me here against my will. It was a diabolical, underhanded, mean trick, and one not worthy of a gentleman!"

He stepped toward her, his eyes blazing. "You little vixen. You drive me too far."

"Don't you touch me," Selene cried, raising the iron rod.

"I'll touch you well enough," he said, starting for her. It was all she needed. She brought the rod slamming down on his head, stunning him, and rushed to the door, turning the handle to pull it open. Ignoring the blow, Wade was right behind her. He grabbed her hand, tearing it away from the handle, and with one arm around her waist yanked her back into the room. Selene struggled wildly, furious that he had caught her before she could get away. Scratching at him, biting him where she could, she struggled in his grip until with one thrust he threw her across the room where she landed against the wall. While she fought to get her balance back and to calm her reeling head, Wade turned the key in the lock and dropped it in his coat pocket. Then he quickly pulled off the coat and dumped it inside one of the chests. Only then did he move to where she had dragged herself up on her knees.

Reaching for her arm he pulled her to her feet. Her back pressed against the cabin wall as he forced his body against hers, roughly kissing her throat and shoulders. There was no gentleness in the way his hands kneaded her body and his weight pressed against her. Selene struggled for breath. As her head cleared she was overwhelmed with fury at the way he had thrown her around. Pounding on his shoulders she writhed in her attempt to get free but his body had her pinned against the wall and the more she struggled the more she inflamed his desire for her.

His hands slid up her waist, roughly compressing her breasts and forcing his fingers into the soft flesh of her shoulders. He closed his hands around her neck, pulling her face to his lips. Selene pursed her lips tightly together, mumbling unformed curses as his tongue traced the outline of her mouth and flicked against the tight closure of her lips. She fought to twist her head aside, but his hands held her fast. The insidious tongue, previously so forceful, became instead a soft, tickling tormenting serpent and Selene's tight mouth began to relax in spite of her determination not to. Finding just enough of an opening, it thrust between her lips, circling her teeth, probing the soft expanse of her opening mouth, exploring the roof, her sensitive tongue, swelling with the need for fulfillment.

She felt her body begin to weaken and she fought back. When, finally, Wade lifted his head from hers, his mind completely focused on the resonance of her body, she found her chance. Reaching back she socked her fist against his temple, knocking him reeling.

"Damn you!" he cried, holding his hand to his head. He felt a soft wetness there and knew it was the residue of the blow from the iron bar. Now he would have a damnable bruise to go with it. "That's the last straw," he cried. Selene had taken advantage of his momentary release to scramble down on her knees and make for the door. She got away from him long enough to get back on her feet at the door where the handle wobbled uselessly in her hand. Pounding on the implacable wood she screamed for someone to help her. Wade caught her in mid-scream, lifted her like a feather—so great was his anger—and dumped her on the narrow bed. Pulling at his clothes, he had them off before Selene could throw herself to the foot of the bed in an attempt to climb out. He got free of his clothes in time to grab her ankle and pull her back up on the bed where he fell on her. Her own clothes were a torment of skirts, petticoats and lace-edged bodice which he ripped from her shoulders. Throwing her over like a fish in a net, he worked the dress from her, exposing her chemise and bloomers. The chemise he did not bother with, other than to work her breasts free. She felt his hands tear into the waist of her lower garments, felt them worked down around her thighs, all the while twisting and writhing beneath his insistent hands.

His body was fierce on top of hers. His fingers dug into her flesh, thrusting between her legs, forcing them apart. Weight like a heavy press forced her down into the mattress. His fingers dug into the wet softness between her thighs, then she felt them replaced by the massive, hard thrust of his throbbing manhood.

Pushing harder and deeper, over and over, Wade drove into her. Dimly she heard the loud, panting cries he made against

111

the depression of her shoulder. Her whole body was filled with this invading, monstrous shaft that pulsated and rammed her, filling her with its pulsating need. Her own exertions had left her heaving for breath and there was at last a point at which she could fight no longer. She was helpless, held in the grip of this man stretched over her, his body violating her own, pressing her to him as part of an extension of his own grasping need.

Selene could not breathe. Wade's heavy body climaxed in a spasm that lifted him slightly, long enough for her to wedge her hand between them and gasp for air. Then he collapsed, shifting slightly to the side and lying inert upon her. There was no sound in the cabin but the loud gasps of their exhausted bodies as the swaying lamp threw shadows across their damp flesh, shimmering it like satin in the wavering light.

Wade slumped exhausted on the outside of the bed. Wedged between his body and the cabin wall, Selene rolled over as far away from him as she could get in the small space and pulled her legs up against her chest like a child. She wondered why she was not crying. Shouldn't a genteel girl, brought up to consider herself a lady, be overwhelmed with shame and mortification? Was she ruined? Dishonored?

Her common sense told her no. What she had just undergone was probably no more than what many a wife endured on her wedding night, often quite willingly. Nor was she a virgin. She well remembered how her own passion had swept her along joyfully that first time. No, what filled her now was not shame but fury that Wade could have forced himself upon her because he was bigger and stronger than she. If there were tears, they were of frustration. If there was a residue, it was a determination to get even with him someday, to pay him back for preventing her from serving her country and for the indignities he had heaped upon her.

She grew conscious of his soft, even breathing beside her and realized he had fallen asleep. For a moment she weighed the possibility of trying to slip past him, retrieve the key and join Mattie up on the deck. The ship was quiet now, with only the mesmerizing motion of the waves and the gentle creak of timbers to break the silence of the sea. Yet even as she lay wondering if escape would be possible her exhausted body gave up the struggle and she drifted into a fitful sleep.

Consciousness came back slowly, drifting on waves of a delicate, silken tracing on her flesh. Like the faintest breath Wade's hands drifted over the long expanse of her outstretched arm, lightly outlining the length of her body under the thin sheet, searching the creamy stillness of her exposed thigh. Only half-awake, Selene gave a shudder of delight. The tickling, silky touch of his fingers on the surface of her skin sent a shiver through her that she was only barely aware of. Still half asleep, she murmured a protest that was not meant to be taken seriously as her body warmed to the wandering, insistent touch of Wade's hands.

Stirring, Selene opened her eyes to see Wade's dark form bending toward her. Over his shoulder the cabin was dark as the lamp had gutted out, though faint light at the window spoke of the coming dawn. She was too tired, too lethargic, and too bemused by the gentle touch of his hands to do anything but lie quietly, allowing her mind to drift on waves of sensation. In serpentine patterns that swirled up and down, then around, and back again, he followed the line of her throat, her neck, and the swell of her shoulder, down the sensitive whiteness of her underarm, around the curve of her waist to circle her breast. The sheet slipped away and Selene, warmed to the music of his fingers, arched her back slightly, carrying the taut nipple upward. She gave a small shudder as his fingers traced the ever-enclosing circle of the brown aura of her upward thrusting breast. Only the sudden cool wetness told her he had lowered his head to circle it with his mouth, his tongue lightly flickering against its awakening passion.

Faintly she heard herself moan and her body stretched like the string of an instrument in the hands of an artist. His lips closed on the nipple, all gentleness and softness, lightly pulling at it, making little sucking noises, awakening her to a crescendo of sensation. She wanted to cry stop, and yet, more significantly, she never wanted him to stop. She wished she could go on forever this way, floating on a sea of feelings. No thoughts, no reasoning, nothing but this wonderful, all-encompassing glorious sensation. She was a vessel of senses, taut nerves, delightful, pulsating forces.

She grew conscious of Wade's other hand, even as he continued working her nipple, kneading the flesh of her breast, and driving her ever more wild with his lips. She was helpless beneath him, powerless to move as she felt his other hand tracing its determined patterns down her body, gently probing her navel, sliding downward around the bony protrusions of her hips. Selene rolled over on her back, unconsciously making it easier for his insistent fingers to entwine her pubic hair, inviting them closer, into her most secret spaces. But he refused to come, torturing her with his endless searching, tracing the inner thigh in an ecstasy of sensation. Her legs opened for him and her hips made small circling patterns as her need grew. Her hands reached for him, circling the broad coolness of his back, beginning their own wandering on his taut flesh. Like a stream they moved over his hips, filled their longing palms with the delicious roundness of his hips, slid around to touch and hold the throbbing shaft, so engorged and ready that she could barely clasp it.

She pulled him toward her. Nothing mattered so much as to take that wonderous, magnificent magic wand inside her, letting it fill her with its sweetness. But he refused. With a control that was almost cruel, he moved away and, instead, thrust his probing fingers into the damp valley between her legs. She could feel the tight thrust of his fingers forcing their way within, practically filling that emptiness that cried out for completion. Then they slid out and instead went to search the magic place that sent Selene reeling. Finding it, they began a hard, ceaseless massage that built wave upon wave of ecstasy within her. She cried out, her body stretched taut, her legs splayed. His lips grew hard on the throbbing nipple as she writhed beneath his determined hands. Her eyes tightly closed, she could see white sparks, changing to red, growing in intensity as her body became one long flame, crying out for him.

And then as suddenly as he had begun, he pulled away. Lying inert, brought to a point so close to ecstasy, Selene almost sobbed. His lips slid up her breast to her neck, her chin, closing against her welcoming mouth. He was breathing harder now, along with her, matching her growing passion. She was

114

desperate for him, wanting him so badly it almost hurt. Her hands closed over his back, her arms pressed him against her. Her legs lifted to cross over his back, lifting his thighs to hers. She felt the stiff thrust of him against her, driving deep until with a joyful force it thrust home, deep inside her. Deeper, probing, searching for that primitive completion. The waves began to build again, carrying her along, her body thrilling at holding him prisoner within her. Now, at last, she was in control. She was the jailor and he was the bound. He was helpless now, unable to stop or pull away. His breathing grew stronger, his body snapped against hers, throbbing with its need. Together, at last, they crashed over the edge, arriving simultaneously at that glorious climax where all is feeling and beauty.

When her mind cleared she realized she was lying in the hollow of his arms, her head nestling in the slight depression between his neck and his shoulders. She was still panting, too wonderfully tired and satiated to move. Wade's breath, too, came in short bursts that gradually subsided. Selene felt so content, so filled with satisfaction, that she unconsciously kissed the taut flesh near her lips. His arms tightened against her, holding her close and she felt his lips on her hair. The hands that pushed away the long strands that lay across her forehead were gentle, moving over her as though she were some fragile vessel which too hard a touch might break into a thousand pieces.

Neither of them spoke. Words, they unconsciously knew, would break the aura of contentment and bring them back to the world they knew was waiting, a world of anger and divided loyalties, of vengeance and resentment.

Selene was unaware of falling asleep again except that she drifted in an easy comfort she had never before experienced in her life. There was something about it that reminded her of her father, of the security and happiness she used to know when he held her snug on his lap and read to her from one of his wonderful old history books. Her dreams were of that time, long ago in Washington, when she was the beloved daughter

115

and she was happy. That time before death, loneliness, grief, and war had shattered her pleasant world.

When she woke sunlight was streaming through the window, giving a brass patina to the plank floor. The bed was empty beside her and no one else was in the room. For a long moment she lay there trying to remember if last night had been a dream or reality. Had it really happened, that contented, almost loving coupling? Then the earlier time came roaring back, when Wade had thrown her down and forced himself upon her. That had certainly been real! The other—well, even if it had actually happened, it meant nothing. It was probably no more than his attempt to convince her he was not the monster she thought him. Either that or it was just another time of self-indulgence at her expense, and she knew better than to be tricked by that.

She threw off the covers and stood in the room, her feet cool against the bare floor. Stretching her arms over her head she pulled her body taut, enjoying the feeling of the tight muscles. She was a little sore and she was dismayed to find herself smiling at the remembrance of where that soreness came from. Mustn't get led along that rosy path, she determined as she sought out her clothes.

To her surprise a clean, plain but serviceable dress and undergarments had been laid out on the chest. Selene put them on, buttoning them up herself as she idly wondered where Mattie had gone to. Then she brushed her hair and tied it up in a chenille net.

She was starving. And, in spite of her anger and resentment, she felt wonderful—alive and well and full of a buoyance she had not felt since her father's death. She stood at the window, watching the sapphire sea rolling below, listening to the whip of the wind on the sails, and enjoying the slight dip in her tummy when the ship plowed through the trough of the waves.

It must be the salt air, she thought, as she went bounding up the stairs.

Matilda was sitting on the deck, turning her face to the sun, a smile flittering about her lips. Selene stood watching her, her hands resting on her slim waist.

"I can almost see the freckles popping out," she com-

116

mented. At the sound of her voice, Mattie jumped to her feet. "Oh, Miss Selene. I didn't see you come on deck. You found your clothes? I'm sorry I didn't stay till you woke but . . ."

"It doesn't matter, Mattie. I managed very well by myself. Isn't this a beautiful day! Look at the sky. I never saw such a deep, true blue before. And not a cloud in sight. But you really should be careful, Mattie, or your complexion will be nothing but a mass of spots."

The girl shrugged. "Oh, I don't care about that, Miss Selene. People expect ladies to have perfect complexions but not girls like me. Besides, the sun feels so good on my face."

Selene plopped down on the coil of thick ropes where Matilda had been sunning herself. "I'm famished, Mattie. Could you see about finding me some breakfast? Oh, and bring up my parasol, would you? Lady or not, I don't want any freckles."

"And you an old married woman, too," Mattie snickered. Selene's face darkened at her frivolous words and the girl, seeing it, scurried toward the hatch. "I'll see about your breakfast," she threw over her shoulder. Selene watched her leave, sensing that something had gone out of the bright day. She was sure of it when she spied Wade Kinsolving coming toward her from the stairs of the poop deck.

"I thought you might want this," Wade said, holding out a large straw hat of the kind popular sixty years before. Its wide brim was the size of a small sunshade and it was fastened under the chin by two long streamers wound around the low crown. Grudgingly Selene took it from him.

"Thank you," she murmured.

"I wouldn't want to see that milkmaid complexion ruined," Wade said, turning away to stare out at the sea. There was something in his manner—an apologetic stance or perhaps it was embarrassment. Selene tied the ribbons under her chin, acknowledging to herself that the wide brim made a welcome dent in the glare. With surprise she realized that she could not meet his eyes. Neither could he meet hers, she thought, with some satisfaction. Served him right!

"Where are we," she asked, not to break the uncomfortable silence, but because she genuinely wanted to know.

117

"Northeast of Florida, by now. Probably off St. Augustine, if you know where that lies."

"I remember. My father was very strict about geography. Will we reach Barbados today?"

He laughed. "Your father was not quite strict enough. We are still several days away from Barbados."

"Oh." She had hoped this ridiculous fiasco might be over with sooner. One of the sailors passing by on the far side of the deck paused to lift his hat to her.

"Good morning, madam," he said politely and Selene recognized Seaman Hawke. "Fine mornin', ain't it," he added, and when her half-hearted reply gave him no encouragement, moved on. "Do they all know about that ridiculous wedding?" Selene snapped, glaring at Wade.

"What if they do? It gives credence to it, doesn't it. And I should think you'd like being Madam and Mrs. Most women, I'm told, long for the time they can have that title."

"Most women agree to it when it's offered! They don't have to be dragged, coerced, threatened, or bribed into it, and . . . and raped in the bargain!"

She caught the sudden flush on his skin. That had hit home right enough. "It was a legal ceremony," he said lamely.

"It was a hollow mockery and you know it. I would prefer to remain Miss Sprague to these sailors."

He turned on her, his eyes flaming. "Well, you have no choice. While we are on this vessel, we will keep up this charade. Once this is over, you can call yourself anything you like, and I can think of a few choice names that would be very appropriate."

He stalked away but stopped by the steps to the deck above, resting his hand on the railing. "By the way. We are to dine with the Captain tonight, and I expect you to be pleasant and to say nothing of our bargain."

Selene studied him standing there. His uniform looked neatly pressed and his hair was clean and combed, in contrast to the unkempt slovenliness of the sailors around him. The lean jaw and firm chin, the strong dark brows, the tall figure and straight shoulders, the self-assured way he moved with firmness and yet with grace—she could almost admire him if

118

she hadn't known his dark side so well. She dipped her head, hiding her face under the brim of her hat, and said nothing. Wade went up the stairs, giving an exasperated click of his tongue that implied he felt she was hopeless. Selene smiled out over the water. Pleasant and quiet! He would see.

"Slavery is not the issue."

The clatter of Selene's spoon on fine china drew Wade's eyes from the rim of the decanter he was holding over Carey's glass. He threw her a warning glance as he watched her lips disappear into a thin line that was a pink slash on her white face.

"That is a ridiculous statement, Wade Kinsolving, and you know it," the ship's master replied in his laconic way. "It was slavery that brought on this misguided war, no matter how much the Confederacy tries to push other considerations to the fore."

"The real issue is states' rights," Wade said, filling his glass.

"The right of states to buy and sell slaves." Both men turned to her, surprised that she had finally spoken. In spite of her determination to be the opposite of the quiet and pleasant lady Wade had advised her to be, Selene had sat through the meal saying little beyond polite responses. She wasn't sure herself why she had done this, except that she wanted to be very certain to take the correct measure of the company. There would be no more wild forays or desperate attempts to escape from Wade Kinsolving. From now on everything would be carefully thought out.

Captain Carey gave a short chuckle. "Well said, Mrs. Kinsolving."

"Virginia's right to be her own master and to make her own decisions," Wade snapped.

"I take it you do not approve of slavery, madam," Carey went on.

Selene turned to him, ignoring Wade and enjoying it. "My father was a distinguished teacher and philosopher. He taught me from my cradle that traffic in human lives that reduced them to no more than chattel is an abomination. I have seen

119

nothing in the years since to convince me that he was not correct. A man or woman, whether their skin is black, brown, red, or whatever, is not an animal to be bought and sold with no more thought than a horse. Indeed, with less thought, for to most Virginians a good horse is far more treasured and better treated."

Carey lifted his glass to her then downed the contents. Though he had remained more sober than usual through the dinner, now that the meal was nearly finished he was well on his way to his customary inebriation. "And how do you answer that, Captain Kinsolving, for what the lady says is all too true. I myself have seen our fellow Virginians be attentive lovers to their Arabians while they watched the backs of their field bucks cut to ribbons for trying to run away."

"Any man who runs a good plantation would never abuse his workers. They are the ones who keep his operation running successfully. I admit there are exceptions—men who take some kind of perverse pride in their cruelty—but the majority of Southerners know the value of contented workers."

Selene sat back in her chair, noticing that he looked slightly more uncomfortable than before this subject was raised. "But you must admit the system allows for such men to take advantage of the power they wield over other human beings."

"Negroes are not to be considered in the same light as cultured, educated white men. There are differences of breeding, training, enlightenment . . ."

"Oh yes, owning and abusing other human beings is very enlightened."

A flush spread upward on Wade's lean cheeks. "It's too bad your father didn't teach you better manners along with his philosophical principles."

"Like yours, I suppose!"

"Now, now," Carey said unctuously, "let's not let our passions override our principles. Madam, you may not realize it, but Wade here is a fine example of the kind of ownership he espouses. We grew up together in King William County, and I know for a fact that his plantation is as neatly and fairly run as any in Virginia."

"You own a plantation?" Selene asked before thinking. The

words were barely out of her mouth before she wished she could retrieve them. Why should she care how he made his living before the war.

"A small one. It was left me by my father who died when I was only twelve. I had to learn early in life what it meant to take responsibility for others, including the welfare and livelihood of over one hundred slaves."

"And a good job you made of it, too. I have often thought how different your life might have been had your older brothers lived. You and I could have taken to the sea together as we so often planned when we were children. Do you remember how we were going to build the fastest clipper on the waves and win the market for the China trade?"

"I remember," Wade said, forgetting Selene for the moment. "It could still happen, perhaps after the war."

"Not while you have the responsibility of Five Oaks on your shoulders."

"My poor mother would have never allowed me near the sea. It was difficult enough for her to see me astride a horse, she was so fearful that I would follow my brothers into the grave. What would she say now if she could see the havoc brought on by this war."

Carey turned to Selene. "It's true, Madam Kinsolving. Madam Esther was always watching out for this lad, but he gave her good reason. I never knew anyone better for taking the highest fence, driving the fastest mount, or searching for the riskiest venture. It was as though he wanted to break his neck."

Wade smiled at the memory and Selene could not help but think how attractive he looked when softness touched his face. "I had to fight her, or she would have swathed me in flannel for the rest of my life. That's no way to live."

Carey reached again for the decanter, a rose-colored glass bulb that glimmered softly in the candlelight. "I don't think we will be able to go back to clippers in the future, my friend, even when this sad war is finally over with. Did you notice that isolated fence at Norfolk with all the noise and bustle behind it? That was the wave of the future. An iron-clad frigate that can bounce cannon balls off its hull as easily as though they were made of leather. It hadn't been tested yet, but if it works—and most of my colleagues are certain that it will—the old sailing ships will be driven from the seas. No, I don't think we will ever have that clipper, even if the war should come to a speedy, successful end."

"I heard rumors of that ship, though nothing that could be verified. But surely, even if it proves successful, it will be a long time before the old ships are gone. And in the meantime, think of the havoc it could wreak on the Federal Navy."

"Unless the North develops one, too, which I have heard they are doing. You see, my friend, that is the real point. The South has the will and the determination, but they don't have what is more sorely needed to fight a war—factories, cannon, ammunition, guns, ships, clothing, even food stuffs . . ."

"As long as we have the Mississippi Delta, we have the breadbasket of the South. As for clothing, we have more cotton than any part of the country."

"Most of it is shipped to factories in other places."

"Ah, but if England—"

He stopped, his eyes swerving to Selene who was closely studying this conversation, watching both men as they talked. She was far too quiet and yet too interested to suit Wade. He threw down his fork. "Enough of this gloomy talk. In the end it does not matter who has the factories or the guns. We have the spirit and the conviction of a righteous cause. Besides, the issue for me, as I said, is not slavery or even states' rights. It is loyalty to my own state of Virginia. I go with her, even if she should lead me into hell itself."

Carey laughed and lifted his refilled glass to Wade. "My friend, I fear that is exactly where she is going to lead you."

Wade and Selene went up on deck, glad to be out of the stuffy cabin with its dark paneling and flickering lamplight, away from the heavy odors of food and wine. Though they moved side by side, there was a stiffness between them as they stood by the taffrail, drinking in the night air. Selene drew her lacy shawl around her shoulders against the coolness of a light breeze.

"Is he going to be in any condition to run this ship?" she

asked, finally breaking the strained quiet that lay between them.

"Oh yes. Carey drinks too much—always has—but he never gets too far under to know what is happening on his ship. You saw him at his worst the night we left Norfolk. He may be in his cups, but should an emergency arise, he will be as suddenly sober as any man. I've seen it too often not to know it's true."

"My father always said that drink was the ruination of many a good man."

"Your father sounds like a self-appointed prig."

"Naturally *you* would think so."

He took her arm angrily, pulling her toward the stairs. "Come on. It's time you retired." She followed reluctantly, but once they reached the cabin door, he stopped, facing her briefly. Reaching for her hand, he brought it to his lips in a gesture that was more sarcastic than chivalrous.

"Good night, Miss Sprague," he muttered and turned to walk back up the stairs to the deck. Selene watched him go in disbelief. She had half-expected to be dragged into the cabin and thrown on the bed again. She stood, wondering if this was a game, and would he soon come thundering back. She opened the cabin door to see Matilda moving around the room. A cot had been laid in the corner, neatly covered with a blanket and pillow.

"Master said I was to sleep here," Matilda said almost apologetically. She looked at Selene as though wondering what to expect. Both these people seemed so crazy at times that she never knew how they were going to react. Had Selene taken a notion to catch her by the collar and walk her out the door she would not have been surprised.

"Good," Selene said and slammed the door shut. Then for good measure she turned the key in its lock and slipped it into her pocket.

The following night passed with Matilda again sleeping on her cot in the corner and Wade somewhere far away. Selene had not been able to learn where since she was too proud to ask. When the next two nights passed the same way, Selene began to feel herself relax. She even felt some small tinge of gratitude

123

toward him, some slight suspicion that perhaps he was a bit more of a gentleman than she had thought. Perhaps remorse had got the better of his baser instincts, or guilt had softened that violent character. Whatever it was, she was grateful. If, now and then, she woke in the night to find herself recalling those other early morning hours when her body had been one long flame under his hands, she quickly forced the memory from her mind. It was simply an aberration anyway, and not indicative of her true feelings toward the despicable man.

She seldom saw Wade as the days flowed one into the other, lost in a melange of brilliant blue skies, towering billows of clouds, the ceaseless motion of the ship cutting through the troughs of lacy-tipped waves. The sun grew hotter each day and Selene learned to wear her lightest frocks and never remove her hat while on deck. Even then her arms turned brown, a not unbecoming brown, though there was a very distinct whiteness below the line of her bodice. Poor Matilda's plain face was a mass of freckles, but it did not seem to make her unhappy as she flirted with the sailors on the decks. If I'm not careful, Selene thought, I'll soon be as dark as a native. How distressed her father would be to see that!

There was an air of unreality about each day as one slipped into another. Selene began to feel as though she were suspended in time, all that had gone before was like a dream, all that lay ahead was a fantasy lingering on the edge of reality. She seldom saw Wade except from a distance, and that solitude helped her to withdraw a little apart from the intensity of her anger at him. She stopped thinking about how she had come to be here, and simply let herself soak up the tranquil monotony of the sea.

Occasionally the ship passed islands which were only glimpsed from afar. Captain Carey evidently thought time was too precious to allow for detours, pleasant as they might be. Selene grew proficient at spotting frequent schools of purpoises cavorting around the ship and the spectre of fins stripping through the water that meant a trailing convoy of sharks. Once they even passed a small school of whales, their spouts like narrow plumes against the sea. It was only when she walked onto the deck one morning to be met by a squawking cacophony of sea gulls, that she knew they were finally nearing their destination. The sea in the bright morning air was a brilliant sapphire green, and so translucent she could almost see the white bottom below. A thick line on the horizon, more green even than the water, rimmed with brilliantly white sand like a narrow lace collar on a jade-colored dress, told her that Barbados lay waiting. And with that thought something of her position came flooding back. The dream was gone and reality lay waiting to be faced.

It was after they had weighed anchor in the roadstead that Wade, for the first time in several days, stepped up to her side. "We'll be going ashore in an hour's time. Can you be ready?" His voice could not have been more matter-of-fact if they had been brother and sister traveling together.

"I don't have that much with me," Selene answered, making it sound as though that were his fault, which, indeed, it was.

"That should make it easy for you then," he said, not rising to the bait. They both stared at the low masts of ships at anchor in the harbor and the roofs beyond, topped by the tall square tower of the Anglican cathedral. Unspoken questions lay between them but Selene was too proud to ask. Where would he take her? Would it be a cell in some stinking tropical jail? Would he put her under house arrest? That might at least be endurable and offer the possibility of seeking help. Wade turned and left her without another word, leaving her to wonder and wait. She would find out soon enough what he planned for her once the lighter carried them to shore.

Bridgetown reminded Selene of Charleston, South Carolina, as her father had often described it to her. There were rows of wooden, fretworked buildings with long balconies and wide open windows. Donkeys pulled small carriages loaded with foodstuffs, so many that they clogged the narrow streets where carriages and pedestrians battled them for space. Native women in colorful dress carried tubs on their head of the spicy mauby-bark brew so popular on the island, or so Carey told her. There were, sprinkled among them, some very elegant-looking Caucasians, dressed in the kind of finery that would have graced a London street. In the main square, where the temporary government buildings looked out over a statue of

125

Lord Nelson—a disastrous fire two years earlier had destroyed the previous offices—booths were set up, some of them looking rather hastily thrown together for the benefit of the newly arrived passengers, selling wares of all kinds from tropical fruits, vegetables, and flowers to coral jewelry, native rum, and brightly dyed fabrics. Even to one accustomed to the large Negro population of Virginia, Selene thought there seemed an overwhelming number of natives. They spoke a kind of lilting English, but in spite of the common language, Selene saw little among their smiling faces to indicate she might solicit help from them.

Wade bundled her into a waiting carriage which he ordered driven down a long shaded street to Government House, the Governor's residence. He disappeared up the stairs and through the wide double doors, leaving Selene and a wide-eyed Matilda under the watchful care of her old adversary, Hawke. This was one time Selene felt there was nothing to be gained by trying to run away, for where could she go? She knew no one, she was utterly unfamiliar with the town or the rest of the island, and she was surrounded by an imprisoning ocean. So she waited quietly, taking in all the strange details of this exotic new world. When, after half an hour, Wade returned to the carriage and gave directions to the driver, Selene suppressed her curiosity once again about where he was taking her. They passed several likely-looking inns, most of them inviting, and continued jogging along a dusty dirt road that eventually left the town behind. Though the low rolling countryside was pleasant enough, her hopes diminished as she saw that they were leaving Bridgetown. An isolated house in the country was going to make it far more difficult for her to get away from Wade, much less find passage off the island.

When at length they left the main road to pull up a long, winding driveway, Selene felt she had marked the route carefully enough that she could find her way back if necessary. She was helped by the fact that the house itself was situated on the drive, close enough to the main road to walk. Wade handed her down from the carriage without a word and led her up on a long veranda to the open door of the house. The jade sea was just visible beyond the piazza and Selene lingered a moment savouring it before entering the house.

It was so inviting that she had to remind herself how much she intended to hate it. Built of the same pink coral as most of the buildings in Bridgetown, it was carefully designed to allow the cool breezes off the ocean to grace every room. The long windows that opened onto the veranda, the high ceilings and delicately worked plaster that looked as though it had recently been painted, the heavy ornate furniture with its highly polished patina made it the most elegant house she had ever seen. She wandered around the rooms, unable to hide her appreciation. Wade leaned against the door frame, crossed his arms over his chest, and watched her. He had not failed to notice her reluctant admiration.

"It belongs to a friend of mine—or rather the father of a friend. Jamie Corbin. I knew him in Virginia. His father has allowed me the use of his house since he is away at the moment, visiting England."

Selene pulled the ribbons of her straw hat loose and laid it on the back of one of the brocade sofas. "It's very grand."

"I think we will be comfortable enough here. My . . . business cannot be completed until a ship that is due from England finally arrives, so we may have some time to ourselves for a while."

"You mean the British ministers," Selene said, looking at him directly.

"I do want you to be comfortable here," he went on, ignoring her remark, "you can go into Bridgetown as long as Hawke is with you. And I think I will also find you another maid. Matilda can stay and even help you with whatever it is you women like to do. But I would be just as pleased to see you accompanied by a native woman who knows the island."

"Another keeper, you mean!"

"There are some fine seamstresses in Bridgetown, too. You might as well have some gowns made up since we will probably be entertaining. We've already had an invitation from the Governor to a dinner next week."

Selene threw herself down on the sofa, her skirt billowing around her. "Really, you are the most infuriating man. Do you expect me to pretend to be your wife, to carry on a charade that

127

we are some kind of devoted couple in front of these people? Well, I won't do it. You can tell your friends that you have a crazy madwoman for a wife if you want. It's immaterial to me what you say. But you'll have to find some explanation for my nonappearance."

Wade walked to the table next to the sofa and picked a long seegar from a humidor there. He seemed singularly unconcerned by her passionate declaration as he lit it and breathed out a long trail of smoke.

"I'll say that if you wish. But first, think what you are doing to yourself. This is a lovely place, very beautiful and certainly different from any you've seen before. The people here, the Bajans, are cultured and pleasant. They will do everything to make you welcome as my wife. As a crazy woman you will end up spending all your time here in a closed room—a locked room, I might add—with no visitors, no entertainment, no exploration of the island, no shopping—in short, none of the things that might make your stay here interesting. However, if that is what you prefer . . ."

He was already half out the door. "Wait!" Selene called. "Do you mean I will be allowed to do all those things, if I go along with this deception?"

"As long as Hawke and your maid are with you."

It was better than nothing, despicable as it was. Locked in a room as a madwoman she would never be able to find a way off this island. And sight-seeing, shopping, all those frivolous things—well, they might at least be diverting.

"Very well," she muttered, barely above a whisper.

"What?"

"*Very well!*"

The satisfied smile that flitted across his lips was infuriating.

"I thought that was what you said," he answered and disappeared.

Selene grabbed up the nearest thing to hand, one of the cushions from the couch, and threw it after him.

Seven

It was not until the next morning that Selene remembered her new servant. When she was roused from sleep by Matilda she opened her eyes to bright sunlight streaming through the long windows of her bedroom. It took her a moment to recall why the room was so sunny and bright. Where was the dingy closeness of the ship? Where was the constant motion? She swung her feet over the high bed and tried to stand, feeling as though the waves had returned. But the day was so beautiful, it didn't matter. Pulling her robe around her shoulders, she stood in the windows and stretched her arms far over her head. With some surprise she realized she was almost happy.

It must be because my "husband" left me alone again last night! she thought to herself.

"The housemaid told me that your breakfast is downstairs on the sideboard, Miss Selene—just as grand as you please. And she said, too, that if you wanted tea first thing when you woke, you was only to let her know." Matilda chattered amiably as she picked up the clothes that Selene had carelessly strewn around the evening before. "I declare, it's enough to make you feel like a real lady, ain't it?"

"Yes. Well, you and I both know better, don't we Matilda? It seems like only a few days ago that I was bringing tea to others in the morning."

"Yes, ma'am, but I believe you might as well enjoy playing the grand lady while you have the chance. Who knows when we'll both be back at your uncle's waitin' on anybody that

129

happens in. Besides, Miss Selene, you always seemed like a lady to me."

Impulsively Selene threw her arms about the girl and hugged her. "Thank you, Mattie. You've made me feel even better than I did when I woke up and saw all that sunshine. Now, help me get dressed and do my hair up so I can go down to breakfast. I'm famished!"

Once she was dressed, Selene threw open the door to hurry downstairs and almost collided with a dark figure that rose from a chair standing beside her door. The height and breadth of the woman caused Selene to step back into her room briefly. It was more than just her bulk that appeared frightening— there was something in her manner, in the dark-lidded eyes that peered impassively down at her.

"Who are you?" Selene asked as she felt Matilda inch up behind her.

"Me Gurda, Missy." The woman had a way of speaking almost without moving her lips that caused Selene to peer closer up at her. Gurda had the blackest skin she had ever seen on a Negro. The whiteness of her eyes were in stark contrast and gave her an unblinking, fixed look of concentration. She wore a colorful turban and a black dress that emphasized the darkness of her skin. Her arms were folded across her massive chest, and under her wide skirt Selene could sense she stood with feet apart, as if daring her to pass.

"Gurda? Oh yes. Did Mister Kinsolving send you here?"

"That right, Missy."

No explanations, no friendly overtures. No apologies. It was enough to make Selene feel the hairs stand up on the back of her neck. Gurda's broad face appeared carved in ebony. The broad, flared nostrils, the strangely contrasting thin lips, the square chin thrust forward as though her jaw protruded over her upper lip. And worst of all, the large silver ring through her nose, that complemented huge circular globes on either ear. She wasn't just ugly—she was savage.

"Gurda," Selene said, recovering. "I can see that you are exactly the servant my husband would have chosen for me. Now why don't you just sit here and wait while I go have some breakfast. After that we can discuss how this arrangement might be terminated. Quickly terminated."

Edging around the massive Gurda, Selene tripped down the hall to the stairs. She was nearly to the front hall when she realized that Gurda was silently, quietly, impassively following her. When she took her place at the table, Gurda sat easily on one of the chairs placed around the perimenter of the room. While Matilda fussed over her, filling her plate from the sideboard, Selene tried to ignore the cold, quiet presence of her watchdog, mentally determined that once she saw Wade Kinsolving she would send this horrible woman packing once and for all.

Gurda's inflexible presence might have been enough to put her off all the natives, except that halfway through the meal Odett, the housemaid, came cheerfully in, to see if Missy Kinsolving found everything to her satisfaction. Odett was a handsome Negro woman with a ready smile and beautiful teeth. Selene was impressed at her excellent English, her starched uniform and cap, and pleasant ways.

"I've been speaking English all my life," Odett informed her when she commented on it. "This is an English island, and has been for almost two hundred years. Missy is sure to like it here and if she don't, she be sure to tell me about anything that doesn't please. Odett will see that everything is right for Missy."

"What about her?" Selene said, gesturing with her fork to the massive, silent figure sitting by the wall.

"Oh, Missy, that's the one thing I can't do nothing about."

Odett leaned over close to Selene to whisper in a loud voice, "The Master hired her . . ."

"That reminds me—where is the Master this morning? I am very anxious to speak to him."

"He went out early, Missy, very early. He say he going into Bridgetown and won't be back until afternoon."

Bridgetown. Of course. He would be off enjoying himself in congenial society while she sat here, a prisoner under the watchful eye of a keeper. From the open window the breeze drifted across the room carrying with it the sweet fragrance of jasmine vines. Beyond them she caught the vivid red of hibiscus swaying gently. Blue plumbagos bobbed against a pure

131

sky and occasional deeper turquoise of the ocean.

There are worse places to be a prisoner, she thought reluctantly. It was a big house with extensive grounds and she intended to explore every inch.

The afternoon was far gone by the time Selene spotted Wade's carriage rolling briskly up the drive. She was in one of the gardens at the side of the house, trying to concentrate on a book she had found in the library. The library and the garden were only two of the places she had exuberantly explored that day in an effort to shake off Gurda's dark presence. And all to no avail. Wherever she went the woman glided behind, never underfoot but never quite out of sight either. Even now she sat at the other end of the long graveled walk with stone benches inside a parallel row of white begonia hedges. Like a pet dog, Selene thought in her ever increasing irritation. Flopping down silently wherever she stopped, jumping up to glide after when Selene walked away. Never out of sight.

She waited nearly fifteen minutes before going inside to seek Wade, not wanting to appear overanxious. By the time she started into the house she ran into Matilda who was bustling out onto the veranda to find her.

"Oh, Miss Selene," the girl said, her eyes wide with wonder. "Come see. Oh, you must come and look. Hurry!"

The girl was almost jumping up and down in her excitement. Selene followed her down the hall, wondering what on earth could have set her off so, then stopped at the open French doors of the parlor.

The room was cluttered with paper carelessly strewn about and a jumble of boxes. Draped over chairs, sofas, and tables were an assortment of fabrics in the most beautiful vibrant colors she had ever seen. It took her a full minute to realize they were actually dresses, fully sewn, and ready to wear.

"I thought you should have a better wardrobe than those dingy tavern things," Wade said, stepping from the sea of cloth to move toward her. "Of course, they might not fit perfectly. The seamstress in Bridgetown keeps a certain number of gowns ready to fit more accurately to the figure who buys them . . ."

"Come look, Miss Selene." Mattie cried, pulling Selene into the room. "Look at the size of those skirts . . . did you ever see the like!''

"I—I don't know what to say," Selene muttered, suppressing her first reaction which was to order him to take them all back. She picked up the brocade skirt of a shimmering green satin, so translucent it might have been sea water. "They're so fine—"

Wade sat on the arm of the sofa and said in a matter-of-fact tone: "We'll be doing some entertaining, after all, and I can't have you receiving the governor, not to mention the British ministers, in a cotton chemise. I have to make an impression."

"You mean I am supposed to represent the South?" Selene said suspiciously, tearing her eyes from the beautiful gowns. "I'm not sure—"

"You can always go back to being a madwoman if you'd rather."

"At least if I was locked up in an attic I wouldn't have that watchdog hovering over me," she said, gesturing to the silent Gurda who was standing in the doorway looking over the array of lovely clothes with no expression at all on her dark face.

"Oh, I don't know. You would still need a keeper."

"A keeper! That's an excellent word. If I had to have one you might at least have found a—a human being."

Gurda comes with excellent references. She knows exactly what I want, and will see that I get it."

"Which is to prevent me from escaping. But that's absurd. Where could I go? Who could help me? You might have a little trust."

Wade's eyes darkened. "You've given me very little reason to trust you. And now, when all my work is about to come to fruition, I cannot risk anything going wrong. But come now. Doesn't all this please you a little? Enjoy it. It will be something to remember when you go back to serving in your uncle's tavern."

Selene glared at him as Matilda came dancing up, waving the lacy froth of a petticoat in her face. "Just look at this, Miss Selene. There's undergarments, corsets, sleeping gowns, caps, everything. Even—even this . . ."

Depositing the lace on a nearby chair, she reached behind the sofa and pulled out a pyramid of wire hoops held together with gauze. Selene stifled an excited cry. Never had she worn so large and impressive a hoopskirt. It was almost enough to make her forgive Wade a little for Gurda.

"Take them all upstairs, Matilda," Wade said. "Try them on, Selene. Tomorrow you can go into Bridgetown to have Mlle. Laurent fit them properly."

Matilda looked to Selene who hesitated a moment before nodding. Why not? She might as well enjoy something about this cursed position she had gotten herself into.

That night she half expected Wade to come striding into her bedroom. It was a relief when he did not, though it was also a little annoying. If her pride was a trifle piqued, she refused to allow the thought to linger in her mind. She was glad he let her alone and she only hoped he would continue to. Perhaps he had decided a marriage in name only was enough for him now that his mission was almost accomplished and she would soon go free. And yet, that was almost too much to hope for. It was also not in keeping with the treatment she had received from him so far.

The following morning, however, when she dressed herself in one of the morning gowns that fit her without alterations and preened at the gorgeous person that looked back at her from the mirror, she was almost pleased enough to forgive him for the way he had treated her. She twirled around, flaring the wide skirt of pale blue dimity that was trimmed with lace flounces and deep blue ribbons. There was a matching ribbon for her hair and a soft lace shawl that matched the color of the dress perfectly to set off the whole ensemble. It wasn't vanity to decide that she looked prettier than ever in her life. If only her father could see her now looking like a princess, she thought. He would have been so proud.

With Matilda's help the rest of the dresses were boxed for the trip into Bridgetown to Mlle. Laurent. Actually none of them needed much fitting and Selene was hopeful they could be done all in one day. There were two ball gowns, one a translucent emerald trimmed with blond lace and tiny green satin rosettes, the other a white brocade with ruby velvet ribbons making a pattern across the billowing skirt and across the scooped bodice. The other morning dress was a smokey rose, almost the color of the coral stone so popular around the island. It was the plainest of the three but it had a fitted short jacket that made it especially appropriate for traveling. Yet Selene could not resist the sunny yellow flowered dimity. It came with a straw bonnet as frilly and lacy as the dress itself, and since it fit her the best, she decided to wear it into town. As the carriage rolled down the drive, she smoothed the skirt over the cushions, opened her parasol, and nodded to the native workers among the garden flowers that lined the drive, feeling like a very grand lady indeed.

Across from her, scrunched into a corner, Matilda hid her face under her straw hat and tried to ignore the dark bulk that was Gurda on the other end of the seat. As usual, the black woman stared straight ahead, looking neither to the right nor the left, oblivious as much as Selene could tell to the beauty of the land through which they traveled. On the seat next to the driver, Hawke's broad back hid the expanse of the road, but Selene did not mind. She seldom took her eyes from the rolling white beaches to her right, sparkling in the jeweled sun and beckoning her with their promise of warm, soft water. She was enchanted with the small brightly painted wooden cottages surrounded by flowers in gorgeous profusion and sprawling in the shade of a mahogony or a bearded banyan tree. The natives they passed walking along the road or driving their ungainly donkeys ahead of them never failed to wave and smile broadly. Selene nodded back as graciously as she could, determined that as long as she was playing the part of an official's wife, she would act every inch of one.

"Such friendly people," she exclaimed to Mattie, whose surreptitious glances at Gurda suggested she did not agree.

They drove straight to Trafalgar Square, dodging the women with tall cans of the native mauby-bark brew balanced on their heads, and a plethora of donkeys and carts, all vying for space along the narrow streets made even more congested by booths whose owners hawked fruits and vegetables. Off the square, on Broad Street, they were deposited at the door of a narrow two-story building with a sign in the window proclaiming Mlle. Marie Laurent, *coutriére*. Selene was a little surprised when Hawke heaved his bulk off the seat to disembark along with Mattie and Gurda, but she said nothing. Let the boredom of a day at the dressmakers be his punishment, she thought.

It turned out that Mlle. Laurent worked faster than Selene expected and they had the whole afternoon to themselves after fitting her new dresses. With her entourage in tow, Selene set about exploring the winding streets with their colorful shops, studying the harbor for any idea of how she might slip away to one of the ships, and wandering around the Cathedral of St. Michael's. The church was very old but the building fairly new, replacing one that had been destroyed by a hurricane in 1831. Gurda, like a wide shadow, stayed close behind her, as silent and impassive as ever, but Selene was able to rid herself of Mattie and Hawke by insisting they sit outside the stone cathedral while she browsed around inside. Since churches were of little interest to either the seaman or the girl, and Mattie's feet were by this time protesting her long walk, they were both willing to oblige. Selene determined to ignore Gurda and simply enjoy the brief solitude and calm the cool church allowed her.

After tea on the outdoor patio of a local tavern, they picked up the dresses at Mlle. Laurent's, then rolled along the beach road back to the villa, tired but pleasantly relaxed. Her trip had convinced her of the wisdom of going along with Wade while they were on the island. Not only was it more enjoyable, but it offered her the only opportunity she would have to find some way to get away from him—not that it seemed there would be such an opportunity. The inlet called the Careenage had held several good-sized ships turned on their sides for recaulking, and out in the harbor there appeared to be at least two packets, both flying British flags, which might offer a hope of escape, *if* she had any way to talk to their captains. As it was, she could see little possibility of doing that unless one of them happened to turn up at one of the parties Wade had mentioned. All the more reason then to wear the new gowns and present a pleasing appearance.

The next two days were very quiet. Selene went back to wearing her Virginian gowns, clean now though shabbier than ever, read most of a novel in the library plus part of a small history of Barbados, wandered the limits of the extensive gardens of the villa, always with Gurda in tow, hovering behind and never out of sight. Once when she attempted to walk beyond the gates of the villa, she was stopped in a firm but respectful way by two of the men working among the flowers who told her they had strict orders not to let her pass. Though she was somewhat bored, she was not unhappy. The cool winds off the glittering sea made the warm air more than comfortable, the exotic flowers and trees of the gardens constantly surprised her to new raptures of admiration, and the calm serenity of the ocean and white beach in the distance were balm to her soul. As long as Wade left her alone, she could not be unhappy in such heavenly surroundings.

And then on the third day, he came striding into her bedroom just as she was sitting propped against the pillows sipping her morning chocolate.

"I'm glad you're awake," he exclaimed, moving to the windows to pull back the long curtains. "I was dreading having to pull you out from beneath the covers in a stupor and then add another deadly sin to your list of grievances against me."

Selene glared at him from above the rim of her cup. He was much too cheerful to be trusted.

"What is it now? Are we to finally have that dinner party you mentioned? Have the British ministers arrived?"

"No, no. Nothing so businesslike. The truth is, my dear wife," he sat on the bed, crossing one leg over the other, "that it is too lovely a day to spend once more among the paneled walls of the government house. I've seen nothing of Barbados since I arrived but the wigs of jurists and reams of papers in the governor's offices. Enough. I'm taking a holiday today to see something of the beauty of this place, and I want you to go with me."

Selene eyed him suspiciously. "I suppose you're afraid that if I stay here while you're out galavanting, I might try to run off. Though how I should do so with that vigilant zombie following my every step is more than I can imagine."

"You do me an injustice, as usual. I only thought you might enjoy seeing something besides this villa and Mlle. Laurent's dressmaking house. However, if you'd prefer . . ."

"Would that woman have to go, too?" Selene said hastily.

137

"Gurda?"

"Of course, Gurda. You've no idea how annoying it is to have her shadowing me everywhere I go. Just to be free of her for an hour would be worth . . ."

"Worth even my company?" Wade smiled, and rose to his feet, standing with legs apart and hands hooked in the broad leather belt around his waist. "I'm glad the prospect thrills you so. Still, I shall put my damaged feelings aside simply because the day is too fine to sulk. So up! I'll allow you half an hour to dress and get downstairs."

He was already out the door. "But what shall I wear?" Selene called, scrambling off the high bed.

"Something simple. We'll take the shay."

When she realized she was scurrying around in order to get downstairs in the time he had ordered, she deliberately stopped and exclaimed, "Let him wait!" Yet the truth was, she was thrilled with the idea of getting away from the villa and visiting other parts of the island, even with Wade. She wore the best of her old dresses—a dark skirt over an eyelet blouse with full sleeves and a wide scooped neck—her new flowered straw bonnet, her parasol, and lace shawl. Feeling pretty but not overdressed, she finally went down the wide stairs to meet Wade who was waiting for her impatiently at the bottom of the stairs.

"Only fifteen minutes late!" he exclaimed, looking at the round watch on his waistcoat fob. "I suppose I ought to be thankful. Well, you look fetching enough to forgive. Come along now. The shay is outside and the horse is restive. If we don't get started right away, he may very well dump us in the first ditch we pass."

Selene followed him outside, wondering where Hawke and Mattie were, and relieved not to see the oppressive Gurda. Wade handed her up into the small carriage, open to the air and with room on the seat for only one other person besides the driver. Climbing up beside her, Wade picked up the reins and flicked them over the horse's back, and with a rolling jerk they went smartly down the drive.

Selene snatched a few surreptitious glances at her companion, enough to see that he as very neatly dressed in beige trousers, a plaid vest, satin tie, and dark brown coat. About the only concession he had made to the island heat was in his hat— a large round straw with a low crown that served as eyeshade protection from the sun. Her thoughts went racing along with the shay. Why was no one else along? Shouldn't Mattie, at least, be present for decency's sake if nothing else? But then, of course, they were supposed to be an old married couple. Why not Hawke then to see that she did not attempt to get away some time during their excursion. But did he really need Hawke to watch her when he himself was there? Selene thought not. He had certainly done an excellent job up until now of keeping her under his control.

A horrible idea came insinuating itself into the gyrating jumble that was her mind. Suppose . . . suppose he meant to get her alone in some isolated spot and murder her. It was a crazy thought, but on the other hand it would certainly solve his problem once and for all. Dead women told no tales . . .

But if he intended to murder her, why go to all that trouble to procure her a wardrobe? And what about the notables who were expecting to be entertained by Captain Kinsolving and his lovely wife . . .

She edged away from him on the seat, but Wade seemed not to notice. He was too intent on negotiating the narrow brick roads that carried them away from the beach and across the island. This was a part of Barbados that Selene had not seen before, and soon her macabre thoughts were overcome by the fascination of what she saw around her.

The roads led through miles of sugar cane, growing so tall that they towered high over the shay running along between the fields. Just when she thought they were never going to leave the sea of cane, they emerged into a broad flat open area containing several buildings. A low house with a wide porch running around its perimeter stood far to the rear. In front of it was a tall, rambling barnlike structure with open terraces and balconies perched at crazy intervals along its high walls. The noise that issued from this building was deafening, though not loud enough to drown out the rumbling of a huge windmill standing to one side on the highest knoll in the flat circle.

Wade pulled the shay to a stop just as a man emerged from

the tall barn and came toward them. He was an Englishman, Selene noted, though his skin was a mahogany tan and his lean face lined under his palm hat. He was in shirtsleeves and suspenders and had a cigar protruding from his lips which he seemed more interested in chewing than smoking.

"Good morning, Jason," Wade called, jumping down to reach up to help Selene from the carriage. "I've come as I said I would to visit your mill and I've even brought my wife with me. I hope that is all right."

Jason swept off his hat and made Selene a polite bow. "Why ma'am, I'm honored. I had no idea the Captain here had such a lovely helpmate. Welcome to Cable's Cobb."

"Jason is the brother of Jonathan Cable, one of the most successful sugar planters on the island, my dear," Wade said to Selene, with all the graciousness of a man speaking to his real wife. She nodded, carrying along the charade. "He invited me to have a look at his mill, and since I've always had some interest in sugar production and its by-products . . ."

"Particularly rum," Jason added, chuckling.

". . . I thought this would be a good place to begin our exploration of Barbados. So. Where would you like us, Jason?"

Jason Cable took his cigar from his mouth and looked around as though wondering what the sugar operation was all about. "Why not start with the mill itself," he finally said, rolling the cigar between his brown fingers. "You may have to lift your pretty skirts up a bit, ma'am—the floor's pretty dingy."

"I won't mind," Selene said as graciously as possible. She left her parasol in the carriage and followed the two men into the barn where the racket of the machinery was even more deafening than outside. While the production of sugar and its products had never interested overmuch—indeed she seldom thought about it at all—she found that as they went along it was more interesting than she expected. A great many men were employed in the mill, most of them blacks, and they appeared to be well treated and industrious. That was because, as Jason explained, most of the jobs done inside were to some extent skilled ones requiring an apprenticeship and a pride of craft. In marked contrast, he went on, to the cutting of the cane which was back-breaking labor and required only the skilled use of a machete.

"Although that's not entirely true," he added as they went up the rickety stairs to a platform above. "Cutting cane requires a kind of skill in itself and is not the kind of thing an ordinary man would take to. A really good cutter can bale up to ten tons a day and earn pretty good wages at it."

It took the most of an hour to tour the mill itself. Afterward Jason Cable showed them around the fields to watch the cutters at work. By the time they left the Cobb (as its owners had dubbed the plantation) the day had grown warm and the open fields were unpleasant. Selene was glad to be back in the shay with a cool breeze on her face. When Wade guided the carriage away from the fields and through a shady grove of mahogany trees and tall cabbage palms, interspersed with small cottages and farms, she was relieved to leave the plantation behind. She began to smell the salt air of the coast before they actually saw it.

"We've crossed the island," Wade explained, "to see something of the Atlantic side. Then we can go back around the coast road."

"I thought the sea was nearby."

"Yes, it's amazing, isn't it, how you can almost *sense* the water? It's something in the air. Or maybe it's just the birds."

"No, it's in the air. This island must not be very wide if we've come all the way across it."

"Fourteen miles at its broadest, I'm told. Less at this end. Ah, there we are. The Atlantic."

He pulled the shay to a stop and Selene strained over the side to see the coastline. And what a coastline it was. They were on a pinacle high above the water. It fell dramatically to the beach where a thundering surf pounded against it. "It's so different from the other side," she gasped. "I never expected this."

"It's beautiful, isn't it. The western side is very quiet and low, but on the Atlantic you have these dramatic heights and wonderful surf. It's the reason no one was ever able to invade Barbados and wrest it from the British. They couldn't land on this side, and on the other they could be seen forty miles away. Come on, let's walk."

Helping her down, he secured the reins and led her toward the edge of the precipice. Selene forgot to be worried about what he had in mind, so absorbed was she in the beauty of the place. The sky all around them was a deep lapis blue with no sign of a cloud anywhere. They were standing on a plunging headland, looking far out over a turquoise ocean. The cliff face fell precipitously below to a thin edging of pink sand where a turbulent surf traced lacy patterns. The waves reformed and crashed restlessly on the jagged coral rocks that lay in the water as though flung there from above.

"I've never seen anything so beautiful," she sighed. She had almost forgotten he was there.

"Nor I," he answered, and she looked up to see that he was watching her intently. She felt a flush spread up her cheeks. "We really ought to go back," Selene said quickly and turned away to hurry back to the carriage. She was embarrassed and annoyed that her appreciation of this lovely spot had been intruded upon by his feelings and his presence. She did not want to think of him at all. She wished he hadn't taken her out this day.

When Wade climbed back into the shay he spoke jauntily as though nothing had changed. "I'll bet you didn't know I brought a lunch with me, now did you? We'll go along this road until we find the right spot and then have our picnic. It's about time for luncheon anyway."

"Picnic?" He was right. She hadn't thought about a picnic or even lunch itself. Now that he mentioned it, she realized that she was hungry, and a picnic did seem a nice idea, even with him.

By the time they found the right spot they were already well along the road to the western side of the island. Here they had long stretches of pinkish white sand and gentle surf. Finally, Wade reined in at a place that for sheer beauty and privacy could not be equalled. It was almost a cove, an indented concave of silver beach surrounded on both sides by promontories of huge trees of banyan and oak. They had seen few houses for the past half hour and passed no one on the road; the secluded quiet of the cove reinforced a feeling of being alone in the world. She had felt it on their ride more and

142

more strongly. Selene stepped down from the shay, and for the first time that day smiled at Wade as he handed her down. He was really rather tolerable when all the rest of the world was suspended somewhere out there.

He pulled down a basket covered with a checkered cloth and handed it to her. While she laid everything out on the sand, he unfastened their horse from the carriage and led him to a patch of grass not far away. By the time he joined her half a chicken, a large loaf of bread, fruit, wine, and cheese were neatly laid out on the cloth, along with knives, tin plates, and two crystal glasses.

"You were very brave to bring these," Selene said as he poured the wine.

"Madeira calls for nothing less." He handed her one of the glasses. "What shall we drink to? To us?"

"I don't believe I care to drink to that," she said with a trace of her old resentment.

"Very well then. To the day. Surely you can't refuse to do that."

"No. It's been a beautiful day and, though I hate to admit it, I've enjoyed it."

"Now why should you hate to admit that I've given you a little pleasure for once instead of pain. It truly is a lovely day. Can't we call a truce, just for awhile?"

She watched him closely, wondering if he was trying to trick her again. Did he have some diabolical plan up his sleeve? Was he only waiting to catch her with her guard down? Was all this elaborate entertainment just a means of setting her up for another form of imprisonment?

She watched as he picked up the bottle to refill his glass. He had removed his coat and was sitting in his wide shirtsleeves and vest, one leg tucked under him. His hair was blown carelessly around his long face. His eyes, when he looked up to see her studying him, danced with the pleasure of the day, and the smile he gave her was beguiling and completely innocent. And he was handsome, she thought to herself as she felt the stirring of her blood. Dear Lord, but he was handsome.

She looked quickly away, aware once more of the telltale flush on her cheeks. For a while they ate in silence, enjoying the food and the chatter of the birds in the trees around them. The waves on the shore nearby made their own music, a throbbing, gentle rolling sigh. Once they had had their fill of the meal, Wade stretched on the sand with his hat over his eyes and appeared to drift off to sleep while Selene packed everything back in the basket. She was drowsy herself, yet she was also too puzzled and disturbed to take a nap. She moved away from him, to the shade, sitting on the sand with her back against the thick trunk of a tree and closing her eyes, wishing she could drift off. But confusion—and she was certainly confused—picked away at her consciousness, and her eyes were drawn over and over to that long body stretched on the sand.

Why must she feel this way, she chided herself? She hated him. He had treated her abominably. She ought to feel nothing but revulsion when she looked at him. She wanted to feel nothing but revulsion.

With a sudden motion Wade rolled over and sat up, moving his arm across his eyes. "Heavens, what a wasteful thing to do," he said, running his hands through his hair. "A day like this and I sleep it away." Standing up to his full height, he stretched his arms over his head, with a loud happy groan, then began pulling at his tie. Selene's eyes grew round as the tie came off, followed by the vest, both thrown carelessly on the sand. When Wade started pulling at the buttons of his shirt, she sat up.

"What are you doing?"

"Going for a swim, of course."

"Now wait a minute . . ." She watched in horror as he bent to throw off his shoes and then began unbuttoning his trousers.

"You can't strip right out here in front of . . . everybody!"

"Why not? After all, you're everybody and this is nothing you haven't seen before."

The trousers were pushed down and he stepped nimbly out of them and stood before her. "Behold, Adonis in all his glory!"

"This is disgraceful . . ." she spluttered, trying not to look at the bronzed length of him and unable to tear her eyes away.

144

In a bound he was at her side. "Come on, you, too. Think how tragic it would be, to be here so close to this wonderful ocean and not try it out."

"Stop it . . ." Selene cried, as he began slipping her bodice over her shoulders. "Now don't do that . . . stop at once, do you hear!"

Wade's laugh was exuberant as he pulled her toward the water, divesting her of her clothes as he went. She could not resist his infectious good humor. "Wait a minute," she cried. "it is not as easy for me as it was for you. Now stop, let me do it." Unbuttoning her skirt, she dropped it in the sand, followed by the voluminous petticoats. Wade danced around her, pulling at her chemise while she fought off his tenacious fingers, trying to divest herself of it. He reached down for a handful of sand and dropped it down the front of her bodice while Selene danced a jig trying to shake it out before pulling away the garment. Modesty was swept away in the delight of the warm sun on her beguiling flesh and the laughter with which he joked her out of her clothes. When the last piece of linen was dropped away, he grabbed her hand and pulled her toward the water.

"Come on, in you go."

"No," Selene cried, wiggling away and digging her heels into the delicate sand. It slid between her toes like soft talcum powder, gentle and downy. It was another of the delightfully sensual sensations she reveled in, so new and different from any she had ever experienced before. But Wade was having no part of allowing her to sit back and soak them up. With a laugh he scooped her up in his arms, her naked flesh soft against his hard arms, and walked into the gentle surf.

"You're going swimming today whether you want to or not!" he announced, striding into the water.

"I can't swim!" Selene cried and tightened her arms around his neck, clutching for dear life.

"You don't have to," he said, now waist deep in the green sea. "I'll hold you up."

She screamed as he walked out far enough that the water was up to his chest, then dropped her with a sudden plop into the sea. Truly frightened, Selene felt herself sink into the tepidly warm water, felt it cover her face, and tasted the salt as she got a mouthful. Splashing wildly she bobbed up and down twice before his sure hands pulled her upright and her feet touched the sandy bottom. The water was only chest high. Chagrined at her ridiculous fear, Selene wiped her arm across her face and pushed her wet hair from her eyes.

"That wasn't nice," she muttered, her good humor almost washed away.

Wade pulled her toward him, cradling his arms about her, and supporting her as her feet left the bottom. "I promise I won't allow you to drown. In fact, if you really can't swim, then it's time you learned."

"I really can't," she answered, clinging to his neck. "I never had an opportunity to learn, and I certainly don't want to start now in this—this ocean. It's too dangerous. There are waves and sharks and—all kinds of dangerous things."

"Ridiculous," Wade said, drawing her closer. "This is the most gentle surf you could ever ask for. There are no sharks to badger you here and the salt water will help support you. Here. Let me show you."

Selene was not anxious for a swimming lesson, yet as long as she had the reassurance of her feet touching the bottom, she went along. When he supported her lying on the water, she quickly went back to clinging to him, finding that being cradled in his arms was both a security and a delight. Before she realized what was happening, she was laughing with him again and even moving through the silky surf in something close to swimming. She refused to go out over her head, and there was no need to since the shallow water extended so far. Wade humored her, showing her how to open her eyes under water and observe the strange world there, so clear and pristine. They swam back and forth, and once her confidence grew, playfully dunked each other. When they finally floated in on the lacy waves, Selene realized she had never had such an enjoyable experience in her life before.

"I think I'm going to enjoy swimming," she said, as Wade took her hand and led her to a grassy knoll near the sand. She stretched out on the soft green blanket savouring the warmth of the sun on her salty body. He fell beside her for a moment

146

then sat up on one elbow and looked down at her. With her eyes closed against the sun she did not see him bend, and did not realize until the cool wetness of his tongue circled her taut nipple what he was doing.

"Ah, I taste the salt," he murmured.

Selene's body became a warm, glowing thing. She did not move, thus encouraging him to go on teasing her with his tongue. She felt rather than saw him move away, and wondered if he had once again decided to leave her alone. A few moments later she came roaring up when a cold stream of liquid poured down on her naked stomach.

"Merciful God!" she exclaimed. Wade bent over her, laughing and holding aloft the wine bottle he had retrieved from the picnic basket.

"As long as I have to taste something it might as well be wine," he said, tracing a pattern on her creamy thigh with his fingers. "Here," he said, pushing her back gently on the grass until her uplifted breast arched toward him. Dexterously he poured a little of the deep burgundy liquid on to her nipple then bent to suck greedily. "That's better," he murmured as Selene stirred in ecstatic pleasure. She felt the coolness of the wine on her other breast, followed by the probing, circling wetness of his tongue. His lips closed gently over the erect brown thrusting protuberance and he pulled at it, taunting her with his lips, teasing her slowly melting body with his lazy, insistent circulating pattern. "Oh," she moaned, stirring beneath him. His tongue, like tiny flames of fire, flicked over the mound of her breast, darted into the caverns between. He gently folded his fingers over the curving sweetness and pushed them together, thrusting the already full roundness into swelling mounds of flesh. With a groan Wade buried his head in them.

Dimly Selene felt the slow trickle of wine rolling down her flank. The sun was warm on her yielding flesh and the sand beneath her seemed as soft as down. But it was Wade who slowly, deliberately blocked all other sensations from her mind as he fondled her willing body, playing it like a musician with a treasured instrument. He was bent over her, his hands smooth as silk, drifting along her stomach and across the concave smoothness of her hips. There was nothing in the world but the

147

sweet sensation of the tickling of his tongue gliding over her bare skin. She felt the telltale dampness between her legs and, without even realizing it, spread her creamy thighs to welcome his probing fingers. Her back arched as his lips slid downward, tasting her flesh, taking little bites that drove her desire to new heights. His arms circled her thighs as his head rested on the soft swelling mound rising from her open legs. With a cry, Selene drew up her knees, spreading them wide to receive his probing tongue, the lips that caught and pulled and sucked at her tender flesh until she writhed in agony beneath him. Her hips made a slow arch, driven by the mounting fire that threatened to burst within her. Dimly she recalled they were alone. There was no one to hear or care, and she cried out in the primitive, aching plea of every woman since Eve, begging for completion, for wholeness.

Wade heard her cry, and though driven by a need and desire as great as hers, yet held back, taking a fierce delight in forcing her to an ever-growing frustration.

"Take me, take me," she whimpered.

"No. Not yet," he murmured, and renewed his devouring on her tortured flesh. She was rolling on the sand now, crazy to have him. She never knew when his lips became the hard, driving fingers or when, after that, his driving shaft, hard and engorged, thrusting into her. Even then he brought her to the edge only to leave her there while he shifted his weight over her, his arms on either side of her shoulders, working his hips to slide into her, and out again, over and over until both were wild with their need. Then, as his own will crumbled, he clasped her in his arms, thrusting wildly until with a cry both broke through that beautiful barrier of ecstasy where all the world is an Eden of pleasure and sensation.

Satiated, the wildness gradually receded but not the joy. Clasped in each other's arms they lay panting on the sand until with a loud laugh, Wade rolled over, pulling Selene on top of him.

"You . . . you are beautiful!" he whispered, burying his lips in her hair. "The most beautiful, wonderful woman I have ever known."

She laughed, too, out of pure joy and satisfaction. "Do you

say that to all the women you have just made love to?"

He smoothed back the hair from her face. Her eyes were as brilliant as the water beyond and as sparkling with vivacity as the sea with the sun. "Only when they make me feel as you just did."

Selene laughed and bit him lovingly on the neck. She leaned over on her elbow to take in the length of his bare body stretched out on the sand. He was beautiful, too, though she would not say so. The firm, broad chest, the lean hips, the swelling length and impressive stature of his phallus, lying flaccid now after its exuberant performance, the long legs, brown with downy tuffs of hair—a body worthy of a Greek sculpture. She looked around at the quiet, isolated cove protected by thickets and trees behind, the gentle sea stretching away to the front. They were two bodies in a pristine world, no clothes, no modesty, simple and pure delight in each other. The first man and woman in paradise could not have been any more blessed, she thought.

And forgetting all "proper" attitudes she had been taught, she gently and methodically began teasing and torturing Wade the same way he had her. She kissed his lips, thrusting her tongue within to explore the cavity of his mouth. "And that was only the beginning," she cooed, as she methodically tasted every inch of his face and throat. Wade lay back on the sand, enjoying, as she worked on him. "It's probably hopeless, you know," he murmured between little groans. "You've drained me."

"We'll see." The hairs on his chest were soft and silky to her face. She swiveled her flicking tongue around his navel, licking the delicious depression. When she slid lower, he moaned and, as she had done earlier, spread his legs. Moving easily, Selene swiveled around to sit between his legs and nuzzled at his testicular globes, like peaches in her hand. She licked the length of his shaft, circling the tender tip with her lips, laughing to herself as it came to life again, firm in her hand.

"I . . . didn't know you were so . . . ." Wade tried to say, but was lost in the mounting waves of lust that she invoked. Still she teased him with her tongue and the light, mouthing suckling of her lips as he moaned beneath her. The elongated

149

shaft grew within her, filling her, a swelling fountain of life-giving sustenance. With a growing fury she pulled and tugged at it while he squirmed on clouds of pure delight, his frenzy holding him prisoner on his back. She could hear his moans and gasps and it drove her to new efforts, working on him and the magnificent extension that had become all of him, until with an exquisite eruption of shining, tossing stars, it exploded in her mouth.

Wade fell back, spread-eagled and exhausted on the sand. "I may never be able to stand up again," he moaned. "Where did you ever learn to do that?"

Selene smiled like a cat caught with its whiskers in the cream. Drawing up her knees she sat beside him, her arms around her legs. "My father had some forbidden books in his library. They included some engravings from India and the Far East and I used to steal glances at them when I knew he wouldn't be home. He would have been horrified if he had known. I just thought that since this was also part of the world, I ought to know about it."

"I can't tell you how happy I am that you did." He picked up a handful of silky sand and dribbled it down her back. "You've got sand all over you, even in your beautiful hair. Come on, it's time for another swim."

Selene did not protest as he grabbed her hand and drew her back into the water. They dove and surfaced, and clasping their arms around one another, kissed, tasting the salt on the other's lips. Selene thought they might leave after that, and determined that even if they did, she would never know any happier hours.

But Wade had other ideas. They ate more of the fruit and cheese, drank more of the wine, and laid a blanket on the sand to drink again from that fountain of delight that had held them so enthralled before.

He wanted to try it a new way this time, and positioning her on her knees, he entered her from the rear, his hands around her, firmly grasping her dangling breasts. Another quick dip in the sea and they went back once more to exploring, trying it this time on their sides, scissors-fashion, Wade informed her.

"How many positions are there?" Selene asked, lying

completely spent and out of breath, sprawled beside him on the rumpled blanket.

"Didn't your father's books say? I'm told there may be something over forty altogether, including a few even I don't know."

"I'll never make it!" she laughed. He pulled her to him and kissed her lightly on the lips. "We don't have to try them all today, you know. There will be lots of time to leisurely work our way through all forty."

Selene sighed and closed her eyes. She was so tired and so satiated that all she wanted was to doze the rest of the lazy afternoon away. "I'm glad to hear it," she mumbled, and sank into the delicious clouds of sleep. When she woke it seemed only a few moments later but she could sense that the evening was approaching. Beside her Wade stirred in his sleep. She smiled to herself at the thought that he had given out just as she had.

Far out over the water the deepening clouds gave the first indication that the afternoon was almost spent. In delicate shades of gray and rose, tinged with a silver iridescent rim, the huge clouds banked like a celestial city, ready to be climbed and explored. Selene lay with her hair spilling over Wade's arm and studied them, searching for shapes, or rather for omens that this magical afternoon was not imagined or dreamed. The breeze had grown cool against her satiated flesh and she shivered, inching closer to Wade's body. The heat from his flesh warmed her as she leaned against his chest and he circled his arm around her, pulling her even closer. Entwined, the sand and salt sticky on their bodies, nevertheless they lay content, as if unwilling to break the spell that had graced itself around them.

The wind picked up, raising gooseflesh on her arms and her long legs. "I think I am going to have to get dressed," she sighed against his chest. "I'd rather stay like this."

"My wanton Eve," he said chuckling.

"It is like paradise, isn't it. Unspoiled. Magical. Before the Fall."

He squeezed her hard then let her go and sat up on the sand. "Unfortunately, the Fall has already occurred, even here. If we don't get back soon the servants tongues will be wagging like the limbs on that frangipani tree. Come, my love . . ."

Kneeling he reached to pull her up to her knees, then with one motion urged her into his arms, lightly kissing her moist lips. "Mmmmm, if I don't stop, we'll never get off this sand."

Selene laid her arms around his neck and rubbed her body against his, the vales and valleys of her breasts pressing the mounds and deeps of his own. "I don't think I ever want to leave. As for the servants, if it gives that horrible Gurda something to talk about, it will be nothing short of a miracle. Must we leave?" she begged, nibbling on his earlobe.

Gurda's name seemed to bring him back to reality. He stood up pulling her after him. "We must. But we'll come back, I promise. And we've got nights and days in your lovely bed to continue what we've had here. I intend to continue it, I warn you."

"It won't be the same," Selene mumbled, kissing him again. Reluctantly she pulled on her clothes, ignoring the uncomfortable sensation of sticky sand under her clothing. Wade helped her into the carriage, climbed up beside her, kissed her soundly, and flicked the reins to start the carriage rolling. Selene looked back over her shoulder as long as she could, watching the lovely cove disappear finally among the leafy branches and the shadows of the early evening. We'll come back, she told herself, and yet she was disturbed to see it fade away. Somehow reality had been suspended while they laid there, loving and lingering. As they rolled down the beach road toward their villa, reality seemed to come thundering back.

Yet what I feel won't change, she thought as she watched Wade's clean profile, intent on driving. The gentle, considerate lover who in this one afternoon had invaded all the physical and spiritual places of her body and her soul would—must—remain. She had given him all there was of herself to give. Surely nothing could ever change that.

They spoke little on the long road home, content to twine hands and fingers when Wade could spare one from the driving. Occasionally Selene laid her hand on his knee, as if to hold him close to her even while the carriage took them back toward the pressing concerns they had so blissfully laid aside this lovely afternoon. By the time they turned up the long drive to the villa's door, the sun was a fiery flaming ball deep on the gray horizon, and the wind was stronger and cooler than ever. She realized with surprise that she was hungry. Somehow she had not thought she would ever be hungry again.

The spell was wrenched completely away by the time they drove close enough to the veranda to see Odett standing on the porch, flapping her apron at them. Behind her Matilda came hurrying out the door. "Damn!" Wade exclaimed. "You'd think we were lost at sea or something. Now what's all this about?"

"Oh, Master Kinsolving," Odett cried, hurrying to the side of the shay before it had completely come to a stop. "Oh, I'm so relieved you come at last." Matilda scurried around the carriage to Selene's side and stood close to her.

"What's the matter, Odett? Did we keep supper waiting?"

"Oh, that don't matter, sir. But Mister Falk, the governor's secretary, he been waiting all afternoon, impatient as could be. And I couldn't tell him where you were and oh, sir, he was so upset . . ."

She was interrupted by the appearance of the gentleman himself striding through the hall to the porch and hurrying down the stairs. Falk was a short, portly fellow who could not move very fast. His irritation with Wade was written all over his face.

"My dear fellow," he puffed, tripping down the low steps. "What a turn you have given me. All afternoon waiting in this beastly dull place for you to appear, and not daring to leave for fear of not seeing you. Very explicit the Governor was. Don't leave without seeing him, he says. Where on earth have you been, dear boy?"

"Hello, Swinton, I had no idea," Wade said as he jumped down from the shay. "Odett see that the groom—what's his name, James—see that he takes care of this horse. Now, Swinton, let's go inside and have a brandy and tell me what all this fuss is about. You haven't met my wife, I believe."

Falk nodded to Selene whom Wade handed down in a swirl of ruffled skirts. She hoped she did not look so unkempt and casual as to make it obvious what they had been doing, but

153

since Wade did not seem worried by it, she decided neither would she.

"Ma'am," Falk gave her the briefest of bows, then took Wade's arm. "There's no time for brandy, dear fellow. We must get back to Bridgetown at once. Without delay. Your ship has arrived."

Wade's look was completely baffled. "My ship?"

"The British, Captain Kinsolving. They dropped anchor in Carlisle roadstead this morning. Your ministers are here!"

Eight

"Oh, Miss Selene, I never seen anyone look so pretty as you do!"

Selene pirouetted in front of the long mirror, turning first to the left and then right, peering over her own shoulder at the elegant creature that stared back at her. "I can't believe it myself, Mattie," she replied without a trace of vanity. She felt almost as though the person looking back at her was a stranger from some foreign land. Her hair was piled high and laced with tiny jasmine flowers enhanced by several sparkling jewels. The dress of deep green satin billowed around her, its color shimmering in the light from the long windows. Her shoulders above the wide beige lace and emerald flowerets seemed as creamy as the frothy lace that surrounded them.

"Do you think this necklace is really all right? Something with real stones would be more appropriate but, of course, I don't have any. This cameo was the best Wade could do on such short notice."

Mattie straightened the exquisite cameo where it hung from a thin velvet green ribbon around Selene's narrow throat. "It sets off the dress perfectly. I think Captain Kinsolving knew just what he was about. Real jewels might take away from the rest of you."

Selene laughed. "Well, I suppose that's one way to console yourself over a lack of finery. But so be it. I think I'll make a suitable impression on Wade's high-tony British friends. And if not—they can go hang."

*   *   *

"But I don't know anything about putting on a grand dinner," Selene had cried when Wade first proposed entertaining the delegation at their villa. "I've never done it. And the cooking and the foods are so strange here."

Wade had started to argue that anyone with an ounce of sense could plan a dinner party, but had caught back his words. Perhaps he had been hasty in assuming that Selene was accustomed to entertaining on a grand scale. "Didn't you learn anything at your uncle's? Didn't your father ever invite his friends to dinner?"

Selene had bristled at the implied accusation in his words. "My father and I lived very simply. There was never enough money to put on lavish entertainments, and he would not have done so even if there had been. And my uncle ran a tavern, remember. He offered simple fare that could be gotten on the table and off again quickly. As quickly as possible."

Wade could see she was growing upset. He fought down the temptation to take her in his arms, and instead said in as kindly a voice as he could manage: "Don't worry about it then. Odett is an experienced housekeeper. Between the three of us we'll manage everything splendidly. All you'll have to do is wear one of your new gowns and look beautiful. Oh, and making pleasant conversation wouldn't hurt. The more we can butter up these English the better."

She thought of this conversation later sitting at the head of a table bright with candles and burdened with silver and fine china. The mauve-pink blossoms of the congea vine laid a heavy scent over the room where they had been strewn along the table. Through the open French windows the fragrance of jasmine drifted on the cool breeze. The servants moved noiselessly among the guests, replenishing wineglasses and offering tasty dishes of English and Bajan food, each more tempting than the last. Selene watched carefully as the meal progressed, determined to learn how to manage an elegant dinner party should the need arise again. The number of courses amazed her, as did the way in which Bajan cuisine was easily worked into them. The fish turned out to be the common flying fish so popular in the island, but cooked in a clever sauce elaborate enough to raise it to epicurean heights. Breadfruit pastries, fried plantain, and oursins sautéed in butter and onions augmented the usual chicken and vegetables. Even the sweet was a coconut concoction as rich as it was delicious. Each course moved easily on to the next, augumented with an appropriate wine, while Selene watched and stored away every detail. The fine Royal Crown Derby china, Waterford crystal, and gleaming silver candelabra and serving dishes danced in the light of nearly fifty candles. She had no idea where Wade had obtained these fineries, but she suspected they had been borrowed for the occasion.

From the far end of the table Wade smiled at her and lifted his glass ever so slightly in silent tribute. He was very striking this evening himself, Selene thought, in his full Confederate uniform with sword and sash, all cleaned and pressed. The ministers sat along the table, three to a side—Lord Candelby, the most important of the group, on her right, Sir Francis Stringer, the Governor General, on Wade's. Lord Candelby was a heavy-faced man with exquisite manners and a jocular wit that belied the shrewdness Selene suspected lay underneath. He kept her entertained throughout the meal with descriptions of England in general and London in particular— an area she was avid to know more about. When he occasionally turned to address the rest of the table, she studied his companions: Lord Hardwick from the Admiralty, a taciturn navy man with a massive lower jaw that gave him the unfortunate appearance of an English bulldog, and Sir Thomas Gregg, a member of the House of Lords appointed to accompany the mission. The other member of the delegation was a Mister Thomas Overton whom Selene supposed by his servile silence to be secretary to Lord Candelby. He sat for most of the meal with his attention centered on his plate, as though he distrusted foreign cooking or suspected an attempt to poison him. Swinton Falk, sitting across from him, was as ebulient as always, but even he gave up halfway through the meal when all his attempts at drawing out Mister Overton had been unsuccessful.

At first it disturbed Selene to be the only woman present,

but when she realized that even hers was a token presence to the really significant business of the evening—breaking ground for the first round of serious talks on the morrow—she relaxed and began to enjoy herself. The obvious admiration in the eyes of the gentlemen present, Wade included, helped to put her at ease.

"We were not appraised that Captain Kinsolving was bringing along his lovely wife, madam," Lord Candelby said, leaning toward her and brushing her arm. "I confess that it has been an unexpected pleasure. You have allowed me to wax poetical about my native country, which I am sorely missing at the present moment, and in addition, you are as much a feast to the eyes as this country of Barbados itself."

Selene felt her cheeks warming at his compliment. "It was a last minute decision, Lord Candelby," she said wryly.

"I can only say that had I such a lovely young wife I, too, would refuse to be parted from her. My own wife is a fine woman, please don't misunderstand. Yet when these separations arise, it does us both good to be apart, rather than prolong a closeness that long ago ran its course, so to speak."

"You've been to Barbados before?" Selene asked, somewhat embarrassed at the frankness with which he discussed his marriage.

"No, not Barbados. But Her Majesty asks me to take on these little missions now and then, and it enables me to see more of the world than I might otherwise. I confess I find this a lovely island. Very romantic, so to speak."

His stress on the word "romantic" made Selene look quickly away and pop her fork into her mouth. Was there more here than just polite conversation, she wondered with a tiny thrill? Of course she ought to be outraged if there was, but on the other hand, it was rather nice to think she might inspire the interest of a gentleman like Lord Candelby, even if he was nearly twice her age.

She glanced up to see Wade watching her, obvious pride in his eyes. The memory that flashed between them carried portents of the afternoon before and brought a tingle to her flesh when she remembered being atop his long torso, seeking out the hidden places of his body with her tongue. She smiled back and for an instant there was no one in the room but the two of them.

"You must come to England someday," she heard Lord Candelby croon in her ear, and Selene pulled her gaze from Wade's. "A woman like you would be the rage of the town. I would be happy to introduce you into society, which I am certain you would take by storm."

"You flatter me, Lord Candelby. But I would love to visit England someday. I heard so much about your country from my father. The apotheosis of civilization he called it."

"He must have been a very astute man. If you do come to London— with or without your husband—please do let me know. I mean that sincerely."

Selene gave him a quick glance, wondering if he suspected her marriage was not all it appeared to be. Yet how could he? On the surface she and Wade must appear the happily wedded couple. They had gone to great pains to look that way.

"I shall remember your kind invitation, my Lord," she said with as much aplomb as possible. She realized that Wade has been nodding at her for the last minute and that the servants were waiting with the port. He must wish her to leave so they could get down to the real business at hand. Murmuring something about retiring, Selene rose and spoke graciously to the group, all of whom jumped to their feet and fastened their eyes upon her. When she swept from the room she knew those admiring eyes followed her through the door. Closing the double doors she leaned against them, briefly wishing she could hear what was being said inside. Somehow she felt sure they were talking about her.

"Did I do well? Was I a good hostess?"

"You were wonderful. I wish you could have heard all the compliments they paid you after you left. What a lucky fellow I was, and so on, ad infinitum. I had to force them to get back to the business at hand."

Selene giggled and stole her arms around Wade's neck. He had slipped into her bedroom sooner than she expected and she still wore her emerald dress. The only thing she had removed was the cameo from her throat and her earrings. Wade bent and kissed her, gently, delicately, as though she were a fragile art object. When he raised his head, he reached up and began to pull the flowers and then the pins from her hair.

"I think Lord Candelby wanted to go to bed with me," she said, as her hair fell in a golden cloud around her shoulders.

"I hope you didn't encourage him. He's got a reputation as a first-class roué with the ladies. I wouldn't want him to get the wrong impression of our Southern belles."

"I'm not a Southern belle! But I didn't encourage him anyway. He's too old and stringy for my taste."

Wade slipped his hands over her shoulders and gently eased down the lacy sleeves of her dress. The bodice drew taut across the swelling mounds of her creamy breasts.

"And what is your taste, madam?"

He bent and licked her skin, his tongue probing beneath the fabric, thrusting it down and over the ripe fullness of her breasts, searching for the flaming erectness of the brown nipple. When he found it, pulling it into his mouth. Selene's head went back and she gave a low moan of sheer pleasure.

"Tell me, what is to your taste?" he insisted, teasing her with his tongue, taking the taut nipple between his teeth and drawing it toward him. She was not able to answer.

When her knees turned to water, he clasped her in his arms, pressing her against him, unfastening her beautiful dress which fell like a pool of seawater around her feet.

"Tell me," he said with cruelty in his voice. She could feel him against her, his firm mound pressing into her thighs.

"You," she sighed. "You, you, you . . ."

He laughed with triumph and joy, picked her up in his arms, and carried her to the bed where he lay her down and fell on top of her. A single candle guttered on the table beside the bed, throwing a coverlet of shadows over their entwined bodies. Selene tore wildly at his clothes even as he stripped her of her own. They rolled together across the bed in a frenzy, wild to be linked once more, lusting in the joyous abandonment of their willing flesh.

"Take me . . . please," she begged as his fingers sought that exquisite spot that brought her to a frenzy of longing.

"I'll take you . . . but not yet," he taunted her. "Beg for it a little longer. Beg!" His hands sought every inch of her thighs, searched the creamy mound of her stomach then slid downward to begin again the insistent gyrations that brought her writhing body to a pleading madness. She reached to enclose the huge firmness of that desired organ, struggling to force it within her, desperate for its fullness, the completion of all her empty spaces.

"Take me . . . oh, please . . ."

And then he was there, thrusting inside her as his body fell over hers, pushing ever more with a growing intensity, again and again carrying them both on a joyous celebration that was all sensation with no reason, no thought, nothing but the merging of earth and heaven in the one great swell of sensation.

He cried out as he came, and her arms went around him pressing him to her. When he slumped, exhausted, his head buried in her shoulder, Selene gathered her own breath, then gently stroked his hair while he recovered.

How is it, she thought, that I am so happy?

He stayed with her that night and she woke in the morning with his head against her shoulder and his arm across her bare breast. She stretched her bruised muscles, reveling in the feeling of utter satiation, so happy with the world that she almost laughed aloud.

Wade was deeply asleep as she stole from the bed and silently dressed. It was early but it was too beautiful a day and too full of promise to lie abed. She slipped downstairs to take breakfast, then went outside to roam the gardens.

She knew that she should be disturbed over the joy that these last two days had brought her, but she refused to think about it. The pleasure, the closeness, and the promise of love was too enticing to remember unpleasant things that now lay in the past. She and Wade inhabited a fairy tale world that could not be touched by war and bitter divisions. It disturbed Selene a little to think how disappointed in her her father would be for so easily turning away from her convictions, but she decided

161

that would just have to be. Her father was dead now and, if the truth were told, she suspected he had never in his long pursuit of intellectual satisfaction, known such sensual joy as she had known these last two days. She refused to let that joy be tarnished with regrets.

When Wade finally came downstairs to find her in the gardens, he chided her for leaving him alone in the wide bed. "We might have started the day as we ended it," he said, kissing her earlobe and cupping her breast with his hand.

Selene felt the old stirring under his nimble fingers. "We can always go back upstairs . . ."

"Alas no," he said, pulling her up to her feet and walking her to the house with his arm around her waist. "I fear the call of duty at this moment is stronger than the call of love. However, there is always tonight . . ."

"And what is duty today?" Selene asked, leaning happily against his broad shoulder.

"I must be in Bridgetown for our first serious discussions with the British ministers. Then this afternoon at four o'clock there is tea at the Governor's palace in honor of Lord Candelby. Most of the important people on the island will be there, including you, my lovely wife."

"Is this another dress-up occasion?"

"Of course. Look your prettiest. Oh, and don't wear that cameo. I made up my mind last night that you should have a proper necklace. What's your favorite jewel?"

"Why, Wade, can you afford something like that?"

"Well, it won't be the black ruby, but it will be something nice. Now tell me, what do you like?"

"As a matter of fact, I've always wanted a sapphire. The color is so beautiful."

"Done. Just be sure you are in Bridgetown early enough to go shopping."

"Wild horses couldn't hold me back!"

All day she looked forward to the trip to Bridgetown. With Matilda's help she dressed as beautifully as possible, wearing the rose concoction that could serve for late afternoon,

162

leaving her neck bare. The only sour note to her happiness was the dark presence of Gurda, who had resumed her watchdog duties that morning once Wade left.

He looked tired when she met him at the square, as though the morning session had not gone well. Yet when she questioned him about it he said little and simply handed her out of the carriage and led her to a jewelers' shop on one of the narrow streets off the square. They had such a good time there, poring over enchanting baubles and selecting one, that his good humor soon returned. In the end it wasn't sapphires they found but rubies—two delicate gold chains, the larger one looped at three places to the smaller and held together by single rubies set in gold and surrounded by tiny diamond clusters.

"Oh Wade, it's beautiful," Selene said as he fastened it around her white throat. "I've never had anything so lovely." The airy grace and delicacy of the necklace appealed to her over the more ornate necklaces with larger stones and higher prices.

He bent to whisper in her ear: "I think rubies are more appropriate. Sapphires are cool and icy. Rubies suit you better—hot, passionate, flaming."

She laughed, turning her head this way and that to admire the way the light caught the rosy stones, warming them to luminescent fire. In spite of the jewels the necklace was not heavy and its delicacy suited her slim throat. She was pleased, too, that it would not look ostentatious but rather in simple good taste.

"I hate to cover it with the high neck of this jacket," she sighed, "but I suppose I must. I can wear it to the Governor's tea, though, can't I?"

"I insist that you do. It will look its best though with a more formal evening gown." Standing behind her he put his hands on her shoulders and bent to lightly kiss her neck. Selene watched him in the mirror as his lips touched her tingling flesh and thought that she had never been so happy.

"Come along now, Mrs. Kinsolving. Enough of this preening in the glass. It's time we got to the Governor's palace. And don't flirt with Lord Candelby this afternoon. I don't want to have to call out the highest ranking member of the delegation.

It would do little to encourage the success of my mission."

His words echoed in Selene's mind when they entered the crowded reception room of Government House a little later. Lord Candelby spotted her at once from across the room and gave her a short bow and a knowledgable wink. She smiled back as her fingers went instinctively to her throat to feel the hard stones of her new finery beneath the jacket of her dress. The room was thick with people, most of them strangers, and she was relieved to recognize Swinton Falk pushing through the crowd toward them.

"Captain Kinsolving," he said effusively. "So glad you're finally here. We've been waiting for you."

Wade stood in the doorway looking around the room as though reluctant to enter. "Who are all these people, Swinton? I didn't expect quite such a crowd."

"An American ship arrived earlier today with the other members of your delegation. They're here somewhere."

Wade dropped Selene's arm. "Mister Weston is here. No one told me."

"It's only been within the last hour that we knew ourselves, and then we couldn't find you. But come, let me get your lovely wife some punch. You would like some, wouldn't you, Mrs. Kinsolving? And I can introduce you to the guests while your husband here looks for his colleagues."

"Would you mind, Selene? George Weston is President Davis's hand-picked ambassador to help draw up the treaty we hope to make. I have to find him. And the others, too. They did all come together didn't they, Swinton?"

Swinton pulled Selene's arm smoothly through his own. "They did indeed. I believe there are two more of them—one an officer like yourself. They're all here somewhere. Come madam. Shall we leave this fellow to his business? I'm sure you would appreciate the opportunity to meet some of the other ladies here. Most of them are residents of Barbados and most pleasant they are too."

Selene smiled at Swinton as Wade disappeared into the crowd and she carefully masked a small tinge of desperation at being thrown to a roomful of strangers without Wade to lean on. Across the room an opening in a group of people revealed a tall man dressed in a spotless Confederate uniform with a handsome red sash and a sword at his side. Swinton pulled her away and she followed, resigned to the fact that Wade was going to have more important things on his mind for a while than squiring her around the room.

"You are most kind, Mister Falk," she said as graciously as she could manage. "I'd enjoy meeting some of your resident ladies."

It was difficult to maneuver through the room, and with the noise of so many voices all talking at once, heightened by the clatter of china and silver, she had difficulty hearing, much less remembering, the names of the women Swinton introduced her to. After a few attempts at small talk with one or two of the ladies, Selene watched again with that feeling of desertion as Swinton was carried off to assist the governor in a conference with two of the gentlemen she recognized as being part of the British delegation. From across the room she saw Wade wave at her as he caught her eye briefly. Sipping her punch, Selene moved near the open doors to the balcony and looked around, wondering who she should try to make conversation with first. She was relieved to hear a familiar voice speak behind her.

"Good afternoon, Miss Selene."

She swirled around. Her eyes widened and her smile faded as she stared up into a pair of humorless eyes, hard as agate.

"Simon Lazar! What on earth . . ."

"Am I doing here? I might ask the same question of you."

It was the same Simon certainly, though dressed much more formally and neatly than when she last saw him. He looked, in fact, as she remembered seeing him in her father's parlor, beardless, in formal black, the suit a little shabby but very neat, the cravat tied in an ornate pattern that almost prevented one from noticing how old it was. Even his hair was different, long and slick with the ends curling toward his face near his shoulders. He looked, Selene thought, like the government clerk she remembered.

"I can't believe it. How did you get here? And why?"

"Your curiosity has outrun your manners, my dear Selene," he remarked dryly, taking her elbow and gently maneuvering her toward the open French doors. "Have you seen the garden from the balcony, ma'am?" he said speaking more loudly. "Most interesting and much cooler than this close room."

Before Selene realized what had happened, she was standing on the balcony, in clear view of the room but unable to be heard. Simon spoke so low that she had difficulty making out his words over the noise of the company behind them.

"You have certainly undergone a transformation since I last saw you. I had no idea you were so handsome all done up in finery such as this. Please look around, my dear. We ought to appear to be admiring the view at least."

Selene felt a sudden embarrassment at standing next to this man from the world of her past dressed as she was. She was all at once back to playing a part, an actress in a charade. It was a feeling she had forgotten these last two days and it made her ashamed.

"What are you doing here?" she said, allowing her irritation to show. "You have no right—didn't you see my letter?"

"My, my. I did fancy you would be happier to see me. Yes, I saw your note, and I followed you as quickly as possible. In fact, I arrived today on the same ship that brought that arrogant deputy Weston. He thinks I am a journalist, by the way, with Southern leanings. I would be obliged if you don't disillusion him."

"Did you give General McDowell my note?"

"That is my concern. I think what is needed now is to remind you of yours. Have your loyalties been bought by a few fine gowns?"

"Of course not," she snapped. "I am as loyal to the Union as I ever was."

"Shh," he warned. "In this company it might be best not to say that too loudly." He studied her with his cold eyes. "I confess, however, I am relieved to hear it. We must talk, Selene. Somewhere private. Do you know what a disaster it will be to our cause if these play-actor diplomats manage to convince England to sign a treaty of recognition?"

Selene fussed with the ribbons on her dress. "I know," she murmured. And she did know. She had just not remembered it these last few days.

"Where are you staying?" Simon asked pointedly, his gaze focused on a brilliant blooming frangipani tree below. From the corner of his eye he saw a gray uniform coming toward them, and raised his voice as he pointed at the gardens.

"What gorgeous vegetation is found on this island. Did you ever see anything like the scarlet of that red hibiscus? I'm told there are even places here where the flowers bloom under water."

"I think they are referring to the sea grottos in St. Lucy," Selene casually observed. "Animal flowers are the name the locals have given to the sea anemones that live in the shallow pools there."

"Here you are, Selene," Wade said stepping out on to the balcony with them. "I thought you got lost in the crush back there. Did you get some punch?"

"Yes, I did." There was a strained quality to her voice she prayed he wouldn't notice. "This is an old friend of mine, Wade. Simon Lazar. He—he used to know my father."

Wade extended his hand but Lazar did not take it. Instead he gave Wade a stiff, formal bow.

"So you are the one who has monopolized my wife. Your servant, sir."

"Wife?" Lazar's brows moved upward as his sharp glance flew to Selene.

"Yes," she said hurriedly. "Captain Kinsolving and I were married shortly after our ship left Norfolk. It was—quite a sudden decision. And Simon was not monopolizing me, Wade. It was just that the room was very close, and I needed a breath of air."

The two men stood looking each other over, an air of distrust growing between them. Selene scooped up her punch cup from the railing and handed it to Wade. "Perhaps I could have a little more . . ."

"So, felicitations are in order," Simon said, ignoring her. "May I offer you my heartiest congratulations, and pray that I may have the honor of calling on you while I am here in Barbados."

"That's very kind," Selene muttered without enthusiasm.

"What brings you to Barbados, Mister Lazar?" Wade asked, moving closer to Selene and laying a possessive arm around her waist. "Are you accompanying Mister Weston?"

"Oh no, at least not officially. I am something of a journalist, it is true, but it was ill health that drove me to seek the islands. I confess, however, that when I learned that Mister Weston was aboard, I did hope for a story, but to no avail. He seems to be escaping the war, too."

Wade appeared to be relieved at his words, and yet it was obvious he did not know whether or not to believe him. "I see. Well, we do not intend to be in Barbados too much longer, but by all means, feel free to call on us while you are here. We are staying at the Villa Corbin in St. James. It's just a short afternoon's ride from Bridgetown. Why not stay for dinner when you come?"

"You are too kind, sir," Lazar bowed. His manner was polite and easy and Selene wondered if the lack of sincerity behind it was only her interpretation. From what she knew of him, she did not entirely trust him, though she could not exactly put her finger on what it was that gave rise to her suspicions. There always seemed to be more going on behind those veiled eyes than his polite conversation indicated.

"I'd be glad of the opportunity to hear how things are going back home," Wade went on.

"I believe Major Gorham can fill you in on that better than I, Captain."

"I suppose he could. Come, Selene. I want you to meet George Weston. Excuse me, Mister—what was the name again?"

"Lazar, Simon Lazar."

"Of course. Excuse us, Mister Lazar."

They moved off, but not before Selene received a very pointed look from Simon. It dogged her steps the rest of the afternoon, though she tried to ignore it while making small talk with the guests and fending off the not too subtle advances of Lord Candelby. An uneasiness persisted, following her like a stray dog at her heels far into the evening, even when she lay hot and writhing in Wade's arms. Afterwards she lay listening to his slow rhythmic breathing, thinking how even he had noticed that something between them was changed because of Simon Lazar.

"I feel as though you are not really here, even though I hold you in my arms," he had said at one point in their lovemaking. And then, as if one thought led to a second logical one: "I didn't like your Mister Lazar."

"He's not mine. I hardly know him."

"Oh? That's not the impression he gave."

"Why don't you like him?"

"I'm not sure, except that there is something about him I don't trust. The eyes maybe. They seem to be mocking everything he sees, even as he mouthes polite pleasantries. Do you have to see him again?"

"You invited him."

"No, he invited himself."

"Yes, but you told him where we live. If he shows up, I suppose I shall have to be polite."

Wade was half alseep. "I suppose you will. Maybe he won't come."

Selene lay awake long afterward, knowing that Simon would come, bringing with him the war, the causes, the divisions she had almost forgotten for a time. They had all slipped away in the euphoria of sensual pleasure, the intoxication of romance. Wade stirred beside her and instinctively she inched away from him. How had she so quickly forgotten the way he had treated her—dragging her with him across an ocean, forcing her to marry him, to sail away from all that she held dear, and finally even forcing his body into hers. How could she have been so shallow as to let this masquerade—for surely that was what it was—drive from her mind the very real allegiance and principles that divided the two of them? It was this place, this magical island that blocked off everything beyond fleshly gratifications. The dreamlike aura of sand and sea had severed her from reality, a reality she now saw with a sharp, new clarity.

Oh yes, Simon Lazar would come, and she would have to

greet him, a girl now at war with herself. Loving and hating, mourning the dream lost, longing to forget all she had believed for the glory and joy of love.

Whatever would her father have said to see her now, forsaking everything she believed in, everything he had taught her, for a man who had deceived and violated her.

She turned over on her side, away from Wade's sprawling body. She was glad Simon had come to remind her of her duty.

Nine

She hoped he wouldn't come but, of course, he did. All day Selene busied herself with foolish activities that served to pass the time without calming the disquiet that had consumed her since meeting Simon the day before. In the back of her mind was the hope that if she forgot about him, he would go away, leaving her to recapture the euphoria of the past days.

But there he was, standing stiffly polite in formal afternoon dress, scrutinizing her with those eyes that seemed to see through to her very soul.

"Would you like some tea?" Selene asked formally while Odett still hovered near the door.

"Perhaps later," Simon answered, fingering the fob of his watch. "It seems a shame to stay indoors on such a beautiful afternoon, and I noticed while driving in that the villa has extensive gardens. Perhaps we could take a turn around them."

His sudden interest in botany was suspicious but only to Selene, who recognized it as a need for privacy. She rose with a sigh, determined to see this annoying visit through to the end. But she was careful to keep a discreet distance between them as they wandered the gravel paths, fragrant with flowers and overgrown in places with fat palm leaves. Lazar waited until they were well away from the house, then lost no time getting to the point.

"What have you been able to learn about Captain Kinsolving's mission? How close is it to completion?"

"I've learned almost nothing." Selene answered quietly. "I met the British ambassadors when they were here to dinner, but naturally we discussed nothing beyond polite pleasantries. And Wade—Captain Kinsolving never talks about his business with me."

"I'm sure he doesn't," he replied, staring down at her in a way that sent her anger surging.

"I resent your innuendoes!" she snapped through clenched teeth. "I did not come willingly to this island. I was forced here against my will. Even this marriage was foisted upon me without my consent."

Surprised at her anger, Simon quickly pulled back slightly. "My apologies. You and I must not quarrel. Our task is too momentous. It was only that the two of you presented such a happy picture together."

"It was all feigned."

"Then you may add actress to your list of accomplishments. That is all to the good, by the way, since you may have to encourage the Captain to divulge more about his business while convincing him of your 'ardor.'"

She glared at him with his deliberate lingering on the word "ardor." The treacherous blood rushed to her cheeks but Simon did not seem to notice. He had stopped on the path to admire a perfect miniature pink hibiscus blossom and took the opportunity to look back down the path they had just walked. "Who is that woman?" he whispered, holding the bloom to his nose.

For the first time Selene noticed the familiar dark shadow hovering behind them. "That is Gurda, my keeper. The Captain does not trust me, so he has installed this watchdog to follow me around, to make certain I don't bolt. Though where I would go is beyond my perception."

"He really expects you to run away?"

"I have given him good cause to believe I would. I hope this helps to convince you of how little ardor there is between us. A true lover would hardly set such an unpleasant policeman on his beloved."

"You have a point. All right then," Lazar said softly, starting

172

off down the path once more. "We must find a way to make certain this treaty is never signed. I don't really believe it will be, but I want to make absolutely certain of it."

"Why don't you think it will? The British ministers have come all this way to meet with Confederate representatives. And England needs Southern cotton, everyone knows that."

"Not so much as the South would like to think. Crops have been so enormous these last few years that jolly old England has stocked reserves. Besides, their broader interests must lead them to see that the Southern cause is a lost one. They will have to make their peace with the Union if they wish to keep an eye to the future, no matter how much their sympathy might lie with the South. In addition . . ."

He hesitated, and Selene waited, feeling certain that he knew more than he wanted to say.

"Well, no matter," he went on, while Selene forced herself not to meet his eyes. He did not completely trust her, she felt sure. "I shall take my own steps to see that this treaty never comes to pass. Meanwhile I shall count on you to learn all you can from your good Captain. And when the time comes, if you still want to leave here, I'll help you get away."

Freedom! Her reaction to the thought was surprising. She had almost forgotten how much she wanted to get away from Wade's bondage and make her own decisions again. Now the intoxicating thought came surging back. "Can you help me?" she whispered. "What about that native woman? What about Wade?"

"I'll find a way. Neither of them suspects, I would imagine, that I would be the one helping you to escape. The Captain does not realize that we know each other very well, does he?"

"You heard what I told him. He knows only that you were a friend of my father's."

"I shall have to elaborate on that a little for his benefit. In the meantime, try to get some information out of him concerning where and when this treaty might be put into effect. I had ample opportunity to observe his two cohorts on the journey down here, and I'm convinced that your Captain is the one to watch. George Weston is an ass, more concerned with his own position than the Southern cause, while Major Gorham is a malcontent who resents being taken away from the battlefield and forced to join a diplomatic mission. Neither of them are likely to convince the British that this treaty is a wise move. But Kinsolving might. He has presence, and he appears to be invested with more authority than his rank would suggest."

"I wish you would not refer to him as 'my Captain.' I've told you what our relationship is."

"Yes. A charade. Forgive me, my dear, but intuition tells me it is a bit more than that. But no matter. This is the time to put aside any personal feelings of your own and concentrate on your country's need. I heard your father espouse that high calling often enough. Can you do what he himself would ask you to do for the sake of a righteous cause?"

Selene glared at him. "You don't have to remind me of my father's principles. They were ingrained in my soul long before you appeared in his parlor."

He gave her a cool smile. "Good. I only wanted to make certain you remembered them. Well, here we are back at the terrace doors. If you don't mind, Selene dear, I believe I will pass on your invitation to tea. Perhaps the next time I'm out this way."

"But Wade expected you would stay for supper."

He took her hand, the picture of civility. "Please give him my regrets and tell him business matters called me away. I intend to leave the Captain to you as much as possible."

"But when will I see you again? How . . ."

He held up his hand slightly, just enough to silence her. "Do not worry. I shall be making my plans, and I will let you know of them in good time. Good day, my dear."

She watched him trip lightly up the steps to retrieve his hat and gloves from the front hall before heading out the door of the house. What an enigma, she thought. Her ally. And yet one whose presence awoke in her the deepest distrust and misgivings. There was something ever so slightly repulsive about him that made her blood chill. And yet it was nothing she could put her finger on. On the surface he was a friend, a compatriot, a means of escape.

Glancing back she saw that Gurda had halted on the path and stood in the shadows watching her. This was intolerable! Wade Kinsolving would soon learn that he could not keep her chained to him.

"That woman makes my skin crawl! Why must she follow me around? Why don't you trust me? She's like one of those zombies the natives talk about—half-dead people who move like ghosts. Why can't you trust me enough to call her off?"

"She's not a mad dog, Selene," Wade said impatiently. With an infuriating objectivity he opened the humidor and chose a long Havana seegar, rolling it lovingly between his long fingers. "She's only doing what I told her to do."

"Then tell her to leave me alone. Have I given you any reason to think I might run away? Haven't I played the part of your dutiful, loving wife well enough? You might afford me a little trust."

He ignored the "playing a part," but he was conscious that her words hurt just a little. She had agreed to act the part of his wife in the beginning, of course, but he rather fancied they had got beyond that. Obviously he was wrong.

"I cannot take the chance," he said, bending to light the seegar by a flame of a tall candle. "She doesn't get in your way. I told her not to speak to you, not to interrupt, not to prevent you from going where you will. Why can't you just ignore her?"

"She's always behind me, like a sinister stray dog. And whatever I do, whomever I speak with, I know she runs right back to you and tells everything."

"And are you speaking with anyone you shouldn't be?"

She turned her back on him to pick up her embroidery, hoping to hide the sudden flush his words gave her. "Of course not. You know very well whom I see, and that none of them are any threat."

Wade sat down heavily in one of the stuffed chairs, crossed his knees, and studied her. Her discomfort was so obvious that it made him curious, where before he had given no thought to Simon Lazar. That strange man was the only person Selene talked with whom he did not know or trust. And yet, as far as he could tell, there was nothing about him that was suspicious. It was more intuition than anything else.

"I'm sorry Mister Lazar did not stay for supper. I would have welcomed the chance to talk with him about things at home. What was the reason?"

"Business matters," Selene murmured, concentrating on her needle. "He didn't elaborate, and I've no idea what the business was."

"He's a rather secretive gentleman, isn't he?"

"I don't find him so, but then I barely know him. And I'm not involved in all the intricacies of diplomacy you gentlemen are so fond of."

"No, you're not. And it's better that way. Well, I'm rather tired. I think I'll turn in. Are you coming up?"

Selene hesitated just a moment too long before answering. "No, I think I'll work for awhile yet."

Impulsively Wade rose and bent over her, lifting her chin to lightly kiss her lips as his hand cupped her breast. "Can't convince you to change your mind?"

She fought down the hot surge that swelled within her. "I'll be up later," she murmured, trying not to sound too cool. He smiled at her, a quizzical smile as full of questions as joy. When I am asleep, he thought but did not say the words. He was as disappointed as much as he was suspicious of her sudden coldness. The change in this woman, who had been so hot in his arms and responded to him so lovingly just two days before, was too startling and too sudden. And it had all come about with the appearance of Simon Lazar. That gentleman would bear watching, Wade determined.

"Good night then, my dear," he said smoothly. He left the room and Selene watched him go, convinced she had given him nothing to suspect.

Looking back, Selene would realize that evening was the last time Wade called her "my dear," except in public. In the days and weeks that followed her first meeting with Simon Lazar, an estrangement grew between them like a fog settling in, filling in

176

all the empty spaces where once for a brief time there had been harmony. He still came to her bed, progressively less than before, and he took her with a ferocity and roughness that was reminiscent of that first night on the *Yamacraw*. Selene began to think that afternoon on the beach had been a dream, had never existed, that it was some romantic fantasy he had foisted upon her. This was the true Wade Kinsolving, the man who had kidnapped her and forced his way into her body with no regard at all for her own feelings or wishes.

It was some kind of irony, she thought, that it had taken Simon Lazar to wake her from her foolish euphoria and recall her to the real work she was meant to do. How could she have been so naive, so gullible, to think Wade had changed? Even that dreamlike experience on the beach had probably been planned to deceive her, to lull her into his trap where she would be no threat to him. Thank God Simon had shown up in time to save her from becoming the complete fool he no doubt thought her.

Yet, even Selene had to admit that Wade's frustration with his mission probably had something to do with his increasing estrangement. She pumped him for details with little success, but it was obvious the negotiations were going nowhere. She heard him arguing late into the night with Major Gorham and George Weston, standing close to the door straining to hear their words until she spotted Gurda lurking down the hall and quickly pretended she was on her way to the kitchen to ask for some warm milk. Later, when the other men had gone, she heard Wade pacing the floor of the parlor until the early hours of the morning. She went downstairs finally, intending to appear sympathetic and concerned, but he only ordered her back to bed with an angry curtness.

"It's nothing. And I don't want anything to drink. I've had enough brandy tonight to make a weaker man roaring drunk. Go back to bed."

"Why don't you come to bed then?" Selene muttered, making what for her seemed the final sacrifice to her cause. In the mood he was in, he might be encouraged to talk once his lust had worn off. He looked at her with some surprise.

"That's an unusual invitation from you," he said cryptically. "I'd begun to think you are not interested."

She shrugged, hoping he would believe she was simply in the mood. But his suspicions were too strong. "I don't think so," he said, reaching for the nearly empty decanter. "Go on back to bed."

The following day Selene accidentally ran into Simon at the outdoor market in Bridgetown. He strolled around the booths with her, pausing to look over the native crafts and foods, all the while keeping a discreet distance from Gurda and allowing the noise of the market to cover their own conversation.

"He was terribly upset," Selene said in a quiet voice, just low enough for Simon to hear. "I think the negotiations are not going well. I've never seen him so frustrated, almost despairing."

"Good. That is an excellent sign that my own little efforts are working. Now if we can just keep the pressure on until I hear from London, our work here will be complete."

"What do you mean, your little efforts?" Selene picked up a large native breadfruit and examined it carefully.

"My dear girl, you don't suppose I have been cooling my heels in Barbados merely to enjoy the sights, do you? I have contacts at home and in England who keep me well informed. In turn I make sure that Lord Candelby—who, by the way, is a doddering old fool if ever there was one—is aware of the meaning of everything that happens in Virginia. The war will begin in earnest soon, now that winter is almost over, and while we still hope the Confederacy will lose on the battlefield, the real test of their survival lies elsewhere. I don't believe the British really believe the South can win and survive as a separate nation, but they are foxy enough to play along, waiting to see how the wind blows. I intend that they shall be very well informed on the nature of that wind."

Selene replaced the breadfruit on its pile and ambled on to the next booth.

"You really enjoy this game of spying, don't you, Simon? Were you always one—a spy, I mean? Did you only come to my father's house in order to carry back reports on what was said?"

"My dear girl, you wound me to the quick. I was a lowly

178

government clerk anxious to better my education in those days. But one must get ahead and I have found that I have a certain talent for subterfuge. If I can use it to do my small part in saving the Union, I will feel my life has not been in vain."

"But if the South cannot survive as a separate nation, is it really necessary to go to all these lengths to deceive?"

"We must do all in our power to ensure that they never have the chance. A treaty with Great Britain acknowledging their government would be a disastrous first step. It cannot be allowed. I only wonder . . ."

Selene fingered a necklace of pale pink coral and said without looking at him, "What do you wonder?"

"That is a lovely little thing, isn't it?" Simon said, taking the necklace in his own long fingers. "It would look very beautiful on you. Might I be allowed . . ."

An image of the ruby necklace in its case at the villa flashed across her mind. "No, thank you," she said, moving on. "I have enough trinkets. More than I can wear." That wasn't true, of course—but she did not want one from this man around her neck, no matter how many others she had. "What do you wonder?"

He strolled beside her, his heightened color the only sign that her rebuff had angered him. "Just that this British delegation does not seem to be clever enough, or of sufficient high rank to be seriously negotiating a treaty with the Confederacy. I made some inquiries in London and expect to hear a response soon. I suspect these so-called ministers might be deliberately making themselves appear to be inept procrastinators for some devious reason. I intend to find out if that is true."

Selene recalled Wade's restless pacing and wondered if he too had begun to have his suspicions. It might explain his bad temper and increasing despair. "I hope you will tell me what you learn," she said with an air of conspiracy. "It might help me get under Wade's defenses at last."

Simon paused beside the next booth and leaned toward her, speaking in even more quiet tones. "When I do hear, it is possible that I may leave for England, rather hastily. Do you still want to come with me?"

She looked up startled. "England?"

"Shh," he warned looking around. The massive shadow that was Gurda stood several booths back, waiting for them to move on again. "Not so loud. If my plan is to be carried out, it must be done in the strictest secrecy."

"I don't know. I had thought you might help me get back to Virginia."

"And I can. But it will be infinitely easier to send you there from England, than to get you away from Captain Kinsolving here in Barbados. Think of it for a moment, Selene. Any ship in this harbor bound for Virginia is going to make him watch you even closer, while a ship sailing for England might never arouse his suspicions."

"But I have no money, nothing. How can I support myself in England or afford passage to America?"

"My dear, you will be under my protection. Any help you need can be thought of as a loan, if it makes you feel better. After all, I admired your father greatly. He influenced my life more than any other person I've ever known. It would be an honor for me to care for his daughter."

Selene bent her head to allow the brim of her bonnet to cover her confusion. Above all things, she wanted to escape this island and Wade Kinsolving. Yet, with this man? And to a foreign country? She hardly knew how to reply.

"Think about it for a while," Simon said, as though he had read her thoughts. "It will be a few weeks before I know when and if I'm going there. That should allow you time to decide what you want to do."

"Yes," Selene murmured. "Thank you, Simon. I'll need to sort this out . . ."

"Just remember, though, not a word to anyone. If you decide to accompany me, I will only be able to get you away safely if we have surprise and complacency on our side."

"I haven't tried to get away for many weeks now. Perhaps Wade thinks I have given up the idea."

"Let us hope so. And now, I fear I must leave you to wander the shops alone. We must not appear to be close friends. Good day, madam."

He gave her a short formal bow and disappeared into the sea

of shoppers. Without a glance Selene went back to studying the booths, trying to calm her tangled emotions. England! What had Lord Candelby told her—a country she must visit some day. She had never expected to have the chance and here it was, offered to her on a plate along with her freedom. But with Simon Lazar—a man she really did not much care for, and whom she was not even certain she could trust.

It was something she would have to think about very carefully.

"No, no, Mister Weston, it won't do. It won't do at all. There's no way we can guarantee Southern ships."

Wade sat silently studying Lord Candelby across the table. Gone was the smooth, genial, lady's man he had come to expect at public gatherings. The ponderous lower jaw rested on his huge satin cravat like a bulldog's collar, and the taut lines around the mouth, not to mention the narrowed, beady eyes, only enhanced his Lordship's stubborn demeanor. Much of the pleasant admiration he had felt for a Lord of the British realm had long since been dispelled, and now, as the odious man dug in his heels to reject every semblance of compromise and a meeting of the minds, the last of it evaporated. Wade flexed his fingers beneath the table, wishing he could strike that smug jaw.

"But your Lordship must realize that if our cotton cannot reach England, the very crux of our agreement would be nullified. Your country needs those shipments every bit as much as we need to sell them to you."

Weston's voice was reedy and too high-pitched, Wade thought. It betrayed the man's impatience. How long had these tiresome arguments dragged on now? It was beginning to get to them all.

Lord Candelby answered amiably as though they were discussing the latest change in the weather. "Yes, but it must be obvious that any sovereign nation is itself responsible for the protection of its shipping. She cannot depend on the vigilance of a sister sovereign nation to safeguard her rights at sea. Suppose her Majesty's government was to ask the

Confederacy to protect our interests in the Indian Sea. I'm sure you can understand the parallel."

"England is not facing a blockade in the Indian Sea. The Union is committing an outrage by preventing our ships from seeking lawful commerce and trade, and no one in the international community seems to care."

Major Gorham broke in, his voice patient. It occurred to Wade that this was how the pattern of negotiation had developed these last few weeks. The British threw out a stumbling block, and the Southerners passed their pleading responses from one to the other, depending on whose patience wore away first. "Your Lordship knows we are at war. Surely this makes the situation somewhat unusual," the Major intoned.

"Yes, but her Majesty's government is very anxious not to be drawn into this conflict between—what shall I say— cousins? I must remind you gentlemen of the painful reality. It is by no means certain yet that you will survive as a sovereign nation."

"We certainly shall not survive without the ability to sell our cotton to England," Weston said testily. "And you know that very well."

Thomas Gregg sat forward, resting his arms on the green freize tabletop. He seldom spoke, but when he did, it was usually to allow Lord Candelby to reorganize his thoughts. "Your ships have run the blockade, I believe. When we sailed from Portsmouth there were three of them in the harbor. Perhaps you exaggerate the problem."

"Some of them manage to get through, but many more are lost. And every consignment of cotton that falls to the United States is a dagger in the heart of the Confederacy, as you well know, gentlemen. All we are asking is a guarantee . . ."

"A guarantee that could lead to English tars fighting Union sailors. It is impossible. This cannot be a part of the treaty."

"I understood it was a point to be discussed when the original plans were drawn up," Wade said smoothly, seeing that both Weston and the Major were about to explode. "That suggests to me that it was at least to be considered by your government."

Lord Candelby shook his head, setting his cravat fluttering. "No, no, no. We were given strict instructions before we left. We can agree to nothing that might draw us into your war. You are involved in a civil conflict, gentlemen. A family fight, if you will. England cannot and will not interfere."

"It is a fight to establish sovereignty," Weston exploded. "A conflict for independence. May I remind you distinguished gentlemen that England has seen fit to become involved in similar difficulties when it was of profit to her."

The color drained from Candelby's face and Wade hastily broke in. "Mister Weston only means that this conflict involves your country's trade, and therefore could be to your profit."

Lord Candelby's narrowed eyes flicked back and forth between the three Americans as he fought down his irritation. At length, like a true diplomat, he decided to ignore the insult. Folding the leather case in front of him, he made to leave.

"I think this matter must be referred to London, as it is obvious you're unwilling to accept our word on it. I shall write to the government at once. I believe there is a ship now about to leave for England and the correspondence can leave with her. Perhaps when you hear it from Foreign Secretary Russell himself, you will believe me."

Weston stood as the three British ministers rose from their chairs. "We would be obliged if you would refer this as an earnest request by our government, one that could have lasting results for both countries."

"What do you take me for, Mister Weston? A dictator? Of course I shall present it in the most polite language possible. Naturally we wish to see these meetings resolved successfully just as much as you. Good day, gentlemen."

When the heavy doors closed behind the British, Wade sank back into his chair. "I wish I could believe that," he muttered, stacking the papers in front of him.

"I'm convinced they don't want to see this treaty signed at all," Weston commented dryly, pouring from a decanter that stood on the sideboard. "They've done nothing but raise objections from the day we walked in here. We've had no agreement on even the slightest proposal. What in the world am I going to report to President Davis?"

"They're waiting to see which way the war goes," Major Gorham said. "Not as I blame them. I'm not so certain I would accept the responsibility for safe trade with a country which might not even exist beyond next year."

"For shame, Major! Surely the success of First Manassas must prove something. And there's little hope that McClellan will do anything with the Federal army besides march and drill. Why, with one more decisive attack . . ."

"I believe that is what they are waiting on," Wade commented dryly. "All this procrastination is simply to delay until the spring and summer campaigns begin. Everything will hang on the outcome of those battles."

George Weston laid a hand on Wade's shoulder. "We must believe, my friend. We have the spirit and the capability. We have to have faith as well."

The major pulled open one of the doors and stood stiffly aside to let Weston pass. "We have to have guns, too. But if we don't get that cotton to England, we won't have much chance of getting them."

Wade was about to follow when he heard his name called and looked up to see Swinton Falk coming toward him down the hall. He stopped as his two fellow diplomats made to leave.

"Well, perhaps tomorrow we can agree on something. We must at all costs keep trying."

He was conscious all at once of how tired he was. Tired of sitting, tired of arguing, and most of all, tired of trying to discern the devious minds of devious men.

"My God, man, you look as though you've been run through a water mill," Swinton said genially, clapping Wade on the shoulder. "Things didn't go so well, I suspect."

"As well as ever," Wade said, falling in step with Swinton. "Which is to say, not very well at all."

"Well, I'm glad to see you. I was hoping we might just nip over to Ploverman's and have a rum toddy before you head for home. You look as though you could use one and, God knows, I could. The governor was in a beastly mood today and kept me running from pillar to post all day."

Wade opened his mouth to protest that he ought to be

getting home, then thought better of it. It was certainly true he could use a good stiff drink after this hopeless day. And besides, home was not such a pleasant place anymore. Selene was quiet and withdrawn, and though she submitted to his occasional sexual moods, there was precious little joy in it for either of them. "Why not," he said to Swinton. "Just let me put these papers away and I'll join you gladly."

Swinton had half-expected Wade to refuse his offer. He smiled broadly, for he found the captain good company and was longing for a relaxed evening. "Excellent, my good fellow. Excellent. Who knows, we might even find a good game of poker in progress. After this horrible day I feel my luck changing. I suspect it will be very good."

"I could use a little good luck myself," Wade answered, setting the papers in a drawer in his desk and turning the lock. If a bad day was the prerequisite for a lucky evening, he should have something tremendous in store.

Looking back later Wade could not be sure how it had all happened. It had something to do with the fact that he was so tired, he was sure. And discouraged almost to despair. And not simply over the damned hopeless negotiations either, but over Selene as well. Discouraged that something so lovely, bright, and promising had faded abruptly into cold estrangement.

There was no suggestion when they entered the tavern of anything unpleasant. It was crowded and hot with men sweating in their frock coats and cravats and even a few who had removed their coats to crowd around the faro and poker tables in their vests and shirtsleeves. Barbados rum, renowned all over the world for its silky taste, flowed freely, and the loud conversation, sprinkled with laughter and occasional hoots, promised an easy camaraderie and a relaxed time. Wade had downed several drinks before he found himself at the gaming tables and by then his head was none too clear. Afterward he could barely remember ambling over to that end of the room and inquiring as to the game and the stakes. But there he was, at a large round table overlaid with a thick pall from half-smoked cigars, and covered with chips, counters, and cards. Across the table the reptilian eyes of Simon Lazar stared a challenge at him.

It was something of a sobering shock to see Lazar in this place. Somehow Wade had never thought of him as convivial, or much interested in evening relaxation among the locals. He only had to play a few hands with the man to realize why he was there. Lazar might not have been interested in drinking and conversation, but he was very serious indeed about gambling, poker in particular. He played with an intensity and concentration worthy of a Mississippi River card shark and it was soon apparant that winning was for him the only thing that mattered.

Wade got a grim satisfaction from beating him one hand almost as soon as he joined the game. Whatever luck Lazar had been enjoying fled with Wade's appearance and, like the treacherous lady she was, settled her fairy hands firmly on the Captain's shoulders.

Wade endured the murderous glances Lazar threw him for a while in silence, then, with the help of two more rum toddies, began to enjoy himself hugely at Lazar's expense.

"Too bad, sir," he said in a voice dripping sarcasm as he pulled the counters into a pile in front of him. "Perhaps you have talents in other areas. Journalists usually do."

"The evening is young, Captain," Lazar said through tight lips. "I demand the chance to win back what I have lost."

"Oh, you'll have your chance, though little good it may do you. The cards are running my way."

"Yes, that's one thing about card games. It requires a deal more luck than talent."

Wade ignored the insult, but it made him crow all the more loudly when he won the next two rounds as well. He could hear the arrogance in his own voice but he ignored the tiny protest of conscience underneath. Lazar was a cold fish, overbearing and ill-humored. Let him suffer.

The other players drifted away or stayed just to watch as the game began to grow into a contest between the two men. The bad feeling between them was almost as strong as the smoke in the low-ceilinged room, and it grew with each new gloating comment Wade made and each bitter reply from Lazar. Wade, by now half-drunk, grew louder and more affable with each win, while Lazar sank deeper into a sullen sulk, peering out at the man across the table with barely disguised malice.

Then, unexpectedly, Lazar won a hand. As Wade spread his full house on the table and reached to sweep the counters into his high pile, Simon shoved his hand away. "I think you'd better see this first," he said savoring the pleasure as he spread four queens on the deck.

Wade stared at the cards, almost without believing. "Oh well," he said dryly, loud enough for all to hear. "Even a blind hog will root up an acorn occasionally."

The color drained from Lazar's face and he leaned menacingly toward Wade. "I beg your pardon."

Through his rum-soaked stupor Wade was a little taken aback at the man's reaction. "Just an old country saying," he muttered.

"Are you accusing me of cheating?" Simon's voice was as cold as his eyes.

"Who said anything about cheating? On the contrary, I only mentioned the law of averages."

"I resent your words, sir."

"And I demand the right to win back what I've lost."

"For heaven's sake," Swinton said at Wade's shoulder. "Both of you have been playing so long you don't know what you're saying. Come on, Captain. Leave this game and go home. You've had too much to drink and you've certainly won enough off these people. Let's go."

"In a minute. In a minute," Wade said, settling back in his chair. "Just a few more rounds."

The game went on with Wade losing the next two hands, one to Lazar and another to the one remaining man on his right. It began to appear that his luck had deserted him, and for the first time he began to notice the pounding in his head and the way the smoke smarted his eyes. Perhaps it was time to go.

Another two lost rounds and Wade tossed in his cards and collected his winnings. He lingered for a while at one of the tables near the door where Swinton introduced him to two planters from Christ Church, then pulled on his coat to go. He ambled out the door and down the steps where he missed his footing and stumbled against the man in front of him, nearly knocking him down. He was about to apologize when he saw it was Lazar again, turning on him furiously.

"Are you too drunk to walk?" Lazar snarled.

"Better men than you are not allowed to call me drunk," Wade replied angrily at the man. Lazar swung his fist at Wade's chin, and as the other men in the street cleared a place around them, both of them began pummeling the other.

"Stop it!" Swinton cried, wading in to separate them before they could do any real damage. He yanked Wade aside and pulled out a handkerchief for him to dab at a slight cut on his lip. Lazar stood back, his suit was torn in one small place and rumpled badly but otherwise he was not hurt. Now, Swinton thought, if he could just get the Captain away before he really went at the man.

Grabbing Wade's arm Swinton pulled him back down the street toward the public buildings. "Come along, Captain," he said smoothly. "You can sleep at my place if we can't find a carriage to get you home. Good night, Mister Lazar."

Behind them Simon watched silently as Swinton, with Wade leaning on his shoulder, disappeared into the darkness. Murderous hatred filled his soul. From the first time he met him he had thought this popinjay Confederate was contemptible, but now there was open insult to add to vague dislike. The Captain would pay for this night. He was not sure when or how but he would pay someday. The first step in that retribution would be to carry off his so-called wife. Up until now, taking Selene with him to England had seemed simply a practical way to allow them both to serve their mutual cause. Now it became a burning obsession. He would see to it that Selene left, oh yes. And he would see, too, that these absurd negotiations were a failure. They would have been anyway, but by the time he was finished there would be not a shred of a chance left that they would succeed.

Captain Kinsolving would find that Simon Lazar was a man to be reckoned with.

The square in front of the Public Buildings was as crowded

as Selene had ever seen it. To the side, in the Careenage, three ships sat in dry dock to have their bottoms scraped and caulked. Their huge bulks had a forlorn air, like spinsters at a party, out of their natural element, as foreign to the congenial business of the market as Selene felt herself.

She stopped at a pungent booth ladened with sea urchins, dolphin meat, and assorted other fish right off the boats, and glanced behind to see that her ever-present shadow had paused as well. Not that Gurda was even pretending to examine the contents of the tables around her. Her dark eyes bored into Selene with the concentration of a snake mesmerizing its victim.

Not yet, Selene cautioned herself. Just a little way farther to go. She was helped by the crowd, that thick, milling clutch of bodies that blocked her now and then from the native woman's view. She could sense without seeing how Gurda, taller than most women, raised herself even higher, straining to keep sight of Selene's chip bonnet. And then, when she feared she might lose Selene altogether, moving closer, following Selene at a pace of two booths instead of the usual four.

It was all Selene needed. She paused beside a few more tables, cursorily examining their wares, each one bringing her nearer the draper's shop, then turned in exasperation and stalked straight up to the startled native woman.

"I am sick to death of being hounded like this!" she exclaimed angrily. "Get away from me, do you hear! Go home."

Gurda cast anxious glances at the people around them, staring at the lady who was suddenly so oblivious to the scene she was creating.

"So sorry, Missy, but I do what Masta tell me. He say to watch."

"Does that mean you have to follow every step I take? Am I never to have a moment's respite? It's like . . . like having the devil himself stalking me every hour of the day."

She could see that hit home. Gurda's tiny eyes were white slits in her grim face. Left to her own devices she would have gladly dealt with Selene in her own way, but duty was stronger. "Sorry, Missy, but Gurda do what Masta say."

It must have cost her something to contain that fierce, burning rage. Good enough, you black devil, she thought with satisfaction. But she deliberately pouted like a spoiled child railing against leading strings. "Well, stay out of my sight then. I don't want to see you at all, do you hear? If I do, I shall complain to the Master in words that won't do you any good at all. I have some influence, you know, and I shall see that it is used against you."

The native woman shrugged, but Selene could detect a slight pulling back even as she stood there facing her. That was all she needed. Angrily striding ahead, she made one more perusal of a booth filled with native baskets and glanced behind furtively. Sure enough, Gurda had moved back some distance, not out of sight, of course, but far enough away to satisfy Selene.

In front of the draper's shop she hesitated as though unsure whether to enter, then casually walked up the two low steps to the open door. The shop had a large window across the front, allowing Selene to glance up at Gurda across the street while she stood examining lengths of silks the pleasant proprietor, a Scotsman with a cheery round face, laid in front of her. After five minutes of this she inched her way to the far end of the counter where a cloth curtain hung over a doorway leading to the back of the shop. The owner left her and crossed the room to climb a ladder and pull down more lengths from well-stocked shelves.

"Well done," a whispered voice spoke from behind the curtain. Selene breathed a sigh of relief at recognizing Simon's voice and inched a little closer to the curtain, all the while fingering a lovely rose brocade satin bolt on the counter.

"At least she didn't follow me into the shop, as she certainly would have if I hadn't made that scene."

"Where is she now?"

"Across the street, watching the door. She can see me very clearly."

"As long as she doesn't see me, we're safe."

"What about him?" Selene whispered, nodding toward the owner.

"He's been sufficiently bribed. Don't wory about him. Now listen closely, we don't have much time. The ship will be leaving a week from today."

She hesitated. "So soon."

"There is a ball in the Public Buildings that night. I assume you will be there."

"I don't know. Wade hasn't said anything."

"Then make sure he does. You say it. But be at that ball. Bring along the things you want to take with you, but not too much or obviously he'll suspect something's up. Can you take that serving girl into your confidence?"

"Matilda? I think so."

"You'll need a maid on the trip anyway. Let her bring what you want to take in that night. But not too much, remember."

"What about Gurda?"

"I'll take care of Gurda. You just be there and be prepared to leave."

"But Wade? He's very clever, you know. If he even has the least suspicion—"

"He won't. Has he seen you with me since that first call I made? Haven't we managed to meet without anyone knowing? You'll have to buy something here today as you have in the past. It must appear to be just a shopping expedition."

Selene held the cloth up to her, then laid it aside, and picked up a bolt of pale gray silk, draping a corner of it over her arm. "Gurda probably believes I am the most frivolous woman she's ever seen," she whispered to Simon.

"Let her. She probably thinks all white women are just like you. The more you can convince her you have fluff in your head the better. We want no suspicions. Especially now."

"Because we're leaving?"

"That, yes, and also because these negotiations are falling apart. I've had word from England confirming my suspicions. This whole thing is a charade, a cover for the real negotiations that are going on in London. There is a second Southern delegation there now, as well as an extremely distinguished Northern one."

"But . . ." She wanted to ask why this elaborate ruse, but she knew this was not the time nor the place for long explanations. It surprised her that Simon, a man she still thought of as a government clerk, would have access to such information. He must have more influence than she ever suspected.

"Do the Confederates here know this?" she whispered.

"No. Not yet. And they must not know until the very last moment. Go now across the room and look at what he's laid out, before that woman begins to wonder why you're over here so long."

Selene picked up the gray silk to take with her. "Will I speak with you again?"

"Not until the ball. Be ready."

"This is a lovely color, Mister McCray," she said loudly, walking across the room with the cloth still draped over her arm. "Do you have any ribbons to match it? Or lace, perhaps?"

As she rode home later in the carriage with her parcels piled beside her, she thought back on what Simon had said and was filled with a strange mixture of elation and distress. It was exhilarating to think of having her freedom at last and to think of going to England. It served Wade Kinsolving right to have her flee his grasp after the way he had used and manipulated her. And yet, she recalled the strained, disappointed lines of his face, so obvious these last few weeks. He had come here expecting to win a great coup for his country and instead . . . But that was foolish. This treaty, if it had been negotiated, would have been a disaster for the Union. It had to fail and she ought to be glad that it had.

But why were the British stringing the Southerners along this way? Did the government in Washington know about the other Southern delegation in England? Surely Simon would have told them if they had not heard it from their other spies. Suddenly she felt certain that Simon Lazar, with his usual efficiency, had done his part in discrediting the Southern ministers, Wade, George Weston, and Major Gorham. It would be so like him. There may have been some hope in the beginning that these talks would succeed, but with Lazar's arrival on the scene, that hope had never stood a chance.

She ought to be glad—she was glad. The tiny voice that somewhere in the back of her mind exclaimed, "Poor Wade" must be stifled once and for all. Once she got away from this island the world was hers for the taking and she intended to enjoy it!

4 BESTSELLING HISTORICAL ROMANCES BY YOUR FAVORITE AUTHORS CAN BE YOURS, FREE!

Kensington Choice, our newest book club now brings you historical romances by your favorite bestselling authors including Janelle Taylor, Shannon Drake, Rosanne Bittner, Jo Beverley, and Georgina Gentry, just to name a few! Each book is filled with passion, adventure and the excitement of bygone times!

To introduce you to this great new club which is part of Zebra Home Subscription Service, we'd like to send you your first 4 bestselling historical romances, absolutely free!   And once you get these 4 free books to savor at home, we'll rush you the next 4 brand-new books at the lowest prices available, as soon as they are published.

The way the club works is that after your initial FREE shipment, you will get our 4 newest bestselling historical romances delivered to your

doorstep each month at the preferred subscriber's rate of only $4.20 per book, a savings of up to $7.16 per month (since these titles sell in bookstores for $4.99-$5.99)! All books are sent on a 10-day free examination basis and there is no minimum number of books to buy. (And no charge for shipping.) Plus as a regular

subscriber, you'll receive our FREE monthly newsletter, *Zebra/Pinnacle Romance News*, which features author profiles, contests, subscriber benefits, book previews and more!

So start today by returning the FREE BOOK CERTIFICATE provided. We'll send you 4 FREE BOOKS with no further obligation: A FREE gift offering you hours of reading pleasure with no obligation...how can you lose?

*We have 4 FREE BOOKS for you
as your introduction to
KENSINGTON CHOICE!
To get your FREE BOOKS, worth
up to $23.96, mail the card below.*

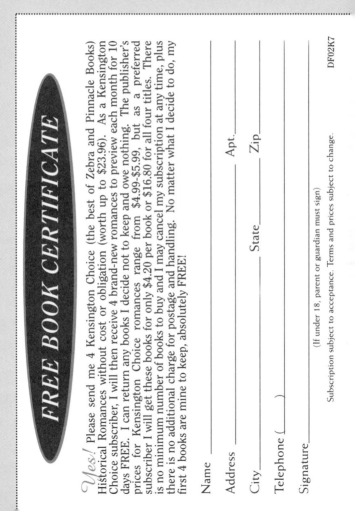

FREE BOOK CERTIFICATE

Yes! Please send me 4 Kensington Choice (the best of Zebra and Pinnacle Books) Historical Romances without cost or obligation (worth up to $23.96). As a Kensington Choice subscriber, I will then receive 4 brand-new romances to preview each month for 10 days FREE. I can return any books I decide not to keep and owe nothing. The publisher's prices for Kensington Choice romances range from $4.99-$5.99, but as a preferred subscriber I will get these books for only $4.20 per book or $16.80 for all four titles. There is no minimum number of books to buy and I may cancel my subscription at any time, plus there is no additional charge for postage and handling. No matter what I decide to do, my first 4 books are mine to keep, absolutely FREE!

DF02K7

Name _____

Address _____ Apt. _____

City _____ State _____ Zip _____

Telephone ( ) _____

Signature _____

(If under 18, parent or guardian must sign)

Subscription subject to acceptance. Terms and prices subject to change.

4 FREE
Historical
Romances
are waiting
for you to
claim them!

(worth up to
$23.96)

See details
inside.....

KENSINGTON CHOICE
Zebra Home Subscription Service, Inc.
120 Brighton Road
P.O.Box 5214
Clifton, NJ 07015-5214

Ten

During the next two days Selene barely saw Wade. He came and went like a phantom, arriving home after she had gone to bed and leaving the next morning before she was awake. She vaguely recalled him moving stealthily around her bedroom, and once when she woke during the night she found him sleeping beside her, restless and murmuring in his dreams.

Then it was Sunday and Selene rose, washed her face, and combed her hair, then put on her coolest dress since the weather was very warm. She found Wade downstairs at the breakfast table, pushing kidneys and eggs around on his plate, still undressed.

"I thought I might drive to church at Holetown," Selene said as she took her place at the table. "Would you like to accompany me?"

"No, thanks. I don't feel very worshipful at the moment."

"Papa used to say that was when we should go to church, not when we felt good about ourselves or the world."

He looked up at her, his gaze like flint. "Spare me Papa's wisdom. I'm not in the mood for it."

Selene felt some of the brightness go out of the day. "Whatever else you're not, you're certainly in a foul mood. I'm sorry I asked."

"You seem to be busy enough with your own pursuits. Go

without me. No one will wonder at it. People are accustomed to seeing the handsome Mrs. Kinsolving without her husband."

"Now that's not fair. When are you ever here to accompany me anyplace I want to go? You're always at the Public Buildings or their extension, Ploverman's Tavern, drinking with your cronies. It's not my fault you never come home."

"I might come home more often given a little encouragement to do so."

"I don't believe you. You have nothing on your mind but those foolish talks. Besides, we never tried to pretend this was a real marriage. I've kept my end of the bargain."

Furiously she dug her fork into her plate, all the satisfaction she had felt at the lovely morning having fled. Wade threw his napkin on the table and rose to stalk to the window, staring out at a Barbadian golden apple tree without seeing its beauty. He was all at once filled with such a rage toward her that it frightened him. With her long golden hair falling down her back, framing her white throat above the lacy bertha of her dress, she looked more beautiful than he had ever seen her. There was a vibrancy about her that gave color to her cheeks and a lively glint to her large eyes. Surely by now she should have got over her childish resentment at the way he had carried her off, and grown to care for him. He was so certain she would.

"You've kept it in public anyway," he said bitterly.

"That's all we agreed to. I paraded myself in front of your pompous 'Lords' and 'Sirs.' I was the gracious hostess for your interminable suppers. I did everything you asked to keep this hopeless charade of a treaty going, even though there was never a chance it could succeed."

Wade turned sharply to stare at her. "Hopeless charade? Never a chance to succeed? What do you mean by that?"

Selene felt her cheeks growing warm as she realized her mistake. She could only hope her indiscretion had not loosened her tongue too much as she concentrated on her plate. "There was never a chance that England would side with such a hopeless cause as the rebel Confederacy. The South cannot hope to win its independence as long as the Federal government is determined to hold the Union together. They don't have the resources to win this war."

"You seem to know a great deal about it. What makes you so certain."

"Common sense. Anyone who knows anything about America can see that the South could never survive as a separate nation. It relies too much on the mills and factories of the North."

She did not at all like the intent way he was studying her. There was suspicion and hostility written all over his face, plus something even more worrisome—the suggestion of a light dawning.

"I've often wondered," he said in measured tones, "how it is the British ministers seem to know so much about what goes on in Richmond, even before the members of our delegation are aware of it. Every proposal they put forward is presented as if they know exactly what the reaction of President Davis and his cabinet will be, no matter what we say."

Selene decided to face him head on. "Well, you can't suspect me. I don't know any more than you do. We arrived together on this island, you know."

"Not you perhaps. But you have some very suspicious friends. That Lazar fellow for one. A scurvy journalist if ever I saw one. It wouldn't surprise me at all to learn that he was actually a spy, carrying letters back and forth between Virginia and Barbados."

"Simon Lazar is not my friend. I've told you before I hardly know him. Even if he were a spy, I wouldn't be aware of it. He's hardly going to confide in me."

"Oh yes. I've heard that before."

Selene slammed her fork down on the table and rounded on him. "What do you want from me! Have I got to vouch for every acquaintance I run into, every person I've met over the past ten years? I didn't ask to be brought here, you know. And I certainly didn't volunteer to be your wife. My views on this terrible war were never a secret—in fact, if I remember rightly, that is why you dragged me along in the first place."

She felt near to tears and, in a futile effort to prevent them, laid her elbows on the table and buried her head in her hands until she could regain control. It was anger, surely, but it was fear, too. Fear that she would betray everything by her strong emotions.

She never saw him move until she felt him standing behind her, bending over her hair. She felt his hands, the fingers firm as iron, stroking her neck. There was nothing gentle in his touch.

"Yes, you've done your part," Wade said in a voice low but dripping with sarcasm. "Even in bed you've played your part very well." His fingers closed around her throat and Selene stiffened. She had only meant to turn his mind from Simon, but suddenly fear of him replaced her calculated fury. She held herself very still, afraid to make any quick moves, and beginning to wonder if he was sane.

Wade's falsely soothing voice, so in contrast with his forceful grip, went on as his fingers tightened around her throat. "Who could ask for a more passionate wife, a more loving companion?" One hand broke away and slid downward underneath the gauzy fichu of her dress. Selene closed her eyes with relief as she felt his fingers slip beneath the fabric to close around her breast. Wade bent his head, his breath hot on her neck. "My dear, Yankee wife . . ." With his free hand he grasped her hair, pulling her head sharply back. She caught her lower lip between her teeth, determined not to cry out. His lips roamed her face, his tongue traced a pattern on her smooth flesh. "So loyal, so responsive, so hot-blooded . . ."

Twisting around he caught her head in the crook of his arm and closed on her lips, forcing them apart with his tongue. His hand kneaded her breast painfully, his body pressed her against the back of the chair. She struggled to wrest away from his lips but his tongue was a hot searing serpent in the cavity of her mouth.

Frantically Selene worked her arm up between his body and her own and shoved with all her might. It caught him off balance long enough for her to push him back against the table edge.

"Yankee mistress, more like. Let me alone!" she cried, twisting out of the chair. "You're nothing but an animal. A viper! I won't be mauled and forced like this!"

To her surprise he merely leaned against the table, folding his arms across his chest and laughed. "Conjugal rights only

196

apply when you wish it, I see. Very well, I won't bother you again."

"That would be a relief," she said, rubbing her neck. She felt a small sense of triumph until she remembered Simon's instructions. Lowering her voice, she moved back to the table keeping a distance between them. "Please, let's not fight," she said trying to sound conciliatory. "I know I haven't done everything the way you wanted, but I have tried. And I've even enjoyed some of it."

"I'm thrilled to hear it."

"The gowns, the shopping, dressing up—that sort of thing."

"Well, that's something, at least. And you did look very handsome in your finery—I'll say that. All right, my Yankee wife. Let's play the charade out to the end. But I'll leave you to 'worship' for both of us."

He moved toward the door, his shoulders a little lower than they were before.

"Wade," Selene stopped him. "The ball next week in Bridgetown. Can we go?"

"Why? Another new gown?"

"Well, I did find a lovely length of gray silk when I was in town last week. It would look so pretty with the ruby necklace."

"Gray silk. Oh hell. Why not. I can think of nothing I want to do less right now than make merry with our friends from Great Britain, but if you want to go, go we shall."

He went out, closing the door behind him, discouragement in every step. Selene waited until she was certain he was on his way upstairs then slumped into the nearest chair. Soon. Soon there would be no more of this subterfuge. Soon her life would be her own again. She realized her whole body was trembling and steadied herself against the table's edge.

Soon!

It was a beautiful dress and Selene knew she would have felt like a princess in it had circumstances been different. Mlle. Laurent had worked her own fingers and those of several of her seamstresses to the proverbial bone in order to finish it in time

197

for the Queen's birthday ball, and when it was finished she thought she had never produced a more lovely creation. The gray silk had a faint rose tint to it which was set off with the palest artificial tea roses and deep rows of gray lace exquisitely worked. Matching roses cascaded in a crescent among Selene's curls. With the rubies gleaming like fire at her throat and a pale pink lace shawl draped around her shoulders, even she felt she had never looked so beautiful.

And yet she worried all the way into Bridgetown, sitting silent and morose next to Wade in the carriage. Would Matilda be able to carry out the plans they had gone over so carefully so many times? She was certain of Mattie's loyalty to her, but the growing friendship the girl had developed with Hawke worried her. Mattie had sworn she was willing to follow Selene to the ends of the earth if need be, but the proof was in the pudding, and if she failed to carry out her part tonight, their whole plan might be jeopardized.

"That time with Hawke was only a little flirtation," Mattie had sworn to her. "Just something to pass the time while you were always out shopping."

Selene rearranged the shawl over her arms and around her shoulders and stared out into the dark night. Pray Mattie was telling the truth and a flirtation was all it was. One word of this to Hawke and everything would be ruined.

All she had to do was bring a portmanteau into town with the barest necessities for a journey. The lovely dresses would all be left behind except for the one she was wearing, for she refused to leave with anything more than the plain garments she had brought here. Her hand automatically went to her throat at the thought. The rubies were an exception. After all, they had been a gift. Wade owed her that much for keeping her part of their bargain. Once she was established in London, she would see that they were returned.

Wade noticed her gesture and seemed pleased that she was wearing his gift. "They look lovely with that dress," he said smiling down at her. "You should be a sensation tonight. Fine things become you and you them."

"Thank you," Selene murmured. There were so many things she might liked to have said, but she was afraid to open a conversation. One thing might lead to another and that was a risk she refused to take. She wanted him to know that she was not ungrateful for all he had given her, but it was better to let things between stay at this strained, cool level. Besides, it was his fault for bringing her to this island against her will in the first place. She must never lose sight of that.

The square was still crowded when they rolled up, filled with other people arriving at the same time, decked out in their finery and surrounded by the native population, watching in fascination. Lanterns gleamed from every post and were strung on festive strands across the streets. The wooden-balconied buidings were ablaze with light and from every open window and door the sound of fiddles and pianos could be heard. The light on the water of the Careenage glimmered with all the brilliance of a hundred moons. Wade hopped out to hand Selene down and tucked her arm protectively over his as they went up the low steps together. The public rooms on the first floor were mobbed but it was a comfort to Selene to see how many people she recognized. Society in Barbados was small enough that everyone soon came to know one another, except for the visitors from the ships that came and went so frequently. Lord Candelby bore down on her right away, exclaiming over her gown and insisting she put him on her card for several dances. She was grateful that Wade stayed by her during the first hour, dancing several reels and a lancer and bringing her cooling cups of punch in between. He seemed to satisfy himself that she was not going to be able to do anything suspicious in this company and eventually he wandered off to visit with the others. Even then Selene did not lack for partners. Swinton claimed her twice. Mister Weston and Major Gorham took their turn, and she even managed to tolerate his Lordship's slavering familiarity by taking nothing he said seriously. It did not please him but it kept him at bay.

Only once did she see Simon Lazar. He stopped briefly by her chair where she was fanning herself after a robust waltz to pay his respects. Taking her hand he bent over it to whisper, "Midnight, on the quay."

Selene caught Wade's eyes on them from across the room. "Good evening, Mister Lazar. I hope you are enjoying the dancing," she said loudly, then whispered, "Suppose I can't get away then?"

Simon straightened to look the room over, his fingers on his watch fob. "Dancing is not one of my favorite pastimes, Mrs. Kinsolving, but I do enjoy seeing the ladies looking so beautiful. You will excuse me, I'm sure," Very politely he bent toward her again, whispering, "I'll wait twenty minutes. No more."

From across the room Selene saw Wade watch Simon walk away, obviously relieved at the very formal and brief exchange. Midnight! How was she going to arrange to slip off without exciting his suspicion? Several excuses churned in her mind but she decided to wait and do nothing until the time came, so fearful was she of making the wrong choice. As the clock moved relentlessly on, she grew anxious and more conscious every minute of where Wade was. And then, with twenty minutes to go, she turned at his hand on her shoulder. "There is a game starting in one of the rooms above and I've been invited to join," Wade said. "Would you mind going into supper now?"

Selene fussed with her shawl. "Why don't you go ahead. I can always get Swinton to take me into supper."

"You're sure you don't object?" he asked, with an obvious eagerness to get to the card table. She only hoped her relief was not too apparent.

"By all means, go ahead. I'll stop in later to see how you're doing."

"No, no. It's no place for ladies. You look as though you won't have any trouble finding partners. You're sure you don't mind?"

She smiled at him, acutely aware that it might be the last time she would ever see him and wanting to leave him with that much.

"I'm having a wonderful time. Please, go ahead."

To her surprise he leaned over and kissed her lightly on the cheek. It was such a strange, gentle gesture, so unlike him lately, that for a moment she feared he had seen right through her. "Enjoy yourself," he said, and she was certain he meant it. He left her to wander the hall back to the dancing rooms, and disappeared up the stairs where some of the offices had been converted into gaming rooms. Selene waited until he was gone and then hurried to the front hall. Both doors stood wide open to allow the breeze off the harbor to sweep the hall. Some of the gentlemen and a few women ambled up and down the steps, cooling off after the more hearty dances. She looked right and left, smiled at a few faces she recognized, and walked casually down the steps to the square along the front of the building.

She had not gone more than ten yards beyond the steps when a dark figure stepped directly in her path blocking her way.

"Masta say you not leave the party," Gurda hissed.

Selene caught back her exclamation of surprise. "Get out of my way!" she snapped. "What are you doing here. My God, did he order you to spy on me even here?"

"Masta say to watch and see you don't leave." The woman's grim face, dappled by the shadows of the lamplight, looked more evil than ever. Selene, in her frustration, longed to shove her aside, knock her down, anything to get beyond her. She forced herself to step back and speak languidly.

"It's beastly hot in there. All I want is a breath of air. He certainly would not object to that."

"Can't do, missy," Gurda mumbled.

"Now that's absurd. Look, you beastly creature, you can follow me if you want. Twenty paces behind. Just don't let me see you." It was the best she could do. Simon would have to deal with her when they reached the quay.

Gurda chewed on her thin lower lip, thinking this over. At length she decided Selene's suggestion was better than wading into that lighted palace to find Wade or forcibly preventing this foolish woman from going any farther and creating a nasty scene. She dropped back and Selene moved on, ambling slowly down the street toward the quay as though she had not a care in the world.

It was darker there, not really out of sight of the bright splash of light in front of the Government Buildings, but far enough away and dark enough not to be noticed. As she neared the water she spotted the mast of a small sloop below the stone walk, and the dark outline of a sailor's cap. Holding her breath,

Selene stepped into the pitch-dark overhanging shadow of a house that bordered the walk. She stooped to look back and saw Gurda behind her, feeling the woman's eyes boring into her back. Then, as she watched in horror, the black bulk of the woman was pulled suddenly down, kneeling in the street while a shadowy figure bent over her. There was a struggle, more perceived than actually seen, and a horrible gurgling sound. Selene, her skin crawling, ran back far enough to recognize Simon, shrouded in a dark cape, with one arm around the woman's throat. A shaft of silver gleamed in the light then disappeared and Selene recognized the flash of a knife. She reached out to grab him, crying out, and found her hand wet with blood.

"Go on. Get in the boat!" Simon hissed at her.

"What are you doing! My God, you don't . . ."

"Get out of here. This is none of your business. Get in the boat before it's too late."

She turned as though in a trance, wiping her hand violently on her dress. At the edge of the quay Matilda jumped up from the rocking boat, relieved to see her at last. Grasping Selene's arm she pulled her down into the gyrating sloop and tucked her dress around her.

"I'm that glad to see you, Miss Selene. I was so afeared you wouldn't come and then I don't know what I would have done."

Selene looked at her dumbly, as though she did not know where she was. "I've got everything here," Mattie spoke in a hurried whisper, "just like you told me. Everything I could bring, though it wasn't enough, I still say. And nobody saw me leave. Nobody at all."

The boat was set rocking again as Simon stepped into it and sat down across from Selene. At an unspoken command one of the two sailors began rowing away from the quay, pushing the boat out into the water. The other one picked up his oars as they reached the middle of the channel and they were soon slipping through the water toward the dark shape of the ship out in the roadstead.

*　　　*　　　*

The windows in the small gaming room were open to the night, but with the smoke of many cigars and pungent oil lamps, the air was stifling all the same. Wade played at piquet with the detached manner of someone who does not care whether he wins or loses and, indeed, expects to lose. It was in far contrast, he thought, to his exhibition at Ploverman's, when winning seemed the most important thing in the world—not so much for the money but to best the supercilious Simon Lazar. But then, he had drunk a lot more rum that night. He had come tonight mostly to humor Selene who wanted to show off her new dress, and in his mind this ball was simply something to get through until such time as she was ready to leave. The gaming room, he had hoped, would make a boring evening more spicy. Unfortunately it had not turned out that way.

"Your bid, Captain," Major Gorham on his right said, interrupting his thoughts. Wade studied the cards in his hand, keeping them close to his cravat even though they contained nothing worth hiding. Then he laid two of them face down on the table, after careful deliberation. Might as well not make it obvious that he was not in the game.

The hand was played out with Wade sitting back watching Jason Cable win again. The congenial planter was having a run of uncommonly good luck.

Major Gorham could not help but detect the discouragement on Wade's face. "Bound to change," he said in his practical way. "They can't go against you all evening."

"I don't know," Wade responded. "perhaps it's my lack of enthusiasm. I'd better retire from the field while my reputation is still intact."

"No, no. You can't do that yet—it's too early in the evening. Stay a little longer," the Major added as he began sorting the cards around the table.

Well, what did he have to lose? If he stayed long enough his luck was bound to turn, he thought, picking up the cards and splaying them out in his hand. Would that be true for the treaty, too, he wondered. Over the rim of the cards he glanced up to see Swinton Falk bending over Cable's shoulder. It took Wade a moment to remember why that seemed strange. "Did Selene go back to the dancing," he asked casually, laying three cards face down on the table.

"Selene? I don't know. I haven't seen her for the past hour or so."

"Why, you took her into supper, didn't you? She said she was going to ask you."

Swinton had to tear his concentration away from Cable's hand—a startling combination of aces, kings, and jacks. "She must have asked someone else. Although, come to think of it, I did not notice her in the supper room either. But perhaps she went in before me."

A cold pricking sensation moved up Wade's neck. Though he told himself he was probably being foolish, he laid all his cards on the table and pushed his chair back. "Gentlemen . . ."

"You can't leave now," Cable exclaimed. "Finish the hand, sir, at least."

"Swinton will finish it for me," Wade called back over his shoulder. "He can't help but have better luck."

Anxiously he searched the ballroom below, taking note of every couple on the floor and the casual spectators sitting along the wall. No sign of a gray dress or golden hair with pink flowers. With a strange sensation in his stomach he moved on to the supper room, bright with light, the long main tables festooned with flowers and groaning under every imaginable kind of dish and confection. Smaller tables were set around the room and out on the terrace, visible through the open doors. Wade searched them all, moving on to the terrace, his concern growing as he found no sign of Selene. Stepping quickly down the terrace steps, he made a cursory tour of the gardens in the rear of the building and then, certain that she was not in the house, went back through the main hall to the entrance.

"Did a lady in a gray dress with pink flowers come this way," he asked one of the liveried footmen. The man thought he recalled such a person only a short time before and pointed out the direction in which she had walked.

With his heart in his throat Wade went hurrying off to follow, asking himself why she would have gone this way unless there was some reason for it. It led to the darkened end of the street by the quay, not a place a lady would usually amble along to get a breath of air. It was too dark and too isolated for that. But perfect for someone who might want to slip away.

Was she meeting a lover? Did she have an assignation with Lazar, if not for love then for spying? The thoughts tumbled about in his mind as he began to run down the darkened street, his anger growing along with his fear.

He never saw the dark body lumped in the road until he stumbled over it. Reaching down he felt the hard tight kerchief on the head, the smooth face, the collar gummy with wet blood. He grabbed a shoulder and turned the body over until a thin shaft of light fell across the face.

Gurda! The white eyes open and staring, the mouth a gaping gash. Horrified, Wade dropped the woman and rose from where he knelt to hurry to the end of the quay. Out in the water he could make out the dark shape of a small boat, the oars on either side working furiously with the tide. And far out, where the moon silvered its top masts, a ship, already in the stages of unfurling its sails for its journey into open water.

He knew Selene was in that boat. He could not see her, but he didn't need to. She was going from him and, unless he was able to commandeer another ship quickly, there as no chance of bringing her back. He heard a loud exclamation behind him as two of the startled footmen stumbled over Gurda's body.

"There's been a murder here," Wade snapped. "You'd better call the authorities."

One of the footmen went scurrying off, the other knelt, looking over at Wade. "Should we get the harbor police too, sir?"

The boat, now a tiny black dot on the sheen of the water, had nearly reached the ship. Another sail went furling out, rocking the large vessel to its leeward side.

"No, I don't think so," Wade said evenly. "it's too late for that now."

So she had finally beaten him and escaped. He had to give her credit for a kind of stubborn determination, if nothing else. Perhaps it was just as well. And if it hurt, well, that would go away in time. He'd be damned if he'd let it bother him.

The wind picked up a little fresher with every stroke that

carried the small boat farther out in the bay. As the waves grew choppier with the strong wind, Selene gripped the sides of the longboat and tried to steady herself against the blackness of the night and the churning darkness within. Her flesh began to crawl anew every time she thought of Gurda's bloody bulk lying so inertly on the cobbled street of the quay. Sitting just in front of her, Simon hunched in his dark cloak, a reminder of the flash of the knife at the native woman's throat. God knew she didn't like the old witch, in fact she resented and despised her. But murder . . .

The somber bulk of the ship loomed up before them almost before Selene realized they had reached it. The little boat bobbed about on the choppy water, churning stronger with every motion of the men within to fasten it to the ropes and harness the sling that would haul the women aboard. Selene forced Matilda to go first, even though the girl's white face was stark with terror in the pale moonlight. Her frightened whimpering was clearly heard above the whistling wind as her form disappeared in a low swinging arch into the darkness. The sling returned to the swaying boat, yet still Selene lingered. Simon watching her assumed it was fear that held her back.

"It's perfectly safe," he said with an irritating lack of concern. "You needn't be afraid. And I think you'd prefer it to climbing the ropes in this darkness."

Selene only looked at him without replying. Let him think she was frightened, she thought. She herself did not know why she hesitated so long, but certainly it was not from fear of the sling. Yet she could not stay in this boat indefinitely, and there was not the slightest chance that they would take her back to land this late in the game. She had made her decision long before and now she had to live with it. She tied her damp shawl around her waist and climbed into the contraption, little more than a canvas seat fastened with heavy, wet ropes. Her hands gripped the ropes so tightly the skin blistered as she bumped her way up the sloping sides of the ship. Beneath her a black void yawned as the longboat disappeared, while above she could make out the barest glimmer of a white face bending over the rail. She felt as though she was suspended in time and space, with all light, familiarity, and happiness gone from her, nothing left but strange hands reaching for her.

Then she felt the hands and they were real enough. They pulled her over the rail and dumped her onto the deck, then reached to haul her to her feet. She stood there, her dress dripping from the wet longboat and the damp air, above her head the snapping of the sails as they unfurled, the creak of the wince and ropes as the anchor was raised.

Lazar came climbing over the rail to stamp on to the deck, pulling his cloak around him, and yanking off his hat to smooth back his thin strands of hair, wet from the spray. Behind her Matilda inched close, her face white as she stared with huge eyes around the strange ship. Selene knew she looked awful— her lovely dress wet and bedraggled, her hair limp from the salt spray, the beautiful pale pink flowers dangling where they had not been lost altogether. A huge net came swinging over the rail and Selene recognized her portmanteau along with several other boxes. The passengers' luggage had come aboard.

Simon took her elbow and guided her across the deck to where a tall gentleman stood, dressed in the full regalia of a British sea captain. "This is Captain Andrews, Selene. He's the one you can thank for your escape."

Andrews removed his cap and bowed slightly. "Welcome aboard, Miss Sprague," he said in a cool voice. She had an impression of a very long, thin face with narrow eyes almost invisible under the imposing brows. She wanted to question Simon's use of the word "escape" in front of this stranger, but thought better of it. There was no telling what Lazar had told the Captain about why she was here, but she was fairly certain she'd learn what it was soon enough. It was a long way to England.

"I am most grateful to you, Captain Andrews," she said with as much dignity as she could summmon under the circumstances.

"I think most of your gratitude should be reserved for Mister Lazar here. You will excuse me if I get back to the matter at hand. Wind and tide wait for no man and both happen to be in our favor at the moment. Mister Lazar will show you where your quarters are to be."

Selene gave Simon a guarded look. "And where are my quarters?"

"You and your maid will have the small cabin next to mine. They are not spacious, but I think you will be comfortable enough. Would you like to go below now?"

"That might be a wise idea," Selene said, pressing a hand to her stomach as the ship gave a lurch. With the anchor raised and catching the wind, the slim vessel broke through the waves with the thrust of an invisible hand, and though Selene was seldom affected by the motion of the water, it might prove handy to let Lazar believe she was. She moved toward the hatch, relieved to know that at least she was to have her own cabin. No telling what that man might have told Captain Andrews, and she was not anxious to get back in the same awkward position as when she sailed into Barbados.

Yet at the open hatch with its dim lights below, she hesitated once again. Stepping to the rail she looked back at the thick blackness on the horizon that was Barbados, slipping away from them. Tiny lights, strung like miniature lanterns, were just visible, clustered around Bridgetown, the Careenage, the Government Buildings.

Had he missed her yet, she wondered. No, engrossed in a card game he would probably not know she was gone until early in the morning hours. And by then they would be well out into the Caribbean.

It was dark now, this place that would be forever imprinted on her memory as a place of sand and light, of shimmering bodies pressed against one another on rose sand, the warm waves lapping at their hot flesh . . .

She clutched her stomach again as a wave of nausea washed over her. A cold hand was laid on her shoulder, heavy against the thin fabric of her gown.

"It's all behind you now," Simon spoke low into her ear. "You can put it out of your mind. The degradation, the abuse, the blows to your principles, they are all falling away. You have a new beginning ahead, Selene. A new life. I intend to make it a wonderful one for you."

She wheeled around, turning on him. "You don't know what

you are talking about," she muttered, conscious of a wetness
on her cheeks. Were they tears or just the residue of the heavy
spray from the longboat cutting through the water. "I want to
go below."

"Of course. So much has happened. You are distraught. A
good night's rest is what you need."

She let him hand her down the hatch and lead her to her
cabin. It wasn't until he left her standing there, under the
swaying lantern in the center of the small room, that she
noticed the long, dirty smear of Gurda's blood on the skirt of
her gray silk dress.

Eleven

It turned out to be another of those cold, drizzly days when the very air seemed to press Selene down. The windows of the cab were flecked with moisture, not quire rain but close enough. The bricks of the road looked slick in the reflected light of afternoon street lamps, lit early to compensate for the darkness. It was the weather she found most difficult to get used to in London. It was such a difference from the warm, pristine brightness of Barbados—like going from daylight into a dim closet. Of course, the fact that it was winter didn't help. Yet, it was more than that. The constant dampness, the cold, and darkness seemed to seep into her very soul, chilling her spirit every bit as much as her body.

Selene slumped on the seat and pulled her kid gloves higher on her narrow wrists before slipping them into the warm depths of her beaver muff. The gray-streaked window pane reflected her mood, she thought. She would rather have stayed home with the dullest book ever written than attend yet another social at Melissa Belton's or, for that matter, at any of the popular London drawing rooms she had come to know so well since arriving in England. But Simon thought it was important for her to attend, and she supposed she owed him that much.

The coach gave a sudden lurch. She heard the horse's sharp whinny and her driver curse at being cut off by one of London's infamous hacks. Though the windows were closed, the rattle and racket of the streets was almost as loud as if she

210

had been sitting up on the perch next to Fenton, her driver. Iron wheels on cobbles and bricks, the interminable rumble of a hundred horseshoes on the pavement, the cries of vendors and urchins, and, over those, the angry expletives of outraged drivers—the cumulative noise was another of the things she had found hard to take after the peace and quiet of the island. There was an excitement about it all, she reasoned with herself, a sense of being caught up in the world's business that, at times, could be rather stimulating and even thrilling. But it was hard on the nerves. There were times when she would have given her soul to return to that sleepy, easy, warm lethargy of island living—that sandy cove with the silken water bathing her bare flesh . . .

Angrily she pulled her beaver pelisse around her shoulders. How useless to linger over the past. It was a waste of time when she had better and more profitable things to think about. Like making herself attractive and useful at Lady Belton's social this afternoon. She allowed herself a satisfied smile as she thought of how well she had done since arriving in London. She was a sought-after guest, with more invitations than she could accept. She had watched and studied and learned everything she could about how to act the lady of quality, even when she knew that her background did not include tripping among the fashionable set. Her careful grooming had paid off and now she moved with ease and aplomb among London's best people, picking up information which she could to pass along to Simon, meeting those men who held the fate of a nation in their hands, and to some small extent influencing them in their decisions.

And now, here she was, bound once more to a gathering of the elite and the influential, set upon making a contact with one Colin Huntworthy, a munitions agent from the midlands whom Simon thought a significant contact. Make a good impression, he had said. Well, again, she supposed she owed him that much.

She was so deep in her thoughts that she was not aware the cab had stopped until the door was pulled open.

"We're here, Mrs. Kinsolving," Fenton said politely, and reached to hand her down—no mean feat in her wide silk hoopskirt. "When would you like me to call back for you?"

Selene looked up at the Georgian front of the house with its exquisite white pediment and half-moon fanlight over the door. The long windows on either side twinkled with the lights within, an inviting contrast to the gray, sombre sky. "Why don't you wait, Fenton? I won't be too long."

"Very well, Madam," he touched the brim of his tall hat and climbed back up on the perch, while Selene hurried up the steps. He was a resourceful fellow and Selene knew he would find a way to get out of the dampness and yet still be waiting when she was ready to leave. She had no wish to be forced to make conversation any longer than necessary simply because her coach wasn't due back yet.

A stiff footman in full livery met her at the door and took her coat and muff, directing her up the stairs to the parlor. Through the open double doors she could hear a symphony of voices, accompanied by an obligato of tinkling glasses. She had to force herself into the room, hoping she would recognize some familiar faces. That was still an ordeal, though she had learned well how to mask her timidity with a dignified exterior.

She needn't have worried for Melissa, Lady Belton, saw her pause by the open doors and came hurrying over to squire her around the room. Most of the people there were unfamiliar to her, though she recognized a few she had met at other such functions. The most noteworthy of these was a Mister Grantham, an MP from Bucks and his long-faced wife, Mercy. Grantham was a garrulous fellow who gravitated to young pretty faces—not surprising, Selene thought, given the unsmiling grimness of Mrs. Grantham. He gushed over Selene for several minutes before Lady Belton was able to lead her on. She paused briefly near a large chair where Mrs. Teague, an obese matron whose whole life seemed to be made up of one social function after another, was majestically ensconced. Today she was accompanied by her daughter, Sophie, a girl Selene had heard so much about that she was interested in finally meeting the paragon in the flesh. It did not take her long to see that dear Mama had Sophie completely cowed, and Selene was grateful to murmur her respects and move on to Lawrence Sopher, Viscount Timms, the most pleasant young dandy and shallowest character she had ever met. He *was* entertaining however, and she was glad that Melissa left her there to be amused by his latest stories and escapades. The Viscount supplied her with tea and cakes and sat her on the brocade sofa near the long windows, next to a heavyset man whose round jowls belled out over his high starched collar. Once Lawrence Sopher left to replenish the cakes Selene turned to her companion and made some casual comment on the crowd and Melissa's socials.

"Not my thing, actually," he said rather brusquely, as though he did not appreciate having to pull himself out of his private thoughts. "The wife likes to come when we're in London. Went to school with Lady Belton, she did."

Something about the accent and his obvious uncomfortable demeanor caught Selene's intuition. "You don't live in London, then?" she asked, trying not to sound inquisitive.

"Good heavens no. We come down a few times a year so my Mrs. can have her season and I can conduct my business. I indulge her in it as long as I'm busy, but once that's concluded, it's back to West Riding for me. She usually obliges me by coming along."

"She sounds like a good wife."

She could see at once she had hit a nerve. He smiled, stroked his whiskers, and almost beamed. "She is that, if I do say so myself. That's her over there, gabbing away with that long-winded Mister Gratham."

Selene gave the obligatory inspection and compliment. In truth the lady, although plump and expensively though not fashionably dressed, had a sweet, cheery face and that suggested a docile and happy spirit. She probably was a very good wife. "What is your business, Mister . . ."

"Huntworthy. Colin Huntworthy, Miss. I deal in iron."

"I'm Selene Kinsolving," she said, extending her hand. She had grown so accustomed to having it kissed that it surprised her when he shook it heartily. Out of the corner of her eye she was relieved to see that Lawrance Sopher had been waylaid by Mrs. Teague with her daughter in tow. That ought to keep him occupied a while. "Iron works sounds so interesting. Do you make bridges, tools, that kind of thing? Did you help build the famous suspension bridge at Avon I've heard so much about?"

"No, we had nothing to do with that bridge. For the past few years we've been into munitions and keeping the army supplied. You'd be amazed, my dear girl, at the need there is around the world for guns and ammunition."

"Oh, I don't think I'd be too surprised. My own country right now is doing its share to create a demand. Of course, I think it's tragic, but men will fight wars."

"And artillery is the wave of the future. Wars are becoming more terrible all the time because of new and better ways to kill. It's too bad, but on the other hand, someone has to supply these madmen with the tools to destroy each other. I do it very well." He sat back, giving her a hard look. "I thought you were an American the moment you opened your mouth. Which side? Are you a Southerner?"

"No, sir, I am not, I hate this war but since it must be fought my fervent prayer is that the Union will hold together. Sometimes I wonder if that will be possible. We haven't done very well on the battlefield this past year."

"Oh, it will hold together right enough. I'm certain of it."

It was Selene's turn to give Colin Huntworthy an intensive once-over. "Why do you say that? Surely England's need for cotton is one of the strongest factors in the survival of the Confederacy. If and when she grants recognition—"

Colin Huntworthy laid a pudgy hand on her arm. "My dear girl, England's reliance on Southern cotton is a myth. The South likes to believe we depend on her supply, and once we did. But not now. That need had been slipping away even before this war began. We are developing our own supply in India—a short-strand cotton more suitable to our mills than the Southern variety. If the American South stopped production tomorrow, we *might* feel the loss, but we would survive. I am not so sure *they* would, however."

Selene thought of Wade's stubborn belief in the Southern way of life. "What do you mean?"

"Only that their whole system of cotton production was based on slave labor and world markets. If they lose both at once, it will mean a difficult adjustment. Perhaps even a whole new way of life. It will not be an easy thing to face."

214

Selene sat down her cup and saucer and realized with some surprise that she had not thought of the war that way. She had assumed that once the rebellion was over, life would go on as before. The slaves would be free, of course, earning a wage instead of being owned by other men, but in all other ways things would be the same. Now she wondered for the first time if that would be possible. It was a sobering thought.

"Were you ever approached by my country, Mister Huntworthy?" she asked. "The United States needs arms, too. Have they tried to purchase them from you?"

"Oh indeed, yes, though not as often as I wish. Very lucrative, those contracts."

"And would you agree to a contract even though the offer came from the wrong side?"

"Right and wrong sides, my dear, are a prerogative of your countrymen. I am in business. I am not hampered by such concerns. My interest is the health of my company."

"In other words, making a profit."

He gave her a searching glance. "That is a rather crass way to put it, but, on the other hand, it is correct. I have always found you Americans to have a disconcerting honesty about you."

Selene gave him a warm smile which she hoped hid her inner dislike. "I assure you most of my countrymen would feel exactly the same in your circumstances. I have very much enjoyed talking with you, Mister Huntworthy. I think my driver is waiting for me. If you will excuse me . . ."

He rose very solemnly and she saw with some surprise that he was shorter than she was. "It has been my pleasure, Madam," he said giving her a formal bow. Before he dropped her hand a commotion at the door drew them both around. A new arrival was being ushered into the room in a flurry of admiring welcomes with Melissa hanging onto one arm and several of the people standing nearby clustered around. He was a tall gentleman with a mane of white hair. He had his back to Selene but there was something vaguely familiar in the stiff stance. She felt her flesh begin to crawl.

"That's an imposing fellow," Colin said near her. "Don't think I've ever seen him here before. Do you know who he is?"

The gentleman turned his profile toward her and Selene felt

her fingers grope for her throat. "Oh, yes," she breathed. "That is Lord Candelby. I believe has has been out of the country recently. He must have just returned."

She saw Mrs. Huntworthy bearing down upon them and took advantage of it to slip away, hoping to ease her way out of the door before his Lordship made his rounds. It was almost unpardonable to leave without speaking to her hostess, and yet she felt she must get away before he saw her. She would make an excuse to Melissa later.

She almost made it. By keeping to the perimeter of the room and hiding as much as possible behind other guests, she almost got through the door before being seen. But Lord Candelby towered over most of the people there and he spotted her just as she reached the hall.

"Why, Mrs. Kinsolving," he called loudly enough to turn a few heads. "Why, don't run away, my dear, before I have a chance to say hello. Melissa, you didn't tell me this charming lady was going to be here."

"I didn't know you knew each other," Lady Belton gushed. "You're not leaving, are you, Selene dear? Why, the party's barely begun."

"I'm so sorry, Lady Belton, but I'm not feeling very well. A headache, I fear. You will excuse me . . ."

"She may but I shall not," Lord Candelby boomed. "We've so much to catch up on. You cannot imagine how dull Barbados was after you left. No sparkle at all. It was as much as I could do to stay on there, it all being so hopeless anyway."

In spite of herself Selene paused. "Hopeless?"

He took her arm, leering into her face, but lowering his voice. "Oh yes. Never a chance that we could conclude anything there. It had to be done here in London, you know. But we were reluctant to say so to those firebrands, your husband and his colleagues. Very pushy they were, if you don't mind me saying so. Very insistent. They simply did not want to believe we could not bring this thing to a head without taking the time required to get official sanctions. Finally had to give up the whole thing altogether."

"Is that why you came home?"

"Yes, that and the fact that I was beastly tired of sand in my food and sunshine all the time. All right for a while that, but not as a steady diet. But, my dear, what a marvelous surprise to find you here. I thought by now you would have gone back to America. I cannot tell you how delighted I am to see you again."

His fingers played a tattoo on her arm the whole time he spoke. She had forgotten his manner of looking at her as though he could eat her with a spoon and the unsettling effect he had upon her. "I really do not feel well, my Lord," she muttered, pulling away from his grasp. "You will excuse me, I hope."

"Only if you tell me where you are living, so I can pay my respects." His hand was like a claw on her arm.

"I am staying with Mister Lazar and his family at Great Ormand Street," she said reluctantly, ready to say anything that would get her away from Lord Candelby. He bent toward her again and she could catch the stale miasma of his breath.

"And I may call upon you?"

"Of course," she said. "Though I am certain you must have a busy schedule . . ."

"Ah, Mrs. Kinsolving, no schedule ever yet kept me from calling on a pretty lady." He leaned close and whispered, "Especially one who is no longer burdened with a husband."

Selene yanked her arm away and ran down the stairs. Throwing her coat around her shoulders she darted outside to see Fenton just drawing up with the coach. She threw herself inside and slammed the door shut. Only as it started off down the street did she realize she was hunched in the cab as far on the other side as she could get.

An hour later Selene sat in front of her mirror, staring at the stranger's face that peered back at her. What had she become since leaving Barbados? Who was this woman, her hair fashionably pulled back and caught in a chenille net, her large eyes outlined by dark circles, her cheekbones more prominent than ever, giving her a sleek, self-contained beauty?

The truth was she did not like this woman very much. It seemed that all that was soft and vulnerable before had grown cautious, wary, even hard. Is this what London had done to her?

She started at a sudden knock on her door. "Supper, Ma'am" the housemaid's voice came muffled through the heavy oak. Selene laid her head in her hands, dreading to leave the peaceful solitude of her bedroom for Mrs. Osborne's mindless chatter and Simon's spartan solemnity. She answered the maid and set about straightening her dress and smoothing her hair with resignation. She had made her bed and now she must lie in it. She had no one to blame for where she was but herself.

Supper was the usual meal—bland food poorly prepared. Letitia Osborne, her ribbons bobbing, constantly babbled on about where she had been that day, the people she had seen, and what was wrong with them all. Selene blocked her out and was grateful that Simon did not show up, kept late by his mysterious business in town, no doubt.

He came in just as the sweet was served, his lowering brows knit together in their customary expression of disapproval. Selene sat quietly while he complained about the food and the service, grateful that at least Mrs. Osborne had grown quiet when Simon appeared. She stole an occasional glance at him, as he cut his stringy beef and speared it into his mouth with the same ferocity and concentration he brought to everything, no matter how mundane. Not for the first time she thought that Simon always looked as though there was a vague unpleasant odor in the room, something not quite defined but definitely unpleasant. How could she have been so foolish as to throw in her lot with this man? Why had she trusted him? Perhaps, she thought absently, pushing her spoon around in her blancmange, it was not so much her trust of Lazar as it was her distrust of Wade. Either way, it seems she had lost.

"I'd like a word with you, Selene," Simon finally said, throwing down his napkin. Thus the general summoned the lowly private, Selene thought. A command, not a request.

"I'd like to have a word with you also," Selene said, trying to assert her own will to some extent.

"Mister Lazar, there are a few tradesmen to satisfy," Mrs. Osborne put in, in her obsequious way. "I try to put them off but they have become so insistent—you know how merchants

218

can be. Perhaps we might take some time this evening . . ."

"For God's sake, woman," Simon exploded, "don't I give you enough to manage your household bills? There is no more this month, I told you that last week, and I want a strict accounting."

Selene watched objectively as Letitia's face wrinkled with imminent tears. Her hands fluttered and she almost cringed in her seat. "My goodness, I only meant—that is, you see, things are so dear!"

Simon pushed back his chair and stood over her, for all the world like a school teacher berating a difficult child. "Perhaps if you devoted more time to running this house—the reason you were engaged in the first place, I might add—and less socializing among your frivolous and useless friends, these confrontations would not be necessary. A more careful woman could manage two households with the generous stipends I lavish on you."

"Well, really, sir . . ." Selene saw the tears rolling down her plump cheeks, fat and wet and so typical of the woman. Yet she felt no sympathy for Letitia Osborne. She had taken this position knowing well enough the kind of man she had to deal with. And she was free to leave any time she had had enough of him. Meanwhile he kept her in fine style. Simon was right. With a little care and forethought she would never have to face him at all.

And that's more than I can say, she added bitterly to herself as she followed Lazar into the small furniture-crammed parlor off the main hall.

He closed the doors, then went directly to a decanter of port sitting on the table near the cast-iron pot-bellied stove.

"Would you care for some?" he asked, not politely but more as an afterthought.

Selene sat stiffly on the edge of a tuffed plush sofa. "No, thank you." She folded her hands in her lap and waited while Simon, with glass in hand, leaned an arm on the marble mantel and studied her.

"Well, did you see him?"

"Mister Huntworthy? Oh yes. We had a very pleasant conversation."

"I don't care about how pleasant it was. What about information?"

"That too. He is in the munitions business as you thought, and he as much as said he would sell to anyone. Profit is more important than ideals, I think, was the way he put it."

Simon's thin lips rearranged themselves into a narrow smile. "Good. I thought as much, but I needed to be certain. You did well, Selene, as usual."

She leaned forward, gripping her hands. "Simon . . ."

"What is it you need?" he interrupted as if to forestall whatever she was going to say. "A new gown? A respite from too many social invitations? You know you have only to ask."

"You know very well what I want. I want to go home. I want to go back to America. How long do you intend to keep me here, fribbling my time away with these eternal teas and socials, trying to pick up a few shards of significant comment that you can use for God only knows what purpose."

"I don't know what you have to complain about," he said coldly, his eyes darkening. "You have been the toast of Society this season. New gowns, parties, foppish young men dancing to your every whim. Why most young women would sell their soul to be in your place, enjoying a London season."

Her frustration brought her out of her seat to pace the small room. "I don't want to be the belle of a London season. I've gone along with you on all this—pretending that ridiculous Osborne woman was your cousin, perpetrating the travesty of a close friendship between our families—all of it only because you promised that if I did, you would send me home again."

"May I remind you that the travesty as you so delicately put it, of a kinswoman in the house and an old family friendship, was solely to protect your reputation. How would it look otherwise? A woman leaving her husband to live with another man. Do you want people to think that you and I are lovers?"

"You know that is a lie!"

"Oh, we know it well enough, but the world would certainly jump to that conclusion."

"Then let me have my own house. Give me my freedom."

"My dear Selene, you are such an innocent. That would only lead to even harsher criticism. Far from being the toast of

London, you would become a social pariah."

"I don't think I would mind that any more than this."

"That is not very flattering to me," he said, his eyes like winter ice. Selene flushed, remembering how fierce his temper could be when aroused. "May I remind you," he went on, "that you have no money at all. Nor any means of livelihood."

"Oh, that's true enough," she cried angrily, turning on him. "The clothes on my back, the food on my table, the bed I sleep in . . ."

". . . the coach, the driver, the fancy gowns, the house, even that useless girl you insist on harboring."

". . . are all supported by you. Out of the kindness of your heart, I suppose."

"As will be your passage back to America when the time is right."

She stopped her furious pacing, throwing him a suspicious look. "That's another thing. Where do you get your money, Simon? How can *you* afford all this?" Her hand took in the well-appointed room. "A government clerk certainly could not manage to accumulate the kind of fortune needed to move in style in London society. And I've never seen you take a regular job since our paths crossed in my uncle's tavern."

His face was like a closed trap. "That is none of your concern. You are only asked to parade yourself attractively and keep your eyes and ears open. And for that you enjoy a very pleasant living."

"Pleasant living!" she could hear her voice rising in frustration but was powerless to stop it. "I hate it! I want to go home."

With a studied casualness Simon walked back to the decanter, his gesture dismissing her. "Tsk, tsk, Selene. You must be overtired tonight to be so wrought up. Perhaps you should omit some of these social affairs from your schedule. Take time each day for a little nap."

In a rage she ran at him, slapping his shoulder with her fist. He turned swiftly, grabbing her wrist in a painful vise, looming over her with a face dark with fury. Selene shrank back, expecting a blow, but Simon caught himself and dropped her arm, stepping back with rigid self-control.

"Don't ever do that again," he said through tight lips.

She fought to keep back her tears, determined not to appear another Mrs. Osborne. "What do you want with me, Simon? I'm useless here. Why won't you let me go back to America?"

When he spoke it was quietly, patiently, like a parent attending an idiot child. "My work here is not yet complete. When it is, you shall certainly go home to Virginia if you still wish it. Remember, Selene, you needed a friend and sanctuary in order to escape that loathsome Captain Kinsolving. I was pleased to provide both." He hesitated, watching closely the myriad of emotions so transparent on her face. "At least, you always said he was loathsome and that you wanted nothing so much as to get away from him. I take it that was the truth."

"He is loathsome. I hated him and I was grateful to leave him. But I thought we would go straight home."

"And we will. When the time is right."

Wearily Selene sat on the edge of the sofa again, her hopelessness obvious in the slump of her shoulders. Then she remembered Melissa Belton's social.

"You knew Lord Candelby would be there this afternoon, didn't you?"

"I had heard he was in London, yes. Then I ran into him yesterday at the House of Lords."

"Why is he here? Did the talks in Barbados end?"

"They were finally dissolved just before Christmas."

"And Wade?"

"Oh, he long ago left for Virginia to make his contribution to Southern idiocy on the battlefield. Considering those battles fought since we sailed from Barbados—Antietam, Seven Days, Fredericksburg—it would not surprise me, my dear, to learn that you are a widow, not a runaway wife."

He seemed to take satisfaction in the thought. Selene looked away, unable to meet his eyes. Her own reactions were so mixed. All that she had read about those terrible battles—the horrendous casualties, the horror of the field, the inefficient Union commanders, outwitted time and again by Confederate generals—only added to her sense of hopelessness and urgency to be home again. And if Wade was dead, well, it would change so much for her.

"All right, I'll try to be patient," she said with resignation. "But there is one thing I refuse to do. I want no part of buttering up to Lord Candelby, so don't ask me to."

"I hope that does not preclude a purely social invitation since he made a point of inviting us to join a party he is taking to the opera a week from Saturday. It's a new work by that Italian fellow—Verdi something."

"Guiseppi Verdi. He's only one of the best known and most famous operatic composers in the world!" Her sarcasm was deliberate and she was pleased when he did not fail to notice it. But it seemed he was determined to be patient with her tonight.

"Forgive my ignorance. Opera is not one of my more happy pastimes, as you well know. However, I do not wish to offend his Lordship in any way, so I think we should accept with grace. I need not remind you of the very delicate negotiations going on right now between Great Britain and the Union. It is imperative that they succeed."

"I don't see what Lord Candelby has to do with them. Apparently all those months he spent in Barbados were nothing but a mask for the real work being pursued in London."

Simon gave her a sharp glance. "Can I count on your co-operation then? You might even enjoy the evening—you spend enough of them at the opera without me. It indicates a certain fondness for the form."

"I like it well enough. Oh, very well. I'll go and I'll be pleasant to him but that is all. And only this once. I suppose I have to, if I want to get home again," she added under her breath.

For several days after her conversation with Simon, the atmosphere in the house was that of a strained truce. Partly to escape the suffocating tension, and partly because it had become her habit of late, Selene took the carriage to Fleet Street where one of the dingy newspaper offices made a practice of displaying a paper from Washington City. It always cheered her, though it was more than a month old. Even the short items for houses to let gave her a sense of home, the addresses were so immediate and familiar.

The day was cold with a thin glaze of snow on the ground. The wind cut like a knife through her heavy fur half-cape and slithered its icy fingers up under the wide circle of her wool skirt. Boots, muff, a warm jacket of blue merino piped with black velvet—none of them helped much against the damp seeping chill of an English winter.

Selene peered through the dirty window, straining to make out the tiny print. The columns on the front page were full of the promise of yet another campaign and made scathing mention of the commander of the Army of Northern Virginia—R.E. Lee. Descriptions of the hospitals chilled her as much as the wind. A brief reprisal of one of Mrs. Lincoln's festival balls sent a wave of homesickness washing over her.

In spite of the deafening noise of the street behind her, for a few moments Selene was transported away from the sooty gray light of London to the bright, warm familiar world of the city in which she had lived most of her life. She bent close to the window, uncaring of the pedestrians on the walk, and did not see the young boy until he careened into her, nearly knocking her off her feet. Grabbing for the brick sill, she managed to steady herself before she could slip in the sleet underfoot.

"Sorry, Ma'am," he said quickly and darted on. She might have thought nothing of it except for the sudden lightness of her arm. Where her reticule had been the strings fell onto her skirt, cut neatly and cleanly through.

"Stop that boy," Selene cried, outraged to have been the victim of such a young thief. "Stop him, someone! He's a thief."

If the child had darted into the street among the clutter of horses and cabs, he would have been lost almost immediately. But he seemed intent on reaching the steps not far ahead that led to a warren of dark alleys along the river. Selene ran a few steps before realizing she would slip and fall if she tried to catch him. She clung to the building while far ahead a heavyset man in a tall beaver top hat went running for the boy. The crowd thinned and she saw that he had caught him, neatly slung under one arm like a squealing pig. The man made his way back to her and deposited the squirming boy on the pavement, one hand firmly gripping the shabby collar of his coat.

"I believe you wanted this urchin, Madam," he said in a bellowing voice that rang a chord deep in Selene's memory.

"He stole my purse," she said, tearing her eyes from the stranger to look over the child. "Why, he can't be more than seven years old."

"They start 'em young in London, my lady. Here now, you filthy brat. Give the lady back her money."

"Ain't got it," the child said with something close to a snarl. His face was grimy, but what touched Selene were the eyes, large and piercing like two anthracite coals in the pale, taut oval of his face. His hair was long and greasy, his clothes tattered and ill-fitting, and there was a gap of cold white skin between the hem of his ragged trousers and the gaping tops of his boots. All at once she felt sorry he had been caught.

"Don't add lying to your sins, you dirty blighter." With a quick swing of his arm the big man upturned the boy and shook him, sending the reticule clanging to the sidewalk.

"Stop!" Selene cried. "Set him down." For the first time she looked closely up at the large man who had come to her rescue. Surely she had seen that broad face with its ribbon of whiskers and thick brows before. And that voice. It was so familiar, yet it did not belong here in this setting.

"But Madam, he tried to rob you," the fellow said. "Surely you're not going to allow sympathy to overcome your sense of justice."

"Look at him," Selene said quietly. "He must be freezing in this weather in those clothes. And starving. When was the last time you had a decent meal, boy?"

The child glared at her, his lips stubbornly clamped together.

"You do want me to call the constables, don't you? Be fair, madam."

"No. Don't call the police. I have my purse back, thanks to you. I won't press the matter any further. Here, child. Take this," she added, reaching into her purse for a shilling and pressing it into the boy's hand. "Buy yourself something to eat."

Her benefactor's heavy chin fell downward. "Madam! Will you reward this thief for stealing from you!"

"And this," Selene continued, pulling her muffler from around her neck and laying it around the child's thin shoulders. "Now go, and try to find a way to live without taking what belongs to others."

The boy hesitated just long enough to look at the man behind him and be sure he was not still gripping his shoulders. Then without a word he darted away, throwing the end of the muffler around his neck as he headed for the steps once again.

"Madam, I cannot believe what I have just seen. Not a word of gratitude or thanks! Running off to steal from someone else. You don't really believe your kindness will turn him from his evil ways, do you?"

"Oh, no," Selene said sadly. "In fact, he looked as though he had only contempt for my weakness. But I don't care. At least I know one less child in London will go hungry tonight."

The man sighed, shifting his own muffler around his thick neck. "I fear you are wrong there, too. He will probably have to hand your largess over to some worthless adult who will use it to purchase gin. Ah, but you have earned a star in your crown today, nonetheless. 'The quality of mercy is not strained. It falleth like the rain out of the heavens . . .'"

Selene looked up at him, startled. "Now I know where I've seen you before. In a coach on the Norfolk road."

"Surely, I am an American, eh? I hear that a lot over here. And you—I thought there was something familiar about you. Unfortunately I don't seem to recall our meeting before, but allow me to remedy that now." He doffed his tall hat and bowed very formally. "Mordacai Granberry, Madam. At your service."

"Of course. You are the actor who rode with us to Norfolk that night in '61. Don't you remember? You stopped us on the road and rode in our coach to the town."

He studied her, frowning. "I recall the ride, of course. Unusual circumstances. Down on my luck right then. As you can see it has improved somewhat now."

"Come walk with me, Mister Granberry," Selene said, slipping her arm through his. "I am so happy to see someone from home. My coach is waiting at the end of the street and I would be honored to drop you anywhere you are going. I'm not too surprised that you don't remember me, but I recall you very clearly."

226

"I do seem to recall a lady in the coach that evening, but she was rather fast asleep the whole time and it was dark. I vaguely remember exchanging a few words at our destination. Do you mean that was actually you?"

"Yes, it was. And I wasn't really asleep. It just seemed wiser at the time to appear to be so. But that is all long over with now. How did you come to be in London, Mister Granberry?"

"I was appearing at a theater in Richmond when I received an offer to tread the boards in this hoary old city—an offer no true Shakespearean thespian can refuse. The very town where the Bard himself wrote and acted!"

"How wonderful. Perhaps I will see you perform. I go to the theater often."

Granberry stifled a sudden fit of coughing. "I don't think that would be too happy a chance, Miss . . . my goodness, I don't even know your name."

"Selene Kinsolving."

"Miss Kinsolving. You see there are the fashionable theaters in Covent Garden and then there are . . . theaters. Unfortunately, the Carlyle is not one of the more socially acceptable. We do, however, present a repertoire of significant Shakespearean epics in between the, ahem, lesser fare. Fine practice for me and, of course, it will sound very impressive once I get back to the States."

"Are you going back then? Oh, how I long to return."

"I shall be here for another season, but who knows what will happen after that. I fear our dear country is not at its most efficacious at the moment. But perhaps by next summer, the matter will be settled."

Their friendly conversation continued until they reached Selene's carriage where Granberry declined to take advantage of her offer. Doffing his hat he left her to settle back against the leather seat and smile at the memory of that strange ride to Norfolk. "The Carlyle Theater," Selene murmured to herself. "I don't care whether it's acceptable or not, I intend to go down there and watch Mister Granberry perform!"

As the evening at the opera drew nearer, Selene had so many things on her mind that she completely forgot about Mordacai Granberry and the Carlyle Theater. She was filled with the greatest misgivings over seeing Lord Candelby again, yet she could not put her finger on just what it was about him that so distressed her. At length she decided it was because he brought back so vividly those days in Barbados with Wade and the brief happiness they had shared. He was a reminder of the one person and the one time she wanted most to block completely from her memory.

Yet once she was seated in the ornate box with the rest of his Lordship's guests, she decided that her reluctance had been exaggerated. His Lordship treated her with the strictest propriety, seating himself two chairs away and directing his attention largely to his other guests. The party was made up of twelve people, most of whom she knew at least slightly. She had dressed carefully, and in the glittering theater, where the furs, diamonds, sequins, brocades, and silks of the spectators outshone the house, Selene felt she could hold her own with the most fashionable people there. She wore a white dress of floating chiffon over damask, spilled with sequins and set off at the neck and waist with black feathers that continued in a long trailing plume across the skirt. A single long egret feather dyed black made a crescent over her long tight curls. She had insisted on wearing her ruby necklace, even though Simon thought it inappropriate and wanted to furnish her with a diamond necklace in its place. But the rubies were the only reminder of Wade she still cherished, and she did not relish the idea of replacing them with anything from Simon's hand.

She enjoyed the opera, ignoring the rest of the people in the box and giving herself over to the melodic strains of Verdi's theatrical genius. Even the intermissions were pleasant, filled as they were with simple refreshments and engaging conversation. She did not even notice at the beginning of the third and last act that his Lordship had changed to the seat next to hers, until she felt his arm across the back of her chair and his light breath on her bare shoulder. Even then she made an effort not to take offense until in the darkened box she felt the light touch of his fingers across her back.

Turning around she glared at him and edged away in her chair. That seemed to help and for a time he kept his hands to himself as the opera came to its tragic close. Selene was the first one out of her seat, picking up her bag and fan hurriedly, eager to leave.

"Lord Candelby has invited us to a small supper at his town house," Simon said, taking advantage of the conversation in the box to whisper in her ear.

"You said nothing about a supper," she snapped back at him.

He draped her long velvet cloak about her shoulders. "It's the custom, I believe, to attend some kind of supper after these performances. You've gone along with it before often enough."

"Yes, but—"

She was interrupted by his Lordship himself who bent over to grasp her hand and press it to his lips.

"Don't know when I've enjoyed an opera more. I find them interminable as a rule, but not while such a lovely creature sits beside me. You will come to supper, Madam Kinsolving. I am counting on it."

Selene removed her hand as graciously as possible. "Well, I wasn't aware . . ."

"Oh, come along, Selene," Lady Belton interrupted. "We're all invited and no one in London sets a better table than Lord Candelby."

"Oh?" Selene muttered with resignation, throwing Simon a withering glance. "In that case I'd be delighted."

Outside she barely managed to escape being bundled into his Lordship's coach by insisting that she had to discuss the next charity ball with Lady Belton and might as well use the ride to begin their plans. Melissa wasn't very happy about it, since she had young Viscount Timms as an escort and was looking forward to cuddling with him in the closeness of the cab, but she could hardly not agree and gave in with a good grace. Selene chattered cheerfully about every subject she could think of, all the while seething underneath at Lazar who, it was obvious, had been only too ready to hand her over to Lord Candelby. She would have something to say to him later.

Lord Candelby's town house was a graceful edifice of columns and tiers, paladian windows and terraces. A domed entrance way plastered with Italian cherubs entwined in grape

229

vines set off a graceful stairway that led to a long hall. Several doors opened off the hall on to some of the most beautiful rooms Selene had ever seen. The dining room held a table laid for only ten people—somehow the others had been lost en route—and was aglow with what seemed like hundreds of candles twinkling like stars in a crystal sky. Selene was on his Lordship's right, a position of honor she could not appreciate under the circumstances. The meal was long, slow, and delicious, and it wore on well into the morning hours. By that time several of the other guests had wandered away leaving Selene, Simon, the Viscount, Lady Belton, a French diplomat who was a houseguest, and Lord Candelby himself to retire to a green and gilt drawing room for coffee.

Twice Selene had expressed a wish to leave, but both times she was talked out of it, once by Simon and the other by his Lordship's insistence that she must see the rest of the rooms. Though she might have liked to see the house under other circumstances, she was reluctant now to accompany his Lordship out of the drawing room for any reason. She was also very tired and sleepy after the long night and the rich food.

At length she could put the man off no longer. "Why don't we all go?" she insisted as he took her hand and drew her up from the comfortable couch.

"Oh, no," Lady Belton waved them away. "I've seen the rooms any number of times. You go."

The Frenchman set his cup firmly on the table and rose. "I'm off to my bed. I have to be at Westminster House in the morning and I must have my wits about me. You'll excuse me, please."

To Selene's relief Simon rose to stand beside her. "I'll go along," he said. "Just a few turns, your Lordship, and then we must be getting home. It will soon be dawn, you know."

"Nonsense, nonsense," Lord Candelby huffed, drawing Selene toward the French doors. "The night is young yet. You youngsters have no stamina. Why when I was your age, it never even occurred to me to think of bed until the sun was high. Come along, Selene. You'll love what this Italian artisan I hired has done with the back parlor."

Reluctantly she followed him, reassured that with Simon along she could not get into too much difficulty. They left

Melissa with her Viscount in the drawing room, closed the doors, and stood in the hall, looking down a corridor that had suddenly taken on the air of a tomb.

"Now this is the music room," his Lordship said, throwing open the doors to a room that though it was deep in shadow appeared to be lined with dark red flocked paper. Two lamps burned, one on a monstrous gilded piano, the other across the room on a table. Did he keep lamps burning all night in all these empty rooms, Selene wondered, or just when he had guests who might wander into them. What an extravagance. She stood meekly by while her host pointed out all the fancy decorations with an air of not caring a thing about them except to show them off. He himself admitted to no interest in music and as far as she knew he had no children to enjoy it. "Does your wife play?" Selene asked pointedly, crossing the room to put as much distance as possible between herself and her host.

His Lordship followed her, murmuring. "My wife stays in the country indulging her one great interest, raising orchids. It does not allow her any other passions."

His stress on the word passions was accompanied by a light tatoo on her back. Selene slipped away, moving to the door, "We really ought to be getting home."

"Nonsense. We've barely started. Now this next room was designed with a classic motif." Unctuously he shepherded them into the hall to the next room where he threw open the doors.

They had barely entered when Simon gave a start. "Oh dear," he said, digging into his waistcoat pockets. "I seemed to have misplaced my watch. Of course, I recall taking it from my pocket and laying it on your dining room table. Dear me, do you suppose it was found when the table was cleared?"

"Why, knowing my staff, it is probably there yet. I'll send one of the servants for it."

"No, no. Don't bother. I'll just hop down the hall and inquire about it myself, then catch up with you."

"Simon," Selene cried.

"No need for that, my dear chap," his Lordship said genially. "Servants are used to tripping about on such errands."

"No, I wouldn't hear of it. You two just go along and I'll be

231

right back. I wouldn't want to lose it. It's rather valuable."

"Simon, can't it wait," Selene said, her eyes pleading.

"It'll only take a minute, my dear." He was already halfway down the hall. Somehow she knew it would be useless to protest. This had been planned, she was certain of it. What had his Lordship given him to get out of the way and leave her alone with him? Well, it would not be enough, she thought, gritting her teeth. She was no meek little innocent, easily overpowered. If he had anything more in mind than showing off his house, he was going to be very disappointed.

They passed through two more colorfully decorated salons where Lord Candelby treated her with polite respect, apparently only interested in pointing out the artistic delicacies he had brought craftsman from all over Europe to create. She was beginning to think she had misjudged him, when they came to the last of the rooms on the left of the hall, the blue room, lit by several tall candles. It looked at first glance like a huge Wedgewood bowl, all soft blues and whites. Selene exclaimed in admiration at the leather-bound books, two long sofas in the Etruscan style, banks of flowers on small round Chippendale tables and, at the far end, two long French doors that opened onto a terrace with gardens beyond. At first she thought the scent that filled the room had wafted in from the gardens, until she saw vases filled with huge bouquets of forced lilacs standing on tall pillared pedestals. She looked around in time to see his Lordship close the door to the hall, turn a key in the lock, and drop it in his pocket. The hairs on the back of her neck suddenly came alive.

She faced him as he walked toward her, thinking she'd be damned if she'd make some maidenly protest. It was useless to ask this man what he was doing when she knew very well what he had in mind. She had known it for a long time.

He stood in front of her, laying both hands on her shoulders. The fingers he dug into her flesh were surprisingly strong. "Selene," he said in a low rough voice. "You cannot know how I have longed for this moment alone with you."

At least he no longer pretended that he ever had anything in mind but this. She tried to step back but he held her firm.

"You are so lovely," he murmured and bent toward her to nuzzle her neck with his wet lips. Selene squirmed and managed to edge her way backward. He only pressed her harder until she felt the edge of the long sofa against her skirt.

"You were made for love," he want on murmuring against her neck. "I knew it the first time I laid eyes on you. And I am a connoisseur, you know. I can always tell."

"This is an outrage," Selene snapped, pulling away from him. "I have tried to show you in every way I know that I am not interested in your 'favors.' Please take your hands off me. If you are a gentleman . . ."

At her protest his hands came alive, stroking her neck, massaging her shoulders, kneading into her flesh. She had never realized what a big man he was, but with his eager body now pressed against her she was all at once filled with an unreasoning fear. He loomed over her and he was much stronger than his lethargic air had ever intimated.

"Oh, I am a gentleman," he murmured, drawing her closer against him and burying his head against her hair. "But even a gentleman can only be pressed so far."

"I never gave you any encouragement!" Selene pressed her fists against his shoulders and struggled to shove him away, losing her balance. For a moment he held her up but then, realizing he had her in his grip, he began pushing her toward the sofa. Her knees buckled against it and he shoved her down, throwing his body over hers.

She was overwhelmed with a sickening, swelling fear. She tried to slap at him but he only laughed and gripped both her wrists with one hand, holding them tight while with the other he tore at her dress. Dimly she was aware of the thought that he had done this before. There was the air of an expert in the way he loosed her fine clothes, never allowing her the chance to strike back at him. She could hardly believe that this man, whose control was slipping away before her eyes, was the same refined, polite host of only an hour before.

"Oh, you're beautiful," he smirked against her bare skin. "I knew you would be." He was like a monster suddenly revealed when the outer disguise is yanked away.

"Let me go," she cried, twisting beneath him, forcing him to tighten his grip. Her struggle seemed to inflame his lust even further.

"And spirited," he said, his wet lips slopping over her

shrinking flesh. "That's right . . . fight me. I love a fight. I knew you'd give me a good one . . ."

Panic swept over her and she screamed, driving him to more inflamed heights. She heard the gauzy chiffon of her dress rip in a long tear and felt the suddenly cool air on her breast. The next instant he closed his mouth over it, biting at her flesh painfully. "No!" she cried, striking at him as she worked one hand free of his viselike grip. His hands kneaded her breast and his mouth slobbered over her waist. Brutally yanking her up as though she was nothing more than a toy in his hands, he pulled her to her feet, reached under her skirt and untied the laces of her hoop, sending it collapsing to the floor. Grunting like a rutting animal, he lifted her like a child away from it and threw her back on the sofa, falling on top of her. Selene, screaming, dug her nails into his face. He reached back and hit her with his fist square on her chin, exploding the candlelight in a shower of sparks. She did not lose consciousness, but she felt her body sag, and was unable to summon any strength against him. For a few moments she was a limp doll he could thrash around as he wished. His hands dove beneath her skirts, thrusting into her undergarments to grip her between the legs, his fingers shoving rudely into her. He was breathing like an animal, heavy and mindless. As her strength began to seep back she wiggled one hand free and reached behind her, her fingers searching for any kind of a weapon. He was tearing at his own clothes now and she felt the cold, tight shaft of his phallus against her flesh, searching, finding, thrusting into her with an urgency that was both painful and infuriating. Her fingers tightened around one of the slim legs of the pedestal standing beside the sofa until she felt her grip secure. Then she yanked at it with all the strength she could summon.

The table careened over, the huge vase of lilacs crashed on Candelby's head, spilling water and cascading flowers over them both.

She felt his body go slack and she used the advantage to shove him to the floor. Her dress was torn and soaked, the black feather lay in ruins on the floor and her elaborate coiffure was a tangle of straggling curls. But as Selene struggled over his Lordship's body, all she could think of was getting away. She could see that Candelby was momentarily stunned and she dimly knew this would be her only chance to escape. Grabbing up her skirts she ran to the hall door, yanking at the handle. But it had been securely locked and refused to budge. Lord Candelby lumbered up on one knee, rubbing at his head, his eyes two pools of black fury as he groped toward her.

"Damn you for a vixen!" the man muttered, shaking his head and showering water like a dog after a bath. Selene edged around the room toward the door to the terrace. He reached out to grab her as she dove past him but she was too quick. She darted through the doors across the terrace and down three low steps to a graveled path that led into the darkness, surrounded on either side by thick boxwood. She ran blindly down the path, her footsteps a tatoo on the sharp pebbles. Her breath was searing her chest. For a moment she thought she heard him behind her, following. Tearing around a bend she saw a tiny light in the distance and against it the outline of a gate. A back entrance! If she could only reach it she could get away.

She was nearly there when she tripped on her dress and went careening into a dark form that loomed up suddenly between her and the gate. For a moment she thought Candelby had tricked her and gone around another way to cut her off. She stiffled a scream as two strong hands gripped her arms.

"Let me go!" she shouted, driven at last into the panic she had just managed to avoid up until now.

"What the devil's going on?" a voice spoke low.

"Let me go," she screamed wildly, flailing at the man with her fists. They both fell back against the gate, still ajar from his entrance. The lamp beside it threw long shadows on the dark figure fighting to restrain her. Suddenly her strength gave way and she slumped to her knees. It was no use. She would be taken back. She had no more strength left to fight.

"What's the matter with you?" said a familiar voice. Selene looked up quickly at the lean face above her and her pounding heart turned over.

Wade!

Twelve

She couldn't move. She stared up at him, unable to believe it was really Wade. His hands gripped her arms, holding her up, as surprised to see her as she was to recognize him. He bent closer and she saw that it was indeed Wade Kinsolving— thinner, angrier, but really and truly Wade.

"You!" she gasped in a breath that tore at her throat. Hearing footsteps running on the graveled path behind her she cried out, looking around, her face stark with terror. Without a word Wade pulled her through the gate and closed it. They were in a narrow alley, almost pitch black away from the dim circle of the lantern hanging over the gate. On the other side of the wall they could hear muffled voices that sounded as though they came from the other end of the garden.

"I must get away from here . . ." she said, in a low strangled voice as she struggled to work free of his grasp.

"Shh," he whispered. "In a moment. They won't think of looking in the alley."

She did not argue with him, though she was not as certain as he that they would not assume she had left through the gate. She cringed against him as the voices drew nearer and he tightened his arms around her, enveloping her in the dark, strong cocoon of his clasp. When the footsteps faded back toward the house again, she let herself relax a little, slumping against him. "Come on," Wade whispered. "It's safe now."

He led her to the end of the lane that opened out onto the street, the pavement slick and mirrored with a thin glaze of rain. Selene stood while he waved down a passing cab, her hair streaked and limp, her dress wilted, the feathers drooping like some drenched exotic bird. Her hoop, cloak, and bag were back in Lord Candelby's elegant house but she would have waded through fire before going back for them. When a hackney cab, just starting its morning run, came lumbering by, Wade hailed it, pulled open the door, and handed her in. Selene scrambled into its confining darkness and scrunched into the far corner. She felt as though she was suspended in some nightmarish void, lost from the real world. Even Wade being there with her seemed more a dream than reality.

To her surprise he crawled in beside her and pounded on the roof. "I don't know where to tell him to take you," he said as Selene buried herself deeper into the corner. She murmured the address, wondering if she ought to go back to Simon's house after tonight. Yet she had no place else. The carriage rolled away and Selene found she was shaking like an aspen leaf, whether from cold or nerves she couldn't tell.

"Here," Wade said, slipping his cloak around her shoulders. "You're chilled through. What on earth happened back there? No, you don't need to tell me. Lord Candelby's reputation as a womanizer is well known throughout London. I'm only surprised he didn't try something like this when we were in Barbados."

Grateful for the warm coat, Selene pulled it around her. "Why are you here?" she asked after they had ridden in silence for awhile and her shivering had subsided somewhat. "I thought you were in America."

"I wanted to be but my government had other ideas. I'm still pursuing their dream, though it appears to be more hopeless every day. However, as soon as I can make certain of that, I'll be on the first ship for home. What about you? Do you have to put up with this kind of thing often? I'd heard that you were a bright ornament of the London social scene and I suppose these little 'incidents' go with it. So far no one has asked me about the similarity in names. I wouldn't want to put a damper on your social life by revealing that you had a husband hanging about."

The bitterness in his voice drove her deeper into her corner.

"You're not very kind," she said lamely.

"Kind! And I suppose that was what you were when you went running off with that Lazar, leaving me to look like a cuckold."

"Why should you care about that? You kidnapped me and dragged me to Barbados. You forced me to marry you. What did you expect me to do? Thank you for it?"

"I expected you to have better judgment about the man you left me for."

"Simon has taken very good care of me since we came to London." She could not believe her own words. Why was she defending this man when he had so obviously bartered her away this very night. "He was my father's friend."

"Then your father had a poor choice of acquaintances. Don't you know the kind of man he is, or is it that you just don't care? I admit it took me long enough to realize that that British delegation was leading us down the garden path and had no intention of working out a treaty. But the information they were given, the encouragement to think that we could never win this war, the underhanded sabotage of all our efforts—your friend Simon Lazar was responsible for it all."

"You don't know that."

"I have no proof. But I will before I leave this country. And I'll settle with him, too. Carrying you away might appear to be the reason but you and I will know the real truth, won't we?"

Selene leaned her head against the side of the cab, all at once aware of how weary she felt. "Don't involve me in this vindictive feud. Hate him all you want, but leave me out of it."

"I would guess it was a very good thing I got involved tonight."

She gave him a long look. "Why were you there? What were you doing entering Lord Candelby's garden at that hour?"

"You're welcome, I'm sure."

"Oh, very well. Thank you. I admit I'm grateful you helped me to get away, even if it is a strange reversal of roles for you."

"Never pass up a chance to twist the knife. I recall you were always very good at that. What do you plan to do with your life now? Remain the belle of society in London. Marry Simon Lazar? You can divorce me, you know, any time you wish.

Such a peculiar marriage shouldn't be too difficult to remove from the books."

"I didn't even know you were alive. How could I be thinking about divorce?"

"Sorry I couldn't make a widow of you. However the war seems to be dragging along with no end in sight and I'll get back to it yet. Who knows, you might get lucky."

The anger she felt toward him had at least the effect of mitigating her shock and dismay over the distressing scene in Lord Candelby's blue room. Thoughts tumbled about in her mind, leaving her to wonder what approach she should take with him, but the cab pulled up in front of Simon's house before she could decide. The street was deserted but, happily, there was a light burning in Matilda's room. If she could just manage to wake her without disturbing the rest of the house this terrible evening might soon end. At least it appeared Simon had not returned yet. She had no wish to see him now. She'd face him in the morning.

Wade handed her down and ordered the cab to wait. He followed her up the few steps to the portico as if he still had something to say. Selene decided not to give him a chance.

"Here's your coat. Thank you. It helped."

"Keep it until you get inside. I can always pick it up later." At the look on her face he added: "Or you can send it around. I'm staying at a little hotel off James Street called the Winston."

"No. Take it now. I'm all right."

She pushed it at him and he draped it over his arm, still lingering. "Selene, if we're going to be here in the same city . . ."

"We don't have to pretend we even know each other."

"But there are people here who know of our relationship."

"Then tell them we are estranged, which, in fact, we are. I won't have any comment to make on the subject if you won't."

Wade looked up at the house, remembering whose it was. "Perhaps you are right. Good-bye, Selene." Abruptly he pressed her hand to his lips then hurried into the hackney.

She stood leaning against the door while the cab drove away, the brisk snap of the horses' hooves on the brick road echoing in the silence. Then trying not to think of anything but what must be done, she searched for several small stones to throw at the window, alerting Matilda to come downstairs and quietly let her in.

"Good Lord, Miss Selene, what happened to you?" the girl cried in hushed tones at the dismal apparition that shuffled through the door when she opened it. "Your beautiful dress . . ."

"I'll tell you about it tomorrow. Right now, I only want to go to bed. Don't let anyone in, Matilda, until I say so in the morning. And take this dress and throw it away!"

It was not until an hour later, tucked in her bed, that she realized Wade had never told her what he was doing at Lord Candelby's house.

As usual the bells of three churches in three different directions from his hotel awoke Wade the next morning. Groggy from only four hours sleep, he dragged himself up, slung a dressing gown over his long drawers, ran his fingers through his hair in an attempt to comb it back, and rang for the porter to bring him his morning roll and coffee. The coffee helped to generate life into his flagging body long enough to accomplish all the minutia of grooming and dressing. Then, as ready as he was ever going to be to face the day, he sat at the round table in his sitting room and finished off the rest of the coffee while glancing over the daily paper.

However, his mind was not on the news, enticing as it might be. There was little from America to indicate anything more than the stalemate that had existed in the war since the end of last year. The real campaign had not begun yet, though all indications were that early April would see it come to life again. At length he folded the paper and threw it aside. Searching in his pocket he drew out the insignificant slip of paper with the hastily scrawled address he had made last evening while it was still fresh in his mind.

Simon Lazar's house. He had not written the number and street down until he got home, but he remembered it well enough. Nor would he forget how to find it. He had been told it was in the vicinity of Great Ormond but he had to be certain. And now he was certain indeed. She had taken him straight to it.

Wade leaned back in his chair and closed his eyes, allowing his mind to conjure up a vivid picture of Selene Sprague. No, it was Selene Kinsolving now, wasn't it. At least she had used his name when she came running to England under that man's protection. At least it was not Lazar!

No, he had never thought she was the kind of girl to pretend to be married to the man of the moment. She had integrity of a sort, he had to give her that. He had forced her to go with him and forced her to be his wife. He could not force her to love him or even to stay with him—she had made that very clear. But she would be honest about her marriage, even one such as theirs. She would not pretend to be someone she was not.

And she was still so beautiful! Even last night—wet, bedraggled, terrified, furious—even with it all she was still so lovely. Her large eyes, so stark against the classic lines of her face, her lips so luscious, every gesture of her arm and hand so graceful, so appealing! He had wanted her there in the cab more than ever, even more than on that silky Barbados beach whose memory still burned like a candle flame in the bleakness of his life.

But they were far beyond that now. Everything had gone so wrong, there was so much residue of anger and bitterness. And she had left him for the protection of that viper, Simon Lazar! He would never forgive her for that.

He would find some way to get even with Lazar for ruining everything he had worked so hard to do in Barbados. And he would get even with Selene some day, too. He did not know how yet, but he would find a way if he died in the attempt.

A quiet knock on his door startled him out of his thoughts. It took him a moment to come back to the present and then he realized who his visitor would be. He opened the door just wide enough for her to slip in, carrying with her the heady scent of Southern gardenias. Her soft brown watered silk spread out around her as she settled on a stool, laying her parasol and bag on the table. The tall crown of her hat, festooned with gently cascading plumes, set off the carefully sculpted lines of her face.

"Where were you last night?" Melissa Belton said quietly. "We waited for several hours."

"Something came up quite suddenly and I had no choice but to go back the way I came."

Her gaze was filled with questions but they remained unasked. "It must have been of great importance," she said in a voice that was at once both injured and rebuking.

"It was."

She knew he was not going to explain further and she busied herself with the buttons on her gloves. "It is going to delay matters some. And you must allow me a small complaint. All those hours with that silly, foolish Viscount. Now that is what I call going beyond the call of duty."

"If he is so silly and foolish, perhaps we should not trust him."

"He only knows enough to be useful. He did not know we were waiting for you, only that someone important was expected. I'm very careful not to allow him enough information to make him dangerous. You should know that by now."

Wade smiled at her. "I do know it and I'm sorry about last night. You must believe me when I tell you it could not be helped. Now, would you like some coffee? I think there is some left and it is still warm if not hot."

"No, thank you. I jeopardized my reputation quite far enough by coming up here to your room alone, though I do believe I managed to get past the porter without being seen. I brought you the letter."

She removed a thick envelope from her bag and handed it to Wade. "Is it wise to carry this about so openly?" he asked.

"I find that the more open one is the less suspicion one generates. I even had it with me last night, right under the noses of the foolish Candelby, that odious Lazar, and your 'ex-wife.'"

"Not ex yet, though she may be soon."

"She is exceedingly pretty but quite foolish, I fear. I noticed that she left rather suddenly last night," she said, giving him a look that was full of suspicion. "I was rather hoping you two

242

might come face to face. I was looking forward to seeing the surprise."

"Yes, you would love that, wouldn't you? Don't underestimate me, Lady Belton. My private concerns are no business of yours. And don't underestimate Selene either."

Melissa Belton leaned forward, resting her chin in her hands and studying Wade while he broke open the letter and scanned it. A second paper fell to the table and on it Melissa recognized the elaborate imprint of Fraser, Trenholm of Liverpool, the English financial agents for the Confederacy. She was pleased to see it.

"Can you arrange a way for me to meet with Colin Huntworthy," Wade said, pocketing both letters.

She had hoped he might let her read them. "Of course, though I don't think it should be quite as public as the socials he has attended in the past. Perhaps a private little supper party."

"That sounds like the right thing. Will he entertain a business proposition over the port, do you think?"

"Colin Huntworthy would entertain a business proposition in the water closet if he thought it could bring him a profit."

Wade smiled in spite of himself. Melissa Belton's earthy humor often caught him by surprise, since she was the outward picture of a perfect lady. "I think over the port will do fine," he said. "But soon. Very soon."

She reached for her reticule. "It will have to be before the end of next week, for he and his wife are going back to Leeds by then. Have you had any word on the negotiations?"

"No. It's the usual foot-dragging and hemming and hawing. We've given them every reason to believe we can win this war. God, we've outfought the Yankees in every engagement. But it's the long haul they're worried about."

"There is something else, Captain Kinsolving," Melissa said rising to go. "I wonder if you are aware of the proclamation President Lincoln made last month."

"Freeing the slaves? Oh, yes, I read it. Though what right he has to free black men of another sovereign nation is beyond me."

"Perhaps in the Southern view of things that is true. But

243

you should be aware that such a proclamation, with its moral overtones, will be very difficult for the British government to ignore. We have been such staunch critics of slavery for so long . . ."

"It never prevented you from buying our cotton, and God knows that was seeded, harvested, baled, and shipped at the hands of slaves. I cannot see why this should be such a problem."

"I just want to warn you. Don't overlook its wider repercussions." She walked to the door and Wade hurried after her to open it. He stood with his hand on the latch looking at her, his eyes dark with intensity.

"You're not changing loyalties, are you?"

Melissa laughed and tapped him playfully with the end of her parasol. "You don't have to worry about me, Captain. I have been partial to Virginia and the Confederacy since this ugly business started. I don't have to remind you of all the ties to your country I enjoy. You just take care of yourself and worry about those who really would destroy all you are seeking to do. I'll send you word later today concerning the date for our little supper. Good day, Captain."

Wade lifted her gloved hand to his lips in a perfunctory way. When she had gone he opened a window slightly, letting in the racket from the street below but relieving some of the residue of the heady gardenia scent left by Melissa. Then he sat down at the table, took out the letter, and studied it carefully.

For three days Selene did not leave her bedroom. If it had seemed a haven before, now it was doubly so. As long as her door was locked and her blinds closed she felt barricaded from the outside world and all the events she did not want to think about, much less face. She told herself she was ill, but she knew that was not the real reason she refused to go back into the world, unless one could actually be made ill from depression. She was increasingly hopeless of ever getting away from these men who had made her life so miserable and of getting home again to America. Matilda did what she could to encourage her to get up. She brought her her meals, combed and brushed her hair, pampered and cossetted her, but to no avail. Selene remained more listless than ever.

She had had no direct word from Simon, though Matilda told her he had questioned her when he returned home from Lord Candelby's party. After her third day in bed he knocked on the door and was curtly told to go away. The following day he knocked again, received the same curt dismissal, and returned with a locksmith who opened the door for him. Surprised, Selene sat up in bed, pulling the covers up around her chin. He came striding angrily into the room and ordered Matilda to leave.

"I don't have to," the girl blubbered as Simon clutched her by the collar and shoved her rudely toward the door.

"You leave this room this instant or you'll find yourself on the street with nothing but the clothes on your back," he snapped. "And close the door after you."

Mattie gave Selene a frightened glance but did as Simon ordered. She had seen his maniacal temper vented on the other servants and she had no wish to have his wrath directed at her, no matter how loyal she was to Selene. To be cast adrift in this strange city was too terrifying a thing to risk.

Once the door was closed, Simon walked to the bed staring down at Selene with a look as black as an Atlantic storm.

"I suppose you're proud of yourself. I hope you realize you have deeply offended Lord Candelby—"

She gasped. "I have offended *him!* What about his conduct toward me? It was reprehensible!"

"—a man whose favor I badly need. You have set back the cause I've worked so hard for by God only knows how many months."

"How dare you stand there and castigate me for running away from a man who was set on raping me. You snake! You arranged the whole thing . . . I know you did."

"I agreed to help him. He is a man of great wealth and influence. If you had played your cards right, you might have reaped any number of rewards, including enough money to carry you across the Atlantic ten times. But no. You must play the righteous virgin, the prim, outraged prude. And now not only will we suffer, but the hopes that were placed in us as well."

"How much money did he give you to lure me into that spider's devious web? I'll wager it was plenty. And don't try to tell me it was all for the sake of your country. I know about that locked drawer downstairs. How much have you salted away there, Simon? Enough to keep you in style for the rest of your life, I've no doubt. And I was the bait."

She spoke impulsively. Though she knew he kept money in that desk drawer and never let the key off his person, never before had it really mattered to her. Now she saw by the sudden blanching of his face that her comments had hit home. He was so secretive he probably thought he had everyone fooled by his parsimonious ways.

Simon reached in his pocket and drew out a handful of white cards, throwing them over her lap on the bed. "These are invitations which have piled up downstairs. Some of them you have already missed but others must be replied to at once. You have spent enough time languishing in bed grieving over your lost dignity. Now get up and get dressed. One of those invitations is for a soiree tonight at the Earl of Devon's. I've already said you'll be there."

"I won't go!"

"You'll go if I have to drag you there by the hair."

His voice stayed low and sombre, but there was that deepening of winter in his cold eyes that warned Selene he was getting very close to the edge.

"Why should I? Do you threaten to throw me out on the street in nothing but my shift? Very well. Go ahead. I'll leave."

Throwing back the covers she made to get out of bed, slipping her legs over the side. He laid a hand on her shoulder and pushed her back, not gently but with the strength of subdued rage.

"Can't you understand? I don't want to throw you out. I need your help, Selene. I thought this cause meant as much to you as it does to me. Remember your father? What would he think if you turned your back, indifferent to the destruction of the noblest country God ever made? What would he say if you went running out in the street, a beggar. Penniless. Friendless."

246

As always the mention of her father from someone who knew him so well and who had sat at his feet, gave her pause. "He would allow me to do anything as long as my honor was intact," she said bitterly.

Simon hesitated, his face a mask that hid his struggle to control his emotions. "Yes, you're probably right," he said grudgingly. "Honor above all, he would say. Surely the honor of our country matters more than anything, though personal honor can never be far behind. Very well. I apologize, Selene, for pushing you into that little difficulty with Lord Candelby. He had me convinced that it was something you wanted as much as he."

She gave a sharp laugh. "That was his imagination at work. I never encouraged him."

"Perhaps. But men will sometimes see hope where there is none when they are determined about a thing they want. And his Lordship is not accustomed to being refused. At any rate, I'm sorry. It won't happen again."

He walked across the room and sat heavily in a gilt chair as though the unusual effort of an apology had exhausted him. Selene could not see his face since his back was to the light, only his rangy figure, a dark shadow, hanging over her life, one she seemed unable to escape.

"All right. I accept your apology. But I warn you, if anything like this is even suggested again, I will not come back. I'll go anywhere else in London except to this house."

"It won't happen again. Now, get dressed and come downstairs. I need to discuss the other guests who will be at tonight's affair with you and go over some of the topics of conversation."

"One more thing, Simon. I will agree to carry on with this espionage game of yours, but only on the conditions that you promise me a date when you will send me back to America. No more vague intimations. I want something specific."

Simon ran a finger along his sharp chin. "It will probably be next summer. If you will accept that, I'll promise you can leave then."

"Will you put that in writing?"

"Come, Selene. Haven't I taken care of you here? Are you in

247

prison or a dungeon that you need a jailer's reprieve? Trust me.
I give you my word as a gentleman and a scholar that I'll send
you home by the end of the summer."

Could she trust him? She wasn't sure. In spite of her brave
words she knew there really was nowhere else for her to go in
this vast city. There was no one to help her but Wade, and that
was an alternative she refused to accept.

"I'll be down in half an hour," she murmured, dejection in
every line of her body. The end of the summer seemed so far
away that it might as well be three years. But it would come.
And at least she might hope.

Simon started for the door. With his fingers on the handle
he stopped and looked back at her, one brow frowning.

"How did you get home from his Lordship's house? Did
someone bring you?"

"No. I was fortunate enough to run into the street just as a
hackney was starting its morning run. I hailed it down and
engaged him to take me home."

He studied her, obviously wondering whether or not to
believe her story. Selene was relieved when he turned back and
without another word left her to get dressed.

Two weeks passed before Selene had a chance to visit the
Carlyle Theater. During that time she dutifully filled all the
responsibilities which she supposed Simon expected of her.
While it was hard for her to be enthusiastic about meeting and
charming people, she carefully hid her real feelings and
managed to convince even Lazar that she was resigned to his
demands and was back to her old self again.

Then came a lull in the invitations and Selene quickly made
arrangements with Fenton to drive her, accompanied only by
Matilda, to an evening performance of Richard III at the Carlyle Theater.

The area of the city was not encouraging. Though it was
situated near Covent Garden with several other theaters about,
the surrounding buildings appeared slovenly and seedy. Tired
stores below dirty three-and four-story houses which had been
converted from once prosperous homes to tiny flats added to

the squalor. A light rain had begun to fall and around the gas lamps a halo mist only emphasized the cavernous darkness in between. There were pubs every few houses from which she could hear music and singing. A vendor on the corner roasted chestnuts over a brazier whose hot coals stared like so many eyes into the dark street. Their pungent odor almost but not quite overcame the heady stink of grease and smog. There were beggars everywhere. A favorite spot was near the theater entrance where they sat poised to pester the playgoers. Selene, who had read a few of Mister Dickens' works, thought he would be right at home in this environment.

The Carlyle Theater looked as shabby as the buildings that surrounded it. She arrived fashionably late for the performance, but since she had engaged one of the few stalls, she had an excellent view of the audience, already assembled. The cramped, crowded auditorium was only slightly less brightly lit than the proscenium, but even that was dim and ghostly. It was a rowdy audience. The people who filled the orchestra below her were having a wonderful time. They had brought their suppers with them and while their eyes were intent on the stage they never ceased stuffing their mouths with an endless assortment of fruits, cheese, and biscuits, washed down with bottles of ale. The boxes were more genteel, she noted. Most of those patrons focused on the play and tried to ignore the noise and catcalls from below. Selene was not there to be seen and she made a point of sitting well to the back of her cramped little stall, deep in the shadows. Matilda, on the other hand, leaned over the rail with a delight that came from having been inside very few theaters in her time. The play seemed to her almost magical and Selene was consoled that if nothing else came of this, at least it would have afforded Matilda a memorable evening.

Selene by this time had seen most of the prominent actors of the day in London. She was therefore accustomed to the extravagant gestures and broad vocal dynamics which were typical of the greats. However, never had she seen them pushed to such extravagant limits as on the Carlyle's drab stage. At times she had to hold her fan in front of her face to choke back her laughter. The play seemed almost a parody of a tragedy and she wondered at first if this production was supposed to be a satire. But in time she saw that the players were deadly serious. The leading actor—whom she was not surprised to see was not Mordacai—was an intense man who, at times, even managed to suggest true emotions. They peeped out now and then from behind the grotesque makeup and long stretches of extravagant overacting. They were completely eclipsed however by the other actors, each of whom seemed eager to out-do the rest of the company in impressing the crowd with their dramatic skills. Of all of them, Mordacai was the worst. His booming voice and wild gestures as the Duke of Clarence were almost comical, and as far from the tragedy Shakespeare envisioned as it was possible to be. Yet Selene noticed her reservations were in contrast to those of the other spectators. The crowd eagerly participated, booing, hissing, applauding as the mood struck them, and all of them having a roaring good time.

Selene soon turned to studying the sets which seemed as old and tired as the building itself. Even the machinery seemed like something left over from one of Mister Hogarth's barnyard performances of a century before. It was going to be a long evening.

During the first intermission she sent Mattie backstage with an invitation to Mordacai. When they arrived at the theater, she had noticed a tavern at the end of the street which at least on the outside did not look quite as dingy and run-down as the others. Fenton was dispatched to arrange a private supper room before she ever took her place in her box, and it was there that she invited Granberry to join her after the performance.

Once the Duke of Clarence was drowned in his vat of malmsy, Mordacai had little to do backstage but wait for his curtain call and wonder what the lovely Mrs. Kinsolving wanted of him. He was only sorry he had not known she was visiting the theater, for his performance tonight had lacked his usual gusto. Had he known Selene was watching he would have put more into it.

When he entered the Garrick Tavern's tiny private room several hours later, he found Selene waiting for him, sitting on one side of a table that was enticingly covered with a white cloth. The tantalizing odor of hot food and a decanted rose-colored bottle of claret standing on a sideboard put a little more lightness in his step. "Madam," he said, kissing Selene's gloved hand with all the courtliness of a duke, "I am enchanted."

"Thank you for coming," she said, smiling warmly at him. There was just a touch of mischief in her eyes. "I'm sorry it isn't malmsy," she added, having seen the way he eyed the claret. "Why don't you pour us both a glass?"

The actor bounded to the sideboard. "I've never really tasted malmsy, though the Good Lord only knows how many times I have been drowned in it on stage." He handed her a glass and raised his own. "With my gratitude," he said. "You have transformed an ordinary evening into one of enchantment."

"I'm sure you could use a little sustenance after the rigors of your performance," Selene said and indicated the chair opposite her own. She removed the covers and Mordacai's eyes grew round at the sumptuous dishes waiting for them. "Please help yourself," she went on. "You must be hungry and I dismissed the girl who would have waited on us. My own maid is just outside, having already had her supper. But I wanted to speak to you alone."

Mordacai dug in eagerly. He was starved and his usual after-the-play supper was a far cry from this. Selene watched as he sampled something from every dish on the table and washed it down lavishly with the claret. She toyed with her food, not really very hungry and anxious to get away from the area and back home to her clean, expensive house. Though he never stopped eating Mordacai regaled her with a running comment on the actors, the theater, the management, and the play, all of it in his booming voice which Selene reckoned must carry down the hall to at least three other rooms. When he had finally eaten his fill, he wiped his broad chin with the end of the napkin he had tucked over his chest, sat back, and sighed contentedly.

"My dear Mrs. Kinsolving, I haven't enjoyed a meal so much since I arrived in England. How can I thank you? To think that a casual meeting on a rutted road in Virginia would lead to this! It is just another of the astounding coincidences of life that surprises us along the way."

"Well . . . I have to admit, I had an ulterior motive in mind in arranging this supper party."

"Ah, yes," Mordacai sighed, "I was fairly certain it was not my acting powers you came all the way to this part of town to enjoy. Nor, I confess, did I believe for one moment that it was my charms you were interested in—more's the pity. My fellow actors, on the other hand, are convinced of it."

"And I suppose you did nothing to convince them otherwise," Selene said, laughing.

"Of course not. Let them think what they will. We shall know the true nature of our assignation. Or am I to ask?"

"Of course you are to ask. You see, I need help and it must be someone who is not known by the people with whom I am currently living. You are an actor, Mister Granberry. Do you think you could play a part for me? Not in a play, but in the real world?"

"Madam, I would be enchanted to do so. It does not involve, ahem, breaking the law or anything like that, I trust? I have no wish to come up against the London courts."

"Oh, no. It's all extremely proper. At least on the surface. However, I must say this, Mordacai. You are a rather flamboyant person. I mean you no disrespect by saying that— how could you otherwise be a successful actor? But do you think you could tone down your . . . your voice and such to appear an ordinary citizen?"

Granberry, far from taking offense, seemed to seriously consider her words. Frowning, he ran a finger along his chin. "You mean sound and act like a lackluster fellow, good-natured but with no authority or gifts? Something like the sober Rowley in *School for Scandal?* A part, I might add, that I have played often to great acclaim. But it would be a challenge. My yes, a real challenge. Naturally I am competent to meet such a challenge. Any actor worth his salt would have to be."

"Yes, but you must not appear to be acting. This is extremely important."

"But that is the charm of it. Acting without appearing to be acting. Oh my yes, madam, you have caught my fancy completely."

252

She sat back in her chair, studying his broad face. Add a few whiskers, lower the thundering voice a few notches, perch a pair of small round glasses halfway down his nose—he would never be exactly nondescript, but he might do.

"Very well, Mordacai. If you really believe you can do it, I have a proposition for you."

Thirteen

There was no spring that year in England. Wet, damp, miserable winter gave way almost at once to muggy, suffocating heat. The famous English gardens bloomed in a riot of color but wilted quickly from the lack of moisture. Emerald lawns faded to brown and even the trees appeared stunted and panting. Selene, accustomed to the violent heat of a Virginia summer, endured it better than most, but even she felt at times that the weight of her skirts and petticoats felt like being wrapped in cotton bunting.

She saw nothing more of Wade. It was nearly a month after her experience with Lord Candelby before Simon learned he was in England, and then he turned on her in a fury, accusing her of keeping the news from him.

"You deliberately suppressed the information. I know you were aware he had come here—you had to know. You go everywhere, talk to all the most influential people. Why didn't you tell me?"

"It never occurred to me that you wouldn't know it. You are far more adept than I at learning what is going on."

"I do not appreciate your sarcasm," he snapped, his eyes narrowing dangerously. She had seen enough of his temper by now to become guarded in her conversation. And she had no desire to antagonize him just now with the end of summer almost at hand. She shrugged and said lightly: "Why does it matter? I care nothing for Wade Kinsolving. I'm not going out looking for him, indeed I hope I don't see him at all. You know my feelings."

He studied her in his heavy-lidded way, like a vulture examining his prey, Selene thought. "I hope you really do hate him as much as you claim, because the fact remains, he is a threat to my plans. He certainly would not be here in England without some reason. A man with his background should be fighting in the war, not running around overseas trying to flag a hopeless cause into life."

"If it is so hopeless, I wonder he doesn't leave. Perhaps your suspicions are incorrect and the British government is encouraging the South more than they appear to be."

Simon rolled up several papers on his desk and slipped them into a drawer, locked it, and pocketed the key in his vest. "That may be what the government is trying to make them think, but it is certain they will never come in on the side of the Confederacy now. The South has already given up on France. It is only a matter of time before they accept the inevitable and give up on Great Britain as well. Which suggests that Captain Kinsolving must be staying for some other reason."

"Well, I'm sure I don't know what it is. Even if I were in contact with him, he would never confide in me."

Since Simon said nothing further on the matter she assumed she had put his suspicions to rest. And then she ran into Wade again.

He was the last person she expected to see. A terse note delivered the day before had sent her to the International Exhibition at Sydenham where for nearly an hour she browsed among the exhibits, chatting with an occasional acquaintance, asking an infrequent question, pretending an interest in the sometimes wild and often astounding displays from all corners of the globe.

Then, as she stood looking curiously at a mind-boggling aerial photograph of Boston, a portly, tall, well-dressed gentleman with wide side whiskers struck up a conversation. They exchanged remarks on the astonishing ability of a photograph to put man up among the birds and then proceeded along the aisle to a second, more isolated building.

"I was glad to hear from you," Selene said in a low voice once they were out of hearing of the other spectators. "I didn't

255

know you were back."

"Only reached London day before yesterday," Mordacai answered in a low whisper. "I couldn't get away quite as soon as I thought—the play was renewed for another two weeks. But once it closed, off I went. Beastly hot in the midlands this time of year. I didn't quite expect that."

Selene paused beside a rainbow display of fabrics colored with the new synthetic dyes. "And did you learn anything?"

"Oh yes. It is certain Mister Huntworthy is filling a large consignment of arms and it is almost equally certain that they are intended for the South. I don't know where the Confederacy got the money, but it was paid on a draft from Fraser, Trenholm of Liverpool."

They moved on to the next booth displaying an experimental mechanical vehicle.

"What do you mean, *almost* as certain?"

Mordacai smoothed his whiskers, and peered more closely at the awkward object in the center of the booth. Selene had to strain to catch his words, so completely had he modified his old, booming voice. "Only that there appeared to be something secretive about the deal. I wasn't able to discover what it was *then,* but I am returning there next Monday and hope that, with your help, I can bribe one of the clerks in the office to reveal what it is. Do you want me to?"

"I don't know. What kind of a bribe? I don't have any money myself, you know, and it is hard to get more out of Simon. Do you think it is something important?"

"I suspect so, but there is really no way of knowing until I hear what this fellow has to say. I do believe it somehow involves your friend Lazar, however."

"Now what would Simon Lazar have to do with an arms consignment for the Confederacy? He is so devious, I wouldn't put anything past him, not even to learn that he is actually working for them. That would certainly be an about-face wouldn't it?"

Mordacai straightened and walked around the vehicle. "Why this is nothing more than a small engine attached to a handcart. And look at that, will you! They claim this contraption can go seven miles an hour. Why, that's ridiculous.

Whatever are we coming to?"

"The world is moving too fast, that is true," Selene answered in her normal voice, then added softly: "I'll get the money somehow. Find out what's going on up there. I need to know as much about Simon's involvement as possible."

"Send it round to the theater by Friday. I'll be back in touch just as soon as I return." He doffed his tall hat and smiled broadly, speaking in his stage voice. "So pleasant talking with you, Madam. Good day to you."

Selene smiled and nodded her head. As he disappeared down the aisle she turned back to the printed explanation of the mechanical vehicle and pretended to read it, her mind on a munitions factory in Leeds. What could Simon be up to now, she wondered. There was not anything she would put past him, and she knew for a certainty that if she was going to be able to force him to send her back to America, she had better be one step ahead.

"Hello Selene," said a familiar voice.

Selene spun around. "Wade! Why—where on earth did you come from?"

"I saw you from across the hall and thought I'd say hello. It's been some time since we last talked."

Selene's eyes shunted down the aisle where Mordacai had disappeared. He had been swallowed in the crowd, but she could still recognize his tall beaver hat wavering above the heads of the spectators thronging the aisle. Had Wade recognized him? She did not have time to wonder, for he took her elbow in his strong fingers and propelled her the other way. "Somehow I never thought of you as someone who would enjoy a scientific exhibition. Do you find it interesting? You seemed pretty engrossed in that mechanical handcart back there."

"I never thought of *you* that way either. Half the people here are only interested in being seen by the other half. You must realize that."

"And is that your only interest?"

"Of course." She stole a sideways glance at his chiseled profile and hoped she was convincing.

"Oh yes. I forgot that you have become quite the social

257

butterfly around London. A remarkable feat for an American tavern wench who is not living with her husband."

"Stop being sarcastic. I'm not a social butterfly at all—I merely get along with people and they seem to like me for it. And I wasn't a tavern wench either. My father was a respected professor and he taught me well. He was very interested in the development of machinery and science. He'd be fascinated to see how far we've come."

His fingers tightened on her arm. Ignoring the crowds, he pushed her toward the door. "Let's get out of here," he said. "I want to talk to you and we can't do it here."

Selene pulled on her arm. "Don't I have a choice? You're hurting me!"

"No, you don't," he said, impatiently propelling her toward the door. "I've got a cab waiting and you're getting in it."

She hurried after him. "Always the abductor, aren't you? You haven't changed a bit."

"I never claimed I had." They went through the wide open doorway and down the steps to the street where a hackney cab waited, its horse somnolent in the warm sunshine. Wade threw the door open and handed her up without ceremony. He barked a command to the driver which Selene could not hear, then climbed in beside her. The cab lumbered off, wending its way through the crowded streets while the two of them sat inside, not looking at each other beyond a surreptitious glance at intervals. Selene fussed with her reticule and bonnet strings. "Well. You said you wanted to talk. What about?"

"There's still time for that. I must say, Selene, you have really become quite fashionable. It is very becoming. Was that Simon's influence?"

"That's none of your business."

"Oh yes, I forgot. Since he is your 'protector' now, I am not concerned with any part of your life."

"Protector is an old-fashioned word."

"What should I say? Paramour? Lover? You tell me the correct word and I'll use it."

Selene glared at him. She would die before admitting that her relationship with Simon was one of mutual exploitation. Let him think Lazar was her lover. What did it matter.

"Naturally you would think that. It's the only relationship between a man and a woman you could understand."

Wade's lips pursed into an angry line. He slumped in the corner of the cab, staring out of the window and ignoring her until he felt the driver pull up on the reins.

"We're here."

"May I ask just where here is? Or am I not supposed to have a choice in that either."

Without answering he handed her down and paid the driver. Selene looked around, not recognizing the street with its neat rows of houses, flower pots with smiling red geraniums, and lace curtains at the windows. She decided running away would be useless since she had no idea where she was, so she followed Wade meekly up the steps to a pleasant front door. Inside he directed her up the stairs to the first landing, where he put a key in a door and opening it, waited for her to enter. She was inside before she realized she had entered his rooms.

"Really!" she protested, turning on him. He smiled weakly, walked to her, and untied the strings on her bonnet, pulling it off.

"Relax. We are married after all. There's nothing improper about having my wife to my flat."

"I don't give a damn about 'proper.' You tricked me into coming here . . ."

He stopped her words with his mouth, closing on her own as his arms slipped around her. It was a long, gentle kiss, and Selene felt herself melting into it as it went on. When he released her and stood back she had to fight to regain her sense of outrage.

"Oh, I've missed you, Selene," Wade sighed, bending to kiss the white curve of her neck.

"You said . . . you wanted to . . . talk . . ."

"I do, and we will. But I never could be around you without wanting you. You drive reason right out of my head."

With his hands sliding sensuously over her back and his lips tickling the hollows of her throat, Selene had to struggle to remember she was supposed to be objective. Her body grew warmer by the second, a delicious glow that spread like a flower opening within her. It had been a long time . . .

"I don't want this," she protested weakly and tried to push him away.

"I don't believe you," Wade murmured as his fingers deftly unfastened the buttons of her bodice. It had been a long time for him as well.

"It's no good . . ." she cried as he picked her up in his arms and carried her into the adjoining bedroom where he laid her gently down, stretched out on the bed. She tried to move but the glowing cocoon of dawning need held her fast.

"Wade," she protested one last time as he stretched beside her, gently pulling at her clothes. "Wade, would you stop if I asked you?"

He slid her bodice off her shoulder and slipped his hand inside it to free the rich, full globe of her breast, filling his hands with its ripe sweetness.

"No," he murmured and closed his lips around the taut nipple, sucking greedily.

Selene's back arched of itself, thrusting the hot orb upward deeper into his mouth. "If I demanded . . ." she gasped.

He pulled his lips away long enough to bury his head in the deep valley between her swelling breasts. "Never," he cried and went back to drink from the fountain, tickling and tormenting her with his expert tongue. Her body glowed with heat, and now separate from her reason and her mind, embarked on its own sweet journey of fulfillment. She groaned and fell back, rolling gently beneath his taut body, allowing him to cover her with the length and firmness of his torso. She lay inert while he worked at their clothes, easing them away and throwing them to the floor, until they lay naked together on the bed. His hands slid over her, searching her as though they could never get enough of the feel of her silky flesh. He cupped her breasts in them, wiping their fullness against his cheeks and lips, sucking and nipping until she was almost crazy with the sensation. Her hands sought him out as well, grasping at his flesh, cupping, clinging, gripping, drunk with the feel of him.

"Say you want me," Wade breathed against her supple flesh. "Say it."

Selene writhed beneath him, almost unable to speak. "No!"

she gasped, stubborn in spite of her growing need. Wade's tongue came alive, tormenting her, tasting, licking, sliding between her breasts. He shifted to his knees over her, his mouth working her body. His head slid lower, lower, until he was poised between her open legs, sucking, tasting, driving her wild.

"Say it! Say it!" he gasped, raising his head long enough to bite at her pubic mound. His growing frenzy only added to the excitement that sent her reeling beneath his insistent hands, mouth and tongue.

"No! No! I don't . . ." With a cry she arched beneath him. he slid up her body, jamming his engorged phallus deep within her, gyrating his body against hers until she felt like one gaping orifice. Her whole body was an open mouth, waiting for him to fill her. "No! Ah . . . h . . ." she cried as he systematically massaged her to a frenzy of need.

"Say it!"

"I want you. Oh, please . . . please . . ."

And he slammed home. They melded into one tormented body, clasped together, moving as one, driving simultaneously toward that precipice of sensuality that would send them flying into wild, uninhibited, soaring space.

"Oh, oh, oh . . ." Selene cried as the torment eased. She fell back in his arms, unable to move, her breathing gradually slowing. Wade buried his head in her neck and her spilling hair, waiting for his own pounding heart to return to normal.

"God, how I've missed you," he murmured against her. "How I've needed . . ." He stopped abruptly, suddenly wary of revealing to her just how much he had needed and thought of her these last months. Selene caught his cautious return to reality and her own priorities reasserted themselves. There were tears on her cheeks, the aftermath of her passion, but she stubbornly wiped them away with her arm. Slipping away from him, she swung her legs over the bed and struggled to regain control. Surprised at first, Wade caught her tone and rolled off to reach for his clothes. Selene grabbed his dressing robe off a chair near the bed, anxious to cover her nakedness.

"You bastard!" Selene snapped, pulling his dressing robe around her shoulders. "You brought me here deliberately for this. I should have suspected you would never be so civil without some ulterior motive."

Wade laughed and pulled on his trousers. His bare chest and firm shoulders looked bronze in the deepening afternoon light. "I seem to recall I was very civil the last time we met. Indeed, I rescued you and delivered you to your door without even demanding a reward."

"There was probably some ulterior motive for that, too. You never do anything without a selfish reason. What do you want with me, beside the obvious need to get me on my back?"

Deliberately Wade walked into the adjoining room where he poured two glasses of sherry and carried them back to the bed. "Here," he said. "Drink this. Perhaps it will temper your sour humor."

She glared at him but took the wine. "You are the reason for my bad humor. And it will take more than sherry to remedy that."

"Come now," he said, sitting down on the edge of the bed. "Let's agree to be civil to one another. It appeared to me that you enjoyed our bedroom antics as much as I did. Surely you aren't that good an actress."

Selene sniffed but sat down beside him. "I won't say I didn't enjoy it, but I think you are a beast to take advantage of me that way. You got me here under false pretenses and only for this."

He grew suddenly serious. "No, it was not only for this. I will soon be going back to America and I admit I hoped to be with you this one last time. That was part of my purpose. But I also wanted to warn you, I fear for you, putting your life into that man's hands. He is not to be trusted."

"What do you know of Simon Lazar? Nothing. This is just your prejudice speaking."

"Perhaps I know more than you think I do."

She sipped her wine, thinking back over the afternoon. "This was no accidental meeting today at all, was it? You planned the whole thing. I'll bet you were even following me."

Wade shrugged. "As a matter of fact, I was. I've wanted to get you alone for some time now, but it was difficult to do. You are so often with friends or with him." He broke off, taking the long rope of her hair that curled over one shoulder in his hand

262

and gently stroking it. "Will you please take my warning seriously? And if, after I've gone, you ever need help, there is someone I'd like you to turn to. I know she'll help you and I cannot feel that Lazar will."

"Who is that?"

"Melissa Belton."

Selene gasped. "Lady Belton? That society matron? Why she cares for nothing but parties and teas and balls. What on earth have you got to do with her?"

Wade shrugged. "Long ago she was a friend of my mother's. I met her in Virginia before the war and have come to depend on her since I've been here. I know she would be your friend, too."

"But she's a Yankee sympathizer through and through. At least . . . that's what she pretends."

He looked away. "And I'm sure she is at heart. We don't discuss the war." Slipping his hand around her neck he pulled her to him and kissed her lightly. But Selene had grown wary and would not be aroused. Firmly she moved away and slid off the other side of the bed.

"This is a waste of time. I have to go."

He watched her pulling on her clothes, his blood warming all over again. With the slightest encouragement he would have taken her once more. Her body had become for him a limitless pool of delight and ecstasy. Yet he turned from the thought, resigned to seeing her leave, finally now and forever. He had forced her many times—he would not force her again. He wanted her but he wanted her to reach for him and that she was never going to do. Perhaps it was his fault. After all, he had never expected to fall in love with her. He had thought of her first as a danger and then as a pleasant pastime. And now it was too late to change all that. Too late for so many things.

"I'll see you home," Wade said wearily. Selene, struggling with the buttons on her dress, said over her shoulder: "There's no need for that. I'm accustomed to getting around by myself."

Wade stepped behind her and fastened the dress. His fingers, once their task was finished, slipped around her waist and he buried his face in her neck, mouthing her warm flesh.

Selene stood like a stone in his embrace and discouraged he

finally moved away. "I brought you here. I'll see you home."

It was not a comfortable trip. They both sat silent and musing while the cab maneuvered through the traffic on the streets, more congested than usual because a light misty rain had begun an hour before. It served to lay some of the dust but it was a far cry from the heavy dousing the country needed and longed for. When they pulled up in front of Simon's house, Selene opened the door herself and made to get down, but Wade stopped her with a hand on her arm. He pushed past her, then reached to hand her down. Standing with her hand in his he looked deeply into her eyes, almost reluctant to let her go. "Selene," he said gently, "whatever the past has been . . ."

She never knew what made her glance beyond him to the walkway. Coming toward them, his face visibly alternating between surprise and fury, she saw Simon, his step faltering only slightly as he recognized Wade, his silver-tipped malacca cane swinging in his hand. "Please . . ." Selene muttered. "Just go."

"But I may never see you again."

"That can't be helped. It's too late now for words. Please go."

She tried to push him toward the carriage but he gripped her hand and held it. "You will heed my warning?"

"Yes, yes," she nodded, shoving him near the cab. Puzzled, Wade glanced up the walk and spotted Simon. "Is that why you are so anxious to get rid of me? I'm not afraid of him."

"Please Wade. For me . . ."

"Why do you fear him? I'm not leaving you here."

"It's not me I'm afraid for."

It was too late. Simon advanced on them, swinging his cane with obvious irritation. "My, but isn't this a tender sight," he said sarcastically as he moved up beside Selene. "I had no idea you two were still seeing each other." His voice was cold, and Selene recognized the icy undertone that indicated barely repressed anger. She quickly let go of Wade's arm. More than anything she had hoped to avoid a scene. She could deal with Simon's anger toward herself, but she was very unsure of his reaction to Wade. And knowing the hot-blooded, proud Virginian, she felt certain Wade was not going to take anything from this man he so detested.

"We ran into each other at the Exhibition," she said weakly, stepping betwen them to face Simon directly. "Wade was kind enough to see me home."

"Oh? That's not how it looked to me. You are not welcome here, Captain. I'll thank you to leave."

Wade's eyes glinted. "I know that is your house, Mister Lazar, but I had no idea you had leased the walkways as well. And I believe it is none of your business what time I spend with my wife."

"A relationship you have abused and neglected, sir. Kindly stand away from her."

"That is for her to say. You presume too much."

"She is under my protection and has been since I assisted her to escape from your tyranical domination."

"Tyranical! This is ridiculous. If we were in America, sir, I would meet you at dawn to repay you for running off with my wife. Unfortunately dueling is frowned on in this country . . . Besides, duels are meant for men of honor. I would never grant you that distinction."

"Wade!" Selene cried. "Stop this now. I asked you to go. Please . . ."

Simon's lips were a thin slash across his narrow face. "You arrogant cad! You abuse this poor girl . . ."

"Oh, and now she is a poor girl. What is it, Lazar? Not jealous, are you? No, I can't believe you would have that much life in your thin blood. I don't know what your interest in Selene actually is, but you won't scare me off so easily."

"Wade, you are making everything worse," Selene cried and pushed him toward the carriage again. "I won't have this." It was obvious to her that Simon was on the verge of losing his carefully controlled temper. There had always been something a little eccentric in his hatred of Wade and it was fast eroding the bounds of his usual self-containment. Lazar reached out to grab her, shoving her toward the portico of the house.

"Go inside, Selene," he snapped officiously.

"Simon, let him go. People are beginning to gawk."

Lazar made one last effort to control his outrage. "Your cab is waiting, Captain. I suggest you leave and never come back."

But Wade was enjoying himself. "Make me, if you can, you sly, two-faced Yankee."

"A good beating is something you could have used long ago."

"Not from the likes of you," Wade said, laughing at Simon's mounting fury. It was the last push over the edge. Raising his cane Simon slapped it across Wade's shoulders with a force that nearly knocked him off his feet. He stumbled forward against the cab, setting the horse dancing and trying to rear in the harness. While the driver struggled to quiet his mount, Wade regained his balance, grabbed Simon's coat and began pummeling him with his fist. Lazar, lighter and thinner than Wade, had a wiry agility and a better understanding of the business of fisticuffs. He dodged Wade's grip and brought his own fist up, slamming it into Wade's stomach. Gasping, Wade doubled over. Simon slammed his balled fist on the back of Wade's neck. Wade fell against the cab, still gyrating at the curb, managed to grasp the wheel long enough to right his balance, then threw himself against Lazar, pounding him on the face.

One blow found its target, knocking Simon back against the stairs to the house, dazing him long enough that his body slid down the wall to the ground. A thin trickle of blood inched its way from Lazar's mouth. Wade rubbed his hand against the back of his neck. He was going to have a bad bruise there. He could barely hold up his head. Lazar had more strength in his blows than Wade had anticipated.

Selene looked from one man to the other, furious at them both. Then she went and knelt beside Simon, still blinking at the blow to his head.

"I hope you're proud of yourself," she snapped at Wade. "The two of you making a public spectacle of yourselves. You've made everything really wonderful now, haven't you? He'll never forgive you for this, and he'll never rest until he gets even with you."

Wade shrugged and reached for his hat which had fallen in the gutter, dusting it off with his gloves. "Then I'll just have to do it again, won't I?"

She stood up, glaring at him. "And you haven't made things

266

any easier for me either. But that wouldn't concern you, would it? Other people's trials never concern Captain Kinsolving. Whatever he wants, when he wants it, is all that matters. I hope I never see you again."

There was some truth in what she said, he realized too late. "Selene . . ."

"Just go!"

Lazar, his senses still reeling, was struggling to get back on his feet. Wade was reluctant to leave, yet he had to admit it would be for the best. There was nothing more he could do for Selene. He had seen her safely home and he had warned her. Whatever possibilities might have once lay between them were completely gone now.

Without a word he climbed into the cab and banged on the roof. By the time it went lumbering off, Simon was standing, leaning on Selene's arm.

"Come inside," she said, none too gently for she was as angry with Lazar as with Wade. "I'll see what I can do about that eye."

Later, in her room, she sat for a long time thinking about the events of the afternoon. She was so angry with both men she would have liked to butt their two heads together. It was disgraceful, standing like a female deer while two bucks went at each other tooth and toenails for her favors. And yet, she was certain they were not really fighting over her at all. In all the time she had known Simon, especially since they came to London, he had never expressed the slightest interest in her body, much less her affections. She did not know, when it came right down to it, what his interest was in keeping her here with him. But whatever it was, it was something more devious, more selfish than a purely healthy hedonism. What had Wade meant by his warning and by directing her to, of all people, Melissa Belton, if she needed a friend? It was all very confusing and disturbing.

She did not trust Simon anymore than Wade did. But neither did she trust Wade. In all the time she had known him his motive in pursuing her had been just as selfish as Simon's had been, though in Wade's case, she knew exactly what he wanted.

Once again she made up her mind that at all costs she had to get away from London and back to Washington. There was nothing for her here. She wanted to get away from both of these men, back home where she could set about putting her life in order on her own. It was now the middle of July. Surely soon Simon would keep his promise and send her home.

Deliberately she set about being as polite to Simon as possible, never mentioning the events of the afternoon, and quietly probing his intentions toward her. He asked her to attend a series of social engagements over the next two weeks and promised that by the first of August she would have the ticket to America in her hand.

"And in return, I must insist that you do not see Captain Kinsolving again, for any reason whatsoever."

"You needn't worry about that," Selene assured him. "I don't want to see him ever again."

"That should be fairly easy for you. The Captain is returning to America in two days' time. He has decided to go back and do his part for the flagging cause of the Confederacy. Good riddance, I say."

"How do you know this?"

"I make it my business to know my enemies' movements. With any luck he'll become one of the growing number of casualties, and we'll both be rid of him for good."

Selene looked at Lazar narrowly, biting her tongue to keep from responding to his bitter remarks. There was little to choose between them, she thought, and yet she was too anxious to keep the peace to say so. Later, sitting at her dresser, she took out the small velvet case that contained her meager collection of jewels and held the ruby necklace in her fingers. It evoked for a few moments the pleasures of those days in Barbados when happiness had touched her—a happiness that held them both in a warmth of understanding and caring they had never regained. She looked at her image in the mirror, staring into her own confused eyes. What do I really feel, she spoke aloud. Tears stung behind her lids. For so long had she told herself that she hated this Confederate Captain who had forced her from her home, that now she could barely allow room in her mind for any different thoughts. Yet what had he done? He had taken her from a bleak, confining life, empty of all joy, and opened up the world for her. He had given her some of the most ecstatic moments of her life. He had taught her how to be a lady, exposed her to the graciousness of life that she would never have had an opportunity to know without him. Perhaps, just perhaps, it was possible that she did not hate Wade Kinsolving quite as much as she had always thought.

She had to see him once more before he left. He had sought her out when he thought it was going to be for the last time, and now she would do the same for him. Otherwise, she might never know what she truly felt for him, and somehow it was very important to the rest of her life that she did know.

Sailing Friday, Simon had said. That meant he would have to be leaving London for one of the channel ports today or tomorrow. There might still be time, but only if she hurried.

Selene threw a light short cloak around her shoulders and left word with the housemaid that she was going shopping. She decided to go by London cab since Fenton would be certain to tell Simon where she had gone if he inquired—as he was sure to do.

She first went to the house where only a few days before she had lain with Wade in his bed. Entering by the main door she found her way up the stairs. The door to his flat stood ajar and Selene peeked in to see a maid whisking a long-handled feather duster over the furniture.

"Is Captain Kinsolving out?" Selene asked tentatively. She hated to speak to the maid, but on the other hand perhaps he would be returning soon.

"La, ma'am," the girl exclaimed, turning swiftly and clutching her hand to her heart. "You gave me a start. I didn't hear you."

"I'm sorry if I startled you. I'm looking for Captain Kinsolving."

"Oh, he be gone, Miss. Back to America to fight in the war, I do believe. Left this morning, he did."

"This morning." Selene fought to hide her disappointment. She thanked the girl and went downstairs where the cab was waiting, wondering what to do next. After some consideration she had the driver take her to Lady Belton's. There was a chance Wade might have gone there before he left London and with any luck she could still catch him.

It was difficult for her to face Melissa Belton whose surprise and curiosity was so evident. There was also something more, a hint of displeasure and a wariness. Selene stared back at her, determined not to be put off.

"I thought he might have come here," she said, going right to the heart of the matter.

"He did but he has already left. Forgive me, Mrs. Kinsolving, but I understood you and the Captain were—estranged—I believe is the correct word."

"That is true. We haven't seen much of each other since he came to England but he is going back now to fight in the war. I—I wanted to say good-bye. He did tell me that if I ever needed a friend, I should come to you."

Lady Belton's brows inched up and her fine eyes widened. "He told you to come to me," she exclaimed. Selene went on quickly.

"He said you were an old friend of the family and would be sympathetic to me."

"Forgive me, Selene, but the truth is that while I have a fondness for Captain Kinsolving and his family, I have no such feelings for Simon Lazar. I don't trust the man. Perhaps that is what makes me hesitate now. You see, I know he would do Wade harm if he could, and since you . . ."

"Lady Belton," Selene cried, clutching at Melissa's arm in her frustration, "I understand your reluctance but please believe me, Simon Lazar does not even know I am here. I only wish to see my—my husband once more before he goes away, perhaps even to his death. Can you understand that?"

Melissa walked to the marble mantel and drummed her fingers on it, turning over Selene's words. Selene waited, twisting her hands nervously. There was just a chance that Wade was still in London or Lady Belton would have told her no at once. If she refused now to say where he was, Selene would have no other place to turn. Her breath was tight in her chest as she watched the older woman struggle to make up

270

her mind.

"Very well," Melissa finally said, drawing Selene to the couch and sitting beside her. "If Wade told you to come to me there must be good reason to trust you. He's at the Greenwich docks. He's sailing on the *Plymouth Lady* with the tide at about five o'clock."

Five o'clock! Only two hours and Greenwich so far away.

"If you hurry," Melissa went on. She stopped abruptly on seeing Selene's crestfallen expression. "You don't have your carriage, do you?"

"No. I thought it best to come here by cab."

"Yes. You were right to do so. No matter. You can take mine."

She jumped up to reach for a small bell on the mantel, jangling it vigorously. "I'll have it brought around right away. My groom, Rogers, is very skilled at navigating the London streets in record time."

"Oh, but I couldn't . . ."

Melissa took Selene's hands and drew her to her feet. "Now don't be foolish. I have a soft spot for Wade and you said this would be your last meeting with him. Besides, the romance of it all appeals to me. My life for the most part is a selfish bore. Indulge me this one opportunity to do something for someone else."

Selene needed no further encouragement. Before she knew what was happening she was bundled downstairs and into a handsome carriage drawn by a matched pair of grays, showing no sign of a hasty harnessing. Melissa's groom was as good as his reputation, yet with the distance and crowded streets, it was almost five o'clock before the lathered horses finally drew up near the Greenwich docks.

The confusion here was greater than the London streets. A forest of masts rose above the heads of the milling crowds that choked the streets and the wharf beyond. Over it all hung the pungent miasma of the river, made even more stagnant by the warm afternoon. Selene jumped down to push her way through the workmen and passengers, stopping only to ask directions to the berth where the *Plymouth Lady* waited on the tide. She spotted Wade even before she found the ship, since he was standing on a platform that raised him slightly above the crowd. He was in his shirtsleeves and without a hat, bent over a listboard beside one of the workmen.

"Wade!" she called, waving to him and pushing through to the platform. He stared down at her in open-mouthed surprise, then spoke briefly to the workman, grabbed up his coat, and bounded down the low steps to her side. "What on earth are you doing here?" he said, taking her arm and leading her away from the ship to a slightly less crowded corner of the wharf.

"Oh, Wade, I was so afraid I wouldn't get here in time. Thank goodness you hadn't left yet." She fought the temptation to throw herself into his arms, partly from the memory of their last meeting, and partly because of the guarded expression he turned on her.

"I thought you never wanted to see me again. I believe those were your words."

"Oh, Wade, you're going back to fight in the war, aren't you? Why? Why give up on your negotiations now? The war will be over soon."

"You're not worried over my likely demise, are you, Selene? How touching. I rather thought you didn't care."

"Please don't be sarcastic, Wade. Not now. What you plan to do is terribly dangerous. So many men have been killed or maimed."

He dropped his supercilious air as quickly as he had put it on.

"I admit the casualties in this war are suggestive of Armageddon. But that's all the more reason I must get involved. You know I've wanted to since the beginning. I can't stand it anymore, wasting my time over here or in Barbados, while better men are dying for their country."

"But you always said that what you were doing was important to your country's cause, too. Surely you are needed here still."

"No, Selene," he replied, staring out at the ship creaking gently in the water. "It's hopeless. England never intended to come in on our side. I know that now. There might have been a chance before, when we won such splendid victories on the field. But there was a terrible battle in Pennsylvania at the beginning of this month. It ended any chance that Great Britain would recognize the Confederacy."

"I read about it. The paper called it a great victory for the Union."

"More like a draw," he said bitterly. "But bad enough to send General Lee scuttling back to Virginia with what was left of his army. We've lost the west now as well. Vicksburg surrendered the day after Gettysburg. It's hopeless and my work here is finished."

"But if it's hopeless, why must any more men die? Why must you go back and risk your life?"

"Because we're not beaten yet. We'll fight until the last man and the last breath. It's a matter of honor."

Her eyes filled with tears. "Honor! What's honorable about dying for a hopeless cause!"

For the first time he smiled at her. "Why, Selene, I believe you *do* care a little what happens to me. Forgive my amazement. You rather had me convinced that I was the last person who mattered to you. As for your thoughts regarding honor, they sound like Simon Lazar. You've been around him too long."

Selene clicked her tongue in disgust and turned from him, forcing back her tears. "You Southerners! You think no one understands honor except you. Well, there are other kinds of honor and integrity besides throwing one's life away for nothing. Of course I care. I'd feel as much for . . . for a pet dog that was about to be run over by the wheels of a carriage."

"Your analogy is hardly complimentary, but I accept your feelings for what they are worth." He looked quickly up as a bell began clanging shrilly aboard the nearby ship. From the high bridge the ship's master called down to Wade, "Time to cast off, Captain Kinsolving." Wade waved to him and began slipping on his coat. "I must go. But I'm glad you came, Selene. I'll remember you here, looking so lovely with the sunlight and tears on your cheeks."

She clutched at his arm. "Wade, why must we always be at cross-purposes?"

"We got started that way and somehow were never able to move on to anything else. Except perhaps once . . ."

273

A silken Barbados beach . . . She knew he was remembering it, too.

"Ready to cast off, Captain," the ship's master's voice boomed again. The sailors on the dock were beginning to loosen the thick mooring ropes. Filled with a sudden panic, Selene gripped Wade's arm. "Wade, please be careful. I saw those awful war photographs at the Exhibition. I never dreamed it was that terrible."

He slipped his arm around her waist and walked her toward the landing walk. Before he could answer her, the workman with the listboard ran down from the platform and thrust it at Wade.

"Captain, would you just check this before you leave so I can have it signed and stamped."

"I checked through it twice already, Sam. It's correct. Besides, I trust you to get everything aboard correctly."

"Oh, I'm sure of my part, sir. Mister Huntworthy don't keep a foreman who can't account for every piece that's delivered. But I want to be certain you're satisfied."

Huntworthy. The name jarred Selene out of her thoughts long enough to glance up at the wooden crates stacked on the deck of the *Plymouth Lady*. She could not make out the name printed on them but she could see, in large letters, the place of origin: LEEDS.

"Wade," she said in surprise. "I know Mister Huntworthy. He's a munitions agent."

Wade handed the listboard back to the foreman. "That's right. This cargo represents the last effort I could make for my country in England, and just about the only good thing that has come of my stay here."

Selene could see rows and rows of stacked crates. "You're taking all these back?"

"Yes. It's no secret. They were honorably ordered and paid for, at an exorbitant price, I might add, set by the benevolent British government. We are desperate for guns and ammunition back home now, from any source. I was determined that if I had to go home without a treaty, I would not go without a shipment of armaments."

"But can you get them there?"

274

"We'll have to run the blockade, but it's been done before. The port at Mobile is still open as far as I know. Once there I'll make my way to Virginia and lay these at General Lee's feet. That ought to assure my welcome at least."

Beside the gangplank a sailor waited in barely disguised patience. The bell began to clang again as Wade slipped his arms around her, pressing her against him. "Good-bye, Selene. Thank you for coming."

Her breath froze in her throat. Her chest felt constricted. He was leaving her forever and she still did not know what she felt for him. Once she had thought she could turn her back on Wade Kinsolving and walk away with no thought at all. Now faced with a final separation, she knew she could not. Thoughts tumbled about in her mind, words she wanted to speak but could not. "Wade . . ." she started but he laid his fingers on her lips, silencing them.

"It's too late, Selene. There's no time left. Take care of yourself. I wish it could have been different."

"Wade, be careful."

He gripped her hands even as the ship creaked easily from its moorings. With a quick gesture he pressed them to his lips, then bent and kissed her mouth. It was a hard, quick, hopeless kiss. He ran up the plank to the ship's deck and stood, holding the sheets, watching her as the *Plymouth Lady* slid easily out into the river. Selene walked along the dock, following the graceful schooner, her eyes riveted to the figure on the deck growing smaller and more distant. Below her the water churned and foamed. Pedestrians on the dock jostled against her but she paid them no mind, watching until the ship was lost among the traffic on the busy river.

Fourteen

For the next two weeks depression dogged her steps like a hungry dog pleading to be fed. Try as she might, Selene could not shake off an overwhelming grief, the feeling that some part of her had been cleanly cut away and lost forever. She tried to take joy from the fact that it was the first of August and time for Simon to keep his promise to send her home, but nagging, impish voices raised all manner of reasons why that was not going to happen, and try as she might she could not shut them out. Simon had not mentioned his promise since the night he gave it to her and it was finally with some trepidation that she reminded him of it, half-expecting him to deny ever making such a promise at all.

"I haven't forgotten," he said coolly. "The plans are made for you to sail the fifteenth on, I believe, the packet, *Arabia*. The tickets are even now safely locked away in my desk. You'll have them in your hand the night before."

"Why can't I keep them?" she said, trying not to reveal her relief.

"Why should you? They're safe enough with me."

"Let me see them then. Hold them in my hand."

"Why, my dear, one would think you didn't trust me. Have I broken a promise to you any time since we've been friends? Try to see this in the proper perspective. Your longing to return to America has clouded your common sense."

She did feel somewhat ashamed, though, in truth, she did not really trust him. But he had kept his promise to take her away

276

from Barbados. Surely now he would not fail her. And she had kept her part of the bargain. She had pursued every person and every lead he asked of her, diligently making every effort to charm, wheedle, cajole, and ingratiate whoever he wanted. She had even forgiven him his part in the dreadful affair at Lord Candelby's.

He *must* come through! More and more she felt as if she had no place here in this foreign country. She wanted to be home. Her country was bleeding and she wanted to help bind up the wounds.

When she had time Selene began quietly sorting and packing her clothes for the trip. She planned to leave most of the elegant gowns and take only those that were serviceable and modest. She had an intuition that her life in Washington was going to be very subdued compared to the gay social whirl of London, but that was all right. She would try to find some kind of work that might supply a modest stipend—enough to support a roof over her head and food on the table. A governess would be nice since the living was included. She was well taught and she suspected she would be a good teacher. But one thing was certain—she would never work in a tavern again, even if she was forced to go back to her uncle and ask for his help.

With her mind full of plans, Selene went about her duties absently, talking about the upcoming voyage with no one but Matilda, and dreaming of a long blue expanse of sea and sky.

And then the note came for Mordacai.

She was to leave the very next day. Her boxes were packed, her spirits were soaring. Simon had said very little about the trip other than to suggest she take the post down to Portsmouth, but that did not bother her. He had been extremely taciturn of late and she put it down to the fact that she would no longer be around to help in his nefarious schemes. She came home that afternoon to find a sealed letter on the hall table. Ignoring Mrs. Osborne's efforts to discover who it was from, Selene took it upstairs and opened it hurriedly. It was Mordacai's handwriting right enough, but there was a brevity and an urgency about it that was unusual and uncharacteristic of the man. He begged to inform her that he was just returned from the north and that it was important she meet him at the usual place that very evening.

There was a little disconcerting since Simon might expect her to be home that evening. However, he had been in the habit of coming in late every night the past month, and she could only hope she would arrive back before he did. Making an excuse to Mrs. Osborne, who made no secret of the fact that she was convinced Selene was off to meet a lover, she dressed as for the theater and took a cab to the Covent Garden area where she hired a sitting room at the Garrick tavern down the street from the Carlyle Theater.

Mordacai was late and Selene, sure now she would not get home before Simon, was making ready to leave when he came hurrying up the stairs.

"I'm so sorry," he said, bustling through the door and filling the small room with his bulk. "I would have been here sooner but, oh dear, I do hate to say this, but I believe I was followed."

"Followed? But why on earth would you be followed? Are you sure?"

"As sure as I am of sitting here. Dear me, it does seem very mysterious and a trifle disconcerting. I never bargained for anything like this. Many's the time I played the criminal stalking the victim, or, indeed, the victim being stalked. But never did I think to find myself in such a position in real life. This is a dangerous game, madam. Dangerous, indeed."

"I don't know what you are talking about. You said you were going back to Leeds to get more information. Does that have anything to do with your being followed, do you think?"

"I suspect it does. At any rate, I was finally able to shake the fellow and here I am. You must listen to what I have to say and then get yourself off as quickly as possible. I don't want to involve you in anything . . . well, unlawful."

Selene leaned toward him, dropping her voice. "Is all this about something unlawful? I never dreamed . . ."

"Listen to me," Mordacai said in a quiet whisper, bending close enough to her that she could smell the tobacco on his whiskers. "A very large shipment of arms was delivered only two weeks ago, destined for the Southern United States."

"I know about that. Someone I know—a friend—ordered them. They are meant for the Confederacy."

"Yes, yes, I know. However, there was more involved here than merely guns and ammunition. Mister Huntworthy, who, as you know, is extremely sensitive to money, irregardless of the source, was, shall we say, encouraged to alter the contract somewhat."

"Do you mean bribed?" When Mordacai nodded, she went on. "To do what, and by whom?"

"Let me answer the first part of your question first. Those guns are part of a stored parcel left from years ago. They are antiquated and inferior and will probably cause more harm to those who use them, than to those they are used against. Mister Huntworthy was engaged to produce a shipment of Enfields from Austria and to add to them the best he could supply from his own factories. Instead he has rid himself of unwanted old stored muskets that he could never sell elsewhere."

The air of the room had gone suddenly stuffy. "Did the buyer realize this?" Selene asked softly.

"Of course not. That was the whole point. Mister Huntworthy was paid and paid handsomely to alter that shipment. It is almost inconceivable that he would do such a thing since it will reflect so badly on his company, but it seems he was convinced that the armaments were to be used in a dying, unworthy cause. A dead Confederacy will never be in the market for guns again. Then, too, the money that exchanged hands must have been formidable indeed. He received two payments from two sources. It was more than he could turn down."

"But who? Who would do such a thing? No, don't tell me . . ."

"That's correct. Your friend and protector, Simon Lazar. You must have known he was up to something. You live in the same house with him. Surely . . ."

"No, I didn't know. I suspected he was up to no good, but I had no idea what it was about. Or that it would be so treacherous. Oh, dear, Mordacai, what a terrible thing! The person who is taking those guns back to the South has no idea. He thinks he is helping his country."

"Is there any way you can warn him?"

"No. He has already left for America. I saw him just before he sailed. Oh, if only I had known this!"

Mordacai shook his shaggy head. "I only found out myself three days ago, and I left at once for London."

Selene patted his hand lying on the table. "You've done a good job—more than I ever expected. I've always suspected Simon was up to something, but I never knew he would stoop this low. Look," she added, reaching into her purse, "this is all I have now. I'll keep enough to get home and you must take the rest."

Mordacai had the grace to look embarrassed. "I don't relish taking your money."

"Nonsense, I hired you, didn't I? And you've done all I asked. Think of it as being reimbursed for an acting performance."

"But you may need this—"

"No. I'm leaving England tomorrow to return home and all my expenses will be taken care of. Thank you, Mordacai, for your help. I hope we meet again someday, perhaps in America."

He rose and pressed her hand to his lips. Selene all at once felt very sad to be leaving behind her a friend, one whom she had come to rely on in the brief time they had known each other. It was rather sad to think that after all her time in England this preposterous actor was the only person she regretted leaving.

To the surprise of the household, Simon came home earlier than usual. His habitual frown was deeper than ever and, had they been able to, both Matilda and Mrs. Osborne would have avoided speaking to him at all. He began by demanding to see Selene even as he handed his coat to the housemaid. Matilda retraced her steps back down the stairs to the front hall to face him, while Mrs. Osborne fled to the parlor with her mammoth sewing basket tucked under her arm.

"Miss Selene went out." Mattie said with more self-confidence than she actually felt.

Simon looked down his thin nose at her. "Where?"

"To the theater, I believe, sir."

"Alone? Why didn't you accompany her?"

"Why, I think she went with a friend," Mattie lied, holding her breath and praying he would not ask which one. Simon only stared at her in his usual way—which implied she was feebleminded—and snapped: "Tell her I want to see her the minute she comes in."

Mrs. Osborne, buried in her sewing, hoped the Master would retire right away or at least involve himself at his desk in the alcove of the parlor. When he came striding angrily into the room to take a chair near the grate and open a book, her heart sank. If only she had followed her intuition and fled to her bedroom upstairs instead of into the parlor, she thought with dismay. Lazar's stormy countenance warned her not to brave conversation, but it was constitutionally impossible for Letitia Osborne to sit in silence for long when someone else was in the room with her, even when that someone was Simon Lazar. She rattled on for nearly five minutes, taking courage from his tight-lipped silence, before a maid interrupted her to advise Simon that a gentleman had come to the door to leave a note for him. Simon tore it open, and scanned the contents while his face grew even darker.

"Not bad news, I hope," Mrs. Osborne said briskly, barely able to conceal her curiosity. "I always dread notes at night, don't you? Try as I might to be rational and tell myself they are probably some trifling thing or other, they still manage to conjure up all kind of dreadful visions. I do hope nothing has happened to dear Selene . . ."

Even she was not prepared for the storm that exploded over her. "Madam!" Lazar roared, "Just for once will you shut your silly face!"

"Well . . . really . . ." Mrs. Osborne sputtered, her face crumbling.

"Don't you dare shed a tear! You're a foolish, babbling old woman and I'm sick to death of the sound of your idiotic voice. Get out, do you hear! Get out this instant."

She scurried up from the sofa. "I only meant to be polite . . ." she sputtered, gathering up her sewing basket.

"I said get out *now*," Simon roared, knocking the basket out of her hand. She gave a shriek and fled out the door which he slammed after her. Then he stalked back to his chair and threw himself into it, his long fingers curling around the arms like claws as he stared at the grate where a small fire had been lit against the dampness of the night. He was still sitting there when Selene got home. At the first sound of her key in the lock, he jumped up and was at the parlor door motioning away the housemaid as Selene stepped through the front door. His thin body was a dark silhouette against the lighted room behind him. "I want to talk to you," he snapped.

Selene deliberately took her time untying the ribbons of her cloak. "And I with you." She was surprised to see how angry he was with her. Though if he thought he had her cowered, he was very mistaken. She threw her cloak on a chair in the hall and walked into the parlor turning to face him squarely. Simon, his glower deepening, closed the double doors before rounding on her.

"Where were you tonight?" he demanded.

"That is none of your concern. I am entitled to an evening to myself once in a while."

"Don't make excuses to me. I know you were with that imposter—that scenery-chewing actor you sent rooting around behind my back for information."

She hid her surprise. "If you know about my friend, Mister Granberry, that must be because you have your own informants."

"And I learned only a short time ago this evening that you were not at a theater at all, but in a private supper room at a tawdry tavern, knee deep in subterfuge with that man. Do you never think about the proprieties of a woman alone in London at night? How it looks to others. How it reflects on me?"

"That's what really concerns you, isn't it? How it reflects on you. You were the one who was having Mordacai followed, weren't you? I should have known!" She turned away, unable to look at him any longer. The long face, the hooded eyes, glaring their distrust, the conniving mind so evident even in the way he carried himself—she was filled with disgust. How had she ever been so foolish to have put her life in this man's keeping?

Deliberately she moved so as to put the marble-topped table between them. "If you were having us both followed, then you must know what Mordacai told me tonight. You bribed Colin Huntworthy to send defective munitions to the Confederacy. How could you be so low, knowing it means death to so many?"

Simon followed her, facing her across the cluttered table. "I cannot grieve for the death of traitors. Fewer guns and ammunition might help to bring about an end to this rebellion that much sooner. What I did was patriotic."

"Patriotism was not your motive and you know it," she cried. "It was revenge, wasn't it. You would go to any lengths to get even with Wade. What were you hoping for—that he might be killed with one of those antiquated rifles? It's what I would expect of a devious mind like yours."

"You're very considerate of the Captain all of a sudden. Up until now you've made a very convincing case of pretending to despise him, claiming you hated him and never wanted to see him again. Rather muddleheaded thinking, I fear, Selene."

Her cheeks flamed at his words. "He's a better man than you. He'd never involve himself in a despicable bribe such as the one you've made. He'd never stoop that low."

For an instant the self-contained mask fell away from his face, revealing the fury behind it. Simon stepped around the table toward her, his fist rising, then caught himself, and deliberately lowered his arm. "Someday, Selene, you'll go too far."

She stood her ground, though in the back of her mind a small voice reminded her that when he did lose his control, he would be as dangerous as a wild bear. "After tomorrow you won't have to be burdened with me anymore. Take consolation in the thought."

A quizzical look flitted across his features and for an instant Selene remembered how dependent she was upon his charity for her hope of returning to America. She held her breath, trying to stay calm, terrified that he had changed his mind. But he only muttered darkly, "It'll be good riddance."

"For both of us," she added, hiding her relief. She supposed that now was the time to try to calm and cajole him, to express her gratitude for his help and for sending her home. With a less

283

cold and calculating man that would have made her position secure. But she was too angry and too disgusted with Lazar to bother or care. "I earned this trip, remember," she said with barely disguised bitterness. "I did everything you asked of me, buttering up every fat old man with influence you asked me to impress. I ran myself ragged in your pursuits. And I never questioned, never demurred—"

"Oh, yes. You flirted and gaped and made yourself cheap with every pair of trousers in London society, damaging my reputation in the process without ever giving a thought to the effect it had upon me. I suppose I am to thank you for that."

Selene gasped. Grasping the table that stood between them, she leaned over it, into his face. "You can say that to me," she cried, "after the odious way you sold me to that lascivious Lord Candelby! You used me without turning a hair, without giving a thought to what I felt!"

His anger was swelling as swiftly as hers. His voice rising, he roared back. "If you hadn't been so prim and prudish you could have used *him*. There was no end to the favors you might have cajoled from that rich old man, if you had played your cards right. But no. You have to be Miss Goody-Two-Shoes, an idiotic, simpering, silly girl without a modicum of common sense. But then what else should I expect from the daughter of that momumental bore, Professor Theophiles Sprague!"

"You hypocrite! One minute you accuse me of being flirtatious and cheap, and the next of acting prudish and proper. You just throw out words because you have no valid argument to use against me. And I'll thank you not to turn your vitriolic tongue against my father. You're not fit to speak his name."

Simon's lips compressed into a smile that was a slash across his narrow face. With a swift swing of his arm he sent the table crashing to its side. A porcelain vase flew across the room, smashing against the iron grate.

"That's what I think of your father. He was a pompous, verbose twaddler, who was never able to make a decent living at anything approaching respectable work. How I used to squirm perched among that bunch of giddy fools soaking up his second-rate philosophy! I sat there with a serious frown knitting my brow and a mask of polite regard on my face and all the while I was laughing at them—their smugness, their half-baked aphorisms, their idiotic pseudo-intellectualism. And the worst of the lot was the great leader himself. A man in love with the sound of his own voice, ranting about Aristotle and Rousseau, when he himself wouldn't recognize an original idea if he walked into it!"

Selene reared back as though he had struck her in the face. "If you hated him so much, why did you come?" she said in a strangled voice.

"Why?" Even his laugh was a sneer. "Why else? I hoped to learn something I could take back to my superiors in the government, some suspicious activity that would enhance my own position. But it was all a waste of time. Those men weren't dangerous—they were merely stupid."

The colors of the room faded together into one bright scream of fire behind her eyes. Not completely aware of what she was doing, driven by a torrent of rage and injustice, Selene swung her arm and slapped his hateful, grinning face with all the strength she could summon. Simon's head snapped back. A veil seemed to lower itself across his eyes for an instant. Then he regained his senses, the color drained from his face, and swinging his fist, he hit her squarely on the jaw. The force of the blow sent her sprawling backwards on the floor. Selene ducked as he came after her, and for the first time she began to be afraid of him. There was something not human in his contorted face as he swung at her a second time. She threw herself back against the wall but he was too swift for her. Striking out like a viper, he grabbed her arm and pulled her to her feet, then slapped her hard across the face. Her senses reeling, she fell to her knees again, shaking her head to try and clear it. Her bruised face screamed with pain. She had to get away from him somehow. She had to escape out of this room, upstairs to the safety of her bedroom. He roared at her, unintelligible sounds, and Selene knew he was completely out of control. She would be dead if she stayed here. He would beat her insensible.

"You spoiled, stupid girl," Simon screamed, slapping her again. "You deserve a good beating. You should have had it years ago."

His fingers dug into the soft flesh of her arm, bruising her painfully as he tried once again to haul her to her feet. Her hand groped wildly for a weapon, anything she could use to defend herself, and found the jumble of implements from Mrs. Osborne's sewing basket that had been thrown there earlier. Her fingers clamped around the long thin blade of the scissors, grasping them in her fist like a knife, she swung her arm just as Simon yanked her to her feet again. His right hand was raised to strike her once more but she got him first, raking the sharp point of the scissors down his cheek, raising a thin streak of bright scarlet against his white face. With a terrible howl, Simon grabbed his face. Selene slid downward as her knees gave way beneath her. She had felt the rip of the flesh, heard the blade slicing through skin, and it had sickened her. She was on all fours, the scissors still clutched in her hand as she struggled for the strength to stand up and run. When it wouldn't come, she began scrambling across the rug for the door fighting her cumbersome skirt. Simon threw himself on top of her throwing her over, howling with pain and fury, his fingers closing around her throat. In a panic Selene drew back her arm and jabbed the scissors deep into his yielding flesh. His breath went out in one sickening gush. He slumped over her. Gasping with horror at what she had done, she rolled away as he collapsed on the rug. Her throat was in agony from the pressure of his fingers, and her face throbbed painfully. She shrank as far back to the other side of the room as she could get and felt her jaw gingerly with her fingertips, hoping it wasn't broken. All the while she stared at Simon slumped in a heap on the floor, waiting with her breath frozen in her throat for him to rise up again and start for her.

The room was unnaturally quiet. Only her deep, gasping breath broke the deadly silence. All around her lay the clutter of their struggle—the overturned table and its contents haphazardly scattered among those of the sewing basket. Furniture was pushed out of its accustomed position, a chair knocked to one side, the rug now a corduroy jumble, half the sofa cushions on the floor. A log fell suddenly in the stove, sending a shower of sparks visible behind the grilled plate.

As her heavy breathing subsided, Selene realized that she was pressed against the wall across the room, staring at the grotesquely collapsed body of Simon Lazar lying near the door. She looked down to see that the blade in her hand was coated with blood. There were splatterings of crimson across her bodice and down the front of her skirt. Little pawprints of red made a pattern across the rug to the still figure on the floor. She pushed back her tangled hair, undone in her struggle. There was a tear somewhere on her dress and her cheeks were still screaming from the force of Simon's blows. But she was alive. She was not that inert, shapeless lump on the floor.

She inched closer, waiting every second for him to come roaring to life again. When he did not move, she reached out slowly to touch his shoulder and turn it so that she could see his face. His eyes stared up lifeless, his mouth hung open, the pink tongue partially extended. His skin was as colorless as the lace curtains on the window behind him.

A faint gurgle escaped the white throat. Selene quickly jumped back and watched his face fall forward again. He was dead. Killed by her hand. And she was not sorry.

Only gradually did she become aware of a soft scratching at the door. She hid the scissors behind her skirt, listening intently. When she recognized Matilda's voice whispering, "Miss Selene?" over and over behind the heavy oak door, she slumped with relief.

"Are you all right, Miss Selene? It's me, Mattie. Open the door, please!"

Very carefully Selene inched around Lazar's body and cracked the doors just wide enough to make certain Matilda was alone in the dimly lighted hall. Then she pulled her into the room, locking the doors behind her. Mattie stood in her nightgown, pulling a wide fringed shawl around her shoulders, staring in disbelief from Selene to the body on the floor.

"Mercy!" she breathed. "Merciful God. Miss Selene, what happened?"

"Keep your voice down. We mustn't arouse the servants or Mrs. Osborne."

"But what happened here? Is he—is he dead? And you—you're all torn up. What did he do?"

"He tried to kill me but I killed him first," Selene answered. Her calm, dispassionate voice amazed even her. "I didn't mean to . . ."

"What are we going to do? Shouldn't we call a doctor or—or maybe the police?"

"No! I've got to think. Oh God, Mattie, if the police come and find Simon here like this, I'll never get back to America. Even if they decide it was justified, I'll lose my trip tomorrow and it might be months, years even, before I get away. I can't do that. I have to go back. I have to find Wade and warn him."

Matilda could make nothing of Selene's near-hysterical rambling except that she was close to falling apart. "Maybe he's not really dead," she said, grasping her arm to support her. "Are you sure?"

"Yes, I'm sure. Look for yourself if you don't believe me."

"No, no. I don't want to go near him," she whispered. "But I can't say I'm sorry. He was a terrible man, Miss Selene. Imagine him trying to harm you. But, oh, what are we going to do?"

Selene edged her way to the sofa and sat down gingerly, fighting to bring some order to her jumbled thoughts. Raising her head she spied the desk in the alcove across the room and stared at it like a shining beacon in a storm.

"Mattie, I want you to go back upstairs and finish packing my portmanteau. Don't worry about the other boxes. We'll leave them all. I don't want anything that man ever gave me. Just bring enough things for the trip."

"Trip? Are we—"

"Yes. We're still going." Her voice was strong now and she was completely in control. Mattie sensed it with relief. "With any luck Simon's body won't be found until tomorrow morning, and by then we'll be in Portsmouth. Be very quiet. You *must* not wake anyone upstairs. If you should happen to, say there was an argument in the parlor but it's all resolved. Can you manage that?"

Mattie pulled her shawl tight around her throat and edged toward the door. She wanted nothing so much as to escape this oppressive room. "I'll take care of it, Miss Selene. You just hurry and come up to change your clothes so we can leave."

"Wait!" Selene stopped her as the girl was turning the key in the lock. "First, we have to straighten this room so as not to arouse suspicion if anyone should look in. Here, help me put the furniture back."

Together they picked up the table, rearranged the objects strewn about, and straightened the rug. "Now," Selene said grimly. "Help me put him in that chair, so his back will be to the door."

"Miss Selene! I can't touch that—that *thing*. Don't ask me to!"

Selene grabbed her arm, digging her fingers into the girl's flesh. There was an unnatural glint in her bright eyes that belied her apparant calm. "You've got to. I can't move him alone. Help me do it so we can get out of here!"

Reluctantly Mattie followed her mistress, forcing herself to put one hand under Simon's arm and help Selene lift the dead weight of Simon's body. They managed to get him up far enough to drag his body into one of the hearth chairs with his legs extending out toward the stove.

"He's slumped down awfully far in the chair, but maybe it will appear he is asleep. It will have to do, anyway. I never dreamed an inert body could be so heavy."

Selene was rambling wildly again and Mattie tried to urge her out of the room and upstairs. She herself could not breathe, she was so anxious to leave.

But Selene had just enough rational thought left to know she was not yet finished. "You go up and pack. I'll be along in a minute." She opened the door just wide enough to shove Mattie through, then forced herself back to Simon's chair. His head hung at a peculiar angle and his tongue was even more distended. Though she hated the thought of touching any part of him, she forced herself to reach out and pull back the lapel of his coat. His waistcoat was wet with blood and her hand faltered. Quickly, she reached into the narrow pocket until she felt the key. Pulling it out, she wiped it back and forth on her skirt. Then she took it to the desk and opened the drawer he had always been so careful to keep locked. She knew her tickets were there and that was all she wanted now from Simon Lazar.

There were two long folded envelopes on top of other

assorted papers and a second set of keys. Throwing the keys aside, Selene fumbled among the papers. Bills of lading, IOU's, a deed to some property north of London—of course he had never mentioned owning property—but then, who ever knew how many pies Simon had his fingers in. She went through them all a second time, and then, more frantically a third, but there were no tickets for any ship going to America. There were no tickets to anything, anywhere. Frantically she tore at the legal documents referring to a suit, plus several letters, one from Huntworthy's munitions clearly indicating Lazar's part in the deceptive arms shipment. But still no tickets. The other folder, she was amazed to see, was stuffed full of money—rolls of English pounds and American dollars. There were several loose gold coins as well. But no tickets there either.

Selene glared at the slumped body in the chair. "You viper!" she hissed. "You never intended to send me home. It was all a lie!"

Angrily she began to pile the jumble of papers back in the drawer but then thought better of it. Taking the folder of bills she carefully separated enough money to pay for the fare to Portsmouth and passage to America for both herself and Mattie. Then she put the rest back. She wanted no more from Simon Lazar then was justly hers. She had earned this, every cent. He owed it to her. But she did not want the police thinking she was a thief as well as a murderer.

Locking the drawer, Selene thought to return the key to his waistcoat pocket but found she could not bring herself to touch him again. Instead, she threw it into the stove. Then, with a last glance at Lazar's frozen face, she quickly hurried out of the room, closing the door behind her.

Fifteen

It was late afternoon when Selene left the War Department on Pennsylvania Avenue. A whole afternoon wasted! Another four hours spent sitting on a hard, uncomfortable chair along a drafty hall, trying not to think of all the more productive things she could be doing. Surgeon Meade at the Armory Square Hospital had been reluctant to let her go anyway since she was needed to help settle a new batch of wounded men arriving from Virginia. More came every day now, wagon after wagon lumbering up from the Sixth Street wharves, and the hospital was badly understaffed. And now it had all been for nothing. Once again, all for nothing.

She moved down the crowded street, jostling among the soldiers and civilians, and, after examining the few coins in her purse, decided to walk instead of taking the horse-car to her lodgings. The air was cool with just that light touch of warmth so common on spring days. The fruit trees were in full bloom now and very beautiful. Spring flowers bloomed everywhere. Besides, every penny counted these days, especially for a woman alone in a war-weary city.

Ambling along the canal, she put her handkerchief to her nose against the offensive smell. Though the waterway bisected the city and ran close to government buildings—including the unfinished Capitol—it still was a repository for raw sewerage, dead animals, and assorted garbage—the source of its pungent odors. They were still claiming it was to be filled in, but they had been saying that every year she lived in

Washington, even before the war. Perhaps someday.

She turned up Fifth Street, nodding at the old woman who had a flower cart on the corner. It was filled to overflowing with colorful splotches of yellow, red, and white, breathing new hope into the cool day. Selene would have liked to buy a few but her money was too precious to squander on such unnecessary pleasantries. She walked quickly by as sudden images of Barbados thrust their unwelcome memory before her eyes. A painful reminder that she had been in Washington nearly seven months now and she was no closer to finding Wade than she had been when she arrived. When her ship docked in Baltimore she knew it was conceivable that she might have made her way South by going west through Pennsylvania, but she had opted for a familiar city and an official pass through the lines, thinking it would not be difficult to obtain. That was a mistake, and a costly one. By seeking out old friends of her father's she had been able to find decent lodgings and work in a hospital. More than that she refused to accept from them. If only the War Department would allow her into Virginia, she could take satisfaction in caring for herself. But what use was her independence when she could not find Wade, when she could not explain that she hadn't known about Lazar's contemptible trick. When she could not tell him how she had finally realized how much she loved him.

By now those guns had probably been used and done their deadly work. What must Wade think of her now? She dared not imagine.

Selene turned down the tree-shaded side street where Mrs. Weldon's boarding house stood, sandwiched among the other dark brick, narrow, three-story houses. She was glad to leave the busier avenues. It was not just that they were crowded—one expected that. But you could not go half a block now without seeing signs of war, mostly in the injured soldiers, many with missing arms and legs, a few with terrible mutilating wounds to their faces. Even she, who was accustomed to helping the horrible casualties of battle that filled the Armory Square Hospital, often had to turn away from these walking, battle-scarred veterans. And always behind her horror was the thought—what if it had been Wade? Was he mutilated, scarred, or even dead? Sometimes she felt that if she didn't know soon, she would go mad.

When she entered the dim hall she met Mattie coming down the narrow stairway. Though they worked together now side by side at the hospital, once they were back at the modest boardinghouse Matilda reverted to waiting on Selene. Not in a servile, obvious way, but a wish-to-be-helpful manner that Selene sometimes found embarrassing. Especially when the other boarders looked at her, their faces expressing the unspoken thought that she was trying to put on airs. Today she was too tired to care and she willingly allowed Mattie to help her off with her coat and bonnet.

"I'd ask if you had any luck, but I can see by your face you didn't," Mattie said, draping Selene's coat over her arm.

"No luck at all, just like all the other times. They are so concerned about spies that they don't trust anyone who wants to go south. As if I'd want to carry information!"

"It's all the fault of that Pinkerton fellow. I heard just today that he's caught three more people, one of them a woman, and sent them to Old Capital Prison. It's getting so you're afraid to breathe for fear someone will accuse you of sympathy for the rebels."

"But they know I have an uncle in Manassas. Surely that's within our jurisdiction now. All the fighting is further south."

"Yes, but that's where you want to go, isn't it?"

"I suppose it is. I should never have told them that. I ought to have said I simply wanted to visit my uncle. Oh, Mattie. I'm so weary of it all. This terrible war, the fighting, the maimed men, the tragedy of it. Why can't people find a better way to solve their differences than by killing one another and causing so much grief?"

Listlessly Mattie followed her up the two flights of stairs to their room. "I'm sure I'm not the one to answer that, Miss Selene. You'll have to ask Mister Lincoln or Mister Davis."

When the boarders gathered around the table for supper, all the talk was of the latest battle in Virginia, somewhere near a town southwest of Fredericksburg called Spotsylvania. Newspapers were passed around with the mashed potatoes and pickled beef, detailing all the horror and severe losses of the battle.

"Butcher! That's all he is," the elderly Mister Werthim muttered between hefty mouthfuls. Nearly seventy, he remembered the war with Britain in the early part of the century and was appalled at the astounding casualties that had come to be taken for granted even in small skirmishes throughout Virginia and the west. "Twenty thousand casualties in one week of fighting! Do you realize what that means? Why the dead were so thick you could walk across them. Butchery!"

"At least General Grant goes on to fight again. It's about time we got someone in charge who refused to be beaten by that devil Lee." Mrs. Bradley was a widow staunchly devoted to the army her husband had served for so many years.

"You said the same thing about McClellan, Meade, McDowell, and Burnside," Werthim said, wiping at his chin with his napkin. "In fact ever since this war started you've been defending any nincompoop 'Father Abraham' puts in charge. And none of them have been worth a grain of salt."

The fold of Mrs. Bradley's chins tinged magenta with outrage. "General Grant won great victories in the West— Vicksburg, Chattanooga—"

"It doesn't take a tactician to throw men into the mouths of cannon. If you have enough men, you're bound to win eventually. Isn't that so, Mister James?"

Ellwood James, a clerk at the *Star* newspaper, who usually kept his comments close to his chin, smiled wryly. "There is some truth in what you say, Mister Werthim. I saw the list of the dead and wounded today which will appear in tomorrow's edition. It fills three full pages, backs and fronts. It's bound to raise a storm of protest."

"That's what I said. Butchery."

"On the other hand," James went on, "General Grant seems to have a quality of determination that was lacking in our former commanders-in-chief. So many times they might have ended the war by moving quickly, but they hesitated. I don't think Grant will be guilty of that. In the end, it just might make the difference. What do you think, Mrs. Kinsolving?"

Selene looked up quickly from her plate, startled. She had heard Werthim's comments and her mind had leapt to visions of Wade lying dead somewhere on a Virginia field. Twenty thousand Union casualties! What must the Confederacy have lost?

"What? I'm sorry. I didn't hear."

James smiled at her kindly. "I was only wondering what you thought about our new commander-in-chief. Are his bloodthirsty tactics likely to win the war sooner?"

Selene appreciated the young man's efforts to involve her in the conversation, for she was certain he did not really have any interest in her opinion. "I don't pretend to understand strategy, Mister James," she said politely, "but I do see that with an apparently endless supply of new troops, General Grant can at least afford such a policy. That is not true of the Confederacy, I'm sure."

"No. I'm told that more and more they are forced to rely on young boys and older men and even their Negroes. Enlisting slaves was something I'm sure they never wanted to do."

"No slave will ever be put under arms," Mattie muttered under her breath. She received a few startled glances from the others around the table who were unaccustomed to hearing her speak at all during these communal meals. Selene, recognizing Mattie's Southern background asserting itself, gave her a warning glance. She was saved by James.

"Do you have relatives on both sides, Mrs. Kinsolving? So many of us here in Washington do."

"Yes," Selene said quietly without elaborating further.

"And were many of them lost in the terrible battles earlier in the war? I myself know of five family members killed between First Bull Run and Gettysburg."

"I don't know. I lost touch early in the war. I've spent nearly two and a half years out of the country—in England."

Mister Werthim, disliking the way the conversation had turned to the women at the table, thrust a long finger in Mister James's face. "Mark my words, young fellow. The country can't take much more of this bloodletting. We're fed up with it. Come the election next fall and that monkey-faced yokel we call president will be out on his ear. We'll put a real man in his

295

place, a man who knows how to fight and how to bring this awful thing to an end."

James smiled at him wryly. "I hope you are not talking about General McClellan. If *he* knows how to fight, this war will drag on until the next century."

The two of them launched into politics while Selene went on mechanically pushing her food around on her plate, her thoughts back in Virginia. Was Wade's body there somewhere, a rotting corpse? Was he lying mutilated in some dirty field hospital? Even worse, was he languishing in one of the cold, foul prison camps scattered around the North, slowly dying of starvation. She had to know. Something in the deepest recesses of her soul told her he was not dead. If he was alive, she had to find him.

Similar thoughts pulled at her mind all that night and into the next week. As she worked in the hospital, going about her duties with half her mind elsewhere, she came to the reluctant conclusion that there was only one thing left to do—slip off into Virginia like so many others and lose herself somewhere in the country. Yet she was frightened to think of it. Even if Mattie went with her, they would be two women alone moving around a war-devastated area, encountering soldiers of both armies, not to mention the terrible scavengers and guerillas who were so notorious in Virginia. It was not a prospect she liked to think about.

"Oh, Mrs. Kinsolving," the matron called, trundling down the aisle between two rows of beds, carrying a tray filled with dishes of beef tea. "There's a gentleman wishes to speak with you out in the front room."

"A gentleman? Did he give his name?"

"No. Said he wouldn't keep you long. And I hope he means it, for I need your help serving all this tea. Do hurry, won't you."

"I won't be long." Selene smoothed her apron over her serviceable merino skirt and hurried to the front of the long room, wondering who in the world would be asking for her here. The hospital entry had only a small foyer where a soldier sat at a desk. Nearby there were several chairs lined along the wall. A tall man, holding his high beaver hat in his hand, stood beside the door, waiting. It took her a moment to recognize Ellwood James away from his customary element in the boardinghouse.

"Good afternoon, Mrs. Kinsolving," he said bowing politely. "I hope I won't be interfering with your duties if I take you away for a brief chat."

"No, Mister James," she answered, trying to stifle her surprise. "We can sit over here if you like." She directed him away from the desk to a corner where two straight-backed chairs stood against the wall. Without quite knowing why, she sensed he wanted privacy and when he began speaking to her, leaning close and in a quiet voice, she knew she had been correct.

"I won't keep you but a moment. I came here because I felt it would be more private than Mrs. Weldon's house. There are so many old people there, you know, with nothing better to do than to be inquisitive about their neighbors. You see, Mrs. Kinsolving, I have noticed you three times waiting at the War Department. Oh, you did not see me but I recognized you. And then, a few nights ago, when you said you had relatives in the South, well, I just wondered if you were trying to get a pass to go through the lines."

Selene inched away from him, her face drained of its color. "Oh, please don't be afraid," he said quickly. "I'm not a spy or anything like that. Nor am I trying to ferret out sympathizers for the war department. I recognize your attempts to keep your personal matters to yourself. I've noticed how reticent you are to speak of your family life at the table, and I don't blame you. It's no one's concern. Nor is it any of mine."

"Then I confess I don't know why you have interested yourself in it, Mister James."

"Because I have an offer to make you. I have at long last been appointed a correspondent for the *Star* and I am going to Richmond tomorrow." He noted the sudden widening of her eyes as her interest flared. "Yes, Richmond. I know it sounds impossible, but I am a newspaper man, you know, and I was born in Petersburg. I still have relatives there. The paper is arranging to send me, hoping I can smuggle out some good hard copy about actual conditions. Anyway, I propose to take you

297

with me, if you want to go."

Selene studied his homely, long face. Was this some kind of a trick? Would this man, almost a stranger, really take her into Virginia, allowing her his protection without asking something more of her? He seemed to read her mind.

"There are no strings attached, Mrs. Kinsolving. Believe me, I want nothing from you myself. My only interest is to be of service to a young woman whose sad eyes betray her misery at being forced to stay in Washington when she longs so much to leave the city."

Selene twisted her hands in her lap. "I can't believe this, Mister James. Why should you offer to do this for me? I have nothing to give you for it. The little money I have would be needed for expenses. And I must tell you this much—the reason I want to go South is to search for my husband who is somewhere there, dead or alive, I don't know which."

"I suspected as much."

"Then why should you want to do all this for me? Why should you even bother?"

She was startled when he reached out and took her hand in his. "Because, Madam, ten years ago when I was very young, I went with my uncle to the parlor of a simple little house on Seventh Street, where I sat with several other gentlemen listening to the most sane, sensible, kindly voice I had ever heard in my lifetime. It happened to be a time in my life when I was beset with great doubts and questions. I went back several times and he helped me resolve them. More and more I felt this was a man whose gentle and reasonable manner was an example to all who knew him."

Selene gave a little gasp. "You knew my father?"

"Yes, and I honored him above all men. I still do. You wouldn't remember me for I was little more than a boy. But I recognized you the very first time I saw you step into the dining room at Mrs. Weldon's boardinghouse. Now will you let me help you? It seems a fitting way to pay back a little of the enormous gratitude I owe your father."

She turned away, unable to look at him. Tears welled hotly in her eyes but she fought them back. "You cannot know how much your words mean to me, Mister James. To think that—to know that—that others felt about him as I did—"

"Why everyone who knew him felt he was exceptional."

Not everyone, Selene thought with bitterness. But then, who would Simon Lazar admire? Attila the Hun!

"I'll go with you, gladly, Mister James. And I'll do my very best not to be a burden to you. If I can get to Richmond, surely I will be able to trace Wade from there."

Ellwood James became all business. "Good. That's settled. I'll have to get a pass for you this afternoon, but that should be no trouble with the *Star* backing me up. Can you be ready to leave tomorrow morning at first light?"

Her smile was radiant. "Oh, yes. I'll be ready. I'd be ready if you wanted to leave this very afternoon!"

The next morning Selene was packed and eager to be off long before Ellwood James knocked softly on her door. She had very little and took only the barest necessities out of that, thinking that traveling light would be the best means of making herself the least trouble to her companion. James took her light pormanteau downstairs as she threw her arms around a tearful Mattie and gave her a hug.

"I'm so sorry you can't come with me," Selene said with all honesty. She had a suspicion that there would be times ahead when she would wish she had another woman along.

"It's all right. I can slip across the river and get home anytime I want. I only stayed here in the city to take care of you."

Selene suppressed a smile at the idea of Matilda mothering her. "You're sure you'll be all right?"

"Certain. You just go and find Mister Wade and make it all right with him. I always knew you two really cared a lot about each other, even when you was acting the worst. And write to me. Let me know where you end up."

"I promise." She smoothed back the straggling strands of hair from Mattie's brow. "You've been a true friend and companion, Matilda Rollins. Thank you."

Impulsively Mattie leaned forward and kissed her cheek. "God go with you, Miss Selene."

With a light heart she ran down the stairs to find James waiting outside beside a small black leather chaise. Both the carriage and the horse that pulled it looked as though they had seen better days, yet in these times of shortage, Selene knew what it must have taken to find a horse and carriage of any kind. She climbed aboard and they started off, jostling among the early traffic toward the Long Bridge. The church bells rang and echoed, telling the hour, and even as they moved the streets filled with pedestrians on their way to work, soldiers galloping on horseback, horse-cars, and carriages. Selene held her breath as the sentry at the bridge examined the papers James handed him, half-expecting him to order her down. But he only waved them on and they clopped across the bridge and into Virginia, as though it was the simplest thing in the world. It wasn't until much later, when they passed the Fairfax courthouse that she began to see how devastating a toll four years of war had taken on Virginia. Ruined fields, an occasional burned farmhouse, stunted trees whose new green growth fought to cover the ravages from cannon fire, and soldiers everywhere. Blue uniforms, sometimes in small groups, sometimes in battalions stepping smartly down the road. Officers on their sleek horses galloped by, stopping occasionally to examine their papers, eyeing their poor horse as though it was a side of beef.

Nowhere were the ravages of battle more apparent than around her uncle's tavern where twice the ground had been contested by two armies. She was appalled to see that mounds of earth, covered with a stubble of green, still bore evidence of the bodies of those who had fallen there. Several of the houses near the site had been abandoned for safer places, but the stone tavern stood yet, showing signs of neglect but still active and occupied. Her uncle stared at her as though his eyes deceived him.

"I figured you was dead!" he gasped, taking her by the arms and holding her from him.

"Why? Did you think I got between the lines and was shot?"

"I didn't know what to think, Selene. You just vanished and not one word for these three years. Where have you been?"

"Oh, Uncle John, it's such a long story. For the past seven months I've been in Washington City, trying to get a pass to come into Virginia. Do you think you might give Mister James and me a late breakfast while I tell you all about it?"

That was one thing Uncle John could do well. He served them both up ham, coffee, and biscuits still warm from the oven, and sat at one of the tables with them while they devoured it. "I guess you aren't home to stay," he said, half-hopefully. "I could use your help. Seems like we get rid of one bunch of bluebacks just to have a larger bunch take their place. It keeps me hopping, it does."

Selene finished off one of Rosie's biscuits. "I can't stay, Uncle John. I have to go to Richmond. But Matilda—you remember her—she should be arriving back here soon. She'll help you, I know."

"That worthless wench? Don't tell me you ran into her."

"Yes, right after I left here. She's been with me all this time and right now she's still in Washington. But she's coming back soon."

"Well, I don't see as how you're ever going to get to Richmond. There's two armies between you and the city, in case you didn't know. If one of them lets you out, the other one sure won't let you in."

James pushed his plate away and sat back, looping his thumbs in his vest pockets. "What's it like down there, Mister Carpenter? Do you ever hear?"

"It's pretty bad," John answered, looking at him as though unsure whether or not to trust him. "They're calling it three of the most bitter weeks of fighting in the war. Grant threw everything he had at Bobby Lee but couldn't get through."

"At Spotsylvania. Yes, we read about it in Washington."

"What's your interest in my niece here?" Uncle John demanded abruptly. Selene, embarrassed, spoke up quickly.

"Mister James is helping to escort me to Richmond. I'm married Uncle John, and I want to look for my husband. I haven't seen or heard from him since last summer and I want to know if he's all right."

"Married! To—"

"That's right," she broke in. "The officer I went away with."

Her guarded looks warned him not to say any more. "I suppose it's no more than I should expect in these crazy times.

But you ought to be careful, my girl, going South. You may think we've got shortages here, but they're nothing to those near Richmond. I hear tell that in the city they're ransacking the garbage for enough to eat. Nobody trusts anybody else. There are spies everywhere, North and South. And those raiders, Mosby's men and the others, they'd just as soon cut you down and burn you out as look at you. It's very bad right now. That horse, for instance, young man. The Confederacy is so short of horses they'll requisition it right out from under you, if the troops don't take it for food first. You'd be better off trying the railroad."

"I was afraid we wouldn't be able to get through," James answered. "But I'll be careful with the horse and with your niece, I promise. We'd better get back on the road, Mrs. Kinsolving, if we want to make any time today."

At the door of the tavern Selene and her uncle paused while James went to bring the chaise around. "So it's Mrs. Kinsolving, is it? I remember that Captain. A fine-looking man, he was. But somehow I didn't think he had marriage on his mind."

"I don't quite know how it happened myself, Uncle John. I only know I have to find him one way or another. He was—is a fine man. I only hope I have the chance to tell him so again."

"Well, if all this works out, and he gets through this thing in one piece, bring him around to see me someday."

Selene could not remember when her uncle had been so kind to her. Whatever the travails of this war, they had certainly mellowed Uncle John. "I promise," she said and hugged him quickly before climbing back up into the carriage.

By mid-afternoon they were well into Virginia and observing everywhere the truth of her uncle's description. The ordered industry of peacetime Virginia had been replaced with weed-infested, unplowed fields, neglected orchards, and a lack of grazing flocks or herds. The houses they passed were silent, not bustling with the accustomed activity of thriving farms. Many were boarded up and empty, others fallen to ruin or lifting only charred embers to the afternoon sky. The civilians they met on the road avoided them, treating them with a wariness and a lack of hospitality that Selene had never seen before. Soldiers, on the other hand, evidenced a great interest in who they were and where they were going. More than once they were ordered down to have their carriage and baggage searched in case some ciphered note was hidden somewhere. It would have been easy to serve as courier, Selene realized. Men and women left Washington everyday for the South with hidden messages revealing the Federal government's military plans. But that was the last thing she wanted to get involved in. And now she was more grateful than ever that they had nothing with them to arouse suspicion.

They spent that night with a family who were friendly with Ellwood James, though he had not seen them since before the war started. Their home was a comfortable but inelegant farmhouse and their sympathies were entirely with the South, yet they made them both at home and shared their meagre fare willingly. They made her feel so welcome that Selene began to feel that hospitality as she remembered it in Virginia was not dead after all. She was surprised, too, at the rather explicit information they seemed to have about the movements of both Grant's and Lee's armies.

"It started in the Wilderness area," their host explained. "Both armies collided in all that brush and woods. I was told it was so thick in there with the tangles and the smoke that half them fellers didn't know if they was shootin' at friend or foe. Then Lee beat the Federals to Spotsylvania and dug in tight as a tick on a hound's rear. A regular slaughter, it was, with the bluebellies gettin' the worst of it."

They sat around the table in the weathered dining room enjoying the last of the stewed chicken and dumplings Mrs. Warren had fixed for their supper. Rafe Warren was a middle-aged farmer whose face was as lined as old leather from working in the sun. All of the children around the table were girls—the boys had long since gone off to war. The eldest was a pretty, fresh-faced blonde whose innocent smile was like a ray of sunshine in the darkened room.

"Who told you about it, Rafe? One of your sons?" Ellwood asked.

"Yes. Mandy. He's with General Ewell. Thank God he come through it with nothin' worse than a scraped hand. He stopped by long enough for a quick meal then went on back. Seems there's pretty poor fare among Lee's boys these days. Would have sent something' if I could of, but we didn't have so much ourselves."

"And what we do have the thievin' Yankees steal," Mrs. Warren added. "Sally, pass Mrs. Kinsolving some more of them dumplin's. That's one thing you can always stretch, Mrs. Kinsolving. As long as we keep a little flour, we'll never go hungry."

"Where's the action now, Rafe?" Ellwood went on. "Have you heard anything more since Mandy left?"

"Oh, bits and pieces, but nothin' very certain. A Federal Lieutenant came through two days ago and said something about Grant trying to turn Lee's right flank. I don't think it worked."

"He must have had a careless tongue," Selene said, wondering at the casual way information was passed around in this war.

"Most of them do, at least once Sally gives them a smile or two. That loosens them up every time."

"Are you sure you won't have some more of these dumplin's, Mrs. Kinsolving," the man's wife put in again in an effort to stem the war talk. Of course a Yankee woman would not take kindly to hearing that her own side's soldiers were so free with information, Selene realized. She knew her presence put a damper on the conversation and besides, she was very tired. She politely declined more food and thought she would just go on up to bed.

"Sally will show you where to sleep. You'll be sharing her bed tonight."

"Hope you don't mind, Mrs. Kinsolving," the girl spoke up with a shy smile. "I'm very still."

"I'm so grateful and so tired that I can only thank you for being kind enough to allow me to share your bed." The girl rose from the table and gave Selene her hand, delighted with her visitor.

"I've got a little brandy, Ellwood, and some good Virginia

tobaccy," Rafe said. "Why not stay a little longer."

"Perhaps I will, thank you, Rafe," James answered, rising to his feet. "You get some rest Mrs. Kinsolving, because we'll have to be off early in the morning again."

Selene left them and gratefully let Sally lead her to an upstairs bedroom. She was very tired and the nearer she came to Richmond, the more she began to wonder if she was doing the right thing. What would Wade say when he saw her again, given the slim chance that she could find him at all? What did he think of her now? Did he blame her? Hate her? Would he welcome her or send her away? She was so unsure that she did not know what to think or expect. She only knew she had to go on.

Her concern did not keep her from falling asleep as soon as her head touched the pillow. The next morning, feeling considerably better, she was dressed and ready to climb into the carriage before Ellwood left the house. As he started to hand her up, Sally came running out, carrying a homemade plaited straw bonnet in her hand, the ribbons trailing. "I made this for you, Mrs. Kinsolving," the girl said offering it to Selene. "I would so love to go to Richmond, but since I cannot, would you accept my gift and wear it for me there."

The modest little hat showed unmistakable signs of being fashioned by an amateur, though the ribbons that decorated it were obviously a pre-war treasure. Selene took it hesitantly, not daring to refuse the girl's kindness and thinking that her one poor bonnet, which was all she had brought with her from England, could use a little rest occasionally.

"I'll wear it right now," she said, removing her own to tie the new one under her chin. "How does it look?"

"It's very becoming," Sally said. "But you are such a pretty lady, anything would look lovely on you. I do hope you'll enjoy it."

Selene squeezed the girl's hand and climbed into the carriage, throwing her old one under the seat. The road was shrouded in a light mist that threatened to burn off once the sun came up. She smoothed the wide ribbons that trailed the front of her dress, admiring their bright color. It was nice to have something fresh and new to wear, she thought. It made

305

one feel pretty and gave a lift to the day.

The haze was nearly gone an hour later when they were abruptly stopped on the road by a small party of horsemen. Selene was relieved to recognize their blue tunics and the eagles on their brass buttons. Yet when the Major in charge ordered them both to step down in a very unfriendly way, she began to wonder if they were on the same side after all. The officer in charge made no attempt to hide his distrust of two civilians, one of them a correspondent, headed for the capital city of the Confederacy, no matter how official their passes looked. He had every inch of the carriage searched and then started on them. Sending Ellwood off into the woods with one of his men to be searched, he turned to Selene without a trace of apology.

"I don't have a woman with me, Ma'am, but if you'll cooperate we should not have to embarrass you unduly. You will please drop your hoop."

Selene stared at him, her eyes growing wide with outrage. "Drop my hoop! You cannot be serious."

"I was never more serious, Madam. Ladies hoopskirts are a very convenient way of carrying messages and supplies through the lines. I cannot number the times I have been through this before, and I assure you, it means nothing to me. If you refuse to drop it yourself, I will have one of my men do it for you."

Selene was aghast. "I have nothing to hide. For heaven's sake sir, I'm no spy."

The officer smiled wryly. "No, they never are. Please, madam, it will be easier for all concerned if you will do as I ask."

She hesitated a moment more, then realized that her very reluctance aroused suspicion. The Major was obviously not going to even turn his back, as a gentleman should, so, resigned, Selene reached under her skirt and released the tape that tied her hoop. It fell to the ground and she stepped out of it. The orderly pounced upon it and examined it thoroughly. "Nothing here, sir," he said, handing the ungainly contraption to the Major. He looked it over carefully, then handed it back to Selene, his eyes carefully scanning her dress. There was so little to arouse his suspicion—a worn jacket that fitted her perfectly, her ridiculous bonnet, her patched skirt.

"I'll just have to look at the cameo," he said and reached for the pin at her throat. "We've found them to be hollow sometimes."

It was only a cheap broach she had picked up at a shop in Washington, and of course it was completely innocent. The Major was beginning to show signs of embarrassment.

"I'm sure you realize we have to do this," he said as he handed the cameo back to her. "The countryside around here is littered with spies and sometimes they are the most innocent-appearing people imaginable. We have to be careful."

"I understand," Selene said, trying not to show her irritation. It was useless to try to tell him that she shared his beliefs, that the Union meant as much to her as to him. He was only doing his job. Ellwood came stalking up to her, his jacket over his arm, scowling blackly. Evidently they had not been as gentle with him as they had with her.

"We'll leave you to dress," the Major said, and turned his back long enough for Selene to pull her hoop back under her skirt. They were both seated in the carriage before the Major handed their passes back to James. "You'd better keep these safe. If you're wise you'll head west to the valley. It's likely to be a lot safer than this road in the next few days."

"Thanks," James muttered. He wanted to ask why, but the men were off in a cloud of dust before he had the chance. However, he and Selene had not gone much farther down the road before they learned the answer.

"Is that thunder?" Selene asked, scanning the sky. The quiet rumbling in the distance rose and fell like a grumbling storm poised over the next line of hills.

"No. It's not thunder. It's artillery. We must be nearer the lines than I thought. That's why that Major warned us away from here."

Artillery! The distant memory of Bull Run became suddenly vivid in her mind. The big guns, the sharp chatter of firearms, the shriek of the howitzers. Nervously she fingered the cameo at her throat.

"We're not going to get caught in a battle, are we?"

"Afraid?" James smiled down at her.

"Frankly yes. I went through that once before, at Manassas Junction. I'd rather not go through it again. Can't we take the western road?"

He patted her hand. "Don't worry. I know exactly where I'm going, and I assure you, you will be as safe with me as in your own home in Washington."

She wished she could be so confident. The loud thunder of the guns grew nearer, ranged farther away, then nearer again as their increasingly nervous horse plodded on down the empty road. They saw so few soldiers, or any people at all, that Selene began to think James knew what he was talking about. And then, just about noon, as they rolled along a stretch of narrow road lined on either side with thick pine forests, their horse shied and reared as several men broke from the thickets alongside to rush around the carriage and pull at the bridle. They were a scruffy-looking lot, their uniforms so tattered and patched that Selene could barely make out that they had once been gray. She gripped the seat as the carriage wobbled crazily while they pulled at the traces, tearing away the leather straps.

"This here horse is r'quisitioned," one of them said, approaching the carriage. "You'll have to walk."

"You can't do that!" Selene cried as James laid a quiet hand on her arm.

"You've no right," he said firmly.

"Right of findin' him," the soldier said. When he came abreast of the two occupants, he pulled off his hat. "Sorry, ma'am, but we need horses too bad to let even the ladies ride out with them. You got any papers on you?" he said to James.

Ellwood took his time reaching into his pocket. "What regiment are you with, soldier?"

"What's it to you?" the spokesman for the group replied as he spread James's pass out against the side of the carriage.

But James had already recognized the man's cap and insignia. "Hampton's cavalry on foot? Well, at least you're not renegades. I was afraid we'd run into one of those lawless bands."

"We're on foot because we don't have enough horses. That nag of yours will help some, though he's a poor one, that's for sure. You're a correspondent, I see, going to Richmond. How do we know you're not a spy?"

Selene groaned, seeing visions of loosening her hoop once again. "Can't anyone travel in this country without being thought a spy?" she said impatiently. "We are trying to get to Richmond because my husband is somewhere with the Confederate army and I am trying to find him. Please let us go on our way."

"Sorry, ma'am, but I can't do that. The Captain will have to decide if you both are what you say you are, or something worse. You'll have to come along with us."

"That's all right, soldier," James said levelly. "We don't mind."

Selene wondered at his calm in the face of yet another delay, but there was nothing she could do but go along. They walked nearly a mile along a narrow road that led off at a right angle to the Richmond road before they emerged into a clearing where several tents stood with open flaps around a crude cooking fire. The guns were louder than ever and soldiers were everywhere, most of them coming and going with purposeful strides that belied the apparent confusion of the place. Near one of the tents an officer was bent over a table while two others looked on. The soldier who brought them in marched them to the open doorway and spoke to the officer who stood near the flap. He handed him the papers and stood waiting while the Captain scanned them, looking up only once to glance at Ellwood James. Then, to Selene's surprise, the Captain walked over to James and extended his hand.

"Welcome back," he said, shaking James's hand energetically.

"Thank you, Captain. It's good to be here."

With a curt order the officer dismissed the soldier, motioned them both inside the tent and lowered the flaps.

"And was your trip productive?"

"Not as much as I hoped. I wonder, Mrs. Kinsolving, if I could trouble you for your bonnet."

Selene, who had been looking from one to the other in total confusion, wondered if James had lost his senses. "It's in the carriage, don't you remember? I put it under the seat."

"Not that one. This . . ." and he extended his hand to touch the narrow brim of the homemade straw Sally Warren had given her. The color began to creep up her cheeks as she untied the ribbon under her chin and handed the hat to James, watching in increasing anger as he tore the ribbon away from the brim and held up the plaited straw to the Captain.

"The message is sewed in between the rows of braid," Ellwood said. "The actual numbers are in cipher, of course, but I can help supplement the general information from what Rafe told me. His son, Mandy, brought it to him from the front so it should be pretty accurate."

"You used me to bring information through the lines!" Selene cried in a choked voice. "And without my consent. How could you! I thought you were my friend."

"I am your friend, Mrs. Kinsolving. And I greatly deplore the fact that I had to put you in jeopardy all unwillingly. But this information is vital and I could not see any other way."

"You couldn't see any better way, you mean," Selene said, glaring at both men. "What could be more innocent—a *sympathetic* Yankee woman with espionage the last thing on her mind. You counted on me to protest my innocence and cover your own perfidy."

"Don't be too hard on Mister James, Madam," the Captain said soothingly. "The fact is that every day both civilian and military personnel in disguise go back and forth between the lines carrying information. The Federals depend on it every bit as much as we do. As it happens right now our forces are gravely hampered by having lost touch with the main body of Grant's army and we desperately need all the information we can get. General Grant appears to be of a different stripe from the Union generals we've dealt with in the past, and we can't count on him retreating to lick his wounds after a good shellacking like the others. We must know what he intends to do next."

Ellwood picked at the closely braided rows of straw with the point of his knife, tearing away a small pouch of satin cloth worked in between. "Rafe was certain General Grant plans to move South to strike at Richmond. If he can't break through Lee's lines, he'll try to circumvent them.

"We suspect that but we must know for sure. You heard about Yellow Tavern, I suppose."

"Yes. What a bitter thing to lose General Stuart just when we need him most."

"Bitter indeed," the Captain answered as he slipped the pouch into a leather dispatch bag. "I'd better send this over to headquarters right away. Corporal . . ." he called, and a young man pushed aside the tent flap and stepped smartly inside.

Selene watched as he gave the pouch and his orders to the soldier, her indignation growing at both men. They acted as though she wasn't even there, just something to be used and thrown aside with no more thought.

"What's to stop me from turning around and going back to find a Federal picket and tell him about your friend Rafe? And about you, Mister James, for that matter. This is outrageous."

"I don't think you will, Mrs. Kinsolving," the Captain said wearily. "For one thing, Mister James here is going to see you safely into Richmond. Once there I think you will find there is more than enough to keep you occupied. Besides, Rafe's usefulness to us is at an end. The Federals have suspected him for months now and it is no longer safe to use him."

"And after all, your mission is actually to find your husband, isn't it?" James added. "I apologize for the deception, but it has served its purpose. Can't we forget it now and go on?"

Selene studied the gray eyes that had always seemed so kind in his long face. "I don't know if I can trust you," she said, feeling suddenly very weary. "Will there be any more such tricks?"

He raised his hand. "I promise, no more. Once we reach the city, we'll go on about our own concerns and I will not involve you in mine again."

The Captain did not allow her time to protest. "Come along," he ordered, lifting the tent flaps. "I'll have one of my men drive you to the rail line. You can catch a ride into Richmond from there. It won't be first class accommodations, but it will get you to the city and out of this dangerous area that much sooner. Oh, and I'll have someone retrieve your other bonnet, Mrs. Kinsolving, if you like."

Selene nodded. She was still too outraged to speak to either of them. It did seem too much that after years of being wrongly accused of it, she should become a spy without even knowing that she was. She knew James had thought it was safer for her if she did not know she was carrying a cipher—her very innocence was her security. But to put her life in jeopardy without even asking her consent—that was sinking pretty low. "I suppose all those remarks about my father were just so much syrup," she later muttered to James when they were seated on the train and she could bring herself to speak to him again.

"No. I meant them sincerely. I did meet your father years ago and I admired him very much. I'm not a complete lout, you know."

"That's the trouble with being deceived. You don't know if you can believe anything of the person afterward."

"Perhaps, circumstances being what they are, you'd be better off not to believe anyone anyway." James answered cryptically. He then pulled his hat down over his eyes and scrunched down in his seat, prepared to take a nap. Selene was far too restless to enjoy anything so leisurely. The train inched along, starting and stopping so many times she began to think they would never reach Richmond. Soldiers came and went between the cars while an equal number seemed to be working on the rails outside. The tracks were in such poor condition that the train was forced to sit idly for long periods while they were repaired. She was the only woman aboard, but she was treated with such courtesy by the numerous strangers that she never felt out of place. Most of them assumed her sleeping companion was her brother or husband and she did not bother to enlighten them.

It was early evening before they finally pulled into the Broad Street depot in the city. Once she embarked with James walking alongside carrying her pormanteau, she realized with surprise that she was very nervous to have finally arrived in the war-torn capital of the Confederacy. She had imagined a place similar to Washington, and perhaps in the days before the war it was. But there was a somberness about it now that almost seeped into one's bones. The wide avenue was crowded

312

with lovely women in worn dresses, civilian men, either very old or very young, and myriads of military men in gray. Wounded were still pouring in from the recent battle at Spotsylvania and they lay everywhere, many of them crying and moaning for assistance. Nurses, women and black servants, moved among them with toddies and teas. Selene recognized the ministrations of a few doctors, all of them who appeared to be elderly, weary men. The street was a jumble of wagons, caissons, and occasional carriages. The buildings appeared to suffer from a lack of any recent painting but the streets were exceptionally clean. Injured men among the pedestrians, as in Washington, bore solemn witness to the horrors of the war for independence, but Selene was so weary she could only turn her eyes from them. A funeral cortege passed slowly by them, the band blaring the mournful strains of the Death March from Saul. Windows, doors and signs were still hung with black bunting from General Stuart's recent funeral, all of it adding to the grimness that pervaded the very air.

Darkness had fallen before she finally located a room at the Ballard House on the corner of Franklin and Fourteenth Streets. It was far too expensive for her limited purse, but she was too tired to care. It was as crowded as the streets had been with both civilians—women and children and older men—and with military personnel looking haggard and weary. Most of the soldiers and the families seemed to be accompanied by their Negro servants, yet no one seemed surprised at her being alone. Perhaps with all the peculiar contingencies created by the war, nothing surprised anyone any more. She later learned that she had been given one of the last rooms available, and only because her money was in Federal dollars instead of Confederate currency.

Selene said good-bye to Ellwood James once she knew she had a place to sleep. He assured her that the government was still functioning, distressed as the city might appear to be, and she made plans to begin the very next morning with a visit to the War Office near Capitol Square. Then she fell into bed without bothering about supper.

The corner of Ninth and Franklin was one of the busiest in

Richmond. In one small area were clustered most of the military and civilian offices and bureaus that made up the heart of the Confederate bureaucracy. The war department was only a short walk from the Ballard house and Selene's visit there the next day presaged many in the week that followed. In the beginning the harried clerks behind their desks either knew nothing about Wade or did not believe she was his wife and pretended ignorance. Selene could sense their distrust, once they heard she had just come from Washington. Yet she persisted, going back each day to try to find someone there who might have an idea where he was. Though they eventually accepted her for who she was, no one knew where Wade could be, especially since she had no idea of what regiment he was with. After five days of this she began to realize that in a city where a pound of bacon cost eleven dollars, when it could be found at all, and a lowly watermelon went for ten dollars, even her United States money would eventually be gone.

She returned to her room after the tenth fruitless day and was counting the money she had left, wondering what on earth she would do once it was spent, when there was a soft knock at her door. Selene looked up, startled. Who would be visiting her in Richmond? She knew no one in the city except Mister James, and she had not seen him since the day she arrived. She had been careful to keep her distance from the friendly women of the hotel, a chatty group made up mostly of refugees from the more war-ravaged sections of the South, who when they found they could not draw her out had learned to leave her alone. Hesitantly she put away her money and walked to the door, cracking it open just far enough to see who was in the hall. It was one of the black porters, an elderly fellow who had served her in the dining room several times.

"Scuse me, ma'am, but theys a lady downstairs what wants to see you."

"A lady? Did she give her name?"

"No ma'am. She say she wait fo' you in the blue parlor. She have on a little blue hat with a flower, sort of yellow like."

"Are you certain she asked for me?" Selene said, frowning. He nodded with assurance, bobbing up and down.

"Sho' was, missy. Miz Kinsolvin'. That's right, ain't it?"

"Yes. Thank you. I'll be right down."

More mystified than ever, Selene took time to smooth her hair and fluff up the wrinkles in her skirts. She still felt disheveled from the day spent in the crowded halls of the War Department, yet she did not have time to change. Her mysterious visitor would have to take her as she was.

She spotted the blue hat the minute she walked into the spacious parlor. A woman rose from a round, tuffed sofa that circled a mahogany column, the focal point of the large room. She was tiny and the wide skirts spread around her gave her the appearance of a miniature adult. She came swaying up to Selene, looking up at her with a fresh face, not as young as it had seemed from a distance, but vivacious and kindly.

"Mrs. Kinsolving? I recognized you right away from Woody's description. How do you do, ma'am," she said, bobbing Selene a curstey. "I can see by the look on your face that you can't imagine who this person could be, accostin' you like this, a perfect stranger and all. I'm Susannah James, Ellwood's sister."

Selene took the mitted hand that the girl offered, so small in her own. "Miss James. How nice to meet you. Excuse my bewilderment but Mister James never mentioned he had a sister."

"I'm sure he didn't. He probably didn't mention that he has a mother, two more sisters and an aunt either, but here we all are, and living right here in Richmond." Susannah took Selene's arm in an easy, natural gesture and drew her to the tuffed settee, chatting away as though to give Selene time to take stock of yet another stranger. "And that's really why I'm here, you see. Ellwood stopped by before he left and told us about you and about how he had—well, played a very naughty trick on you coming down to Richmond. We were so ashamed that he would do such a thing, even if it was for a righteous cause and all. But anyway, he asked us to look after you, so that's why I'm here. I've been to the hotel several times before but you were always out, and I didn't want to leave my card, being a perfect stranger and all. It seemed better to explain face to face."

"You're very kind, I'm sure, Miss James. I'm really quite

settled," Selene said a little lamely. "And I'm quite over my anger with your brother now, though I admit I did resent his using me that way at first."

"I don't blame you a bit," Susannah said, bending forward to tap Selene's arm. "Tell me, have you had any word of your husband yet?"

So James had told them about Wade, too. "No. So far no one I've spoken to has any idea where he is."

"That's too bad, but not surprising considering the confused state everything is in. I mean, once we began to hear the guns so close and all, we thought our old city was gone for good, but here we still are. Our poor army has suffered terribly, but so far they've kept the Yankees from the gates. Oh, dear me, I quite forgot!"

It was Selene's turn to smile. "That's all right. My sympathies are with the Union, I admit, but what I've seen so far of the devastation this war has brought about makes me wonder if any belief is worth it."

"I do declare I'm glad to hear you say that, Mrs. Kinsolving," Susannah said. She had a way of smiling that lit up her eyes like candlelight suddenly catching fire. "For you see, I've come to ask you to stay with us. Oh, I know this sounds very unexpected and sudden and that you don't know anything about our family and all, but believe me, Mrs. Kinsolving, we would be so happy to have you. And you cannot be too comfortable here at the Ballard with everything being so crowded and expensive these days. Dear Woody made us promise we would watch out for you."

"Miss James," Selene cried, taken aback by her enthusiasm. "I don't understand. Are you saying you want me to come live with you?"

"Oh yes, that's exactly what I'm trying to tell you. We have such a grand house on Grace Street, not far from St. Paul's. At least, it was grand before this terrible war started—you never saw such parties and balls and entertainments. But I do run on. Mama always says I can't stick to the point any better than butter in August. What I really mean is, we've plenty of room and you can't want to stay in this old hotel so full of strangers and all . . ."

316

"But, Miss James, you don't know anything about me. I couldn't possibly take advantage of your hospitality in such a way."

Susannah bounced toward her on the seat, grasping Selene's hands. "Oh, but you won't be taking advantage. Mama told me to tell you straight out that you could be such a help to us. You see, we have so many wounded men in our house now, because the hospitals here are filled to overflowing and more come in every day. And Ellwood said you had worked in a hospital in Washington and know how to nurse wounded men. Of course, naturally they'd be Confederates, but you wouldn't mind that, would you? We're all the same, really, under the skin and . . ."

"Stop!" Selene cried, pulling away her hands. "Just be still a moment, Miss James, and let me get this straight. Your house is a hospital?"

"Oh, but it's still a house, too."

"You are caring for wounded soldiers in your house, and you'd offer me a living there in return for my help?"

"Well, that's not the only reason. You're Ellwood's friend, after all, and our home is as open to you as it would be to any of his acquaintances."

"But in return then for your hospitality, I could be of service to the wounded?"

"That's correct. You put it ever so much more simply than I can. Do say you'll come, Mrs. Kinsolving. I can tell just from our short acquaintance that we'd get along famously, and I'm a very good judge of such things. Mama says . . ."

Selene took both the girl's hands and squeezed them, laughing. "Thank you, Miss James. I cannot tell you how welcome your offer is. I was beginning to think I might have to go back to Washington without ever finding my husband. However, I insist that I pay something for my room and board."

Susannah looked at her aghast, "Why I wouldn't hear of such a thing. You're a guest . . ."

"Of course," Selene said quickly. "What I meant was that I do have a little United States money left, and I can already see by my stay in Richmond that it would come in handy for purchasing supplies and medicines. I insist that I be allowed to

317

contribute it."

"Well, I admit supplies are hard to come by and very, very dear. Medicines, of course, are almost nonexistent except when they can be smuggled through the blockade. And Federal money would be most welcome. It has come to the point where it takes forty-eight dollars just to buy four pounds of butter!"

She rambled on about the high price of everything from firewood to cabbages while Selene sat back listening with one ear and thanking providence for this lovely surprise. Young Mister James had more than made up for his abuse of her on the trip down. She would have a place to stay, useful work, acquaintances if not friends and, as long as her money held out, a way to live. And given time, she felt in her heart she would find Wade somewhere with the Army of Northern Virginia. Susannah James, with all her sprightly, loquacious ways, was the answer to a prayer.

Sixteen

Selene's first impression of the James house was of huge shade trees and iron fretwork—a placid, comfortable, unpretentious elegance. The house was one of the tall, narrow brick mansions that stood cheek to jowl on the pleasant street near Capitol Square. The family had sent round their carriage for her, driven by Tom, an elderly black servant who had spent all his life with the James family. He smiled and bobbed and handed her up into the carriage as though she had been a friend for decades rather than for two days. Chattering away in his hybrid Virginia drawl all the way to Grace Street, he filled her in gradually on the people she would be living with, though clearly that was not his intention. When Selene found herself standing in the front entryway, watching a thin, middle-aged woman attired all in black coming toward her, she knew at once that this had to be Cecily James, Susannah and Elwood's mother.

Cecily James had a serene beauty that was heightened by her gaunt cheeks and weary eyes. She stood straight and tall as she extended her hand to Selene. Selene, who had not really yet given up the thought that she might be sent from the house as a detested Yankee, smiled in her relief. "Mrs. James," she said taking her hand gratefully.

"Welcome to our home, Mrs. Kinsolving. Come in, my dear. My daughter has told me all about you."

The soft gray eyes had a permanent cast of sadness about them which was untouched by her pleasant smile. "I would have recognized you at once," Selene said as they started down the hall, "by your resemblance to your son. He favors you greatly."

The sadness lifted ever so slightly. "I'll take that as a compliment. Come along to the morning room off the kitchen, Mrs. Kinsolving, and we'll have a quick cup of tea. I regret that I cannot receive you in one of the parlors but, as you can see, they are required for more pressing matters right now."

As she walked down the hall toward the rear of the house, Selene could see that the large, gracious rooms on both sides were filled with rows of cots and makeshift pallets. The furniture appeared to have been either removed or shoved into a corner to make room for more beds. None were empty. Some of the men glanced up as she passed, staring at her with feverish, questioning, haunted eyes, but most appeared to be sleeping or restlessly tossing about. There were occasional groans while the sickly sweet odor of chloroform—aggravated by the heat of the afternoon—permeated the rooms, reminding her of the Armory Square Hospital in Washington. Her brief scrutiny left her impressed at the neat, clean appearance, for she well knew how difficult it was to attain and keep a degree of good hygiene in a large sick room.

"This all seems very familiar," she commented as Mrs. James led her into a small room at the rear of the house that held a round pine table and several chairs. The walls were lined with cupboards from top to bottom, their glass windows revealing stacks of stored china, crystal, and serving dishes.

"This used to be the butler's pantry," Mrs. James said as she motioned Selene to a chair. "Now the family has meals here, when we can get away. I only have a moment right now myself, but I did want to acquaint you with the household and the work we are trying to do. Dilly," she called to a young Negro woman in a white turban who appeared at the door. "Bring us a little tea, please. We don't have any real tea, Mrs. Kinsolving, but we've found for some time now that the leaves of the raspberry plant make an acceptable substitute. You've had your breakfast?"

"Please call me Selene. And yes, I ate at the Ballard House."

The relief in Cecily's eyes was obvious and Selene knew she

had guessed rightly in sparing the family one meal. With only a brief time available to discuss the household and ways Selene might contribute to it, Mrs. James talked quickly, almost nervously, as though she was anxious to get back to the beds in the parlor. Yet, in spite of her hurry, she seemed so accepting and friendly that Selene thanked providence all over again that she had been invited here.

A few moments later Susannah came bustling in in a flurry of non-stop conversation to welcome Selene again. She was about to take her upstairs to show her their room when a commotion in the front hall told them someone had arrived. The sound of a cheerful male voice carrying on a banter with Dilly brought both Mrs. James and Susannah to their feet.

"It's Woody," Susannah cried with delight. "He's back at last. Oh, come on, Selene, let's show him you're really here."

A little embarrassed, Selene was nevertheless prepared to express her gratitude to Mister James when the words froze in her throat. There in the doorway stood Ellwood James, attired in the full gray uniform of a Captain in the Confederate artillery—scarlet sash, sword, gold braid and hat. The uniform was obviously not new and the color was the off-gray of walnut dye that had been used by Southern women since good broadcloth became unavailable early in the war. But he looked splendid and proud as his sister fussed over him and his mother beamed.

"Forgive my astonishment," Selene sputtered. I had no idea . . ."

"That you were harboring a spy at Mrs. Weldon's boardinghouse?" James laid his hat on the table and faced her squarely. "I make no apologies, Mrs. Kinsolving. I really was a correspondent with my father's paper when the war started, and it seemed a useful way to continue to help my country. But I've done with all that 'behind the lines' work now. Once I got back to Richmond I went right around to the War Department and got myself assigned to the front. I received my commission and was made a member of General Hill's staff before I knew what was happening. And here I am."

"I had almost given up hope of seeing you wear that uniform," Mrs. James said, brushing off the shoulders with motherly pride. "We made it a year and a half ago, Selene, and it's been tucked away all that time. So often I was tempted to give it to someone who could use it, but I couldn't quite relinquish the hope that Woody might wear it."

"Now we can brag about you, Ellwood," Susannah said, arranging the folds of his sash. "It was beastly having everyone think you had gone over to the enemy."

"Careful," Ellwood warned, glancing at Selene.

"I'm not the enemy, please," she said quickly. "It's true my political sympathies are for preserving the Union, but you have all made me so welcome and offered me so much, that I can only thank you from the bottom of my heart and hope that you will consider me your friend."

"Well said, Mrs. Kinsolving," Ellwood beamed.

Susannah gave Selene a quick, impulsive hug. "I can't speak for Francine or Aunt Lavina—who are prejudiced in their way, though heaven knows they have reason to be—but you can be certain that mother and I will always consider you our friend."

"It was very kind of you Mister James—I mean Captain James—to ask your family to take me in. I'm truly grateful to you."

"I can do better than that, Mrs. Kinsolving," the Captain said gravely, though his eyes twinkled. "I may have word of your husband."

Selene had not been at the Grace Street house a week before she felt as though she had lived there all her life. Captain James's knowledge of Wade proved to be more a matter of rumor and guesswork than actual information, but he went back to the lines near Cold Harbor confident that he would know something more substantial soon, leaving her to settle into the routine of the house that was part home, part hospital. The stream of wounded men who poured every day into Richmond from the ever-shrinking crescent of the embattled army of Northern Virginia had filled all available public buildings and most private homes. Through her work at the Armory Square Hospital Selene was accustomed to the sights, smells, and sounds of battlefield casualties. Shattered limbs and faces, fevers and infections, surgery softened only by precious drops of chloroform of teaspoons of whiskey, slops and nauseating bandages—sometimes so congealed with blood they cut like a knife—the ever present miasma of sickroom odors—they were the same everywhere, North and South, where shattered men were cared for. Even when it was all reduced and compressed into a private home, there remained a dismal certainty about it.

However, Selene was not accustomed to trying to nurse the wounded with such a shocking lack of the basic necessities. Tablecloths, sheets, petticoats, even curtains had been torn and scraped for lint and strips to make bandages. And still there were not enough. Chloroform was almost gone, morphine had not been seen for two years except for small amounts smuggled in through the blockade. All able-bodied surgeons were with the army in the field, leaving only the old and weary doctors to carry the burden of the sick. The James's family physician was nearly seventy-five and withering under the heavy load of wounded soldiers. Civilians had of necessity to wait, and often died in the process.

Selene was moved to admiration for the women of Richmond who, like those in the James household, went around the town daily with sunken, haunted eyes and thin bodies searching out enough food to make soups and stews. A few vegetables grown in patchwork gardens in the backyard supplemented the scraps of meat and makeshift flour scrounged from the shrinking markets of the city.

Shoes were nonexistent. Cloth was unavailable and what they had was turned, patched, improvised, and stretched, for there was nothing to take its place. In fact, there was a shortage in Richmond of everything but people. Though many of the wives and daughters of the ranking cabinet members had been sent farther south as the realization dawned that the city must eventually be taken, yet they were more than made up for by the never-ending stream of refugees and wounded, plus the long lines of prisoners crowded into Libby prison where they starved and suffered, lacking food and medicine even more than the rest of the city. Daily the church bells tolled announcing more deaths which did little to relieve the population glut, since new arrivals more than filled the gaps created by the dead.

Selene soon found that the unusually warm welcome she had received from some members of the James family was not going to be typical of them all. Before the war began Ellwood James's family had been large and close, apparently happy with each other and devoted to the well-being and future success of the children—the boys in their chosen careers, the girls in good marriages. The focal point of all the children were the eldest twins, Francis and Francine. Two more boys and two more girls had followed in perfect order. Ellwood was not the shining star his older brother was, yet he showed promise; Susannah cheerful and happy from her cradle; a third boy, Robert, a gifted musician; and a few years later, Lucy, now only ten years old and utterly confused by all the upheaval that had devastated her family. Their father, Ashley James, had been a professor of history at William and Mary College before giving it up to run a more lucrative small publishing company in Richmond. When the war came he considered secession a last, unhappy resort for his native state of Virginia, but in spite of his personal beliefs, he had been among the first to join General Beauregard at First Manassas. He survived that terrible day only to be shot down in a hopeless charge in the battle of Seven Pines. Francis, true to form, had joined J. E. B. Stuart's cavalry and died at Antietam. After his death and with Ellwood off in Washington, Robert fled home and enlisted even though he was underage. The last letter his mother had from him had been written just before Gettysburg. After that, silence, more terrible and poignant and heartbreaking than the knowledge of his death would have been.

On reflection Selene could see that it was no wonder that Francine James went out of her way to avoid having to pass her in the hall or to be forced to acknowledge her presence in the house in any way. A tall, vivid girl with striking green eyes and titian hair, Francine had lost a father, a beloved twin brother, a younger brother, and a fiancé in three years of war. Still striking, her beauty was a pale shadow of what it must have been in better times. Selene, whom the others might accept out of hospitality or because she was married to a Southerner, was

324

too much of a Yankee for Francine. She pulled her bitterness and resentment around her like a cloak, using it to keep the fires of hatred glowing. Selene wisely let her alone.

Lucy, who seemed to adore her oldest sister, was ambivalent toward the new visitor. She could not quite harbor the hatred Francine felt when Selene seemed such a nice person, and yet she did not want to appear disloyal to the memory of her father and brothers. So she remained mostly quiet and aloof.

The most implacable member of the household was, as Selene had sensed from Susannah's first conversation, the terrible-tempered Aunt Lavinia, Ashley James's sister. This indomitable elderly lady had been a force to reckon with in the James house long before "that ape, Abraham Lincoln, and his arch-fiends" had robbed her of her brother and nephews. A sour spinster, Lavinia had at last with the war found a focus for the emptiness of her life. The fates had finally metamorphosed in the form of Yankee invaders and she now loathed Northerners with all the vehemence she had once turned on hapless servants, providence, shopkeepers, and, indeed, anyone with whom she could not get her way. Fortunately she kept mostly to her room on the third floor, so Selene had little contact with her. When they met once accidentally on the stairs, one gray morning. Selene faced the woman straight on, smiling a greeting. In return she received a grave, withering, silent scowl. Aunt Lavinia was older than Selene expected, barely five feet tall, and shriveled. Her figure was bell-shaped, high-waisted, all skirt. She was attired completely in black except for two white side ruffles framing her sunken face beneath a large old-fashioned cap. Her eyes were the most alive part of her, they blazed with a searing, implacable hatred. Selene tried to slip quietly by her, but Lavinia was not about to allow a victim to escape so easily. She unleashed a stream of invectives that rose with her mounting outrage until Mrs. James heard her and broke in, telling her sister-in-law that in her house she would allow whomsoever she pleased as a guest, and she expected Lavinia to honor her wishes. The old lady simmered but held her tongue, and after that Selene barely ever saw her.

Selene often wondered how it was that after all they had suffered, Susannah and Cecily James could accept her so readily. She finally came to the conclusion that Susannah was simply incapable of hating anyone while Mrs. James's grief had gone far beyond resentment and anger. The pain in that lady's heart never left her eyes, yet the warmth of that heart was a light on her face. Selene soon found that she had never worked so hard in her life as she did in the makeshift hospital, simply in the hope that these two gracious ladies would be relieved of a little of their burdens.

She was trying to encourage a listless young private on a cot near the wide double doors of the dining room to take a little bread soaked in wine one morning early in July, when the doorbell began to clang. Though Selene was near the hall, Francine James jumped up from her post by the window and moved to answer it, ignoring Selene as though she wasn't there. Because she was near the door, Selene could hear the voice of a young man inquiring for a Mrs. Kinsolving. "Captain James sent a letter for her, ma'am, since he knew I was comin' to the city. Hurt my leg early this mornin' and had to have it looked after. Can I leave this here for her?"

Francine did not reply but took the letter and coolly laid it on a table in the hall. With exquisite politeness she asked the soldier in, but he explained he had to be at the hospital for there were two other letters to deliver there. Without a word Francine closed the door and went back to her post while Selene finished the punch and hurriedly went to open her note. It was short and to the point:

Major Wade Kinsolving now with the Mahone brigade, near Mt. Airy Station, Petersburg. Good luck,

E.J.

So Wade was now Major Kinsolving. And he was at Petersburg! Only a few miles away. Selene slipped the note into the pocket of her apron and went to find Mrs. James to tell her she would be away all the next day.

She had planned to try to go down by rail but Cecily James would not hear of it. She sent Tom to drive her down in the carriage, using the only horse they had left and hoping its poor condition would not make it useful to the army. It was just as well Tom drove her, for once they neared the town the confusion of military personnel and equipment was so bad Selene knew she would never have found her way. It had been one of the hottest, driest summers of recent memory in Virginia as though the fates had compounded the misery of those men and women laboring under the usual sufferings of wartime. Dust raised by the horses and men trafficking the roads to Petersburg lay thick on Selene's clothes and dry in her throat. The heat was stifling, as only Virginia could be. Perspiration ran in a thin trickle down her back and she dabbed at her face with a handkerchief sprinkled with rosewater, hoping she would not look too hot and disheveled when she finally saw Wade. Her heart went out to the soldiers they passed laboring on the road or digging at the long warrens of trenches and earthworks they passed. They appeared utterly lethargic and worn down by the blazing sun and dry air. Their tattered uniforms were dusty and soaked with sweat and their caps thick with the brown dust of the road. At constant intervals the big guns would thunder forth, setting the earth shaking and frightening the old horse nearly out of its senses. The seige of Petersburg had begun to settle now with the Army of the Potomac barricaded in a crescent facing an entrenched and well-fortified Southern line. The devastation from previous attempts to break that line and take the town—the latest only a few days before—had left a stunted landscape of shattered trees and broken ground. But old Tom had lived in this area all his life and he knew the town well. With a deft hand he negotiated the picket lines around the trenches and brought her to the Mt. Airy Station, surrounded by a sea of tents. The young sentry they asked directions of was so impressed that Wade's wife had come to see him that he offered her one of the staff tents in which to wait. It had been hastily assembled but it was large and airy and afforded some privacy from the business of the camp going on all around it. When he left her there to go find Wade, Selene took her courage in hand and suggested that he not tell the Major who was waiting. "I'd like to surprise him," she said, trying to sound coy, though actually she was afraid that if Wade knew she was there he might refuse to come. The young man smiled at her suggestion, imagining how pleasantly surprised Major Kinsolving was going to be, and went away. For ten minutes Selene paced the tent until she heard Wade's voice, laughing in some careless banter with one of the sentries as he approached the tent.

She stood in the middle of the room, gripping her hands as the tent flap was pulled back and Wade bent to enter. Her breath froze in her throat as he stepped inside, staring at her in disbelief. Thoughts tumbled wildly in her mind. He had lost weight since London. His uniform hung loosely on his tall frame and there were dark hollows beneath his eyes. He must have been working outside for his uniform was caked with the brown dust she had noted on the soldiers they passed coming into Petersburg. It was smeared on his face where the sweat had mixed with it, enhancing the deep tan of his cheeks. Some of the same weary misery she had seen on those men was apparent in his eyes once they recovered from the surprise of seeing her standing there before him. His fingers froze around the pommel of his sword and he stood, speechless, gawking at her.

"Hello Wade," Selene murmured. After all this time and all her longing, it was the only thing she could think of to say.

"How did you get here?"

"I came looking for you. I've been searching for you for months and only got word that you were down here yesterday. I had to see you, Wade. I had to explain."

As she feared his eyes began to darken and the scowl on his face became etched on his tanned skin. "Explain! I'd like to hear that explanation. How do you excuse murder, Selene? This should be interesting. Go ahead."

"Oh, Wade, don't be sarcastic with me. I truly mean it. I wanted to find you sooner but I couldn't get out of Washington."

"You were in Washington? How convenient. What's the matter, London too far from the center of things. Couldn't do enough damage there, I suppose. Or did Simon Lazar engineer this, too. What's he sent you for now? To finagle information out of me? Well, it's too late. I don't know anything worth carrying back. I've given up espionage, you see, not being terribly successful at it anyway. Now all I want is to fight for my country as long as there is any fight left. You'll have to go elsewhere for your spying."

"Stop it!" she cried, moving toward him. He backed away and she stopped suddenly, horribly sick inside. He hated her more than she had feared. "Please listen to me. I didn't come here to get information out of you—I don't even care anymore who wins this war. I only wanted you to know that I had nothing to do with that bogus shipment of arms. I didn't even know about it until after you had left and by then it was too late to get word to you. As for Simon . . ." the name caught in her throat. "He's dead."

She could see that surprised him. "That's no loss. What happened? One of his cronies get double-crossed once too often?"

"There was an accident and . . . I killed him. I didn't mean to but he . . . well, it doesn't matter anymore. He was the one responsible for those guns. He bribed the manufacturer. When I learned of it, I followed you, hoping I could find you in time."

He studied her for a moment, wondering at her words. "What kind of an accident?"

"It doesn't matter," she said, turning away. "It's all over now."

"How did you get here?" he said in a cold voice.

"I'm staying with a family in Richmond and they sent me down with their servant. Otherwise I don't think I could have ever found you. Oh, Wade, it's horrible in Richmond. No food, no medicine, and so many sick and wounded. I never dreamed it could be so bad."

Wade walked to one side of the tent and sat casually on the corner of a table, folding his arms. "Don't tell me you are ministering to Southern soldiers? Or is it Libby Prison where you can ease the sufferings of your own kind?"

"Of course it's Southern soldiers." Selene snapped. "What does it matter whose side they are on, when they are so horribly hurt?"

"Did you ever think that perhaps some of those horrible wounds were caused by antiquated, rusted guns that exploded in their hands? Or by hammers locking as they faced a bayonet. You should have been there, Selene. More casualties were inflicted from their own arms than from the cannonade or charge of the enemy. Oh, it was something to see. I was feeling so confident and happy that I had been able to replenish our meagre supply of guns. How do you imagine I felt."

"I've told you, I had nothing to do with it."

"Of course I was nearly executed. It took some tall explaining and a lot of risking my neck in future engagements to convince my superiors to trust me again, and then they made me a Major. Fortunately, we didn't actually lose the engagement the only time we used those guns. Lazar would be disappointed at that. But that's because it takes a lot to make a rebel line cave in."

Selene felt a sickness in her stomach. "Wade, can't you forgive me. Truly I *didn't know*." She crossed the space he had put between them and looking up into his eyes, her own brimming with tears. If she could only convince him of her innocence. If she could only let him know somehow that she loved him, truly loved him beyond anyone else in the world. Yet she dared not say the words. They would be an abomination to him now, even if he could hear them above all his anger and bitterness. He looked coolly down at her hand without moving.

"I think I liked you better when you were screaming about the way I kidnapped and forced you. Go back to Richmond, Selene. What was between us was always a sham. It belongs to another time and another world. There's nothing left of it now. There's nothing left for us."

She turned away, forcing back her tears, determined she would not let him see her cry! Yet her body felt as though he had slashed it with one great swing of his sword. All her hopes that he might understand—might still care—were beaten down. There was only an emptiness left where her heart used to be.

"Yes, I should go back. There's no point in staying here."

"No, no point at all. I must get back, too. There's much to do, but then I suppose you know that. You'll forgive me if I don't escort you to your carriage."

He gave her a bow that was a mockery of respect and civility, then swept out of the tent. She stood looking after him, gripping her hands, sick inside. She had accomplished nothing

330

except to break her heart and end all hope. Worst of all was the knowledge that in all the time they had stood there he had never once touched her. In fact, he had shrunk from her touch. That would be the hardest thing to get used to, to stop remembering.

It haunted her as she sat in the hot, stifling carriage all the way back to Richmond. And as she neared the house it underscored even more the question of what she was to do with herself now that there was no hope of living with Wade. Where was she to go? Should she stay at the crowded mansion on Franklin Street, despite the fact that at least two of its members despised and ignored her? Should she go back to Washington where at least she would be familiar with the city and some of its people, even though the changes brought on by the war were pervasive. Or would it be better to go back to Uncle John, working in his tavern and trying to pick up the threads of her life that were so brutally unraveled when Wade Kinsolving swept suddenly into it. She knew he would welcome her back. But the thought depressed her. Somehow it seemed that if she went back to Manassas or even to Washington, she would be giving up all hope of ever winning Wade's confidence again. Not that there was any hope—she cringed when she recalled the way he had looked at her in the tent. There was a barely disguised hatred in his eyes.

Her confusion lasted into the next day when, still undecided as to what she should do, Selene took the last twenty dollars of her money and went at first light to a market where a shipment was expected in bringing flour and greens from the Shenandoah Valley. Of course there was already a crowd there, jostling one another with grim-lipped courtesy to get near the stalls. As the wagons lumbered in from the depot with the food, the push became desperate. Several military officers forced some degree of order on the shouting, shoving crowd and saw to it that everyone got a little while it lasted. But as she neared the platform a riotous group of several women, clamoring and shoving, caught Selene in a crush toward the train doors. There was nothing to do but push along with them, for she was determined to take something back to the James house with the last of her money. She felt a sharp searing pain in her side as she was jostled against a wagon and the faint sound of a rip in her dress. There was no time to pay attention to it then. She managed to fight her way to the stall where she got a small bag of flour—real wheat flour!—a can of lard, and a few potatoes and assorted greens. It was more than she had expected, and certainly more than her twenty dollars should have bought. She suspected it was because she had U.S. dollars that the soldiers in charge had given her so much. Clutching her precious parcels she fought her way out of the crowd and back to the house where she left them in the kitchen with Dilly and the James's old Mammy exclaiming over them.

She was exhausted from the ordeal and from a sleepless night of worrying and wondering. It was not until she fell into one of the chairs in the morning room that she remembered her dress and looked closely at the tear. It was a clean cut straight down the bodice under her arm and Selene gaped at it with dismay. The cloth was worn already and would be difficult to repair. And it was her last good dress.

Somehow that seemed the last straw. She laid her head on her arms on the table and wept for the first time since seeing Wade.

"Why, Selene dear, what is it?" At the sound of the kind voice Selene looked up to see Mrs. James bending over her, one hand on her shoulder.

"I didn't hear you . . ." she muttered, wiping her sleeve across her eyes. She had hoped to vent her unhappiness in private and hadn't heard anyone coming. "I didn't mean . . ."

"I'm sure you did not mean me to hear you crying, and I do not wish to intrude. But, my dear, I have felt for some time that you are carrying a heavy burden and you seemed so upset yesterday when you returned from Petersburg. I would be so grateful if I could help, you have helped us so much."

"Have I helped you?" Selene said, fighting back her tears. "I wanted to, but so often I felt as if I was just in the way."

"Selene," Cecily James exclaimed. "We should have suffered so much more than we have if you hadn't come to us. You are wonderful with the wounded men. Your expertise from the hospital in Washington—not to mention your easy, gentle ways—have been such a relief to all of us. Any extra pair of hands would have been welcome, but yours were so skilled and willing we would be lost without them. And the money you contributed toward the house has made all the difference. I saw what you brought us today. Real flour! Ambrosia from the gods would not mean as much in these times. How could you imagine you have not been a help to us?"

"But Francine and Aunt Lavinia—they hate me. I'm certain they would be happy to see me leave."

Cecily's lips tightened and she lowered her voice as if unwilling to speak. "I hope you can find it in your heart to forgive Francine. She has been terribly hurt by this unhappy war. More than the rest of us. She adored her brother and she was so in love with Stuart Appleton. I don't condone the way she has treated you, yet I can understand it a little. As for Aunt Lavinia, well the truth is she was a sour old woman long before the war started. She will never change. You musn't think of leaving us. We need you."

"I thought perhaps I should go back to Washington."

"If you feel you must, of course I would not try to stop you. Do you have a home there?"

"Actually, no. I don't have a home anywhere. Not now."

Cecily studied her face for a moment, the large eyes brimming with tears, the cheeks drawn and thin now like most of the women in Richmond. She reached out and smoothed back Selene's hair from her brow.

"Forgive me for being impertinent, Selene, but does all this have something to do with your visit to your husband yesterday?"

Selene nodded. She tried to turn away and hide her head in her hands but the tears overflowed. Though she longed to talk to someone about Wade and all the pain her visit had caused her she could not bring herself to speak aloud all the tawdry details. She wept against Cecily's shoulder hoping the older woman would think she was crying over the danger Wade was in rather than the estrangement that lay between them.

When Selene's tears finally subsided Cecily laid her arms around her and hugged her. "So many lives have been altered by this terrible war. But one day it will be over and life will return to normal. In the meantime, I want you to think of this

333

house as your home. We need you here and we want you. You seem to be able to detach yourself from the rigid divisions that have been spawned by this struggle for independence and if you can continue to help our Southern boys and assist this Southern family, then rest assured we need you and want you."

Selene rested in the older woman's arms for a moment, savouring the comfort and closeness of this gracious lady who had become almost like the mother she never remembered. "My money is all gone," she said finally in a small voice.

Cecily laughed. "Then you shall have to eat gruel and greens along with the rest of us."

They could hear Dilly and Mammy laughing in the kitchen over the luxury of real flour for the day's baking. "They're already making bread," Cecily said, looking toward the open door. "We're going to have real bread tonight, thanks to you. Now, come. We've spent enough time with our own concerns and there's much to do. Tom told me a little while ago they're expecting another wagon train of wounded men from Reams Station this morning and we can expect to receive our share. Go up and dry your eyes, my dear, and come down when you feel you're ready to face it all."

Selene squeezed Cecily's hand. "Thank you," she said simply. She managed to get upstairs without seeing any of the others who were all busy in the sick rooms. She pinned the tear in her dress and hid it beneath her apron, then splashed some water on her face to hide her swollen eyes. As she started back downstairs, she thought to herself that at least as long as she stayed in Richmond she would have a chance of knowing how Wade was and whether or not he was safe.

Eighteen sixty-four had been a terrible year for both sides in the bitter struggle that was dividing the Union. The new commander of the Army of the Potomac, General U. S. Grant, by doing the one thing that his predecessors had failed to do— persist—managed to draw an ever-tightening noose around Lee's embattled Army of Northern Virginia. Both sides were dug in now around Petersburg with neither able to break the stalemate. The guns went on incessantly and sporadic fighting, bitter and violent, occurred often, but there was no frontal assault. After the terrible losses of the spring campaign it was almost a relief to the men in the trenches to be bogged down, even with the heat and boredom. More than anything Grant wanted to cut the railroad lines through Petersburg that linked Lee with the deep South and its meagre supplies. General Lee was just as determined to keep this lifeline open. For the defenders siege meant dwindling supplies and time on the side of the aggressor. Richmond, twenty-five miles away, knew well enough that Lee's army was all that stood between them and Federal occupation.

On July 30th the Federal soldiers blew up a mine they had tunneled under the rebel works, creating a huge crater. It was their best opportunity to date to break the Southern line, but it was badly mishandled. Lacking strong leadership, the divisions that poured into the vast hole were pinned there in confusion and cut to pieces by the rebels, once they recovered from their surprise. The long lines of wounded and prisoners from that engagement filled the road to Richmond and the hospitals and houses overflowed with maimed and dying men. More engagements came in the months that followed as the summer finally gave way to drenching autumn rains: Globe's Tavern and Ream's Station again in August: Fort Harrison and New Market in September. North and south of the James River General Grant hammered at Lee with coordinated attacks that softened the Confederate lines but were unable to force through them. Every new battle brought a new wave of wounded and dying until Selene thought there must be nothing in the world but blood and suffering. She worked alongside the James women as hard and as long as any of them, determined to prove her gratitude and stamina. She would never believe in their cause, but she would earn their admiration for her willing service to their men in their great need. She worked until she was ready to drop in her tracks from weariness, until she fell on her bed and then was too tired to sleep. She cajoled, pleaded, bartered, and begged to bring in food and medicine when she could find it. She fought along with the rest in the market and shops, giving up dignity and pride in her effort to feed the men and those who helped them. Though Aunt Lavinia was as implacable as ever on the rare occasions they came face to face, she fancied she saw now and then a glimmer of admiration in Francine's eyes, even though the young woman persisted in treating her as though she did not exist. Mrs. James and Susannah, on the other hand, never missed an opportunity to tell her how grateful they were for her help, and by careful cultivation, she eventually was able to make a guarded friend of Lucy. Ellwood James's frequent reports kept her informed about Wade but she made no more attempts to see him.

And then, on a cloudy, drizzling evening in mid-September, he walked into the front hall of the James' Grace Street House.

Even in the worst deprivation, the human spirit manages to inject something of humor and gaiety into the most terrible of circumstances and Richmond was no exception. In the long lean days between military engagements there was always some kind of entertainment going on. Dances were held, amateur theatricals performed, even private dinner parties given, though the fare was a pitiful imitation of those held before the war. When she could get away from the sick beds, Selene enjoyed these diversions as much as the rest. With Susannah's encouragement she often visited other houses where a single fiddle or a worn piano supplied the music for reels, polkas, and even now and then, a waltz. Once there she found herself laughing and flirting and remembering that once there was a life full of these pleasantries. They never failed to lift her spirits, at least temporarily. The officers on the lines attended these light-hearted opportunities to forget the war as often as they could get away, bringing with them news from the front, and inspiring a rash of romances and weddings among the belles of Richmond.

After attending many of these parties at other houses the women in the James family finally decided it was their turn to play hostess. They spent an exciting week discussing how to roll the cots to one side in order to leave a space in the parlor for dancing, what meagre tidbits they could prepare to serve as refreshments, and how they might spruce up their worn wardrobes to look their best.

"It doesn't seem right to shove the men aside," Francine said gravely as they sat around the table planning their party.

Susannah refused to let her enthusiasm be dampened. "Nonsense. It will do them good to hear some music and see some gaiety. We are too sombre anyway. This house needs some laughter. What do you say, Mother?"

Cecily looked from one to the other of her daughters. "I say Susannah is right. If we can manage it without causing any inconvenience to the men, then it's worth a try. Selene?"

"I'll help," Selene said quietly, not anxious to get involved in what was essentially a family decision.

"I don't know," Francine demurred. "It seems awfully frivolous for such desperate times."

"Francine," Cecily said, kindly, "if you are not comfortable with the party, you can stay upstairs in your room. But I think we ought to try to have it. It will give all our spirits a lift."

Susannah's high spirits found an outlet in planning and setting up the party, set for the following Saturday. She found an ally in Ellwood who showed up on Monday and exclaimed that it was a capital idea and he would help. He knew a private in Weisiger's brigade who played the banjo like you've never heard. Add the piano, which Francine had always played so well, and they would be able to offer the best music heard in Richmond since Christmas last.

"I suppose I could come down to play the piano," Francine said with a little urging.

"And I'll try to find some whiskey," Ellwood added. "And maybe a little sorghum so we can make a punch."

Selene soon found herself caught up in the plans and even looking forward to the evening of the party. She borrowed Susannah's curling iron and did up her hair for the first time in months. She took the ribbon from one of her dresses that was almost useless from darning and made bows for her dress and her hair. And after much agonizing, she brought her ruby necklace from its hiding place and put it around her throat. She had held on to it almost religiously because it was the last thing she owned of any value and because it was a symbol of Wade. Now as she watched the way it caught fire in the lamplight, she decided that after wearing it this one last time she would give it up and try to sell it to buy food for the house. Why not? What it had stood for was dead now, as dead as though the donor himself had been killed by a Federal sharpshooter.

The downstairs rooms were so crowded with men from the lines, ladies from the town, and the wounded convalescents, that all the doors and windows were thrown open to the cool night air. It was a lovely party and Selene was beginning to really enjoy herself when she heard a new group of arrivals and walked into the hall to see Wade standing in the doorway.

He spotted her at the same time and for a few seconds their eyes locked. Then he calmly turned away to speak to Susannah who had come running up to greet them. Selene tried to listen to the comments of a lieutenant who had partnered her on the last dance but it took her several moments before she could concentrate. When Wade disappeared into the crowd in the opposite room she shook off her dismay and decided that she would enjoy herself in spite of him.

After that she was more animated than she had been in months. Ignoring Wade, she flirted shamelessly with any pleasant man who showed her attention. It gave her thin face a vivacity and charm which had not been noticeable before, and soon she had a long group of admirers clustering around her, begging her for a dance and requesting to bring her a glass of weak punch. When Francine, who had also managed to shake off her sombre gloom in the enjoyment of the moment, was encouraged to play a waltz, Selene found herself suddenly on the tiny floor alone with Ellwood James, whirling to the gracious music in a perfect concert of flowing movement. They were a good team. He was a strong leader who loved to dance and she followed his movements with perfect accord. The others stood back watching in appreciation, obscuring Francine's view so that she was not aware she was playing for a solo on Selene's part. The lovely strains went on for five minutes and when they finally came to a crashing end, Selene was nearly out of breath. The room filled with applause for the couple and Selene edged back to the wall to catch her breath, very happy and feeling rather good about herself. As Ellwood moved off to bring her some punch she felt her arm gripped tightly. "Come with me," said Wade, pulling her toward the door. She followed him, stumbling through the crowd as he dragged her along the hall to the morning room and out into the back yard. He pulled her ungraciously down the back steps and along a graveled path toward the rear of the garden. There was a huge old oak tree there whose heavy limbs splayed out over the vegetable plot and where the hedges by the rear gate were just visible in the darkness. Light from the house spilled out near the steps casting shadows on the few couples who wandered near them. In the rear under the tree it was darker and more quiet. It was cooler as well, though Selene barely noticed it.

"What do you think you're doing?" she cried, once her surprise was gone. Yanking her arm away from his grip, she rubbed at the bruised flesh with her hand, her eyes flashing.

"Keeping you from making more of an exhibition of yourself."

"I was doing no such thing. It was a waltz, that's all. And very nicely done too. Woody is a wonderful dancer and . . ."

"Oh, and it's Woody now, is it. How do you think it made me feel? My wife . . ."

"Your wife! And who do you suppose even knows that I am your wife? Not one of his sisters nor his mother. I never told them who you were, and they've certainly not seen you here before."

"Ellwood James knows."

"Yes, but he has not made an issue of it. Did he bring you here tonight?"

"No. When I heard there was to be a dance at this house I suspected you'd be in the thick of it."

Her temper flared at the injustice of his attitude. "You have a nerve, treating me as though I did not exist for weeks and then, when there are other men about, deciding to act like a husband. Well, you can go to blazes, Wade Kinsolving!"

He grabbed for her arm again, pulling her to him. "I won't have my wife flirting outrageously and acting like a hussy around the men I have to face every day. I won't allow you to shame me."

"And how do you suppose you've shamed me. Leaving me completely alone here in this city, dependent on the mercy of this family."

"Then go away. Go back to your uncle or into Washington. You don't have to stay in Richmond."

He had a tight hold of her arm but she leaned furiously into his face. "I'll go where I please. Mrs. James invited me to stay here and if I choose to it's none of your business. Damn you anyway, Wade Kinsolving!"

She tried to strike him but he caught her hand. Anger was so strong within them both that for that moment they hated each other with a searing passion. Then, as quickly as it had come, their wild fury exploded into a flaming surge of white hot need. Wade had thought he was done with her forever, but in that dim light, with her face so near his own, all at once he wanted her more than anything on earth. Roughly he crushed her to him, pinning her hands behind her back and brutally forcing his lips down upon hers. Her mouth opened in surprise and his tongue thrust inside, his lips expanding to hers as he searched the soft, wondrous cavity of her mouth, thrusting into her in a symbolic gesture of the completion he really wanted and needed so badly. His lips buried into hers, forcing her back against the rough trunk of the oak, bending her against it until she slid downward and his hands released hers to grope at her bodice and her skirt.

Selene was caught up and swept along in the torrent of his needs. This was familiar territory, this was a homecoming she well knew and longed for with every fibre of her being. Her hands searched his tunic, sliding underneath his coat to clutch at the hard rising of his throbbing manhood. She bent back as he freed her breast from its low confining bodice, closing around it with his soft, succulent damp lips, pulling at the eager nipple. Dimly she wondered if anyone could see them and then, just as quickly, she did not care. All that mattered was this man, these lips, these hands, this hot, thrusting wondrous shaft to fill the terrible emptiness within her. Her arms went about him. "Wade, oh, Wade," she cried as his mounting hunger swept them both up in its torrent.

Their clothes were an imprisoning barrier. She pulled at the swelling mound beneath his trousers, he thrust into her, impaling her on his fingers. Her body melted to his, his lips to her eager flesh. He kissed, sucked, nipped at the exposed flesh where he could find it, tasting of the sweetness of this remembered feast. His nearness, his longing filled her heart and sent it soaring beyond desire, beyond completion, to that realm of absolute adoration and worship where two souls meld to one spirit.

"Oh Wade, you do care! You do love me!"

Had she thrown cold water over him it could not have had a more disastrous effect. Releasing her so abruptly she stumbled against the tree, he stood away from her, silent for a moment, calming his heavy breathing. "You could always get my blood up, I'll grant you that. But I wouldn't call it love."

The cold acidity in his voice ate into her heart. She hated him then and hated herself for revealing her heart so openly. Nothing had changed, she realized bitterly. Everything was just as it was before, and she had been foolish and idiotic to throw herself at him the way she had.

Wade deliberately straightened his tunic. "Who ever designed those silly hoops you women wear must have been some kind of straight-laced puritan. They are certainly not conducive to making love."

"Not conducive to rape, you mean," Selene snapped. "You had better go."

"Yes. I never should have come here in the first place. My instincts warned me not to but I ignored them. But then I wasn't sure I'd see you. I felt certain that you'd have gone back to your own people by now. Why haven't you anyway? There's nothing for you in the South and it certainly can't be pleasant living in Richmond at this time with things as they are."

Her voice faltered. "I stayed because Mrs. James needs my help in the hospital. Not because of you, in case that's what you're thinking."

"Oh. Well, I suppose that's as good a reason as any." He looked back at the porch where light spilled from the doorway and the lilting bounce of the piano could be clearly heard. "I can't go back in there. I'll slip out through the alley. Damn! I forgot I left my hat on the hall table."

Still smarting from her disappointment and hurt, Selene snapped: "I'll get your hat for you. I agree. It will be better if

341

you don't come inside."

Straightening her bodice she stalked off down the graveled path, her wide skirts swaying as she walked. Inside on a table in the hall she located Wade's hat with Dilly's help, then went back to the rear door of the house. Flinging back her arm she threw it as hard as she could into the backyard. If any of the couples browsing around the garden saw her, she didn't care.

To hell with Wade Kinsolving!

Seventeen

The presidential election was close at hand and while Selene saw the Southerners around her praying for Lincoln's defeat, she kept her peace and prayed silently that he might be returned to office. Everyone wanted the death and suffering to end. But while the good people of Richmond longed for an end without the utter humiliation of defeat, she could see little chance of peace unless the President—who had made preservation of the Union his talisman—was allowed to see the thing through to the end. The cold rains of winter were beginning to come more and more often and with them the hope that Grant's constant battering at the thin, stretched Confederate lines would let up. She had almost decided that this had already happened, there had been such a lull in the fighting. Then, near the end of the month, the dull thundering of guns was heard to the southwest and reports began to filter in of another engagement—yet another attempt by Grant to sever one of the few remaining railroad lifelines to Lee's army and the besieged city of Petersburg. The battle was fought around the end of the line near the winding stream called Hatcher's Run and it was as bitter and fruitless as all the others. It did buy the South some time, and with the onset of winter, both sides settled down to long months of siege.

In Richmond the rumors of a fight were, as usual, soon confirmed by long lines of wagons of wounded men being carried into the crowded hospitals of the city. There was no more room at the James house, yet they managed to push some

343

cots together and crowd a few more pallets on the floor. There was general relief when Ellwood showed up three days after the fighting had ended, grimy and thin from life in the trenches, but still whole and alive. He had been with Mahone's division that had slammed into a Federal brigade commanded by Brigadier General Thomas Egan. The fighting had been fierce, but for once the Federals had regrouped and held until darkness allowed them to withdraw to their original lines. Ellwood had been in the thick of it but came out with only a few scratches and the hardened attitude of a veteran who had fought the war for years.

During this time Selene received a letter from her uncle at Manassas informing her that Matilda had returned to her old home from Washington. "She's quite arrogant, she is," Uncle John wrote, "from having traveled all across the world and hobnobbed with Londoners. Sometimes I fear she's got somewhat above her station. But she's a help to me and I need her well enough. There appears to be more soldiers traveling through this way than ever before." There followed a two-line deletion which Selene guessed was not made by her uncle. It no doubt included his forceful views on how the Federal troops could do more to end the war. The last lines intrigued her: "There was a woman come through last week asking about you. Wouldn't have thought much of it except that she was the ugliest creature God must have ever made. A veritable old hag if ever I saw one. What kind of people were you among anyway while you was gone? I told her you was in Richmond with the rebels and she went away saying she was sorry she missed you. You wouldn't be sorry. I'm sure, had you seen her. Anyway, God willing, this war will end soon and you can come home. I need some more help in the tavern. Business is as good as it's ever been—trust mankind to never want for drinking, especially in wartime."

For a moment Selene wondered if perhaps by some miracle Gurda had transposed herself to Virginia from Barbados, for certainly the black woman was the ugliest person she had ever known. But no. Gurda was dead. It was probably someone from Washington whom she could not even remember meeting.

The James women had worked out a duty schedule which

allowed as much as possible for everyone to have some time off for rest or a walk. Selene was about to change her place in the cot-filled parlor with Cecily James one morning, when a young boy in a tattered uniform rang the bell, announcing he had come from Dr. Tracy requesting that they take in four more wounded men.

"I don't know where we shall put them," Cecily said, "but bring them in anyway. We'll find a spot somehow."

"We could take the table out of the morning room," Selene said. The wagon with the wounded was already standing at the curb since Dr. Tracy knew Cecily James would not fail him. "That would make room for three. Then if that Georgia corporal gave up his bed—he is up and about enough now that he might go to the hotel—we could manage it."

"The morning room will be so crowded we won't be able to turn around in it, but you're right. It will have to do. I'll speak to that corporal, Selene. Oh dear, one of them appears to have had an amputation. And we've nothing, nothing to help him with. If only we had some medicine."

Selene peeked around Cecily standing in the doorway. The boy and a black helper were unloading a stretcher whose occupant tossed restlessly. His moans and cries were clearly audible from the street. His whole upper side was covered with bloody bandages.

"Isn't there anything left?"

"No. I used the last of the laudanum this morning and Susannah finished the chloroform last night."

"Listen to him. We've got to have something. I'm going off duty now. Suppose I run around to St. Charles and see if they have anything left."

"I'm sure they don't, none of the hospitals do. But you might try. I'll get Susannah to help me with these men and see what you can do. Try the druggists, too. Is there any money left?"

"Some confederate bills. It's better than nothing."

Cecily called to Dilly to come and hold the door while she started toward the rear of the hall to begin pulling furniture out of the morning room. "Tell them to put these men on the floor until I can get this room ready. And hurry, Selene, find some kind of drug for us, please, even if it's only whiskey."

Selene saw the men safely disposed of in the hall, then tied on her bonnet, wrapped her warmest cloak about her shoulders, and went out into the streets. It was a gray, dreary day with a seeping rain suggestive of slow tears. The guns were rumbling far off toward Petersburg, and the earth shuddered with them under her feet. The cold should have kept people inside, but the streets were filled with men and women, searching for food, drink, or medicines, looking for doctors, milling in and out of the War Department and Capitol Square. She had almost become accustomed now to the people she met when she went out—the young men with crutches or empty sleeves, women with tight lips and thin bodies, few children for all who could be sent away had been, and streets that were as clean as any place she had ever seen. Garbage was not allowed to accumulate in Richmond, for anything that could be eaten was used.

She tried the druggist first since the shop was on her way, and found as she had expected that he had nothing at all to sell her even if she had U.S. dollars. One of them suggested she try again in two days for he thought some medicine might be coming in through the blockade. She was grateful to know that, since it meant she might be able to get there before they were all grabbed up. Yet she needed something now. The rain increased as Selene hurried on to St. Charles Hospital and up the stairs into the building. The noises that met here there were a louder, harsher cacophony of those at the James house, since the hospital was crowded to capacity and more with wounded, dying and convalescent men. She was accustomed to it now, and to the smells—that offensive miasma of blood, putrefication, rancid breath, fevers, and a thin lingering sweetness of ether. The matron almost laughed when she asked for medicine. "We have so little left it's pitiful," the woman said bitterly. Of course there was nothing left to share with the private home care hospitals. What they had was so little, and so precious, she could only suggest that Selene try somewhere else.

Selene turned away without comment, knowing there was no place else to try. With the cries of the amputee still fresh in

346

her ears, for the first time she felt enraged that her own people would not allow drugs to come through the lines. Such needless suffering! How was it going to contribute to ending the war. It only increased the pain of the dying and added to the bitterness that separated a people who shared a common heritage and country. Stupid, foolish men, she mentally raged as she walked back along the rows of beds toward the entryway. She never knew why, with her mind so engrossed in indignation, her eyes lingered over one form out of so many in that room. He was three rows away, near the wall with its streaked gray windows, lying on his side, his white face staring blankly at her. She stopped abruptly, staring back. Surely not!

She had no memory of getting around the crowded rows of beds and over to him. There was barely room between the cots for her skirts, but she pushed in to his side and lifted his head from the grimy pillow.

"Wade! Oh, Wade, what happened to you?"

He stared up at her blankly and with a shock she realized he did not know who she was. His eyes were veiled, glassy. His breath was foul and his head lolled limply against her arm. She pulled back the sheet to see that his shoulder was covered with a gray bandage that wound under his arm and across his throat. It was dirty and caked with blood. But his arm was still there. Thanking God silently, Selene worked her fingers around the bandage. She had seen enough wounded men by now to recognize the early signs of putrefication when she saw it. The wound itself was bad enough, but it was the lack of care and proper medicine that had brought him to this pass.

"Don't worry, Wade," she said grimly. "I'll get you out of here. I'll take care of you."

Though she knew he could not hear her, she spoke firmly, hoping it would comfort him. Tearing herself away she rushed to the matron and informed her that she had located her husband among the wounded and intended to take him back to her home. If she expected an argument, she was disappointed, for the release of one man only made room for another in the overburdened hospital. With the matron's blessing Selene ran back to the Grace Street house to collect Tom and the James carriage to bring Wade back to the house. As she was leaving to return to the hospital she encountered Cecily in the hall.

"Is it all right? I can bring him here, can't I?"

"Of course, Selene, dear. But I don't know where we'll put him. These last four men have filled every corner."

"We could put him upstairs," Selene said, for she had already given some thought to the matter. "We are married, after all. He can have my bed and I'll sleep on a pallet or a chair. Perhaps Susannah could squeeze in with Francine and Lucy. Do you think she would mind?"

"Of course not. He is your husband, as you say. You must bring him here and make him well. Don't worry about the girls. I'll work something out with them."

All the way back to the hospital Selene sent up a silent invocation that God would bless Cecily James. Somehow she felt hopeful in spite of the fact that Wade appeared so sick when she saw him earlier. If she could give him the loving care he needed, she felt sure she could make him well. And if, later, he still hated her, well, she would worry about that then.

By evening Wade was lying in the darkened upstairs bedroom where Selene had lived for the past four months. He was not aware of where he was or who was bending over him, yet already he seemed quieter and his delirium more like sleeping. She had bathed his face and given him fresh clothes but she waited until Dr. Tracy could get around to visiting the house before she tackled the wound and the dreadful bandages.

"How was he hurt," the doctor asked as he began cutting away the stiff cloth by the soft light of a lamp.

"The matron said he was brought in with a large group of wounded after the battle down at Hatcher's Run. She didn't remember too much about him, but then there had been so many."

"But that was over a week ago," Dr. Tracy shook his head and very gently pulled away the dirty dressings. "My God. Didn't they even bother to wash this? What have we come to."

"Is it very bad?" Selene breathed. If Wade should lose his arm, it would be devastating to him.

"I don't think it was in the beginning. It looks as though the bullet tore through mostly muscles and tendons. Someone removed it, thank God for that, but they must have been very hurried to do such a botch of a job. It was probably a field surgeon."

"Is it gangrenous?" she almost whispered.

"Not yet, but it soon will be without some proper care."

Selene reached behind her for a chair and sat down on it, sighing with relief. She had not realized how much she feared that his wound had already putrefied.

"He'll get good care. But if only we had some medicine!"

"He seems strong. Perhaps his own system will see him through. Here, burn these. I'm going to put on a fresh dressing and I want it washed and changed every day—twice a day would be even better. Do you have any bandages in the house?"

"I have a petticoat I can cut up. It's my last one, but that's all right. I want him to get well."

"That'll do. He's lucky to be up here and away from the others. Keep him quiet and give him as much nourishment as you can in this city where there is little to be found. I'll stop in again tomorrow."

The doctor was so pressed attending to others that he did not return to the house on Grace Street for another four days. Yet Selene found that he was not needed. She watched over Wade's bed closely, attending to the frequent change of dressings, attempting to get some nourishment down him, watching his sleep, and calming his moments of delirium, all of it so diligently and carefully that when the doctor did return there was little he could add.

"But he's no better," Selene said, twisting her hands in her apron. "His wound has improved but he still doesn't know where he is and doesn't recognize me at all. I don't understand it."

Dr. Tracy noticed the dark shadows under Selene's eyes with sympathy. Cecily James had told him on the way up that Selene was trying to continue her hours in the hospital rooms below and devote every other moment to caring for her husband, and it was beginning to take its toll. She asked him to order her to get some rest.

Yet later when the two of them came back downstairs, Dr.

Tracy's grave countenance was not reassuring. He took Selene, Cecily, and Susannah aside and spoke to the three women in a hushed voice.

"Major Kinsolving has the typhoid," he said, without softening the blow. "He must have picked it up at St. Charles. It's the fever and not his wound that concerns me, for we don't want it to spread down here."

Susannah gasped and glanced quickly at Selene, while Cecily, in a calm, unruffled way, said softly: "Thank heaven we took him straight upstairs. What do you want us to do?"

"I think Mrs. Kinsolving should stay with her husband. You'll just have to get along without her for a while. The rest of you avoid their room. I may be getting a little opium tomorrow and I'll send some right over. Do you think you can manage?"

Cecily nodded and never had Dr. Tracy more appreciated the quiet competence of this lovely woman. "You go straight back up, Selene. I'll send up your supper. Call me if you need anything else. I can spell you when you need your rest. I'm not afraid of typhoid."

Selene stumbled back up the stairs and into her room. Closing the door behind her she moved to the bed where Wade moaned and tossed beneath the covers. It was chilly and damp in the room, even though the evening was dryer than anytime within the past three days. Yet beads of perspiration stood out on his hot forehead. She straightened the covers and went to sit in a straight chair near the window. She had never been so bone-tired in her life, nor longed more to stretch out and sleep for hours. And yet, at least his wound had not gone putrid and he was not going to lose his arm. Typhoid was a specter as dreadful as any disease that struck silently and suddenly. But in these times of wholesale mutilation and death, there were worse things.

The next two weeks were for Selene like being suspended in some gray limbo. She was no longer aware of the war except when the dim thunder of guns rattled the windows or the sounds in the streets turned to the hurried marching of men and the clatter of their horses. The rest of the time she sat by Wade's bed, sponging his hot body, calming him when demons of bombs and shells brought him straight up, crying and yelling, fighting imaginery battles all over again. When he did lie silent and unstirring she worried and watched for every sign of breath, however slight. He never seemed to know her and yet he often spoke her name. She never knew how to feel about that, but mostly found herself thrilled to hear the sound on his lips. He spoke other names, too, most of them unfamiliar. They seemed more to come from memories of his early life, his parents and his home in King William County. As near as she could tell he never mentioned London or Barbados, though twice he said *Yamacraw* quite distinctly. Once when she was utterly overcome with fatigue, she laid her head on the bed near him and wept quietly, tears of worry, of regret, of weariness. When she felt his hand lightly on her hair she did not recognize it for what it was at first. "Don't cry, poor girl," he said very clearly and rationally. Selene looked quickly up, but the eyes that met hers were as veiled as ever. Then they closed and he drifted off back into his nether world of gray delirium. She saw no one else in the house except Cecily who brought her her meals and begged to spell her at Wade's bedside and Dr. Tracy when he was able to come. She refused to allow Cecily to stay, partly because she feared the fever might spread, and also because she felt she could catnap often enough in between Wade's restless times to manage. Yet she was tired. Everyday more so. There was supposed to be some kind of crisis the doctor explained, but when it would come, and whether or not he would survive it, was anyone's guess. When it did come, she was not prepared, though it was all she had thought about for days. Late in the evening on a day when the guns had been worse than usual, she sat leaning on the bedcovers beside him, and felt so weary that she laid her head down and almost fell asleep. The sudden difference in Wade's breathing brought her suddenly awake, not so much anything tangible as a knowledge that he was sinking.

Frantically she grabbed his hand. "Wade," she called. "Wade, you can't die. Come back! Don't leave me. I love you. You've got to know it, you've *got* to forgive me. Wade! Come back!"

His lashes fluttered against his white skin. Almost imperceptibly his fingers moved against hers, as if to grasp them.

Selene went on calling, demanding, insisting that he fight to live. She never knew when Cecily and Dr. Tracy came into the room until she felt the doctor forcibly remove her hands from Wade's and Cecily's hands about her shoulders.

"I won't go," she cried, tears flooding her eyes. "He must live. I won't let him die!"

"My dear," Cecily said gently, "you're worn out. It's in God's hands now, and Doctor Tracy's."

"No!" Selene threw herself back across Wade's body, shaking his shoulders violently. "Wade, come back to me, you hear me! You musn't die. I love you . . ."

"For God's sake," Dr. Tracy snapped. "Don't shake the poor man to death. If the typhoid doesn't kill him, you will. Take Mrs. Kinsolving to her chair, Cecily. I'll handle this patient."

As Cecily forcibly pulled Selene away, the doctor bent over the bed feeling Wade's pulse, lifting an inert eyelid, studying the impassive face. "He's still alive anyway," he said quietly. "And he seems easier. Perhaps there's hope . . ."

A long whispering sigh escaped Wade's lips and the pulse beneath the doctor's fingers steadied and strengthened. Selene watched through brimming eyes, not daring to believe the doctor's words. Then the old man looked back at her, nodding his bald head. "I think he's going to make it."

Selene wept out her weariness and relief against Cecily's shoulder. Gently the older woman led her to a chair near the window and held her until her thin, tired body finally lay slack in her arms.

"Selene," she crooned. "I'm going to demand that you go up to my room and sleep for a while. You're not helping the Major by making yourself sick. I'll watch him and call you after you've rested."

For once Selene did not argue. "Do you think he really will be all right?"

"He won't be dancing any jigs for a long time to come," Dr. Tracy answered from across the room. "But I don't believe the fever is going to kill him."

That evening marked the turning point. Though Wade remained weak and unconscious for long periods of time, Selene was no longer afraid that he would die. She began taking turns watching him with Cecily and even, now and then, Susannah, and went back to helping in the ward when she could find the time. Though the patient began to improve from that night, he remained very weak and helpless and spent most of his time sleeping. Selene was sure he still did not know her.

She was wrong. The first time Wade opened his eyes and actually realized where he was he thought he must have died and gone to heaven. Curtains at the windows with sunlight streaming through, a bed, soft and clean with lace-edged pillows, a faded flowered rug on the floor—his mind refused to accept it. Somehow he felt he should be back in the trenches, cold, hungry, wet, and miserable. He drifted off to sleep again without really knowing whether or not it had all been a dream.

Gradually that changed and he learned from the lovely Mrs. James that he was in her house. The first time he woke to see Selene sitting across the room sewing, he found himself smiling, filled with a glow that taxed his heart with happiness. And then he remembered. All the bitterness, the estrangement, the betrayal came rushing back to crowd out all other feelings and he turned his face away from her and pretended to be asleep.

As he got better and stronger he fought hard to keep up that pretense. She smiled at him and spoke kindly but he either refused to answer or mumbled some cold response. Soon Selene quit trying. They might not be friends, but she would see that he was cared for. More and more she turned her energies to the men below and let Cecily and Susannah care for Wade.

No one was more surprised at this than Cecily herself. She had expected something much different once the Major was on the road to recovery, and it took several days of studying the growing coolness between Wade and his wife before she realized how bad the situation was. She still did not know the reason and was not concerned to know it. But she felt in her bones that something had to be done.

Accordingly, the next evening when she brought up Wade's supper and helped him take it, she raised the subject.

"I was very surprised to see her here," Wade said quietly. He pushed the bowl of thin soup aside and fell back against the

353

pillow. His strength was returning, but so slowly as to be frustrating and disappointing. Cecily knew that with the proper nourishment he would have been almost well by now, but at least he was lucid and she felt he had enough strength to face the subject.

"I don't know why you should be surprised," she answered. "Selene has been living with us for some time. It was she who found you at St. Charles, nearly dead from fever and lack of care. She brought you here."

Wade turned his head against the pillow to stare at her. "I wasn't aware of that. She never said."

"I'm sure she didn't. Nor would she tell you how she took care of you, night and day, when the rest of us were forbidden to enter this room for fear of the typhoid. She wore herself out watching over you, Major Kinsolving. And when you nearly died, she brought you back, by her determination and her love."

"Love? There has never been any love between us."

"You had an arranged marriage then?"

Wade almost laughed. "No, not quite that. But Selene has spent most of our relationship hating me."

Cecily shook her head wondering how men could be so obtuse. "And what are your feelings for her, Major?"

Wade turned away, refusing to let her see what was in his eyes. "I'm not sure. I thought I loved her once but . . . so much has happened. I thought I hated her sometimes, too."

Cecily rose and took the tray. "You have much leisure, Major Kinsolving. I think it would not be unwarranted if you used some of it to figure out just what your true feelings for Selene are. She nearly killed herself trying to make you live. Now, more and more, I get the feeling she doesn't really care anymore whether *she* lives or not. Good night, Major."

She was gone before Wade could answer, leaving him to lie there in the dim twilight, wondering at her amazing comments. Later, much later, he heard Selene quietly enter the room. He wanted to call her, talk to her, ask her if what Cecily said was true, but she went softly about shedding her clothes, turning down the lamp, and stretching out on her pallet on the floor. He lay there in the dark, fighting the urge to call her to him, longing for the first time in weeks to hold her in his arms, and yet unable to utter a sound. Finally, more from weakness than a desire for rest, he drifted to sleep not knowing Selene was staring up at the dark ceiling, as restless as he.

Though Wade never saw his wife all the next day, he had time to think quite a lot about her. Many things came back to him, comments he had not wanted to believe or hear before. Against those he recalled Cecily's words.

The following morning, after Mrs. James had helped him get up and sit in the chair by the window, he asked if perhaps she would send Selene up.

Cecily tried to mask the pleased surprise she felt at his request. "Of course," she said lightly and hurried downstairs. Selene was spooning a thin mush for one of the men in the parlor. Cecily gently took the spoon from her hand and asked her to take Wade's tray up since she herself was feeling a little tired and didn't want to climb the stairs.

Though Selene had been avoiding Wade since he was on the mend, she was resigned to having to face him someday. She went to the kitchen and filled another bowl with the mixture of milky corn gruel—all they had at the moment—then took it upstairs.

She hadn't expected to see him sitting in a chair and she could not hide her pleasure. Without mentioning it, however, she put the bowl on a table by the chair. "Do you want me to help you with it?" she asked, hoping he would not.

"Yes, please."

Though surprised, Selene pulled up another chair to face him and picked up the spoon. She lifted it to his lips and Wade sipped at the contents, then, when she started to get more, caught at her hand.

"Selene," he said, so softly she barely heard it. Her startled eyes flew to his face. His grip on her hand was no stronger than a kitten's clasp but she made no effort to remove her arm.

"Selene," Wade repeated more strongly. "Mrs. James told me all you did . . ."

She looked quickly away. "It was nothing. I couldn't let you just lie there and die in that crowded hospital. She shouldn't have . . ."

His fingers slid down her arm, gently, like a butterfly's wing. "No. I owe you my life. I realize that now. But why? When I insulted you so. After I . . ."

His hand fell away and she caught it in her own. "Wade, I tried to tell you that day in Petersburg. I didn't realize it until after you had left London, when I thought you might be killed by that cruel deception Simon played upon you. I love you, Wade. My heart nearly broke in two when I thought you were gone and I might never see you again . . . might never explain. When you looked at me that day in the staff tent with such hatred and bitterness, I didn't want to live. Then when I found you so ill in that terrible hospital, it seemed God had given me a second chance to prove that I really do care for you."

She didn't want to cry but the tears brimmed in her eyes. Her head bent and Wade reached to pull her against his shoulder, stroking her hair. "But Selene, how can you love me? I dragged you away from your home, forced you to marry me, took advantage of you every chance I got. You've every reason to hate me."

"And I ran away and went to England with Lazar, shaming and humiliating you. I refused to act the part of your wife. And that terrible trick Simon played . . . I didn't know *any*thing about it, yet I felt so responsible."

Weakly he moved against her hair, brushing her cheek with his lips. "I guess we both made some pretty stupid mistakes. Oh, my dear girl. Even as weak as I am, just having your warm flesh so near makes my blood run faster. Selene, I tried so hard to hate you, but it's no use. You're part of my blood, part of my body, part of my very soul. You're my girl and nothing will ever change that."

She pulled back, staring into his eyes. "Do you really mean that?"

For an answer he slipped his arm around her shoulder and pulled her lips against his own. It was a gentle, warm kiss that stirred them both until Wade's taxed strength began to fail. Selene slid to her knees, clasping her arms around him, holding him with gentle strength. Her tears mingled with her laughter, the joy of resolution and fulfillment after a long, empty, lonely night.

"Wade, my dearest, dearest husband. Oh, I love you. I love you!"

And Wade laughed with her.

Eighteen

It was the first of the year before Wade was well enough to return to the trenches outside Petersburg. To Selene that austere, joyless Christmas was made more than bearable by the fact that he was with her, warmed by the glow of their love for each other. She dreaded seeing him get well enough to go back to the fighting, yet she knew it was what he wanted. The long tedium of waiting in safety while his friends were facing hardship and death was almost as difficult for Wade as the illness itself.

It was a miserable cold and wet winter and Wade had not been back in the huts and dugouts three weeks before he suffered a recurrence of the fever and had to go back to the house on Grace Street. Though his recovery was swift, by the time he returned spring was waiting over the horizon bringing with it the renewal of the war.

Each time Selene thought things could get no worse in Richmond, it seemed there were fewer necessities than ever. Firewood was as hard to get as United States greenbacks. Food supplies still trickled into the city through the one rail line still intact and the efforts of smugglers, but there was so little that often her day's rations were what would have been breakfast in better times. Her clothes hung on her thin frame and she often suffered spells of dizziness along with constant fatigue. But she kept going, sharing what she had with the sick men in the house and keeping just enough for herself to make life bearable. Like all the women in the city, her hardships were made more tolerable by the thought that the men on the lines facing Grant's well-fed and adequately supplied army were even worse off than she.

As everyone expected, along with an easing of the weather came a new burst of fighting. Lee's lines were spread so thin and had suffered so through the winter that it was an unspoken assumption the end must come soon. If Richmond fell, it meant the death knell of the Confederacy. Everyone knew it, even when they spoke bravely of a way out for the Army of Northern Virginia. There was so little food coming into Richmond that even rats were scarce and hard to find. Still the spirit of rebellion burned in the thin, tired breasts of those who saw it not as revolution but as freedom. Selene honored the women she had come to admire by not speaking of what was sure to come, and by working tirelessly to help ease the suffering around her.

Her quiet efforts finally won her the respect, though not the friendship, of Francine. That indomitable lady finally unbent enough to recognize her presence and include her in family conversations. The first time Francine spoke directly to her to ask her a question about one of the sick patients, Selene felt she had won a major victory. Of course to Aunt Lavinia she would always remain the enemy and she would never be a real friend to Francine. Yet she treasured the respect of the proud girl with the tragic eyes for she had fought hard to win it.

Wade had just returned to the lines after his second bout of fever when Selene set out one morning to the market to see if anything had come in that might stretch their limited larder. Almost immediately she noticed a subtle change in the city. The guns in the distance were going almost nonstop, sometimes so close as to seem across the river, at other times like distant thunder presaging a coming storm. The streets were full of people, women with baskets on their arms, young boys hurrying on errands, old men stopping to talk in hushed voices. She recognized one of the Cabinet members—Judah Benjamin, the Secretary of State, standing on a corner talking earnestly with two military men, his usually benign face etched with concern. Soldiers clattered up and down the streets, couriers on their way to the capitol or riding pell mell for the lines. Beneath it all was a dark sense of urgency, undefined but felt strongly. Even Selene caught the spreading sense of panic and said a silent prayer for Wade.

There were many people milling about the market, but no food. She turned away thinking she might try the second market near the depot. The manager there had relatives outside the city who sometimes brought in dried peas or greens when they were available. It was a long walk, but there was nothing else. As she ambled beside the iron railings of the Capitol Square something drew her eyes to the other side of Bank Street. There were crowds of people there, grouped in small clusters, but her gaze fell on a figure apart, standing in the shadow of an overhanging oak. At first she thought she recognized the woman, standing tall and severe with a bonnet that shaded her face. Somehow Selene knew those eyes were fastened on her, and for a moment they held her immobile. A fear seeped through her, completely unreasoning and absurd, yet riveting. She strained to see the face under the bonnet brim but could not make it out. Surely she did not know this woman, and yet there was something oddly familiar about her.

Gurda! That was it. She reminded her of Gurda. The same dark mysterious emanation of evil. Selene shuddered, remembering her uncle's letter about an ugly old woman asking after her. Yet, try as she might, she could think of no one from her past this person might be.

She started on her way again, shaking off the strange misgivings as the result of too little food and too much fatigue. Yet as she rounded the corner on Ninth Street she kept close to the house fronts, pausing now and then to glance behind her. The tall woman was not there among the pedestrians so intently going about their business. Selene smiled, thinking she was growing overly suspicious, but when she reached the end of the block and turned on to Broad she looked back to see the woman crossing the dusty street behind her.

Anxiously she crossed Broad Street, dodging the wagons, keeping behind the shade trees, merging into the crowd. Yet everytime she glanced back she saw the tall grim figure of the woman dogging her steps. By the time she neared the market she was certain she was being followed and an unreasoning fear consumed her. She began walking very fast though her exertions tore at her breath. Ignoring the entrance to the market she ducked down Marshall and darted back up Fifth. Crossing Broad she ducked into an alley that would take her diagonally to Grace and two blocks away from home. Filled with an unreasoning panic she ran down the alley, ducked into the next block long enough to cut back across another way and ran to the end. There was a large stand of lilac bushes that bordered the back fence of one of the houses. Selene slipped behind the tangle of limbs where she could not be seen and stood, breathing hard and watching the other end of the alley. After what seemed hours but was in fact minutes, the tall figure did not appear. She decided she must have outfoxed the woman following her and headed back with a quicker step than usual toward Grace Street.

If the woman was indeed following her, she corrected herself. Was she only being foolish or paranoid? She could not explain the sense of horror the strange woman had awakened in her, the way the hairs on her neck came alive when she looked back to see that tall figure still behind her. Racing up the front stairs she let herself into the house, closing the door tightly behind her and fighting down a desire to run up and lock herself in her room. Within an hour her panic was slowly ebbing away and Selene began to think she was giving way to the vapors. She gave herself a mental shake and kept very busy the rest of the day.

It was two days before she ventured out again, looking around frequently to see if there was anyone behind her. There was no sign of the mysterious woman that day and she began to think she had dreamed the incident. Then, nearly a week later, she saw her again. Once more she stood across the street, her face hidden by the old-fashioned bonnet. Once more she kept well behind Selene, sometimes merging invisibly into the crowds, sometimes brazenly following at a distance with no attempt to hide her presence. With her panic growing, Selene decided to confront the creature. Turning a corner she stopped and waited, ready to step out boldly and ask why she was being followed. When the continuous stream of pedestrians came round the corners but no mysterious woman appeared, Selene went home wondering if her mind was playing tricks on her, and whether there had actually been anyone there at all.

Yet whenever the front doorbell jangled, her heart stopped. If it should be someone asking for her, what would she do? She was filled with a foolish panic that the strange woman might walk right up to her door, confronting her. Noticing how pale and haggard she was beginning to look, Mrs. James insisted that she take a day to lie in bed and rest—something Selene was glad enough to do since she felt safer in her room than anywhere in Richmond. She was lying there in the late afternoon, feeling a good deal more rested in body and mind when she heard the bell below. A few moments later Susannah knocked softly at her door and came in bearing a small box.

"This came for you, Selene. I don't know who sent it. A little lad from one of the mill houses brought it and said he was told to deliver it to you here."

"Who told him?" Selene said, her breath tight in her throat.

"An old woman, he said. Open it. Perhaps it is a gift from the Major."

But Selene knew this small box had not come from Wade. All the old panic swept over her again as she untied a dirty strand of ribbon and lifted the top. Inside, nestled in a jumble of gray paper, sat a small block of mahogany carved in a crude shape of a beetle. The eyes were painted red and tiny wooden claws protruded from the rounded head. Selene gasped and dropped it on the floor.

"What is it?" Susannah asked, retrieving it and holding it up. It was attached to a leather thong, stiff and dark with age. "Is it some kind of necklace? My heavens, but it has an offensive odor. Who would send you such a dirty old thing?"

Selene slid across the bed as far away as she could get from the black thing Susannah held up. "I don't know. It's horrible. Take it away, will you, Susannah. Burn it. Bury it. Do anything but take it out of my sight!"

Susannah looked at Selene strangely, wondering how the ugly but apparently simple talisman could effect her so. But it would not have been polite to ask, so she merely laid it back in the box. "Are you sure?"

"Yes. Yes! Throw it in the stove. Burn it."

Susannah picked up the box top and slipped from the room, leaving Selene to lie frozen in horror on the bed. She had recognized that little piece of wood almost immediately. It was one of the charms Gurda had worn about her neck. How many times had Selene seen it jumbled there among the other weird charms and talismans Gurda habitually wore. Would they all be delivered to her one after the other, gifts that awoke in her torrent of horror and fear?

She pulled the covers close around her throat. Wade! She must see Wade. He would know what to do about this strange business. She would send for him first thing tomorrow morning.

Yet when the day dawned warm and sunny, the birds riotous outside her window singing a welcome to the coming of spring, Selene took stock of her shattered nerves and decided she had been foolish. She was tired and hungry—that must have more to do with giving way to unnamed terror than any real threat or ghostly vision. Gurda was dead and whoever this strange woman was, whatever she was trying to do, there had to be some rational explanation for it. She decided not to send for Wade, who must have a thousand more pressing matters to deal with, and resolved to see this thing through alone. She would be waiting today if the doorbell rang and she would answer it herself.

Of course nothing happened. Word came of some heavy fighting near Hatcher's Run—the same ground so fiercely contested last October where the Confederate lines got the worst of it. General Lee was desperate to break his army out of Grant's encircling noose and to reach North Carolina to join the only other remaining Confederate army under General Johnston. Grant, that determined, feisty fighter, was just as adamant that the Army of Northern Virginia would not escape. Everyone agreed matters could only get worse.

The following day Selene ventured out once again, hoping to confront the mysterious woman. She looked right and left, searching the crowds that clamored around Capitol Square for information and food, but there was no sign of the tall, shrouded figure. She made stops at two of the hospitals and the War Office without obtaining medicines of definite word of

362

Wade's regiment. The crowds were heavy, and they moved restlessly, unceasingly. Again she noticed that urgency in the air, the sense of impending calamity. As she started down the steps of the War Department, her attention was drawn to a commotion at the corner where several private carriages, piled high with boxes and bundles of families trying to leave the beleaguered city, had blocked the passage of several military wagons. The harassed drivers of the carriage traded insults with soldiers on horseback and clusters of civilians trying to get information on what was happening around Petersburg. Across the street, a group of officers clattered up and dismounted. Selene recognized Ellwood James among them and called to him. He waved back before turning to tether his mount while the rest of the group scattered, leaving one tall soldier standing near the iron rail, staring straight at Selene. He wore a round, battered officer's hat pulled down over his eyes, yet she could feel their cold gaze boring into her. His thin, tight lips bore the ghost of a mocking smile and along his cheek a thin white scar glowed pale against the dark skin.

Selene gasped and groped for the stair rail. People, horses, shade trees, the gritty dust of the road—all began to swim in a blur and she wiped her hand across her eyes trying to clear her head. When she looked back there was only an empty space where the man had stood. Was she losing her mind? Had reduced rations and fatigue driven her senses from her, opened the door to an unreasoning, all-consuming terror? She walked down the steps, faltered among the jostling crowd, groped for Captain James coming toward her. The whirling colors that washed her eyes swirled to black and she fell unconscious to the ground.

She came to, hearing Cecily's gentle voice: "I should not have allowed her to go out. She's not strong enough."

Someone was chafing her hands and there was a cool cloth over her eyes. She moved it away to see that she was lying on one of the sofas shoved against the wall in the James's parlor. Over Cecily's shoulder she could see two wounded soldiers peering at her anxiously, and above them Ellwood James.

"Thank God I was there," he was saying. "She might have been trampled otherwise, there were so many people milling about."

"She's coming round," Cecily said. "Selene dear, are you all right? No, don't get up. You must lie here and rest."

"No," Selene cried in a choked voice. "Wade. Tell Wade . . ." She tried to rise but her body refused to move. "Simon. Simon Lazar. Keep away. Keep away from Richmond. Tell him, Woody!"

"What does she mean?"

"I think it's delirium caused by lack of proper nourishment. We've simply got to see that she eats more."

"Simon . . ." Selene went on muttering. "Tell Wade . . ."

Then she saw that Ellwood was gone, and Selene wondered if she had dreamed that, too. But he had only walked to the front door with his mother, explaining that he had to get back to the lines. The push by Grant to take Petersburg was expected any moment and Ellwood had been sent into the war office with strict instructions to return immediately.

Cecily clung to his hand. "Take care of yourself. Don't do anything heroic. We've already given your father and brother to this cause."

Gently he brought her fingers to his lips. "I'll be careful. Take care of Selene. I think—I'm certain the city will fall soon. If it does, stay inside the house. Don't leave for any reason. If you promise me you'll do that, at least I'll feel you're safe."

"I promise," Cecily said and kissed him quickly. When she went back to Selene lying on the sofa she found she had fainted again.

Later that day Tom went out into the city and returned an hour later with the thinnest, scrawniest chicken Cecily had ever seen. Yet gold itself would not have been more welcome. She cooked it and saved some of the broth for Selene, serving it with what was almost the last of their meal. Tom informed her of disturbing rumors filtering about the city that the military commissary warehouses were full of food meant for the army but at the moment lying there unused. There were ominous rumblings that if the army didn't have it, why shouldn't the people of the city? It had fueled an angry undertone to the crowds milling about the streets. They were full of what Tom called trash, which Cecily determined to be gamblers and low-

364

caste women. It was even rumored that some of the convicts in the prisons had been turned loose. She had the servants barricade the windows of the house that night, and when the cannonade began from the distant town of Petersburg, the sounds were muffled by the shutters.

By the next morning it was apparent that a major offensive was underway in the trenches surrounding Petersburg. It was a Sunday and the churches were full. Selene didn't feel strong enough to go out but Francine and Susannah slipped through the front door of the James house and made their way to St. Paul's nearby. When they returned later, it was to tell of a disturbing scene during the service when President Davis had been brought a note and had immediately risen and left the Church. One by one the remaining Cabinet members followed, all of them obviously intent on making their way from the capital.

During the day the clatter of wagons and horses on the street mingled with the tramping of soldiers, the cries of civilians, and the constant clang of the tocsin in Capitol Square. There was a frantic agitation that could be felt even behind the shuttered windows of the house. When Tom or Dilly or, at one point, even Francine ventured out to try to learn what was happening, each returned more grim than before. The Confederate lines had been broken at last after ten months of holding fast; Lee was pulling his army out of Petersburg, trying to escape the Federal noose and make his way westward; the city was doomed and would fall before midnight. The crowds on the street were increasingly made up of the riffraff of the town, angry, vengeful, hungry, and lawless. Decent people who had been unable to leave the city were now barricaded in their locked houses, hoping to wait out the worst.

By afternoon the streets were filled with long lines of ragged, hungry men in gray streaming through the town on their way westward. The women opened their doors to stand on the porch or run along side the stumbling men, asking where they were from and where they were going. They learned that the rumors were true and Lee was abandoning Richmond to save the last of his army.

"Better lock y'er doors, ma'am," one of them cried to

Selene. "There's nothin' behind us but the dregs."

Some of the wounded men in the house who were ambulatory took off with the army rather than wait to be captured prisoners. A few simply decided to head away from the fighting and to make their way back to their homes. One or two left to join the crowds roaming the city. Those who could not walk stayed with the household, all of them sitting together and listening to the racket outside their windows with increasing anxiety.

More than once Selene had to force herself to sit still when everything in her longed to go running out to search the columns of the retreating army for some sign of Wade. It was the not knowing that was so horrible. Had he been part of that last fierce fighting? Was he on his way west along with Lee's remnants? Was he in the city, part of that last contingent of soldiers whose job it was to destroy what had to be left behind? Had Ellwood given him her message? Was the man she saw Simon . . . Simon in a Confederate uniform? Yet Lazar had always known how to use disguises. Could he still be alive? The tall mysterious woman made sense if he was. It was not some ghostly apparition of Gurda. It was Simon trying to drive her crazy, taking his revenge. Or was she imagining it all? Was it the result of her weakened state and the stress of this dying war?

As the afternoon wore on into evening, Tom came pounding on the rear door, crying for Miss Cecily.

"God aw'mighty, Miz James," he cried, the whites of his eyes stark against his dark skin. "Dem soldiers gone an' fired de warehouses and de liquor, it flowin' in de streets. Doze trash, de done gon crazy!"

"I don't believe it," Cecily cried. "Our own men burn their stores? It can't be." The women hastily threw open the front door to stand in the darkened street. There were few soldiers now among the confused crowds and those who straggled by had the look of opportunists or deserters. Down over the rooftops toward the river they could see spiraling black smoke and the first tongues of flame rising above the commissary buildings. "Look," Francine pointed. "Tom was right. It looks as though the whole warehouse district is on fire!"

366

"Don't they realize what they're doing? Those buildings are so close."

"Mama, what will we do if it reaches our house?" Susannah said, clutching her mother's arm.

"Stay calm. It's nowhere near us now. We'll see what happens."

Selene had never appreciated Cecily's calm, controlled manner more than at that moment. It would be so easy to give way to panic and fear and yet that would be the worst thing they could do. The people hurrying up and down the street were enough to give one pause. Rough-looking thugs and hard women racing toward Capitol Square, laughing and calling to one another as though they were at a revelry rather than presiding over the death of a city.

It was dark now and the high, swelling flames were a vivid band of color against the darkened roofs of the town. Cecily shepherded her family together to retreat back inside the house, Selene in the rear. She had just walked up the front steps and was about to enter the doorway when a young boy darted across the street and came running up to her.

"Miss Selene," he called and she turned, wondering. "Are you Miss Selene?"

"Yes," she answered, straining to think if she knew the child.

"I was told to give you this at this address," he said, handing her a dirty wrinkled piece of paper.

"Told by whom?"

"Just told." He shoved the paper in her hand and ran off, lost in the crowd almost at once. Selene stared down at the note, almost afraid to open it as Cecily came back to take her arm and draw her into the safety of the house. The light from the front hall was just strong enough to make out the words scribbled on the paper:

At St. Charles Hospital. Caught a ball in the leg. It may have to come off. Urgent you come. Wade.

Selene stared up at Cecily with huge eyes. "It's Wade. He's been hurt."

367

"You can do nothing about it now, Selene," Cecily said anxiously, pulling her into the hall. "We must lock ourselves in. I promised Ellwood. It's not safe to be outside."

Selene strained against the older woman's grasp. "No! He's been hurt. He needs me. I have to go!"

"Selene, you can't," Susannah protested. "It's too dangerous out there."

"He's at the hospital. Anything could happen. It could catch fire. I must go to him."

"If you can even get there. Think what you'll have to go through!"

"Let me send Tom," Cecily pleaded. "He'll bring the Major back to the house where we can care for him."

Selene was already halfway down the steps, desperately trying to free her arm from Cecily's determined fingers. "I have to go. Don't you understand, he wants me there with him."

"Selene, it's not safe!"

"I don't care," she cried, yanking her arm free. "Lock yourselves in," she called over her shoulder as she ran into the street. "I'll try to bring him back here."

She caught a glimpse of the three women, dark silhouettes standing against the white light of the hall. Then the door closed and she realized she was alone on the street. Alone among the noisy, rowdy, angry mob, the confusion, the wild revelry. And over it all, the insidious cloud of billowing smoke, blowing up from the river, that choked her lungs and filled the air with throat-searing cinders. Alone, though there were people everywhere. Selene pushed her way through them, trying not to get caught up in the riotous fever of excitement and fear that spread like a plague through the crowds. When she reached Main Street she found that what Tom had told them was true and the very gutters were flowing with the whiskey that had been dumped farther up the street. Many of the people there were scooping it up with pitchers and cups. Some lay face down on the walk, cupping it in their hands, and not a few were already showing signs of drunkenness, even some of the women. Selene kept close to the buildings, shoving away the occasional hands of an amorous man who assumed that because she was out on the streets she was seeking as much merriment as could be found in the face of disaster.

She had to pass through the rioting to reach the hospital and the pillage and disorder grew worse as she hurried into the business area. Looted stores had left a carnage of broken glass and stripped cartons along the walk. The heat from the burning stores and warehouses was nearer now and terribly intense. Yells of drunken men, shouts of roving pillagers, wild cries of distress made the night hideous. But she pushed on, forcing herself up the steep hill to the hospital.

The matron behind locked doors was reluctant to open them until Selene's stubborn pounding finally forced her to crack one door just far enough to allow her voice to be heard.

"Go away! We haven't any more room or medicines."

"I must get in. My husband is here. He was wounded and brought in today, facing an amputation." Recognizing Selene's voice, the matron inched the door open a fraction wider.

"You're mistaken. We've had no wounded for the past two days and no amputations are being done. There's not space on the floor to put another body. You'll be better off with Mrs. James, Mrs. Kinsolving. Try to get back home."

"But I can't. Look, I had a note from him. He said he was here and he told me to come."

"I know your husband, Madam, and he is not in this hospital. If you want to come inside and wait out this riot, I'll let you in, though heaven knows where you'll find a place to stand, much less sit." The door cracked open a tiny bit more.

Selene looked around at the busy street. A carriage came clattering by and several men, all of them apparently far gone in their cups, ran out to stop it. The horse shied and reared and the driver swung his whip at them, but they only laughed and pulled him from the seat. It wasn't safe out here. But perhaps Wade had mistaken the name and was in one of Richmond's other twenty-eight hospitals.

"Thank you, Matron. I'll go on back home."

The door slammed without further comment and she heard the bar slide heavily in its lock. The night was completely dark now but the streets were bright with the pine knot torches carried haphazardly by many of the rioters and by the glow of the flames in the distance. Selene hesitated a moment before starting down the steps. Ignoring the crowd she pushed on down Franklin Street, stopping at the several hospitals within walking distance. Wade was not in any of them.

She had retraced her steps back to the St. Charles when one of the men in the street ran up to her, grabbing her around the waist, and tried to kiss her. Frantically she shoved away the clawing hands and began to run, her panic growing. Without being aware of where she was going she careened around a corner right into a dark figure standing squarely in front of her.

"Get out of my way!" she cried, trying to move around the tall man blocking the walkway.

"I think not," said a calm, contained voice.

Selene looked up startled into the white face of Simon Lazar. In the flickering light of the torch he held aloft, his face was shrouded, the long searing scar stark against his skin. "You!" she cried and shrank back. "It *was* you!" He gripped her arm painfully.

"Oh yes, dear Selene. It was me all the time." He leaned into her face, smiling his cruel smile. "I had a hard time running you to earth. Wasted a lot of time in Washington before I remembered that uncle of yours. And then, getting to Richmond wasn't too easy. But I managed. I always do. A tattered gray uniform will get you a welcome anywhere in the South."

"But . . . you were dead. I killed you!"

His fingers dug into her flesh. "You very nearly did. You thought you had left me there to die, didn't you? But I lived. It took me a long time but I did recover from your scissors-wielding tantrum. And now, at last, I'll take my revenge."

His eyes flickered yellow in the fire glow. There was such a look of satanic satisfaction on his face that Selene cowered from him. "You're mad," she muttered.

"Not mad. Just determined to get even. To make you pay, you and your rebel lover."

Somehow Wade's name brought her back to reality. This was no apparition, it never had been. It really was Simon Lazar, come back to kill her. And Wade, too, if he ever found him.

370

That must not happen. "You sent that note," she said, edging back around the corner where the crowds were larger. He held her fast but followed just enough to be in the pathway of the mob.

"Oh yes. And you fell right into the trap. How convenient it is that these riotous thugs should be on a rampage tonight. Between them and the fire—which will surely finish off this city before morning—you'll be just another accident. A victim of circumstances. Even Fate has played right into my hands."

Selene looked frantically around. A large group of revelers, men and women, were moving toward them, jumping and dancing around each other and passing around a large bottle. Twisting her arm, she managed to get far enough out on the walk that they were forced around her, jostling up against her and breaking the hold Simon had on her arm. She yanked free and ran, shoving through the crowd, not even glancing behind her to see if he was following until she reached the end of the block. Then she saw him, bounding toward her, held back by the crowd but making headway in spite of her headstart. She tore down Tenth street and came out on Carey, nearer the fire and more turbulent and crowded than Main had been. Halfway down she got caught in the crush herself and looked back to see Simon gaining on her.

"Let me through," she cried, pushing through a distraught family trying to protect their household goods piled on the road from a gang of thugs circling it like vultures. She drove through them only to find herself enmeshed among a group of looters fighting over the contents of a draper's shop they had just dragged onto the walk. "Where ya' goin', ma'am," one of them drawled, reaching out to grab her. "Look, I'll find somethin' pretty for ya' . . ." Selene sidestepped his arm and pushed frantically through the crowd. Simon was behind her now, held up by the same group. He reached his long arms over their heads, thrusting around their bodies, trying to grab Selene. He was close enough that she felt him clutch at her hair. With a cry of pain she turned and slammed her fist against his arm, driving him away. Then with one last push, she broke free and darted across the street where there were not as many people.

She was fortunate in that a platoon of soldiers came tramping by just then heading for the bridge and she got them between her and the crowd that still held Simon on the walk. She made her way to the other side, diving into a group going the opposite way and attaching herself to them, hoping she could not be seen. When she glanced back, she saw Simon in the street searching the crowd and she took heart. At the first opportunity she broke away to dash up another cross street. Zigzagging as much as possible, from one side of the street to the other under the cover of groups of roving revelers, she came at last to Capitol Square. The open space inside the iron railings was jammed with families who had set up campsites on the grass. They were refugees from the fire and the drunken rioters on the streets below, the homeless and the frightened citizens of the town. Selene moved through them far to the back of the square, keeping in the shadow of the Capitol Building where she could not be seen but could observe. She could not go back to Grace Street for that would be the first place Simon would go looking for her. He must have been following her before when she went on that useless tour of the hospitals and she had never known it. Could he be behind her now, unseen, waiting for the chance to pounce? Just beyond her secluded hiding place a family sat clustered together with piles of their belongings around them. They had a basket filled with loaves of bread and cheeses. One of the children was sent over to Selene, holding out a large piece of bread.

"Ma says it's from the commissary stores and you look hungry," the child said. Selene nodded her thanks to the woman sitting nearby and took the bread, holding it close to her as she peered anxiously around the building to the rear of the square. At length, when Simon did not appear, she slipped farther back in the indentation between the low steps and the foundation, scrunched down in the corner as far back as she could get, and nibbled on the bread. She was hungry and she was bone-tired. The strong wind out of the southeast off the river, driving the fire deeper into the city, swirled the air with smoke and flying sparks like fireflies. Her corner was a little warmer out of the wind, and eventually, in spite of her determination to stay vigilant, she slumped against the

372

building, letting her taut body relax and her deep breathing ease. It grew harder and harder to keep her mind on Simon and her eyes focused on the path out there ahead. She was not even aware when she drifted into unconsciousness.

Long lines of men in gray wound wearily across the Appomattox River from Petersburg trudging southward across the James then westward toward Amelia Court House. Wade sat on his horse by the side of the road along the James River with his hat brim pulled down close to his eyes. The withdrawal was proceeding in a swift and orderly way, yet he viewed it with a restlessness he could barely hold in check. Standing and watching a defeated army forced to flee for its life was much worse than action—any action that would keep his mind from the bitter fact of defeat. He felt as though a stone lay heavy in his chest. Unless they found supplies at Amelia, there was nothing left to support these starving men or even the skeletal horses they rode. They were outnumbered, they had nothing to subsist upon, and they had a long, wearying march ahead if they were going to escape Grant's noose. But they were not outfought. And they still had the magnificent leadership that had brought them this far. If anyone could save them, it was Bobby Lee. Surely he'd pull one more miracle out of his hat. Off to the right an artillery caisson lumbered over a hole in the rutted road and rolled crazily to one side, nearly toppling. The troops around it struggled to catch and right the cumbersome cannon, one of them barking orders at the others. Wade looked closer and recognized the voice and figure of the officer.

"Ellwood," he called. "Captain James! Over here."

Ellwood James turned sharply to see Wade and waved. After making certain the caisson was righted again and back on its way, he loped through the ranks of marching men up to the knoll where Wade had swung off his horse.

"I thought you must have gone on ahead," Ellwood said, pulling off his hat and wiping his arm across his forehead.

"Not yet. Have you any news of Richmond? Are they safe?"

"I was there just two days ago. It was crazy then and must be even worse now. I made Mama promise me she'd keep

373

everyone inside with the doors locked. They should be all right."

"Selene? Is she well?"

"As a matter of fact, no. Not really. It chanced that I was at the War Office with her when she fainted from hunger and weariness. I carried her home."

"Fainted! My God, man—"

"It's all right, Major. She was fine when I left and Mother assured me she'd care for her and make her rest."

Wade's horse, sensing his anxiety, danced nervously. He pulled on the reins and smoothed the animal's thin neck. "You're sure she was all right? She shouldn't have gone out when she wasn't strong enough. I only wish I'd been there."

"Major Kinsolving!"

The voice belonged to a young private hurrying along the side of the road past the ranks of the marchers, his dispatch bag bouncing at his side. Wade called out to him and he ran up the hill.

"Major Kinsolving? General Mahone sends his compliments, Major, and request that you join the rear guard at Chesterfield Court House."

Wade looked down at the lad, his fresh face shining in the fading light. He couldn't be more than fourteen. "How did you find me, private?"

"The General said you'd be guarding the crossing."

"You did a good job. My compliments to the General and tell him I'll leave right away."

"Yes sir," The boy went loping off and Wade reached for his horse's reins. His foot was in the stirrup when Ellwood, who had already started to rejoin his company, turned back.

"Major, I forgot. You wife gave me a message for you. Something about keeping away from Richmond. She was pretty insistent. 'Tell him keep away from Richmond,' she kept saying. She also kept repeating a name—Simon, I think."

Wade stopped abruptly. "Simon?! Are you certain?"

"Simon Lesser or Lasiter . . ."

"Not Simon Lazar?"

"Lazar. Yes, that was it. She was a little vaporish after her fainting spell, but she said that name quite clearly over and over."

374

Wade swung up into his saddle, his thoughts racing. Simon Lazar in Richmond! If he was alive and here, what reason lay behind it? What intentions—evil intentions, no doubt—did he have toward Selene? The thought of confronting Simon Lazar, of getting his revenge for those defective arms and the trouble they caused, set his heart racing.

"Thanks, Captain," he called, whirling his mount.

"Major, you're going the wrong way!"

Wade did not bother to answer. He'd follow General Mahone's orders after he made certain Selene was safe from Simon Lazar.

A shattering explosion near the river startled Selene back to consciousness. The ground beneath her gave a tremendous shudder of shock and surprise and she sat up, wondering where she was. She could feel the walls of the building against her back tremble with the force of the blast. She stumbled to her feet as a second explosion thundered on the heels of the first, throwing her against the wall. Clinging to the building for support, she ran to the open space beyond her hiding place where the air was alive with dust and cinders. The square was in pandemonium with women screaming, clutching their crying children, their white faces turned toward the river in questioning horror. Selene picked her way among them, heading for the gate. Though the explosions were ear-splitting and frightening, it was obvious to her that they were coming from the warehouse area bordering the river and not farther up the hill. The fire had come closer now and was threatening the offices one street over. She thought absently that she must look a fright in the scarlet glow of the torches on the square, her hair tangled and straggling and her dress covered with dust from her hiding place. Where was she going, she thought groggily before remembering the James house. And Simon. She ought to be watching for him. If only her head would clear. If only those terrible blasts would stop their infernal roaring.

Wade had gone straight to the James house on Grace Street only to find that Selene had been missing for hours. With his heart in his throat he set out to find her. The city was wild now, taken over by thugs and whores and even convicts from the

375

penitentiary let loose when the building was threatened by the fire. Small groups of soldiers marched hurriedly through the streets heading for the river, paying no attention to the lawlessness around them. There was no authority even attempting to restore order and Wade had not the time nor the inclination to try. He avoided the worst of the mobs and searched faces on the streets, straining for a familiar countenance. Cecily had told him Selene was wearing a green dress and he strained for a glimpse of that color anywhere in the crowd. The fires were spreading from the warehouses up into the town, giving the scene a look like something out of hell itself. Cinders thick in the air blinded his eyes and dust choked his throat. He ignored the frightened faces of decent citizens driven from their homes by the fire, stepped over the drunks sprawled on the walkways, looked away from those who had suffered a broken head in some useless brawl, shoved aside the clutching hands of the painted women who tried to hold him. He focused on every tall, thin-faced man, hoping to recognize Simon and every golden-haired girl, praying it would be Selene. But it was no use. The commotion and growing panic in the streets was all around him and though she was caught up in it somewhere, he had not the slightest idea where to look.

Then he thought of the square. The tocsin was clanging incessantly, calling men to help with the spread of the fire. Below, at the War Office he could see they were readying explosions, hoping to break the spread of the fire and in the process prevent any records from falling into Union hands. Wade ran up Ninth Street toward the Square, encouraged by the sight of families who had taken up refuge inside the iron railing. He had just dashed through the gate when he spotted Selene making her dazed way below the statue of George Washington.

"Selene," he shouted, his voice charged with his joy and relief. Her head came up sharply and she saw him ahead, running toward her. She tried to move to him but her leaden feet refused to budge. Then he was there, clasping her in his arms, pressing her to him, covering her face with frantic kisses. She clung to him as to a lifeline in a storm.

"Are you all right?" Wade finally said, gripping her shoulders and putting her from him long enough to stare into her face.

"Oh, Wade, you can't know how glad I am to see you."

He smoothed her hair away from her white brow, concerned at the disheveled state. "Are you hurt? Did anyone . . ."

"No, I found a place to hide. But Wade, Simon is here. He's in Richmond. He's not dead. I thought I had killed him but I hadn't."

"I know he's here. That's why I came."

"I saw him. He tried to catch me but I managed to get away. I'm so frightened," she said, burying into his coat. Then she remembered and thrust him away. "You shouldn't be here. You shouldn't have come. He wants you as much as me."

"I won't let him hurt you. Come on, we have to get you back home where you'll be safe."

"No, no. He knows the house. He lured me from there with a note that was supposed to be from you. He'll be waiting." Her voice rose on waves of panic.

"We'll just have to take that chance. It's the safest place to be and I'm with you now." He laid his arm around her shoulders and started toward the gate as another huge blast thundered from the river. Selene tucked her head against his chest and her body trembled as the people around them screamed and ran. "We're being bombarded," she cried.

Wade's voice was level and soothing. "No. It's our own people blowing up munitions and stores and anything else they don't want the Federals to get. Keep walking, Selene. We've got to get you inside."

He stopped abruptly as they stepped outside the railing. Clinging to him Selene looked up as Wade's grip around her shoulders tightened. Not ten feet in front of them, just across the narrow street, stood Simon Lazar, his sword in one hand, the other lightly on his hip.

"So, you've done my work for me," he said, arrogant delight in every tone. "I suppose I ought to thank you for that, Captain, or is it Major now? I knew you'd show up if I waited long enough. Now I can conveniently rid the world of both of you at one time."

There was resignation and even relief in finally coming face to face with Simon Lazar. Wade felt it and something in him soared at the prospect of taking on this detestable man who had

377

robbed him of his wife, his men, and his reputation. Even Selene, now that the dreaded confrontation was here, felt her strength returning. Better to face evil and fight it than to run. Wade pushed her to one side and with a sharp, metallic slide, drew his sword from its sheath, moving across the street to face Lazar. "It's going to give me great pleasure to kill you, Lazar, you swine. My only regret is that I will have to bring you to justice myself and can't have the exquisite enjoyment of seeing you hang."

The two men edged around each other while the firelight danced off the tips of their weapons like lightning. Simon lunged and they were hacking and slashing at each other in a fury of hate while Selene stood gripping her hands, watching in growing fear. While they were both decent swordsmen, there was no finesse in the way they went at each other. It was pure aggression and hatred. Of the two Wade was the better swordsman, but Simon was in better condition and that gave him an edge. Twice Wade forced Simon back and once nearly ran him through before Lazar could dodge aside with agility and fly back to the attack. Then Simon somehow got his sword tip underneath Wade's and flipped it out of his hand, sending it flying up in the air to land four feet away. Selene gasped but Wade, without pausing, reached down and grasped one of the broken wooden cartons lying on the ground and slung it at Simon as he thrust his sword forward to run him through. It knocked him off balance and he fell backwards, landing heavily. Wade grabbed up his sword with one hand and Selene's wrist with the other and ran, not caring in what direction, only obsessed with getting her out of there. Without thinking, he cut across Bank Street and headed toward the basin. Tenth Street was pandemonium. The fire had begun to threaten the YMCA hospital halfway down the block, forcing the patients out into the street. Those who could walk helped those who could not, while others lay haphazardly on stretchers, crying piteously. The women from the brothel directly across from the hospital had piled their meagre belongings in the road where they hovered over them in their cheap, gaudy dresses, howling like banshees. Gripping Selene's hand, Wade pushed through the crush, heading for the corner. Once there, he looked back to see Simon gaining on them.

Dragging Selene, he ran onto Carey and headed toward the bridge and the warehouse area. The air was hot and full of smoke but the worst of the fire had passed them now, leaving only sporadic flames among the ruins. But he knew they would never be able to make the bridge before Simon caught them. Ahead stood the shell of a tobacco warehouse, standing like a horrendous skeleton against the devastated landscape. He pushed her inside.

"Get up the stairs," he ordered, turning away to face their pursuer. The building was still half-intact though all the large windows had been blown out. The staircase stood with no railing against a still hot brick wall, rising three flights above. Selene edged up it wondering what she would do if she was trapped there. The building adjoining it had been destroyed as well and was still burning along its shattered foundation. The acrid smoke choked her lungs as she slipped up the steps, trying not to cling to the brick wall. As she looked down Simon came crashing through the doorway and Wade pounced. The clang of their weapons was barely heard above the bells from the town. Slowly Simon, slashing furiously, forced Wade back and up the stairway as Selene scrambled to the first landing. The floor stretched out nearly twenty feet then abruptly fell away to emptiness. A window running nearly to the floor by the landing had been blown away and its glass littered the floor and crunched ominously under her feet. The fires from the adjoining building were fiercely hot through the gaping hole forcing her up the stairs to the landing above. It too fell away to nothing after a short intact ledge, but the smoke was lighter and breathing easier. Selene could see Simon trying to force Wade out on the ledge below and she called to him, warning him. Wade slashed around his opponent and backed up the second flight of stairs, moving up to where she stood pressed against the brick wall, oblivious to its heat.

As they reached the third landing Wade, with a circular slashing spin, caught Simon's sword and flipped it from his hand, sending it flying through the air two stories below. Without a pause Simon laughed and threw himself at Wade, grabbing for his throat, his fingers digging into flesh. Both men fell near the open window, then struggled to make it back up on their feet, grappling furiously with one another and dangling near the edge. Selene, horrified, could visualize them both going over, locked together. Grappling together they struggled on the ledge, swaying in, then out over the precipice. Frantically Selene threw herself at Wade, trying to grab him as both men swung out over the flames below. Her fingers closed gropingly over his wide leather belt, dug frantically beneath and held. She pulled him back to her, holding him fast as Simon's grip loosened, giving Wade just enough balance to grab the window frame. With a horrible cry Simon toppled backward, landing with a thud in the flames two stories below. Selene slipped down the wall, all her strength gone while Wade, breathing heavily, scrambled on his knees to her, closed her in his arms, and they clung together.

"He's gone," he muttered, between long gasps of breath. "You're safe now."

She wept as she clung to him, feeling as though all her bones had turned to water. When they both were quieted and their labored breathing had subsided, they edged toward the window to peer below. They could see Simon's body spread-eagled on the rubble as the great tongues of fire leaped and danced around him, finally engulfing the still figure.

Wade pulled her to her feet. "Let's get out of here," he said, holding her tightly as they made their way down the stairs. In the street the smoke was thicker than ever. The ironclads on the river were being destroyed now and the din from the explosions was unbearable, forcing Selene to cover her ears with her hands.

"The whole city's going to burn," Wade muttered as he looked back toward the city and saw how the fires had engulfed the business and residential areas up Shockoe Hill. Hotels, homes, shops, warehouses—it was bad enough to lose them. But the departments, offices, and archives of the Confederacy were going up in that blaze as well, symbols of the dream and the cause that were dying beneath those searing flames. All that was left was the remnant of a shattered, starving, but still unbeaten army. "It's the end of everything," he murmured, sick at heart.

Selene was not aware that he was leading her toward the bridge until she looked up and saw it stretching ahead, long logs and pine knots standing ready for the torch.

Wade kissed her gently. "I must go," he said. "I want to take you home, but if I go back up that hill I'll be taken prisoner. The Federal columns are probably near Chimborazo by now. Do you think you can make it alone?"

"Oh, Wade, must you go back? There's nothing there for you. You said yourself this is the end. Come back with me. You can hide in the James house."

He shook his head. "No, I've come this far. The end may be near, but we're not finished yet and I'll not turn my back on my country. I'm not going to quit until the rest of the army lays down its guns. Can you find your way alone?"

"Yes. Don't worry about me. Without Simon to fear I won't have any trouble." She threw her arms around his neck and hugged him furiously. "I love you, Wade. Don't get hurt. Come back to me."

He returned her embrace with that surge of fierce passion she always awoke in him. "I'll come back, I promise." Kissing her lips for the last time, he was gone, racing for the bridge even as the soldiers there put the first torches to the kindling. A last contingent of cavalry from the city's defenders clattered just ahead of him while their commander, whom Wade recognized as General Gary, stood by, keeping his restive horse under rein as he waited for Wade to move after them. The blue-clad Federal cavalry chasing them were within sight in the distance.

General Gary touched his hat as he rode after Wade onto the bridge, nodding to the men ready with the torches.

"All over, good-bye," he shouted to the militia captain waiting beside the kerosene, tar and pine logs, "Blow her to hell."

Selene stood at the foot of the hill, watching a wall of flame and smoke envelop the bridge, blotting out her view of the men who had dashed across. The tears streamed down her cheeks mingling with the soot and grime on her face. "I've got to get home," she muttered as she struggled to gain control of her trembling legs. She turned and saw behind her along the city's skyline, a bulging wall of fire and smoke, bright and vivid against the night sky. She started up the hill, forcing herself to make the steep ascent. Halfway up she stumbled and fell, bruising her knee. Dragging herself up, she went a little farther, fell again over a clutter of rubble, and sank to her knees. This time she could not rise. There was no strength in her legs and her arms refused to push against the crumbled bricks. She was kneeling, wondering what to do, when she heard a horse whinny. Looking up, Selene saw a mounted rider coming toward her, picking his way daintily through the ruins. The soldier's back was to the flames so it took her a moment to recognize the neat blue uniform of the United States Cavalry. The officer smiled at her from beneath his forage cap and shifted his weight in the saddle to extend her a hand. He looked healthy! Fit and strong. And his face was kind.

"Are you all right, miss?" the soldier said, reaching down to lift her to her feet.

"Yes," she said gratefully. "But I need to get home. Can you help me?"

"Certainly, miss. You just tell me where home is, and if it's not burned or burning, I'll take you there. You don't mind riding pillion, do you?"

Selene looked up into his young triumphant face. He was the enemy and yet not the enemy to her. More than anything he meant order and peace and an end to this tragic war. "Oh, sir," she said, supporting herself against his mount's healthy flanks. "I've never been so glad to ride pillion in my life!"

General Lee's valiant army kept up their defiant flight for another five days. Hungry and exhausted, they evaded the huge Federal army that dogged their heels but were pushed ever westward in the process. Constant fighting erupted, skirmishes and clashes as bitter and fierce as any in the war, but they avoided a full-pitched battle which would end it all and struggled on to the west. Finally Lee turned toward Lynchburg only to find his way irretrievably blocked at Appomattox. There, after four years, General Lee could finally see no way out that would not involve more slaughter and gain them nothing. At that point he surrendered his army to the victorious Union Commander, General Grant.

Thanks to the dying wind and the efforts of the Federal soldiers to build a firebreak, most of the city of Richmond outside of the commercial district was saved from the flames. Order was swiftly restored and food distributed and by the time word of the surrender reached the stunned city, it had already settled into a resigned defeat.

General Lee and his staff slipped quietly back into Richmond early one morning, five days after Appomattox. The streams of paroled soldiers from the Army of Northern Virginia followed, often singly or in small groups, sometimes marching almost in their old formations. One such group arrived the day after Lee, not marching but moving still as a single unit down Franklin Street before dispersing at Capitol Square.

Selene, Cecily, Susannah, Francine, and Lucy, along with Tom and Dilly, hurried over to Franklin to stand with the sober people of Richmond, watching their men return. Many searched the ranks for the faces of those they loved, Selene among them. There had been no word from Wade since he flew across the Mayo bridge the night of the fire and she knew there had been lives lost in those last fierce clashes between the two armies. With her heart in her throat she scanned the bleak faces of the men moving listlessly down Franklin, hoping every moment to recognize Wade among them.

Though the fine houses of the upper town were still intact, the city was a ruin farther down the street. Shells of burned buildings stood like frozen corpses on the landscape sweeping down the hill from the Square. The Federal troops had been generous and considerate after putting out the fire and restoring order, and though many of the men and women of the town still looked on them as devils incarnate, Selene felt only a deep sense of gratitude. They had brought peace to the stricken South, held the Union together, and now perhaps would restore the man she loved to her willing arms.

She had been granted a brief glimpse of General Lee after his arrival and the grief on his face was something she would never forget. It was on the faces of his men as well, a solemn, stricken knowledge that they had lost everything they had fought for. Selene wondered if they suspected that, beneath the bitterness of defeat and the injury to pride, their whole way of life had been destroyed. The devastation and change brought on by this war was going to take a long time to heal, if it ever did.

The march was solemn and quiet, a sober contrast to other flag-waving, band-playing parades Franklin Street had witnessed over the past four years. Ellwood had sent word to the James house that he was safe, so there was no anxiety in the faces of his mother and sisters as they searched the ranks for a glimpse of his tall figure. But Wade? Surely he could not have died when the end was so close. Surely God would not be so cruel as to take him away from her now, just when they were finally able to face a lifetime together without recrimination, misunderstanding, or separation.

And then she saw him.

Tired, thin, ragged, but her Wade. She broke from the walk and started running among the lines, calling to him. He looked up and saw her, a sudden light kindling in his eyes. When she threw herself into his arms he hugged her fiercely and pulled quickly out of the ranks to stand by the side of the road, kissing her face, her cheeks, her lips, as though he could never get enough of their sweetness.

Tears of joy and relief ran down her cheeks. "Oh Wade, I was so afraid you were dead. Thank God you're all right," she cried, pressing him furiously to her. He stood in her arms silently for a long moment, then pulled away and faced the road, clasping his arms around her shoulders as he watched the men move by. The haggard, defeated look in his eyes hurt her heart. "My dear girl," he said quietly. "We've lost. Everything is gone."

Selene reached up to kiss his cheek and turn his face away from the haggard men, so near the end of their journey. A light of hope shone brightly in her eyes as she looked deeply into his.

"No, my love. It isn't over. It's just beginning."